AZRAEL'S
Assassin

Stephen H. Provost
Sharon Marie Provost

STEPHEN H. and SHARON MARIE PROVOST

Cover and interior images from Pixabay, public domain; front cover background: Stephen H. Provost
Cover and interior design: Stephen H. Provost

Based on an idea by Stephen H. Provost
Developed by Sharon Marie Provost and Stephen H. Provost

ISBN: 978-1-949971-63-7

"Whoever fights monsters should see to it that in the process he does not become a monster. And if you gaze long enough into an abyss, the abyss will gaze back into you."

— Friedrich Nietzsche

"The more devout [people] are, the more they see murder as negotiable... It depends, you know? It depends on who's doing the killing, and who's getting killed."

— George Carlin

"The older I get, the more clearly I remember things that never happened.."

— Mark Twain

Contents

Trigger warnings? I'll give you trigger warnings: A lotta triggers are gonna be pulled, shots'll be fired, and there's gonna be blood. One more thing: I cuss like a drunken sailor on shore leave. Get over it. If you can't take the heat, I'm always packin'.

— Elijah T. Kirk, private investigator

The Client

Stood Up

At the Roxy

Half an hour late? This wasn't like Olivia. I'd been waiting at the Roxy downtown, and the movie had already started. Father didn't let me attend many movies: One a month was his limit. And then, they had to be what he called "wholesome"... which meant G-rated. I was 21, but that didn't matter. I was still daddy's little girl, living at home, where Father's word was law.

It didn't help that he was the Prophet, the founder and minister of the Compassionate Truth Temple. He'd called it the Chapel of God's Word at first, then the People's Temple, before finally settling on its current name. It was nondenominational. Father was a control freak and didn't like the idea of answering to some ecumenical council in another state. He'd started off as an itinerant preacher when he was just 19, then had started holding tent revivals, and when the tent couldn't hold all the people who came out to see him, he'd built his church.

He'd founded the church when he was in his early twenties, before he'd even met Mother, and he was nearly 70 now. Mother was 58. That meant she was underage when they got married, but that was common where they both grew up, and no one talked about it now. Angering the Prophet was the same thing as angering the Almighty. That was how the members looked at it, and he did nothing to discourage them.

So yes, I was one of those later-in-life babies, which made Father seem all the more imposing. He and Mother had tried to have other children, but it never worked out for them, either before or after me. That was another thing no one talked about, especially with the church so devoted to the command that we be fruitful and multiply. Father believed that the more large families we had in attendance, the stronger our bonds would be, and the faster the church would grow. He wasn't wrong in that. I remember overhearing him once admit he was envious of the LDS church and its sister wives… even though they didn't do that anymore.

Father and I never had a close relationship; parents were meant to be parents, not friends. It was his role to serve as an example, provide discipline, and set forth principles that were to be followed without question. I looked up to him, even feared him. He quoted the proverb often: "The fear of the Lord is the beginning of wisdom, and the knowledge of holy understanding." And this attitude was to extend to him. He made that perfectly clear.

He didn't exactly have a tender side, which was kind of odd considering he'd chosen to include the word "compassionate" in the name of his church. He never spoke of love, but rather of earning trust; and once that trust was earned, you would be rewarded. He rewarded me for getting all A's in school by giving me my job as church secretary and treasurer. It wasn't just a reward for me, though. There was something in it for him, too: He didn't want to see me go away to college and risk my mind being "corrupted from the simplicity that is Christ."

"My kingdom is not of this world," he said, quoting Jesus in the Gospel of John, but he used it to refer to the kingdom *he* had built as much as God's. The world was full of fornicators and idolators, covetous men and extortionists, and I was to have no part of it. I attended public school growing up, but I wasn't allowed to have any friends there. I was expected to come straight home and do my homework, eat supper, help Mother clean the kitchen, then go to my room for an hour of reflection and Bible study. Bedtime was 8 o'clock.

That meant all of my friends were members of the church, and I only saw them at Sunday school, church potlucks, or on outings where our family would join others from the church, like the Dunphys, and go camping or picnicking together. I'd always been closer to Olivia Dunphy than anyone else at the church. And that was probably why my parents were close to her parents, Michael and Patricia. By getting close to them, they were keeping an eye on me. Making sure I wouldn't "stray from the path of righteousness." Olivia was two years younger than me, and we did everything together. With her blond hair, long legs, and willowy look, people often mistook us for each other—or swore we must be sisters.

We went to the movies together on the third Saturday of each month, and being late wasn't just out of character for her, it went against the church's "encouragement" that its members always be prompt. "Better three hours too soon than a minute too late." My father said. That one was from Shakespeare. It wasn't in the Bible. But it might as well have been. Every word that flowed forth from the lips of the Prophet was considered the gospel truth.

Five more minutes passed, and there was still no sign of Olivia.

I decided to call her house, but the call wouldn't go through. That was strange.

I waited ten minutes after that, but by then the movie had already started, so there was no point in sticking around any longer. I got in my car—it was actually Father's, but he let me use it as long as I told him when I'd be back—and headed back home.

Father was sitting on the sofa in the living room when I got there, reading his Bible and listening to *Hour of Decision* with Billy Graham. He wasn't necessarily a fan of the evangelist; to Father's way of thinking, he could learn from anybody as long as it was on *his* terms. Graham had a successful radio show, and I'd heard Father talk about the possibility of getting on the radio himself, or even television. Sitting around the dinner table one night, he'd told Mother and me that Graham had raised $24,000 in donations to start his radio show, and made a lot more in donations after that. Anything Graham could do, Father reasoned, he could do—and better.

"You're home early, Daughter," he said. He usually called me that instead of Claire. It might have been because Mother chose the name, and he didn't like it, but it was also a way of keeping things less personal between us.

"Olivia never showed up at the Roxy," I said. "I waited for forty-five minutes before I finally gave up. I even tried calling the Dunphys at home, but the call wouldn't go through."

"I would not fret over it, Daughter," he said. "I am sure she will turn up."

That wasn't like Father. Something like that would usually make him wonder whether something was amiss in his flock. He wanted to know where everyone was and what they were doing at any given moment.

"What if something happened to her?" I pressed.

"God's will be done."

How could he be so callous? This was my best friend in the whole world, and it was like she didn't even matter to him.

"Don't you think we should do something?" I said.

He still had his nose in the Bible. I wanted to go over there and rip it out of his hands, but of course, I didn't. I couldn't.

Mother came into the room, carrying a platter of gingerbread cookies and a cup of milk. She set it down beside Father, who put his Bible off to one side so he could pick a cookie up and take a bite. He didn't offer me one, and neither did Mother.

"Oh, Claire, dear, I didn't expect you back so soon, or I would have made some for you."

"I'm fine, Mother." I was trying my hardest not to sound upset, but I must not have been doing a very good job.

Father fixed me with a glare. "That's not how you talk to your mother, is it?"

I lowered my eyes and murmured, "No, Father... But what about Olivia, Father?"

"Olivia? Is something...?" Mother said, but she couldn't get another word out before Father interrupted her, raising his voice. "I'll hear no more of it, Daughter. Is that understood?" He said it with the same kind of righteous indignation he used when anyone mentioned something about him being so much older than Mother. Or about me being their only child. It was almost like Olivia's disappearance—because that's what it was—was something he wanted to keep secret. Like he was embarrassed or... I didn't know what.

That night, I went to my room at 7 o'clock, but I was too distracted to study the Scripture. I'd tried calling Olivia again after dinner, but I hadn't gotten through then, either. I couldn't stop thinking that something was wrong. What if she'd been abducted?

Instead of opening my Bible, I lay down in bed and looked up at my Sunday School class picture, which was hanging on the wall just over my dresser. There was something strange about it. Something was missing.

Or someone.

Where was Olivia?

She was gone! But I knew she'd been there when we took the photograph, so that was impossible.

I ran out to show Father the picture, fully prepared to receive a tongue-lashing for not being there in my room. And I did: but not for leaving my room. "How dare you interrupt my quiet time with the Lord?" he nearly shouted. He certainly was *not* being quiet now. And I didn't see his Bible in front of him. Instead, he had the church ledgers spread out on the dinner table, and it looked like he was making entries... or maybe erasing them. That was supposed to be *my* job as church treasurer. He'd said he was giving me that position because I was so good at math, and so he wouldn't have to worry about doing it himself anymore. I had been so proud, but now it seemed clear that he didn't trust me as much as he said he did.

Still, I had to show him the picture.

"I'm sorry, Father. I wouldn't have come to you, but this is important. You told me I should always come to you..."

Father sighed and put the ledgers aside, not even addressing the fact that he wasn't allowing me to do the work he'd assigned me. But in the moment, that didn't matter. I was only concerned about Olivia. "Suffer the little children to come unto me," he said, quoting Jesus. *He* was not Jesus, and I was no longer a little child, but I ignored this as well. "What do you have there, Daughter?"

I showed him the picture.

"I don't understand."

"See there?" I said, pointing. "Olivia's missing."

He grimaced, and I could sense his irritation rising. "She must not have been there that day. What of it?"

"But she *was* there, because *I* was there, and I remember seeing her there too. She was standing right next to me."

"Memory can play tricks. I am sure you are mistaken."

"Father, I know what I saw."

"Or perhaps you are being deceived by an unclean spirit, which has entered into you and must be cast out with prayer and fasting... lest it bring seven more evil spirits to reside there with it."

"Father!"

"Do not test me, Daughter. Put away these childish things and go to your prayer closet. Ask for forgiveness."

"Yes, Father," I said, holding back tears.

I didn't know why he was acting this way, but I did know he would be no help in finding Olivia.

So I would have to find someone who would.

The Assassin

Second Sight

hen is he going to get home? I've been waiting out here in the shadows of the tall trees, in the cold and damp for three hours.

WI looked down the road when I heard the hiss of brakes as the bus stopped at the corner. Several people disembarked, but I couldn't see who they were yet. After a few moments, I heard a tapping sound and watched his slow measured steps as he came down the street. Finally! He was humming a tune as he made his way up to the house and unlocked the door.

I waited twenty minutes for the activity on the street to die down before making my way across. I tried the door and found it unlocked, as I had suspected it would be. No one in this neighborhood locked up at night. It wasn't exactly a small town, but it wasn't a big city, either. Everyone knew almost everyone—and trusted them. It made my mission that much easier.

I crept into the house and quietly closed the door behind me. A floorboard creaked as I made my way down the hall past the kitchen, headed toward the sitting room.

"Is someone there?" his voice called out from the room ahead on the right.

I waited a moment, scarcely breathing, before continuing my trek. As I turned the corner into the small sitting room, I saw him seated in a leather Art Deco chair.

"I can hear you. I know someone's here. You don't need to steal nothin' from a blind man. I'm a generous man. I will help you if you talk to me."

My anger boiled over at his words... to presume I was some common thief... a sinner. I rushed across the room, grabbing his arm, my fingers digging into his skin. I jerked him up, twisting his arm behind his back as I did so. Leaning over his shoulder, I growled, "Are you Jud Williams?"

"Ooooww! Please stop. There's no cause for violence. I'll do whatever you say."

"I asked you a question," I said, my voice filled with rage.

"Uh... yes. What's wrong?"

I wrapped my arm around his neck and increased the pressure until he fell across the chair, unconscious. I pulled him up into the seat again before fishing the rope out of my backpack. I tied his hands together behind him before securely fastening his ankles to the chair legs and his torso to the back of the chair. Jud already had a roaring blaze in the fireplace, so I placed the poker from the rack into the flames.

He began to stir as the sharp tip of the poker began to glow red. I stared down at him as he struggled against the tight ropes binding him. I could see he was trying to sense if I was still in the room. He jumped when my voice boomed at his side. "I'm right here."

"What's going on? Why did you restrain me?"

"John 9: 1-3: 'And as Jesus passed by, he saw a man which was blind from his birth. And his disciples asked him, saying, Master, who did sin, this man, or his parents, that he was born blind? Jesus answered, Neither hath this man sinned, nor his parents: but that the works of God should be made manifest in him.'"

"What does that mean? I'm not a man of God. I'm a good and honest man, but I've never been one to go to church on Sunday." Jud fidgeted in the chair, disarmed by my silence. "Hello. Are you still there?"

"I am. You *will* be a man of God when we're done here."

"What are you going to do to me?"

"Very soon you will *see*." I reached down and pulled the hot poker from the coals. Turning to Jud, I recited, "Colossians 1:13: 'Who hath delivered us from the power of darkness, and hath translated us into the kingdom of his dear Son,'" as I pushed the red-hot tip into the globe that was his eye.

Jud strained against the ropes, screaming out in pain as the tissue and tears sizzled on the hot metal. His other eye kept blinking and squinting as tears poured out of it. He tried to squeeze his eye shut, as if that could stop the iron spear. I pushed harder, and the tip pierced the eyeball, unleashing a great gush of vitreous fluid and blood that ran down his face. Jud let out a howl that reverberated throughout the room. With one final shove, the hook on the fireplace iron broke through the orbital socket, impaling his brain.

Jud's body began to flail as he went into a seizure. Rivers of blood flowed from his mouth when he bit down on his tongue, nearly severing it. As I yanked the tool out, the eyeball was still attached to the optic nerve. With a jerk of my hand, the eyeball was ripped from the socket, flinging bits of brain matter across the room.

His body tensed one final time, and then he slumped into unconsciousness, his breathing growing shallower. I placed the poker back into the fire. While it heated up, I removed the last three items so I could complete my ritual and set them on the side table. Picking up the fireplace iron one more time, I plunged it into his other eye until it was buried deep inside his brain matter, before ripping the eyeball out, spraying the room with blood spatter.

I wiped his face clean before picking up the glass eyeballs. I placed his new eyes, gifted from God, in the vacant sockets to restore his sight. As he breathed his last few breaths, a trail of bloody tears slid down his face at the sight of his Savior. I placed a cross in his hands along with my calling card.

The small piece of parchment contained only the symbol of my mission:

I cleaned the blood and bits of brain matter from my gloves and picked up my backpack; it was time to return home to prepare for the next phase of my mission. There were others who needed to be dealt with.

The Detective

The Church Mouse

Sometimes I think I shoulda stuck it out in the seminary. Not the Catholic kind. Presbyterian. Celibacy ain't my cuppa joe. Religion ain't really, either. But at least with a name like Elijah, I woulda fit in.

The church is crooked, but so is John Law. They don't got principles on the force. You fuck with the wrong cop and you get fucked with right back—only harder, and by all his cronies.

They called me a stoolie 'cause I ratted out my partner, Henry Stiles. He'd been on the take for years, turnin' a blind eye to the Carboni Boys and their network. Me? I never said shit. It's against the code. But the code don't cover havin' your way with a lady and then offin' her when she threatens to squeal.

So I squealed instead. Shit. Hit. Fan. He pinned it on the dame's abusive boyfriend, then said *I* was the one on the take. He knew people. I didn't. The damn muckety-mucks listened to him, not me.

Funny thing is, bein' drummed out of the force as a dirty cop gives you a rep as a PI. A *good* rep. They hire you *because* you don't toe the line. I never tell a client I'm clean. That'd be bad for business.

Not that business is good in this backwater shithole, starin' out the window at the railyard across the tracks. This town is the kind that don't know what it wants to be. It ain't no big city, and it ain't really a small town. It's stuck in some kinda limbo between the two. There's a bowling alley and a worthless excuse for a baseball team in the Cubbies' farm system. We got A&Ps, a Piggly Wiggly, a Woolworth, a Kress, and a W.T. Grant. There's an auditorium where they hold fights an' wrestlin' matches. There's some radio stations an' a UHF TV channel that useta be DuMont but now runs independent.

Most o' the folks here got religion, an' there's a tent revival here every spring. They love their church picnics.

The mob likes it here 'cause they don't hafta deal with big-city exposure. They got their fingers in the Apple an' Hollywood, but they ain't exposed the way they would be there. They send out their goons to do the dirty work for 'em while they sit back an' pull the strings, runnin' small-time operations here that fly under the radar—especially since most of the cops are on the take.

I keep my nose outta that shit too. I ain't Martin Kane or Philip Marlowe, and I sure as hell ain't Peter Gunn. Most of my cases are missing persons the cops won't look for and cheaters the cops don't care about. Not that I care about 'em either, but I work for cash, not kicks.

But it does help to have a little extra motivation... which brings me to my present case.

This dame walks into my office one day, the kind of leggy number who oughta be dressed to the nines. But she ain't. Plain gray dress. White collar. Flats. Sexy librarian look, without the glasses. Like a church mouse with tits and no tail. Superman may have x-ray eyes, but he ain't got nothin' on me when it comes to picturing what's underneath.

Claire Cassidy *acted* like a church mouse too. Introduced herself by way of a soft knock on my office door. When I told her "come," she poked her head in and commenced to be lookin' this way and that—everywhere but at me. Like a rodent comin' out of a hole in the wall.

"Shouldn't be here," she said in a near whisper.

I stood and raised my own voice, in hopes it might put her at ease. "Elijah Kirk at your service, ma'am. Pleased to make your acquaintance."

She took a step backward. Not the desired effect. I decided to dial it back a notch.

"What can I do you for?"

"I shouldn't be here," she repeated, shaking her head, but this time starin' straight at me, sizin' me up. My x-ray eyes were tellin' me this dame was *not* as shy as she let on. But something had her spooked. Or someone. Probably someone who raised his voice like I'd just done.

"Well, here's where you are, so there must be some purpose to it. Spit it out."

She swallowed hard and told me her name, which I already mentioned. It suited her.

"People have been disappearing," she said, sounding a little more sure of herself, like she'd just now decided to come clean about her intentions.

I sighed. Another fucking missing persons case. Just what I needed. "What people?"

"Members of my church. The Compassionate Truth Temple. All in the last month or so."

A church. That explained her mousiness. I'd heard of this particular one too. Had a rep of helping bums and druggies by takin' 'em in. The muckety-mucks liked it, 'cause it got the lowlifes out of their hair. But the members kept to themselves. Bein' in their "prayer closet," they called it. Except they almost never came out of it. That's too much prayer for my taste.

"How many people are we talkin' about?"

"Three so far."

My eyes narrowed. "And the boys in blue won't help you out? Seems like they'd be keen on a case like that."

"No cops," she said.

"Why?"

She didn't say nothin' to that. Just looked at the floor.

"Look," I told her, "this is my fee." I spilled on the cost, figuring it would throw her off. But she nodded.

I shrugged. It was her money. Now it was gonna be mine, and I had abso-fucking-lutely no problem with that. "Up front," I added.

She didn't flinch. Just reached into her purse and pulled out a wad of bills in the required amount.

This was gonna be interesting. At least more than your run-of-the-mill gone missin' case.

The next time I saw Claire, she looked... different. She'd changed out of them schoolmarm clothes and into a black turtleneck and a short skirt, which left plenty of leg to look at. And believe me, I was looking. She wore a blazing red wig, too, that fell down her back the way a guy's tongue would be falling out just to look at her. On top of the wig was a black beret, and she topped off the outfit with the one thing *everyone* wore when they didn't want to get made: big, bug-eyed shades.

We met at the greasy spoon on Norman Avenue, where the trolley tracks ran straight through the middle of the street, between Top Dollar Pawn Shop and Joe Don's Bail Bonds, just across from Fourteen-Carat Fashion Jewelry. The seedy side of town. Last place you'd go lookin' for a whitebread dame like her—which was the whole point of it—a dame who hadn't even been once around the block yet, by the looks of her.

Yeah, Claire was young. Not jailbait, but too young for the likes of me to be lookin' at the way I wanted to look at her.

She was already waiting when I got there, sitting toward the back in a booth made up in fake gold vinyl. The kind with cracks in it that eats your change when it falls between the cushions and looks a whole lot more inviting that it is. Punctual. The 'goody-two-shoes' kind of punctual that put the lie to everything she was wearing.

"Those holy roller friends of yours really got you spooked," I said as I wedged my way into the too-small booth.

"I'm not scared," she hissed under her breath. "These people are my friends."

Freida, the afternoon waitress, showed up just then. They put their worst help on in the early p.m., because that's when they didn't get much business. Claire didn't want too many other customers in the place when we were talkin', which meant we got shitty service, aka Freida Lombardi with her beehive hairdo, strawberry perfume, and bad memory. She took pride in rememberin' all her orders without writing 'em down. She would've been better off takin' pride in something she could actually do.

Freida slapped down two menus in front of us. I handed mine back.

"I'll be easy on ya, Freida," I said. "Coffee. Black."

"Coca-Cola. Over ice," Claire said, giving hers back too.

Freida nodded once. "Comin' right up."

I leaned over and whispered to Claire, "In twenty minutes, if we're lucky. And the coffee will be cold."

"I guess you should've ordered the soda pop then," Claire said with a devilish smile. Maybe the new duds were rubbing off on her.

Fizzy drinks gave me gas... I wasn't gonna tell her that, though. I wasn't gonna say I drank beer anyway, 'cause it was a whole different animal and was worth the sacrifice.

"These friends of yours," I said. "If they ain't got you spooked, who does?"

"It's not 'who' so much as 'what,'" she said. "My best friend disappeared last week—she's one of the three people I told you about. I don't know the others much at all. The thing is, no one in the church will even admit they've gone missing. And it's worse than that. They act like none of these people ever existed."

I swatted at a fly buzzing near my ear. Missed it. It landed on my head, which I shook, but it kept a foothold. "OK," I said, "let's focus on your friend. Got a name?"

"Olivia Dunphy. She's a couple of years younger than me, and she's like the little sister I never had." She was fightin' back tears now.

"Do people sign a register or somethin' when they go to your church?"

"Oh, yes," Claire said firmly, pullin' herself together. "Our church prides itself in keeping meticulous records. We track attendance at Sunday school, morning services, and board meetings. Members have to disclose their addresses, and their telephone numbers and exchanges. It's not required to disclose anything else, but most even give us their birthdays and anniversary dates, so the congregation can praise the Lord for their continued health and fidelity."

I pulled out a pad of paper and started takin' notes. "Us. You said us, like you're the one who takes down this shi... information."

She nodded. "I'm the church secretary. I didn't go to college because Daddy said he needed me here."

That was convenient.

She was going on though: "But when I said 'us,' I meant it. The church is one body: the body of Christ. When one member suffers, so does the whole body. When one grieves, so do we all."

She'd served me up a smorgasbord of questions to ask—the first of which was which of the others to ask first. I decided to get the background out of the way. "Your father. He's in the church?"

She sat up straighter, her face beamin' with pride. "My father's the Prophet, Hugh Cassidy. I'm sure you've heard of him."

I had. I thought there was probably a connection, but word had it that a lot of people in that church were related. Inbred even. Maybe that was just a sick rumor, but you could never tell. The Compassionate Truth Temple played everything close to the vest... unless it was good PR, that is—and made Hugh Cassidy look like the Prophet he claimed to be. From what I could tell, all his predictions were either made after the fact or were so fuckin' vague they could've been made by that fortune teller, Madam Allegra. Who the hell knows? Maybe they were.

His biggest prediction? He said the world was gonna end. According to Cassidy, it would happen at midnight exactly fifty-two years, three months, and seven days from the time he predicted it. That was convenient as hell, it seemed to me, 'cause he could scare his members into forking over loads of loot to prepare for the so-called end times... and he'd have years to rake in the dough. Of course, he'd be stiffer than morning wood by the time it was all supposed to come down, so he wouldn't have to answer for it. And he'd have spent it all by then—probably on high-class hookers, John Barleycorn, a fleet of Mercedeses, and a mansion with phony Greek columns holdin' up the porch. His prediction fallin' flat? That would be a problem for one of his patsies to deal with down the road.

I didn't say any of this to Claire, who didn't need me talking shit about her old man. The point was to get info outta her, which I couldn't do if I shut her down.

"He's got a rep, that's for sure," I said, hoping she'd take it as payin' proper respect, not as a dig.

She must've been fine with it, 'cause she let it pass.

Freida arrived with the coffee. It was cold as a call girl who just got stiffed, and chock full of cream and sweetener. "Just the way you like it," Freida said.

I tried not to grimace. Was that fuckin' cream curdling?

She put a soda pop down in front of Claire, but it wasn't even soda. It looked like Delaware Punch. She pretended not to notice, and smiled with a thank-you that spoke volumes. This gal didn't like to make waves, even on rocky shores. Maybe especially then.

Freida left, and I got back down to it: "If you're the church secretary, you must have access to the records of members who went missing. Right? Getting me those records would help me find your friend... Olivia, wasn't it?"

I fully expected miss goody-goody gumdrop to say she

couldn't possibly do that. That it was against church policy or her father's directive or some such. A place as cagey about its comings and goings as the Compassionate Truth Temple would never let intel like that go public. But that's not what she said. Her answer was a curveball low and tight that the batter never saw comin'—the batter bein' one Elijah Thomas Kirk.

"I've looked in the records," she said. "I can't give you anything, because there's nothing there."

I frowned and sat back. "I thought you said the Truthers kept all that info in a file or somethin'. They don't strike me as the kind of folks who would take their eyes off it."

"We aren't," Claire said. "And please don't call us Truthers. That's what the heathens call us. We are sons and daughters of God Most High and followers of his only true Prophet."

"Which is who's spooking you. Your daddy."

She didn't respond, which was all the response I needed. But it didn't explain why the files on those missing members were just as *missing* as they were. And it didn't help when the next thing out of her mouth was even more unbelievable: "The files aren't just gone. The ink's been wiped clean off the pages: the registry, the weekly attendance records, all of it—at least where it concerns our missing members."

"And now the church uppity-ups say these people never existed. What about your friend Olivia?"

Claire looked down at the table in front of her. "She's not there either. It's like she never even existed."

Either Claire was lying or the church was covering something up. In deciphering which of these potentialities made more sense, I had two factors to consider. One was Claire's sanity. She sounded loonier than a beer barrel full of sauced monkeys, but she didn't have motive to lie. The church on the other hand, was always covering shit up. It was what they did. If they were covering up these disappearances, they probably had the motive Claire lacked... and the added motive to make her look batshit. If she kept poking around, they'd probably put her away in the Oak Patch Asylum to keep her from talking.

That didn't make her story ring any truer, but when there's rats in the cellar spreadin' the plague, you don't worry so much about if there're bats in the belfry.

"I'm gonna need some proof, kid," I told her.

A smile played at the edges of her mouth. "I know just where to find it."

The Assassin 4
Missing In Action

I returned home to find Sally enraged with me, which was the last thing I needed. Things were proceeding faster than I'd anticipated, but there was still much work left to do. I had already eliminated three of my targets. There are many more to go, but they would take more work... more research. I still needed to track them down, and then there would be more traveling involved. All this boiled down to more time away from Sally, and that was all she cared about.

"Brantley, where have you been? We were supposed to have lunch today."

"I'm sorry, Sally. It slipped my mind."

"Slipped your mind? Did I hear that right? I thought you loved me. How could you forget about me?"

"I didn't forget you. I could never... I just have a lot on my plate right now. You know I have a calling... that I have been tasked with a mission. It's very important to me."

"You never told me who assigned you this 'mission'? I want

to talk to them."

"It's not that easy. There's no..."

"There's no what?"

"No one for you to talk to."

"How can that be? They need to understand your family obligations are important, too. I'm part of your family, aren't I? Haven't we been discussing our future together? You told me that the situation with the rest of your family is complicated. It's important to me that we unite our families at our wedding."

"I know, but..."

"But what? Explain how there is no one I can talk to about your so-called mission."

"This mission wasn't assigned to me... exactly. At least not in the way you would understand it. All I can tell you is that I've got to fulfill it. Others came before me and failed. I *have* to succeed."

"Or what? You're scaring me. I don't understand."

"It's difficult to explain. There's a lot about my past that you don't know."

"So tell me."

"I will."

"When?"

"When I'm done. That's all I can say right now. This situation is extremely difficult. I need to right some wrongs. Some sins can't be absolved simply through repentance. I've taken this on myself. I can tell you everything when I'm done; then I'll be able to give you all the details."

If you're still here when I'm done.

Sally just stared at me, her angry eyes boring into mine. "This just doesn't make any sense. Aren't you supposed to be able to tell your life partner anything?"

"Yes." I put both hands gently on her shoulder. "And soon I will do just that... when we are married... once I am done. But before that can happen, I need to fulfill a higher calling."

She pulled away. "You sound like you're joining the priesthood for Pete's sake. So help me, if you do..."

I couldn't help but laugh. *Wrong move!*

The glare returned. "Brantley Donovan, don't you laugh at me! This isn't funny. I'm serious."

"I know, I know. Rest assured, I'm not Catholic now, nor will I ever be. But that doesn't mean I don't take my faith seriously. It is imperative that I finish this task—for my peace of mind, for my soul, for God, and, most importantly, for you. You always said you admired me for my honor. I wouldn't be true to myself or anyone else if I quit now. The sooner I finish, the sooner I can devote myself to you... alone."

Sally smiled and walked into my waiting arms. "I love you, Brantley. I'll try to be more understanding. And patient."

"That's all I can ask. And I will try to be done with all this as soon as possible. Speaking of that..."

"Damn it, babe! You aren't seriously telling me you have to work right now?"

"I'm afraid so. If you can just give me an hour, I will be out to make dinner."

"Fine... whatever. Go!"

I gave her one final squeeze and walked down the hall to my office, fishing the keys out of my pocket to unlock it.

I jumped when her voice sounded from right behind me. "For such an honorable man, why do you have to keep your office locked? What are you hiding from me?"

"Nothing, doll. I swear."

"So?"

"You know I'm a therapist, and my clients are guaranteed confidentiality."

"So, you don't trust me not to go snooping?"

"I never said that. What if I forgot to lock that door, and we had company over? It really doesn't matter the situation. I owe it to my clients to make sure their records are protected from everyone, even if *I* know *you* can be trusted."

"Arghhhhhh! You drive me insane. I'm going home. I'll talk to you tomorrow."

"Yes, I'll..."

Her voice echoed down the hall as she turned the corner. "If you can make time for me, that is."

"I'll call you later. I promise."

"Don't make promises you can't keep. *God forbid* you were to tell a lie." The front door slammed shut as she said the last word.

I sat down at my desk and pulled out my notebook to see who was next on the list.

Ah, yes. Candace Matthews. I need to do some more research and go to the zoo to check some things out.

The Detective 5

Picture Imperfect

"Y ou wanted proof? I'll show you proof."

Claire walked into Nick's Lamplighter dressed in her beatnik attire. I couldn't tell if she was still tryin' to lay low or if she actually liked it. This one was hard to read.

Nick's was a bar near the end of Fifteenth by the old brewery, a dingy hole-in-the wall with postcards from all over pasted to the walls and ceiling. You could barely see 'em though.

Nick needed a *real* lamplighter to chase away the shadows that clung to this place like sticky black tar. Why meet here? It'd been her idea. Did she want a shot of Jack or Wild Turkey to see how the other side lived? Or did she already *know* how the other side lived and didn't wanna admit it?

Nah, she was drinkin' a Coca-Cola. At least Nick got the orders right here.

I ordered a shot of Wild Turkey with a chaser of Pabst and retreated to where she was sittin', in a booth as far away from the bar as you could get.

I downed the shot and took a swig of the Pabst. "Let's see that proof of yours."

She slid a manila envelope across the table. Inside was an eight-by-ten photo print. It looked like one of those class pictures they take at school.

"What am I lookin' at?" I squinted and held it up next to the dim amber glow from the wrought-iron lamp that was stickin' out of the wall beside us. It wasn't much help. Damn it all to hell. If she was gonna show me a picture, why couldn't we have met someplace I could actually get a good look at it?

"It's a picture of our Sunday School class. From nine years ago." I could at least make out that there were three rows of children, with a young woman—musta been the teacher— standing behind them. Claire came around to my side of the table and slid in next to me. "There," she said, pointing as she leaned over my shoulder. "See that?"

"Yeah, it's an empty space." She was pointing to a gap in the front row, just off to the left side, between a young girl in pigtails and some kid who looked like Alfalfa from *The Little Rascals*. It looked weird, I had to admit, but... proof? Of what? That the kid who was supposed to be there had called in sick that day? That he'd run to the head just before the shot was taken? That they'd noticed an anthill swarming with red ants? Any one of those things made sense… a lot more sense than what Claire was about to tell me.

"That's where Olivia was sitting."

"So why'd she leave?"

"She didn't. She *was* sitting there. When the shot was taken. See the girl in the pigtails? That's me. I was right there next to her."

I turned to face her. "Look," I said, "there's no one there."

"There was, but there isn't now." Her face was dead serious.

I shook my head. "You're tellin' me someone did some kind o' hocus pocus on this photo? I don't buy it. I've seen my share of doctored-up shit in my day, but this image is clean."

She took a deep breath, shiftin' in her seat like she was antsy. "That's *not* what I'm saying. I'm telling you that my friend Olivia was sitting right next to me when this photo was taken. And I saw her sitting there in the photo when I looked at it the other day. But then when I looked at it again later, she was gone."

Now *I* was the one gettin' antsy. I wanted to say, "This ain't proof," but I bit my tongue. Instead, I asked her, "Can I borrow this picture?"

"You can have it," she said. "I've got another copy at home. Here's a picture of most of the current church membership, too. If it'll help…"

"Is Olivia in this picture too?"

"No." Claire pointed to another empty space.

"You gotta be shittin' me. And don't tell me: You were standin' right next to her in this one too."

She frowned. There were guys, one on either side of the empty space. "I was the one who took the picture."

That was no help. If Claire had been in that photo, at least I'd have been able to confirm she was there when it was taken.

The girl with pigtails in the other pic? Looked like her. Kinda. But 12-year-old kids look different than full-grown broads, so it mighta been someone else.

I tried a different tack. "What about the other two people you said went missing?"

"They weren't in the picture. They're new, and this was taken before they joined."

I downed the rest of my beer. "I'm gonna have to talk to Olivia's parents. Maybe they've got a line on her."

"You can't do that," Claire said.

I scowled. "Why not?"

"Because they're not here."

"You're shittin' me." This was just my luck. "Don't tell me they've gone missing too."

Claire shook her head. "They're off on vacation. Liv told me they were going to Maui for two weeks. They're always going on vacation somewhere. Like the day this picture was taken, they were in Ireland. I remember it because Olivia was staying at my house while they were gone."

"Lucky them," I muttered.

"So what now?" Claire asked.

I drummed my fingers on my empty beer glass. "Well, I got your friend's name, so let me do some digging and see what I come up with. I'll call you when I got somethin'. Deal?"

"Sure," she said, sounding a little disappointed.

There wasn't nothin' I could do about that. I was hoping I could do somethin' about finding Olivia Dunphy. It woulda helped if I'd had a picture of the dame, but all I had was a blank space where she'd been that I was gonna have to fill in myself. That was a bitch for me, but it was mighty convenient for her. And the church, if it was tryin' to cover somethin' up... which I suspected they were. Whatever the case, there was something fishy as hell goin' on here, and I was bound and determined to find out what it was.

Chris Reynolds was one of the few guys I could trust down at the station. He didn't exactly stick up for me when they railroaded my ass outta the force, but he didn't say anything against me either. I couldn't blame him for keeping mum. If they'd fucked me over for gettin' in the way of Henry Stiles' dirty ass, they'd fuck him over just as quick if he chose the wrong side.

Besides, he'd made it up to me since. He'd helped me out more than once, like that time with Ellie Righetti. Came to me complain' that her husband Doug, the councilman, was cheatin' on her with some bottle-blonde wannabe bombshell. Chris made sure I knew when and where ol' Doug would be with said bombshell so I could catch 'em in the act. How'd he know? I didn't ask. I knew a gift horse when I saw one. Mouth? What mouth?

Chris had fed me info on the QT when I asked—at least most of the time. I didn't wanna wear out my welcome by askin' for too many favors, but I told myself I'd let him have some peace and quiet for a while if he helped me out on this one. What was it about this particular case? Well, workin' for a young, leggy looker who paid my fee without even blinkin' was incentive enough. But something about the case itself had sunk its teeth into me. Nothing seemed right about it, and when things don't add up in a case as wacked as this one, you figure you're onto something. Maybe something big.

The other thing about Chris, besides bein' dependable, was that he used to be in Claire's church. It'd been a long time ago, and he was pretty tight-lipped about the whole thing, but if he had anything of a personal nature to offer, it'd be a plus.

Chris was decent enough to drop by my office after his shift was up; he knew I had no love for the stationhouse and even less for the cockroaches who worked there. Bad memories. No need to dwell. Maybe that's how Chris felt about his time in the church.

"Why'd you finally leave? Weren't a bunch of your family involved there?" I asked, pouring him some Jack.

"Yeah. My grandparents on my dad's side, Obadiah and Nadine Reynolds, were two of the founders, going all the way back to the beginning. I never liked them much. He was always tellin' my dad to whip me with a belt when I got out of line, and she bragged about bein' great in the kitchen, but she overcooked her steaks and undercooked her pies. I joined the church 'cause my dad guilted me into it, but I left first chance I got. Too much Big Brother. Everyone always lookin' over your shoulder and never sayin' nothing if I asked the wrong questions."

"Like what?"

"Like did Christ rise on the third day or after three days? It's two different things, but the Bible has it both ways. There's tons of shit like that. And the Temple folks say the Bible is the only thing you outta be readin'. Not the Post. Not Ellery Queen. Not even the fuckin' Reader's Digest. They say everything you need to know is right there in the Good Book. And when they don't know the answer, they just say 'have faith, brother.' First of all, I ain't their brother, and second of all, it made me out to be the bad guy if what I prayed for didn't happen. Not enough faith."

I waved a hand in front of my face. "Sounds like the papists ain't got nothin' on these guys when it comes to holy guilt."

Chris laughed. "No way. At least the papists let you go home and fuck your wife—or even your girlfriend, as long as they don't hear about it. The Temple? You can't look the wrong way crossin' the street without them knowin' about it and tellin' you to 'get on your knees before the Lord' and repent. And the church has its fingers in every cookie jar you can imagine. A few people know about it, but they don't say shit 'cause they're afraid of the Prophet and the elders."

"What cookie jars? You think they're cookin' the books?"

"I'm pretty sure of it, but there's no proof."

It was my turn to laugh. "I know about that shit."

"You comin' up empty on a case?"

"You could say that." I cleared my throat. "A client retained me to track down a missing friend. They're both in the church, but I can't find anything on her—the missing friend, that is. I was hoping maybe you could help me."

"I'll do what I can. Chris took a swig of his whiskey. "Got a name for me?"

"Olivia Dunphy."

He sat up a little straighter. "I remember Liv. She was always one of those straight-laced types who never got in any trouble. You know? Like a teacher's pet. She was still pretty young when I left the church, but I remember she was always palling around with the pastor's kid. Or the Prophet, as he likes to be called." Chris chuckled. "One high and mighty son-of-a-bitch. But his daughter was nice enough. She was about Liv's age, and was a goody-goody just like her. How could she not be, bein' a pastor's kid? But you know what they say about a minister's daughter. When they come of age, all bets are off. Sometimes before that, if you know what I mean."

I shifted uncomfortably in my seat as I looked across my desk at him. Claire had told me not to involve the cops, but she didn't know how things worked. When a cop's on your side, it can open up a bunch of dead ends. Still, that didn't mean I wanted Chris to know who she was. I wanted her to trust me, and it'd be bad enough if she found out I'd involved one of the boys in blue without tipping him off about who she was. I'd come damn close to doing just that.

A thought came to me, and I switched the subject. "You said members are afraid of the elders. What do you mean? Is it possible the Prophet and the elders are making these people disappear?"

"People?"

Foot in mouth again. I took a deep breath. "My client says three people have gone missing, but she doesn't know the other two well. They're new. The only name I have is Olivia's. Can you help me track her down, at least? I think the church is behind this somehow, but I can't put my finger on how. If Prophet is cookin' the books like you say, and if he wants to keep a lid on things, maybe he's been disappearing these folks 'cause they got too close to the truth."

Chris bit his lower lip. "Not his style. At least not when I was there. He used threats of hellfire and the wrath of God, not thugs and enforcers. But who knows? Something might have changed. Especially if he thinks the church is at risk of being exposed for his financial hanky-panky. Let me know if any other names turn up, and I'll go lookin' through the files for 'em. Meantime, I'll run a check on Olivia Dunphy and see what turns up. Can't give you any federal records, like her Social Security..."

"I know. I used to be a cop, remember?"

Chris ignored my sarcasm. "...but I can look at her DMV records and maybe get an address, and check the local property records to see who's on the deed. That kinda stuff."

"Perfect," I told him.

Maybe I'd start getting some answers that would clear up this mystery.

Except I didn't.

The next time I saw Chris, four days later, he came back with exactly... nothing.

"I went through the DMV records for car titles, license renewals, anything. But it's like she doesn't exist—and never did."

"Maybe she doesn't drive."

"It's not just that. Her name isn't on any piece of property, and there's no record of her ever attending city schools."

"Maybe she went to a private school, like at the church."

Chris shook his head. "They don't have a private school, and they wouldn't let their kids take classes at another parochial school. They're run by heretics, at least that's what they think, and heretics are worse than heathens in their book."

"Jesus, Chris. There must be *some* record of her."

He shrugged. "If there is, I sure as hell can't find it. She's never got a speeding ticket, never been cited for jaywalking, never even violated curfew. I can't even find a birth record. Looks like you're dealing with a ghost, Elijah. Unless you can get the names of those other missing members, or give me your client's name, there's not much I can do to help you."

"Thanks anyway. I guess that's why they pay me the big bucks."

With the money I was charging, Claire would stop anteing up pretty soon unless I came up with something. Problem was, I didn't know where to start.

STEPHEN H. and SHARON MARIE PROVOST

The Assassin

Swimmin' With the Fishes

I hit paydirt on my trip to the zoo. They had just what I wanted. As I walked out of the large Reptile Rotunda, I entered the Amazonian Jungle exhibit, and there they were, right at the entrance.

Now I just needed to find a way to get my next target here. According to the schedule, the zoo would be closed the next two days, leaving me plenty of time to implement my plan.

I'd made a call to Candace's job, and I had no problem finding out her shift ended at 7. This town is maybe a little too trusting for its own good. Then again, that's also what makes it a nice place to live. I appreciate my neighbors... well, most of them anyhow.

I walked to the outskirts of town to find Lily Street. Not being familiar with this area, I was pleasantly surprised to find it was a quiet little street with only a handful of homes. No barking dogs to alert anyone to my presence. No nosy neighbors with prying eyes and open ears, just waiting to eavesdrop on the next bit of town gossip. No children running from house to house. In fact, it appeared that most, if not all, of the residents were still at work.

Not that it mattered, I was dressed in a manner befitting my mission as a defender of the true faith, ready to walk among the shadows until the moment arrived to reveal my identity. I wore black jeans and a black T-shirt with black leather gloves, my face concealed by the hood of my long black cloak. In this guise, to the general public, I was forgettable... an outsider unworthy of notice. To my targets, I instilled fear and panic. The face of the reckoning they were about to incur.

I found 2201 tucked at the dead-end; it was set back from the road and in the middle of a copse of weeping willow trees. Brushing aside the low-hanging branches, I made my way to the back of the house, where I let myself in and began to look around. The tidy little home was sparsely furnished but provided a cozy environment just the same. A hand-embroidered decoration hung beside the front door, bearing the words "Bless this house" and a cross surrounded by white lilies.

I saw numerous framed photos on the mantel, the centerpiece of which was an 8-by-10 wedding photo of Candace and her husband in his full-dress blues. He had recently shipped out on a sub assigned to patrol the west coast and the Hawaiian Islands. They'd moved to town just before his deployment, and she was still settling in. A small painting of Jesus hung above the mantel.

These are good people. I hate that it has come to this, but I have no choice. I cannot ignore my edict.

As I continued down the hall, I found the perfect place to conceal myself until the proper moment to take Candace unaware. I returned to the kitchen to grab a bite to eat while I waited for her to come home.

Just before 8, as I was cleaning up, I heard a car coming down the road. I trotted back toward the bedroom and concealed myself in the hall closet, leaving it open just a crack.

I heard her enter through the front door and cross to the kitchen, where it sounded like she might be putting away groceries. Then I heard the clank of dishes as she prepared herself a meal. This town rolled up its streets by 9, so a little delay would ensure that there would be no interruptions. After some time, I heard the sink running as she cleaned up. I peered through the crack, waiting for her to pass by.

Just after she passed the closet, I leapt out and wrapped one arm around her waist snugly, placing my other hand over her mouth. I didn't want to cause her any more pain than what was already in store for her. With my mouth near her ear, in a menacing whisper, I said, "Don't try to scream or fight me. I don't want to have to hurt you. Nod if you understand."

Tears cascaded down her face as she nodded slowly.

"I'm going to let go of your mouth now. Not a peep!"

I removed my hand and pulled on the rope draped over my

neck. She gasped as she felt the rope in my hand when I reached around and pulled her arms behind her back. I tied them securely so she couldn't escape, but not so tight as to constrict the flow of blood. "Are you Candace Matthews?"

She turned her head slightly, her wide eyes looking up at me, filled with fear and uncertainty. I nodded.

"Yes, I am," she whispered.

I reached back into the closet and grabbed a strip of fabric to gag her. But before I could do so, she let out a rush of pent-up breath. "You can have whatever you want. Just please don't hurt me. I haven't seen your face in the darkness."

"I'm not some petty thief."

"But then what do you...?" Her question ended in wracking sobs as she considered the most likely alternative. Her shoulders hunched as she tried to pull into herself, shielding her body from me.

"I'd never do that to you. It's much more complicated than I can explain to you. It's time we get going."

"Where?"

"That's of no concern to you right now. You'll see soon enough." I reached up and wrapped the fabric around her mouth and tied it behind her head, gagging her. "Your car keys are in the kitchen?"

She nodded.

I grabbed her elbow and led her down the hall, turning into the kitchen. The keys were sitting on the countertop. I scooped them up and led her out the back door. We walked through the darkened yard and around to the car parked in front. I popped the trunk and helped her climb inside.

It was a 15-minute drive across town to the zoo, about three miles outside the city limits. I heard a couple of thumps against the trunk lid after I shut it, but otherwise, the ride was uneventful. I pulled up into the darkness of a dirt path cut into the line of trees across from the zoo. The area was deserted and tranquil, other than the noises from nocturnal creatures. An owl hooted from far away, and a frog croaked enthusiastically from an unseen pond somewhere beyond the trees.

I jogged across and picked the lock at the entrance to the zoo gift shop, then returned to the trunk to release Candace, leading her across the street and into the darkened building. Pulling the flashlight from my backpack, I shone a narrow beam in front of us and directed her through the maze of racks and shelves in the shop. The exit brought us out into the zoo's main pavilion.

We began a brisk walk to the back corner of the zoo, where the exhibit I had chosen was located. Candace had begun crying again and hyperventilating, making it difficult for her to breathe with the gag in her mouth. "Remember what I said," I growled as I slid it down. I gave her a minute to catch her breath before we resumed.

"Where are you taking me? What are you going to do to me?"

"Jonah 1: 15-17: 'So they took up Jonah, and cast him forth into the sea: and the sea ceased from her raging. Then the men feared the Lord exceedingly, and offered a sacrifice unto the Lord, and made vows. Now the Lord had prepared a great fish to swallow up Jonah. And Jonah was in the belly of the fish three days and three nights.'"

"I know the verse. But what does that have to do with me?"

I kept walking through the snake enclosure and then stopped as we entered the next exhibit. Candace looked up at me, anger flaring in her eyes. "I asked you a question," she repeated. "Why are we stopped here?" She looked over at the tank next to us. It held hundreds of gallons of fast-flowing water and was surrounded by rocks and dense jungle shrubbery. Her eyes widened with fright. "No, no, no! You can't mean... you wouldn't?"

I had no intention of backing out or changing my plans, but it was still hard to meet her eyes. I'd taken a solemn oath, but that didn't mean I had to enjoy inflicting pain on someone I'd never met. "I'm sorry."

"I thought you weren't going to hurt me! I did what you said. I haven't fought you or screamed. You can't do this... I'm pregnant!"

"What?"

"I'm with child. I don't know what I've done to anger you, but my child is innocent. You and I have both had a chance to live, but she hasn't even been born yet. You can't take that away from her. I don't believe you are that cruel."

I looked away, my emotions and resolve waging a war inside me. I hadn't anticipated this complication. I empathized with her pain. The mother-child bond was sacred—at least, it should be. But our feelings didn't matter. None of this changed my divine mission.

When I turned back to her, she saw the determination in my eyes. "What kind of a monster are you? This is inhuman."

"You're right," I said as I wrapped my hands around her throat and squeezed. Her face turned red and her eyes bulged as she fought to breathe. Her mouth gaped open, and tears slid down her face. Blood vessels burst in her eyes from the pressure I exerted.

She slumped into my arms, lifeless.

I untied her hands and lifted her up, placing her into the water, leaving one of her arms draped over the side of the tank. I secured that arm with rope and tied it around a planter nearby, so she wouldn't sink below the surface entirely. I pulled a cross and another small parchment calling card from my backpack and placed those in her hand, securing her hand closed with tape, so they didn't fall from her limp grasp.

A large school of piranhas broke the surface of the water, splashing about madly as they swarmed around Candace's body. Piranhas have an unfair reputation of being killers, but in reality, they're heavy-feeding scavengers. The least I could do was not subject an innocent woman to being eaten... alive.

But would she remain so innocent?

I shook my head.

In a feeding frenzy, the ravenous fish ripped bits of flesh from their newfound food source. The water grew murky as blood oozed from the torn flesh. By the time employees came back to check on the piranhas, her skeleton should be picked clean.

I shouldered my backpack and walked out of the zoo to return home. The next targets would take some preparation. And I needed to call Sally; I owed her a night out on the town. She'd been a little distant the past couple days since our disagreement. I had to try to patch things up.

STEPHEN H. and SHARON MARIE PROVOST

7

The Detective

Twilight Zone Time

*T*he leggy dame was due to meet me at Nick's in ten minutes. Given her obsessive punctuality, I was surprised to not find her already seated in the back. I sat down in the corner booth and drew the file out of my briefcase. I thanked Nick when he brought over my usual without havin' to be asked. There's a benefit to havin' your reputation... for knockin' back drinks... precede you.

I opened the file as I threw back the shot of Wild Turkey and nearly choked. The two photos the little church mouse had given me had slid out across the table, revealing more gaps. Ones that hadn't been there before. I was countin' the missing people when her voice drew me back from the fog of confusion I had been lost in.

"You look so serious. What are you looking at there?"

She sat down across from me, distracting me from the pictures with her long legs. She had them peekin' out from a mid-thigh-length green-and-yellow plaid skirt, which she was wearin' with a lime green button-up shirt. Always had a thing for the sexy schoolgirl look. More meetings like this, and I was gonna forget about the age difference.

"Hmm..." she questioned.

"Umm... yea... these photos here you gave me. You looked at them today?"

"No. Why?"

"It's the damnedest thing. You seem to have some more missing church members. By my count here... four, maybe five."

"Oh my! What are you talking about? Let me see."

I turned both photos to face her and slid them across the table, pointing out the absences.

"There's two here... one over here... and this one. Then on this school photo, there's another gap. Any idea who used to be there?"

"Well, this spot on the school photo was Delilah Matthews, the Sunday school teacher. And let's see... yes... she was right there in that gap on the other photo."

"Did you know she was missin'? Or anybody else?"

"No, I didn't. Is that why you called me out here to meet you?"

"Nah. I wanted to give you an update on my findin's. I just found this right before you came in. Now what about these others?"

"Senior members of the church are in back, so that gap was... Now that's strange."

"What's that?"

"That one belongs to Candace Matthews."

"She any relation to that schoolmarm?"

"Yes, she was Delilah's mother."

"So? By itself, I don't see nothin' odd about that."

"Well, she's gone to be with the Lord."

"She's dead? Then how was she in the picture in the first place?"

"No, I mean she was in that picture we took about a year ago. But she passed away from diabetes six months after that. Why would she disappear from that picture? She isn't missing like the others."

"I still ain't seen nothin' like it, but maybe whoever is doin' this *is* some kinda photography wiz and just tryin' to mess with our heads. You know, removin' all the people who ain't around no more as well as these ones gone missin'. But then, how would he know *I* had these pictures? And they were locked up in my desk this mornin', just where I put them the other day. This case ain't makin' no damn sense."

"I'm so confused. This really has me worried. People are disappearing faster and faster. And what you said a minute ago... he isn't removing all the people who've passed on."

"No?"

"Ezrah Phillips, right there," she pointed. "He passed from a heart attack six weeks ago. And Phoebe Wallace, over there, passed from pneumonia after breaking her hip just after this photo was taken."

"This damn case gets weirder by the minute. Okay, now what about these last two gaps together?"

"Let me think a moment. Mother says I have the memory of an elephant. Oh yes, Randall Williams was there, and his brother. I can't remember the brother's name. He only came that one time because we were having a big family celebration and picnic. Family is very important to us. We've kept detailed genealogy records of all our families for as long as the church has been around."

"That's very interestin'. You've never mentioned that before. Any chance me getting' a look at 'em?"

"Oh no! That's simply not possible."

"And why is that, sugar? You're not makin' it very easy for me here."

"They're sacred. Nobody has access to them—except for the elders and the Prophet, of course. I shouldn't have even mentioned them."

"You tellin' me that even you, the church secretary, the one who keeps all the records, can't get to 'em?"

"Uh... yes. I do. But I simply cannot give you access."

"Ain't your father the Prophet? Couldn't you ask him?"

"Absolutely not, I told you that I was here in secret. He wouldn't be happy if he knew I was spreading the church's private business. Besides, he'd never agree to it."

"Did you ever look to see if all traces of those other two missin' people had disappeared?"

"No."

"Well, dollface, then I need you to do me a favor. Look into all those meticulous records of yours, including that genealogy, and see if the records have vanished for them as well as these new ones. We need to find some relation of theirs, outside the church, that might be a little more... forthcoming."

"Does that mean you didn't have any luck finding info on Olivia?"

"Olivia who? My friend couldn't find hide nor hare of her."

"Your friend? Who is that? You weren't supposed to tell anyone else."

"You can trust him. I know him from way back. He's a cop..."

Claire jumped up from the table and turned to flee like a scared little rabbit. I grabbed her hand.

"Please, just wait."

The touch of her soft skin sent an electric jolt through me. I held her hand a moment too long. She looked down at my hand, unease pulsing through her body.

"Sorry about that. Please don't run off. Just let me finish, will ya?"

She sat back down, scooting across to the far side of the booth. "I suppose," she whispered nervously.

"Chris is a good man and, more important, a good, honest cop. That's hard to find these days. I knew he would be discreet. 'Specially since he was once a member, too."

"No, no. 'Chris?' Please tell me it's not Chris Reynolds?"

"Yeah."

"That man is an apostate. He's a Judas to his family. To the congregation. And the church. He was cast out of the body—The Prophet himself expelled him."

"Wow. I didn't know it was quite that extreme. That doesn't change anything though. He's good at his job, and he has access to the records I don't."

"What did you tell him?"

"Nothin' really, except that Olivia was missin'."

"So he doesn't know I hired you?"

"Of course not. You take me for some rank amateur?"

"I still don't like this, but what did he find?"

"That dame is a ghost. Vanished like a puff of smoke from a cigarette in the breeze. She's missin' from all the public records. Was never even born, as far as we can find."

"Damn it!" Claire said, then flushed red at her outburst. "I'm sorry. I'm just so worried about Olivia."

"I get it. Probably won't do no good. But what are the names of the other two missin' people? I want to have Chris check out all of 'em."

"Alfred Sanderson and Elsa Franklin. They both recently moved to the area and joined the church within the last year. I hate to admit it, but I don't really remember anything else about them. With my busy schedule and them being so new to the church, I hadn't really gotten to know them yet."

"I don't understand what's goin' on here. It's like an episode of the *Twilight Zone*. You ever seen that show? It's a damn good mystery, anyhow. I'm gonna take this all to Chris. Then I'm gonna take these photos to a friend who's a photography expert. See if he can find any signs of hanky-panky. In the meantime, see what you can find in those records. I'll give you a ring in a few days so we can meet back up. Got it, sugar?"

"My name is Claire."

"Claire it is, doll."

The Assassin

The Storm Cellar

I've always been exceptional. It took me just six years to earn three degrees: a bachelor's in philosophy, then a master's and a Ph.D. in psychology.

I've always had a passion for learning. When no one ever listens to you, you learn as much as you can without them. Then you astound all those people who ignored you with everything you know. That's the idea, anyway. But it doesn't work like that in practice. No matter how much you know, they'll never fucking listen. They don't care about what *you* know; they only listen to the voices in their own heads reinforcing their ignorant biases.

Cognitive dissonance is their best friend, and you're the enemy for trying to burst their precious bubbles.

So they try to discredit you—not with facts, but with harassment and peer pressure. Then they ridicule you when you keep to yourself because they don't accept you, let alone understand you. How could they, though? They haven't gone through what I've been through: being fed through the meat grinder of the foster care system, where most of your surrogate "parents" couldn't give a shit about you. All they care about is the money they'll get for taking care of you.

The less of that money they spend on your food, clothes, and, heaven forbid, recreation, the more they get to keep for themselves. All they have to do is get you a new set of clothes every time their case worker comes around to check on you, then parade you in front of them like you're some sort of kewpie doll they won at the county fair. It's sickening. And the worst part of it is, you're none the wiser. Not when you're a kid. You think it's normal, because it's the only thing you know.

Not all foster parents are created equal, though. Some foster parents actually do try, but they're usually the ones who send you packing because of a death in the family or because they find out they really *can* conceive after all. Blood is thicker than compassion. Then there are those on the other end of the spectrum. The ones who don't just want you for the money, but as a virgin to sacrifice up to their demons.

That's where I ended up when I was thirteen years old. Orion and Mary Bauer never could have children, and she was past childbearing years when they took me in. They took all their bitterness out on me, as though I'd made him infertile—although he blamed her and never would admit it was *his* medical issue. People say ignorance is bliss, but they've got that wrong. It breeds contempt far more effectively that familiarity ever did.

And bitterness inflicted on an innocent victim breeds resentment.

Or acceptance.

In my case, it gave rise to both. I tried to insulate myself from them by making them as anonymous as possible. They didn't want me to call them "mom" and "dad," so I just referred to them in my mind as "the woman" and "the man." But I couldn't insulate myself completely. I depended on them for my food and clothing, even though meals were usually things like stale bread, overripe bananas, and lukewarm water. Sometimes I got cold oatmeal or what they called "stew" without any meat in it. The clothes were hand-me-downs from the man's own childhood, which meant they were full of moth-eaten holes and stained in unusual places. But I wore them, and I *appreciated* them... because I had to. The man told me I should be grateful I wasn't out on the streets, and the woman told me to listen to the man—not because he deserved to be listened to, but because he was the head of the household.

"We're all one family here," she said. "We have to stick together and love each other. That's what families do."

So I did. I later learned I'd developed a coping mechanism I like to call "if you can't beat 'em, join 'em" syndrome." I used it to deal with being held prisoner. I developed feelings for them. I wanted to protect them and make excuses for them, even though they'd never do the same for me.

Make no mistake, I was a prisoner.

The man and the woman took me into their home, a two-bedroom bungalow in an old subdivision on the edge of town. They slept in one bedroom, but did they give me the other? No. Instead, they put me in a storm cellar lit by a 40-watt, unshaded bulb hanging by a cord from the ceiling. I remember globs of mold clinging to the walls like bats waiting for night to fall. But it was always night down there, underground with no windows. There wasn't any carpeting, either; just a cold concrete floor. Then there was that pungent musty smell that invaded my nostrils every second of every waking hour of every day. You get used to some smells; I never got used to that.

I had a twin bed with a sagging mattress that had one coil poking out near my head. When I turned the mattress, the man came down and yelled at me, demanding I turn it around again. He never gave me any reason, but I did. And I loved him for making me do right, even though I knew I could never satisfy him.

The woman was better. She came down more often, sometimes with a cup of tea or an old blanket. She brought me a book, too, with tales of kings and dragons and wizards and demons. I had to squint in the dim light to read it, but I soaked it up like a sponge. I could see in her eyes that she felt something like pity for me, but she never said an unkind word about the man, no matter how loud he screamed at me—or at her. It was his right, she said, to do as he saw fit. "He has a hard job," she said. "He's responsible for looking after us."

I believed her the same way she believed him, contrary to every shred of evidence he provided by being a pure and unadulterated asshole to both of us. That's how cognitive dissonance works. You believe what you're told to believe in order to survive. In order to preserve your sense of "doing right." Soldiers do it every day. They don't just kill for the ruler who sends them out to die, they kill with the kind of zeal that can mean just one thing. They aren't just obeying that ruler, they love him.

It's sick. I didn't know that then, but I do now.

And still, nobody listens to me.

They put a dog down there with me, a mongrel that already looked hungry.

"This is Azrael," the man said. "A stray that keeps coming around, begging for scraps. Has his name and this weird symbol for a dog tag. He's yours now. Don't say we never gave you anything. Look after him. If he bites you or dies or gets sick, that's on you." He brushed his palms together as though he were washing his hands of the whole affair. "This is *your* dog, your responsibility."

And it was.

They never brought any food or water down for Azrael, so I gave him some of what they gave me, and we both ended up hungry. He'd come over and put his head on my leg, and I would rub him behind his ears. When he shit in the corner, I had to collect it in a paper bag and give it to the woman to dispose of. I had to pick it up with my hands; at least the woman brought me some gloves. I didn't mind anyway. Azrael was helping me as much as I helped him; maybe more.

I got taken away from the man and the woman after about six months when social services realized I hadn't been enrolled in school and a social worker came around to question them. They told her I was too stupid and rebellious to attend school, so they'd been teaching me at home. She didn't buy it, so she had me removed. I remember crying and screaming that I wanted to stay, grabbing a bookcase to keep the social workers from taking me and pulling it down almost on top of me. The man yelled and screamed at me the way he always did, but they literally had to drag me out of the home.

As they took me away, I heard the man say, "Good riddance," and I thought I heard the woman crying.

They must have left the door to the storm cellar open, because Azrael came bounding up the steps and bolted through the door, barking and snarling as the two men put me in the social services van.

They shooed him away. I don't know what happened to him then, but I never stopped thinking about him.

I never told Sally about any of this. I never told anyone at all.

As far as I was concerned, my life began after they took me

back to social services. They had problems placing me after that, so I wound up spending the rest of my teenage years in a group home for troubled teens run by the Lost Hills Orphanage. The people in charge there gave me more books to read, and I devoured them just like I devoured the one the woman gave me. Textbooks, history books, novels, science books. They brought teachers into the home and assigned us classwork there because they said we were too "socially maladjusted" to attend a real school.

It didn't matter to me. I had little use for other people my age, with their silly obsessions with being popular and "scoring" with the girls. I never looked at girls in the home because they never looked at me. And people who wanted to be popular? They'd sell their souls for it, which was something I wasn't willing to do. They'd sacrifice their true identity and their potential for doing anything original, meaningful in life on the altar of base conformity. I wasn't about to do that, and I didn't need them.

My intelligence was my secret weapon; my flamethrower to use on the cold hearts and frozen minds of those who had become mindless minions. I breezed through my GED and aced the SAT with a score of 1,560 out of 1,600, which wrote my ticket into the hallowed halls of higher education.

That's where I met Sally. Unlike everyone else, she actually listened. The irony was I couldn't tell her about what was most important to me. She already thought I was neglecting her, but she didn't understand how my mind worked. Everything was a product of cause and effect, an unbroken chain of events dating back to an ultimate first cause. If you followed the chain back far enough, everything could be explained. It was my duty to continue the chain, which was why my objectives had always been linear; I didn't move on to the next thing until I'd accomplished the task at hand... and I couldn't tell her about the task at hand. She wouldn't understand that, either, and I couldn't put my mission in jeopardy.

I'd already slipped up by calling it an assignment. "You've got your own practice," she said. "Who's there to assign you anything?"

I couldn't tell her who it was. She'd never believe me. She'd never understand how my assignment was revealed to me in my quest to understand things as they once were—in the whispers between the lines of ancient texts, echoing down through the ages as a secret shared by few. I was entrusted with this secret, and was promised assistance by the one who shared it with me.

His goals and mine were in full alignment, and that assistance had been delivered to me, as he'd promised. My course was now set; the die was cast. I loved Sally, but I *needed* to accomplish this. I could only hope that she was patient enough to wait for me, and that she would understand when my task was complete.

STEPHEN H. and SHARON MARIE PROVOST

The Assassin

Till Death Do Us...

My next assignment would be more difficult. More complicated. But I was in no position to argue about what needed to be done. The path laid out before me was clear, and it was not my place to question it—just follow it.

This time, I had two targets: Joseph Edwards and his fiancée Sarah. They'd been engaged for six years but had waited to get married while Joseph got enough money together to go into business for himself. He'd been working part-time at his father's shop since he was a teenager, and his father had promised to hand him the reins once he had enough money to buy 51 percent of it.

That's what Joseph had been working toward. He saw himself as an honorable man. He wanted to start a family but wanted to be sure he could provide for them before taking on that kind of responsibility.

Joseph and Sarah were the kind of couple who waited until they were married to become intimate. That was the "right way to do things," but it also meant they didn't risk bringing a newborn into the world before they could afford to care for it— which would be all the more difficult if they had to deal with the withering looks of disapproval and the whispers about their "bastard" child.

To help him reach that goal of buying his father's business, he had been managing Waverly Waves, a public swimming pool out by the Fairview Country Club. It was better money than you might expect; backyard pools were a luxury for the rich, and hot summers demanded cool recreation. Public pools like Waverly provided that. Families with young kids and teenagers flocked to the pool on ninety-degree scorchers. For the teens, it was a good excuse to meet up with sweethearts away from their parents' watchful eyes. For young single men, it was ample reason to make a beeline for the place and scope out sorority girls in their form-fitting one-piece bathing suits.

That's how Joseph and Sarah had met each other. I'd known them both off and on for several years, and I'd heard them mention it myself—more than once. More than mention, actually. It made me sick the way they droned on about it, like they were bragging about how smart they were being. Joseph wanted to be congratulated for waiting until they got married, and being so frugal with his money, saving up to pursue his dream instead of blowing it on booze at Nick's Lampliter or longshots at Brightridge Downs. It didn't take a genius to do any of that; it was the kind of thing idiots did, and it was certainly nothing to brag about. Especially when he didn't keep such a tight rein on his checkbook when it came to other pursuits.

That gave me a good laugh.

A friend you trust is a lot more likely to stab you in the back than a stranger you keep at arm's length.

I'd heard that once; I'm not sure where, but it had always stuck with me: a message to help keep me on task when pursuing my mission.

As manager of Waverly Waves, Joseph was expected to close up every night and make sure the place was secure. I'd watched him for the past two nights, and Sally had come down to meet him both times. Sure enough, she was there again on the third night.

The pool complex stretched out over a couple of acres, complete with a large building of showers and changing rooms, a wading pool for younger kids, and a bandstand for nighttime concerts. Rows of folding wooden chairs had been piled up against the side of the building in preparation for a Dixieland band's performance the following night.

After the last customers left for the evening, the lights went off, and before Joseph began making the rounds to lock up, I snuck in through the side gate, carrying an insulated container. It held my secret ingredient, purchased for just this occasion; I'd needed a good bit of it, so it was pretty heavy, and I was glad I didn't have to walk far with it. I took it over to the bandstand and hid it underneath the steps that led up to the small circular stage.

The only sounds came from cicadas and crickets, buzzing and clicking and chirping relentlessly as they awoke to conquer the night. Moths that had been whirring and flitting around the incandescent bulbs dispersed now that they'd gone dark, though I could still see the insects in the light of the full moon. It wasn't ideal to have such good visibility, but I'd grown accustomed to hugging the shadows, even in bright daylight. I was confident I could remain undetected until my task was complete.

I lurked behind an L-shaped brick wall that created an alcove at the entrance to the men's room and waited until I heard the sound of footsteps. They were heavier on the concrete path, so I knew they had to belong to Joseph.

He would be first.

I reached into the inner pocket I'd sewn inside my cloak and removed the thick two-foot-long strip of canvas that I had prepared for just this occasion. I wound it around itself like a tourniquet and took hold of it with both hands, pulling it tight. The tension invigorated me, and my muscles tensed, ready to spring. I knew he was a short, squat man, about six inches shorter than I was, so I was prepared to strike at the proper angle.

I counted the steps as they approached. Then, a split second before he passed in front of me, I sprang out of the shadows, whipping the taut canvas over his head and down to his neck in the same motion and pulling back sharply. He tried to cry out, but the pressure I applied was acute and immediate; all that came out of his mouth was a sputtering wheeze.

I pulled him back tight against me. "This is your payment for the filthy lucre *you* paid to fund the sins of their avarice," I whispered through gritted teeth. "For you hearkened unto those who wished to build a tower, yet you did not first sit down and count the cost. And when it was built, it was built on sand."

I slammed my knee into the small of his back and pushed him

to the ground, keeping the canvas tight around his windpipe the whole time. He was gagging and flailing, but I wasn't nearly through with him yet. I loosened it, just a little. "I am going to tell you a parable of my own making," I hissed. "There once lived a man who was very rich. He was so wealthy, in fact, that he bought a large plantation and gave it to his good friend, knowing that friend to be a wicked man. The friend, who had been impoverished until this time, bought slaves for his plantation. He stuck them in a hole in the ground and fed them a dog's rations. He ranted and raved and whipped them when they displeased him—even though *nothing* could please him. Then, one day, the slaves were set free, and the slaveowner was called to judgment for his malice."

Joseph was flailing with his arms again, so I yanked the canvas tight. "If you resist me, it will not go well for you. Do you understand?"

He managed a small nod and stopped flailing, so I loosened the canvas again.

"Now, I insist that you answer a single question. I will loosen this noose around your neck a little more so you can answer it, but if you cry out, I will slam your head into the concrete. We wouldn't want your missus to hear us now, would we?"

Joseph's body went limp in resignation. "She ain't my missus," he said.

I smiled. "But she's going to be. I've seen how you look at her. And I wouldn't want to ruin your reputation as a provider and *protector* by having her see you like this."

"How have you seen... Have... you... been stalking... us? Wait... who... are you?"

"I'll ask the questions here," I said. "And my question for you is this: Is the slaveholder's friend, who sold him the plantation, responsible for the atrocities visited upon those slaves?

Remember, the man would never have even owned the plantation, let alone the slaves, if it was not for his friend, and the friend knew full well his malevolent nature. The slaveowner was called to judgment, so what do you say should happen to the wealthy friend who was his benefactor?"

"He... should... share in... his... judgment," Joseph rasped.

"Very good! Very good indeed! You have understood the point of my parable precisely. It's a pity, though, that you have closed your ears to the parables of Christ. "You have sown your seed among the thorns, which have choked the young shoots that sprang from them before they could reach their full potential. That's why I'm choking you now. But don't think I'm done with you. I'm not. Not even close."

I pulled the canvas tight again and listened to him try to gasp and choke until he finally passed out. Then I grabbed him underneath his arms and dragged him over to the chairs beside the bandstand. I pulled out some rope I had in my other inner pocket and bound his legs to the legs of the chair and his arms together behind his back with constrictor knots. Then I opened his mouth and shoved the canvas in it, pulling it tight and tying both ends around the back of his head.

Now all I had to do was wait.

It wasn't long.

First, I heard Sarah calling for Joseph, then her voice grew louder and she exited the locker complex, shaking her head. "I swear, you're always ignoring me!" she huffed. It reminded me of what Sally said to me. But I wasn't like Joseph. I was nothing like him.

"Joseph, where on God's green earth have you got to?" she said, annoyance mingling with growing concern. "If this is one of your jokes, it's not funny. I know this place is locked, but I'm still a woman, an attractive woman, out here alone at night by myself... Wait, you *did* lock the gates, didn't you? You didn't tell me... Good lord, am I talking to myself? Joseph, I swear..."

She was interrupted by a muffled sound from a few feet behind her and off to one side. She hadn't noticed Joseph was there, and he had just now awakened from the state of unconsciousness I'd put him in.

Her head whipped around, "Oh, my God!" she gasped.

"Now, now," I said, stepping out of the shadows, "it's a sin to take the Lord's name in vain."

She started to scream, but I cut her off by wrapping my arm around her throat and pulling back.

"Who...?" she sputtered.

"I am the thorn choking off the seeds the devil has planted. The one to whom I am sworn has given me this task, to visit upon you just recompense for choking off the seed of many innocents. As it is written, an eye for an eye, a tooth for a tooth... a life for a life! You and Joseph paid handsomely to ruin *my* life, and the lives of many others. Now vengeance will be mine!"

I shoved her backward, into the pool near the steps, her head striking the metal handrail with a *thunk*.

She wasn't dead. Just out cold, lying face-up in the water.

I heard a clattering behind me and spun around. Joseph had managed to tip over the wooden chair and was scrambling to his feet, still tied to it. Bent forward like a hunchback bull, he charged at me, but he was still weak and dizzy from the ordeal I'd put him through, so he couldn't run in a straight line. I dodged him like a matador and brought my two fists, balled up together, down hard on the small of his back.

He hit the ground with an *oomph*, and I pulled him back into an upright position at the edge of the pool. The knots were all secure, and the canvas was still firmly in place. "Try that again, and I'll kill you here and now." It was a lie, but a necessary one. I

65

had to complete the living—or dying—parable I'd begun. It was an indispensable part of my mission. And I needed him to *think* I was willing to kill him on the spot in order to keep him compliant.

He quieted down, his eyes fixed on Sarah's floating body.

A small whimper escaped from beneath the gag.

"Don't worry," I said. "She's alive."

But not for long.

As Joseph watched, I walked down the concrete steps into the water until I was standing waist-deep next to her. I hooked my arms underneath her, raising her unconscious body up out of the water. She was light and petite; even with the water dripping from her clothes, I could have lifted her—or someone twice her weight.

"I hereby baptize you in the name of my master, who has charged me to carry out true justice in his behalf. As he has helped me, I in turn provide him succor in bringing to pass our shared objective. As Noah was carried to safety by the raging waters, these same waters consumed the depraved and iniquitous, purifying all the earth in a single act of baptism. In this way, I baptize you now, purifying the earth of you, that your sins may not be visited on your offspring yet unborn."

With that, I pushed her under... and held her there, locking eyes with Joseph.

He was tensing his muscles, grunting and straining with all his might against the ropes.

Still I held her under.

I counted the time off in my head—*one one-thousand, two-one thousand, three one-thousand*—until five minutes had passed. Then I let her rise to the surface, turning her face-down just to be sure.

Joseph was wincing and crying uncontrollably. If it hadn't been for what he'd done, I would have felt sorry for him. But pity had no place in my mission.

I strode up out of the water and walked past him, retrieving the insulated container I had brought with me and setting it beside him.

His eyes, filled with new tears, looked up at me, questioning. I wondered whether these tears were for his fiancée or what he had realized was about to befall him. Either way, he wasn't a man to cry easily; I'd never seen him cry in the time that I'd known him. He was too proud. *But pride goeth before a fall.*

"The stench of you sickens me," I said. "You, too, must be cleansed."

I knew he thought I was going to drown him the way I had drowned his fiancée; I *wanted* him to think that, to make him panic. He deserved that. But I wasn't going to drown him. Instead, I stepped over to the supply shed beside the pool and found a plastic bucket, which I filled with pool water and dumped over his head. "There now," I said. "That wasn't so bad, was it?"

He scowled at me. He knew I was toying with him, and he wanted no part of it. It was time to end this.

"We're almost finished now," I said. "As it is written, 'Those who have bathed need not wash, except for their feet. Then he shall be clean. And you are clean... but not every one of you.'"

I donned a pair of thick rubber gloves I'd brought with me. Then I removed the lid from the container, which was the size of a large bucket, exposing the clear oily liquid and setting it in front of him.

I lifted the chair—with him in it—and set it down again so that his feet, and the chair legs to which they were bound, were both in the wide container. The minute his feet hit the liquid, he began writhing in agony, trying to thrash and kick. But I pressed down with all my strength on the back of the chair, holding it firmly in place to ensure he wouldn't spill the contents by kicking the bucket. It would have been easier to knock him unconscious first, but not nearly as gratifying. This man had played a key role in what the man and the woman, Orion and Mary, had done to me, and it was my right to see him suffer. My master had agreed to grant me this privilege.

Before too long, the pain of the sulfuric acid eating away at his flesh and through to the tendons and ligaments underneath became too much for him, and he passed out from the shock of it.

Once again, the only sounds were the sounds of the night, the droning and clicking of the cicadas and the constant chirping of the crickets. They were my only witnesses. I knew Joseph would never regain consciousness. He would bleed out before the pool was scheduled to open for business at 10 o'clock the following morning.

Another stage in my mission was complete. I reached into my pocket and withdrew a small cross and my calling card, setting them in Joseph's lap. I had to give credit where credit was due.

The Detective
Elijah In Wonderland

*T*he morning had started out quiet, maybe a little too quiet. That should've been my first warning that things were about to go cattywampus. I'd received a call from Chris down at the station. To no one's surprise, he'd found diddly-squat about any of the missing people. They were all more dust in the wind. This town had an ever-growing population of phantasms. This case had got me usin' words that weren't even in my vocabulary before. Who the fuck believed in ghosts?

I was startin' to believe that girlie's feminine wiles extended beyond makin' me contemplate a little private time with her... if ya know what I mean. I was beginnin' to think she could make me believe anything she said, like the fact that there were seven missing people, who, conveniently, no one else in the church would acknowledge. I'd have thought she'd sent us on a wild goose chase lookin' up these names if Chris hadn't known Olivia.

The day blew up the second Claire came breezin' into my office, the door bouncing off the wall. Without an appointment... or disguise. Her already rosy cheeks were flushed a flamin' red. I couldn't take my eyes off her.

"Whoa there, sweet cheeks! What seems to be the matter? Aren't you afraid of bein' seen?"

"No... well, yes... I guess I wasn't thinking straight. Something's wrong."

I grabbed her hand and led her over to the chair by my desk, shutting my office door behind us. "Take a load off and catch your breath. Then tell me what's wrong."

She gave me a weak smile as I sat back down behind the desk. "Thank you. I'm sorry I didn't call first."

"Relax, doll. No skin off my nose... it's your dollar. Now tell me what's wrong."

"On Sunday, we're having a big potluck like we do after service every week. My mom's making pot roast."

"Let's cut to the chase here, dollface. Daylight's a-burning."

She gave me a hard look and continued. "I *am*. I was expecting Nathan from Prime Cuts Butcher Shop to deliver the briskets this..."

"Oooh, they do have the best meat in town."

"I *know*. Can you quit interrupting? Now who's wasting time?"

I raised my hands in mock surrender. "Proceed, sweetheart."

"Claire!"

"Got it, baby. Claire."

She shook her head angrily, her hands twisting in her lap. "Anyhow, he never came. I had a busy morning and didn't realize until two hours after he was supposed to make the delivery. I tried calling the shop to see if Nathan was out sick, and I needed to pick up the meat, but it didn't ring through. I talked to the operator, and she said there was no such listing."

"I see."

"Doesn't that concern you? Isn't that strange? Clearly, you have been there. They've been in business for over sixty years."

"True. My ma used to send me to that market to pick up the meat every week. Isn't it owned by members of the church?"

"Yes, it is."

"Did you try goin' down there?"

"No, I came right to you. I was just so flustered... and scared."

"Let me go down and check it out. They know me well. Can't beat a nice, juicy steak!"

She rose quickly and grabbed her purse. "I'll go with you."

"Aren't you worried about bein' seen?"

"I'll wait in the car," she said as she pulled those large, silly shades from her purse and tied a kerchief over her head.

"You're the boss lady."

We arrived downtown a few minutes later and parked in the back lot. I used the rear entrance and found the shop nearly empty. Strange for this time on a Saturday. Usually, it would be bustlin' with everybody shoppin' for the coming week. Even odder that I didn't recognize any of the people runnin' the meat counter. Prime Cuts was a family-owned business, a large family at that. I'd never seen anyone workin' there besides one of the family members.

As I looked around the store, I noticed they had done quite a bit of remodelin' since I was last there... not all of it appealin'. The store now had a cutesy western theme. Red-and-white checkered tablecloths covered every table displayin' the spices and marinades. Knick-knack shelves had been hung on the wall, with old metal watering cans actin' as vases for sunflowers.

Alongside all this were cartoons of little boys in jeans and cowboy boots lassoing cows, haulin' hay and such.

The few customers in the shop looked as lost as I felt, wanderin' around the store as if they didn't know where to find anything. As I stood there, slack-jawed, a young man behind the counter broke through my thoughts. "Can I help you, sir?"

"I think so. I need to speak to Joe."

"I'm sorry. We don't have any employees by that name."

"The owner for Christ's sake! Never mind. What about his wife?"

"And who would she be?"

"Sarah... you know, the other owner... your boss," I shot back, frustrated.

"Sir, you don't have to be rude. I'm not sure if *you're* confused, but the owners are Frank and Edna Pierce. Frank is disabled and no longer actively involved in the business. I can go get *Edna* if you like."

"Yes, please."

I couldn't understand what the Sam Hill was goin' on. When did they hire staff? And such an imbecile at that? Didn't even know his bosses' names. I'd just been here two weeks ago, and it hadn't been like this. As I turned back toward the counter, I saw Claire come stridin' in.

"Thought you were waitin' in the car."

"It was taking so long. I got impatient. I'll just pretend I'm here to pick up my order."

"Whatever you say... it's your show."

Just then, the young man returned with an older woman in tow. Who in the hell was she?

"Excuse me, sir. How can I assist you?" she asked, all full of herself.

"I was asking this *boy* to get me the owners, Joe and Sarah

Edwards. I need to speak to them. It's important."

"I am the owner here. My name is Edna Pierce. Now what seems to be the problem?"

I was gettin' damn tired of this game. Just what was going on in this town?

I tried to keep a measured voice as I asked, "Isn't this Prime Cuts Butcher Shop owned by the Edwards family?"

"Oh, now I know what you mean. This *was* Prime Cuts, but Old Man Edwards sold it to my husband and me 'round about twenty years ago."

"Twenty years ago! But what about Joe and Sarah? They bought the shop from him, you know, keepin' it in the family."

"I'm afraid not. They were *going* to buy it after they got married that October, but then tragedy struck."

"Tragedy? What do you mean?"

"Let's see... it was twenty-five years ago, back in June, that they were murdered."

"Murdered? What in the hell are you talkin' about? I just saw Joe here two weeks ago!"

Edna looked at me like I'd lost my mind. Her brow furrowed, but she kept talkin' as if I had never interrupted her. "I'm afraid that's impossible. It was a terrible affair. That awful serial killer murdered both of them over at Waverly Waves. It was quite the scandal. Old Man Edwards kept the shop for about five years after that, but then he started going downhill. He never could get over the loss of his son."

"I can't believe this!"

"I know. It was such a shock to the whole town. But getting back to your visit, is there something I can help you with?"

"No. Thank you."

I rubbed my temples as I turned to leave. Felt like I had a whopper of a hangover comin' on, but I hadn't had a drop to drink. Or had I? It was gettin' harder to know what was reality anymore. Or *when* somethin' occurred... even though I'd been sure only a day or two before. Another young man behind the counter was tryin' to get Claire's attention to see what she needed. She didn't seem to hear him because she looked as confused as I was. As I walked out the back door, I heard Claire fall in step behind me.

I stopped in the middle of the parking lot and spun around. "Jesus Christ on a cracker! What the fuck is going on this shit-ass town? Forget *Twilight Zone*! I just know any moment the music is gonna start playin', and Allen Funt'll come out, mic in hand, and say, 'Smile, you're on *Candid* Camera.' They just wanna see us react to this insane, impossible bullshit!"

I looked up and saw Claire staring down at her feet, shifting uncomfortably. "Please don't take the Lord's name in vain."

"Sorry, kid. I wasn't made for this hocus pocus shit. Give me good ol' solid ground any day. How're you doing?"

"I'm not sure. Miracles should be left to the Lord. This seems more like the work of Satan."

"Amen to that, sister."

Claire's lip twitched, trying to hold back a smile. She burst out laughing when she heard me snicker. "Now that's more like it. I think we both needed to let off a little steam."

I looked up to the sky, sighing. I couldn't believe my eyes as I looked back at Claire. "Holy shit! Will you look at that? Did you notice that on our way in?"

"What?" Claire asked, all puzzled like, as she turned to follow my eyes.

"The sign. The logo has changed to that ridiculous little cowboy with a lasso, and it's called Pierce Meats."

"That wasn't here two days ago. I'm sure of it. I picked up chicken for dinner on my way home from the church."

"Am I stuck in a nightmare an' can't wake up? None of this is possible. It just ain't! Guess I gotta just keep lookin' for clues until we solve this damn case or hell freezes over."

"So what's next, Detective?"

"Seems like you're gettin' wrapped up in this, eh?"

"God forgive me my selfish thoughts, but yes, I have enjoyed your company today, even if has been a bit strange. This investigation thing is very different from my day-to-day duties at the church. Don't get me wrong... I love my work."

"But it can be a bit tedious?"

"Yes. I'm worried about Olivia and the other missing parishioners, and heartbroken by this news about Brother Joseph and Sister Sarah. But until all this happened, there was very little change in my routine from one day to the next. The biggest conundrum I had each week: Would it be meatballs, pot roast or fried chicken served at the potluck after services? If the Prophet heard me say this, I'd be on my knees for days begging forgiveness."

"Heard what? I didn't hear anything."

"Thank you."

"But seriously, your father would really do that to you?"

"He is the Prophet first... last... and always."

"That must have been a hard life for you growing up."

"It's all I've ever known. Besides the Lord is my savior. I'm happy to serve him."

"That makes one of us. Now back to your question... what's next? You up for a trip to the newspaper office? A double homicide this big woulda been front page news twenty-five years ago. Still would be, for that matter. Let's hit the stacks."

STEPHEN H. and SHARON MARIE PROVOST

The Detective

Three Strikes an' I'm Out

We drove downtown and pulled up in front of the offices of the *Tri-Valley Tribune*. The secretary at the front desk looked up when she saw us comin'. "Welcome to the *Tri-Valley Tribune*. How may I help you?"

"We need some help finding a story about some murders that occurred here about twenty-five years ago."

"Let me call down to the archivist. He'll be able to help you with that."

A short while later, a short, balding man with Coke-bottle glasses came down the hall and greeted us.

"I hear you need some help researching an old news story."

"Yes, that's correct. We need to see about the murders of Joseph Edwards and Sarah..."

I looked over at Claire at a loss for Sarah's maiden name.

"Danvers," she interjected.

"Yes, Sarah Danvers. They occurred here in town twenty-five years ago in June."

"I can certainly help you with that. If you'll just follow me downstairs to the morgue, we'll look through the archives to find that story."

"Morgue?" Claire questioned, her eyes wide with concern.

"Not that kind of morgue. It's what these newspaper guys call the room where they archive all the old issues."

"Oh!"

We followed him down and took a seat at a table there, where he told us how to look through the microfilm. It took a bit of searchin' but forty-five minutes later, a gritty image was up on the screen. The headline "Azrael's Assassin Strikes Again" was emblazoned on the front page, along with a picture of Waverly Waves surrounded by officers, an' photos of Joseph and Sarah.

"Azrael's Assassin? Who the hell is that? I've never even heard of him."

Claire looked at me and shrugged her shoulders.

I read the story and turned to Claire.

"Apparently, a serial killer they called Azrael's Assassin drowned Sarah in the public pool, then gruesomely murdered Joseph after making him watch."

"Wait... Azrael's Assassin? Does it say why they called him that?"

"Apparently, he left some kinda calling card with a sigil on it... Not sure what it means. You ever heard of a sigil?"

"And how was Joseph killed?"

"I'm not sure you wanna hear the details."

"Yes, I do. It could be important."

"His feet were soaking in a bucket of sulfuric acid. He bled out."

"Oh my! That's horrific. But somehow the staging of that crime plus that name Azrael and the sigil. There's significance behind that. Spiritual significance."

"Look who's the detective now. So what does it all mean?"

"Give me a bit to think about it. I can just about see it, but I need some more time to interpret. What about that headline? Strikes again?"

"It says this was his third murder here in town. He killed a woman named Candace Matthews seven years prior, and Jud Williams four years before that."

"Oh dear! You said Candace Matthews?"

"Yeah. What about it?"

"Candace was Delilah's mother. Delilah is the Sunday school teacher who disappeared, remember"

"Shit! This is getting curiouser and curiouser."

Claire stared at me, a puzzled look on her face.

"Cut me some slack. I'm tryin' to be respectful and lay off some of the cursin' and blasphemy."

Claire laughed and actually appeared to relax for once.

"I appreciate that. You're a good man, Detective."

"Don't you go ruinin' my reputation now. I'm as jaded as they come. Crooked too, if you talk to those other assholes down at the station."

"I would've never guessed you'd read *Alice in Wonderland*."

"Hey, I was a child once too... long time ago. Seems like we've hopped down the rabbit hole in this town. Smoked a little too much hookah with the Caterpillar. Drunk too much of the Mad Hatter's tea. I swear, if a disembodied grin appears above us, I'm gettin' myself fitted for a straitjacket before checking myself into the looney bin."

Claire giggled. "Better make that a reservation for two then."

"Now let's get back to work here. We need to look up these other murders and see if they describe the scene. I got a theory, and I wanna see if it pans out."

Another hour later and I had the details down.

I turned to Claire. "You sure you want to hear what happened? It's pretty hair-raising."

"Let's do it. I'm ready."

I took a deep breath and let her have it. "Jud had his eyes poked out and brain scrambled with a hot poker and then replaced with glass eyeballs. He had that same calling card plus a cross in his hand."

Claire took a deep breath. "Okay. I'm afraid to ask, but what happened to Candace? She was such a sweet woman."

"She was strangled to death an' fed to a tank of piranhas at the zoo. He left one hand out of the water claspin' a cross and the calling card."

"That's..."

I hated to interrupt her, but there was no choice. "There's somethin' else."

"What?"

"She was pregnant at the time."

Claire's hand flew to her mouth, and she gagged. "I have to get out of here," she moaned as she took flight up the stairs, leavin' her purse behind. I collected our belongings and followed her out, thankin' the archivist as I left.

Claire was huddled on a bench outside, still lookin' green. I set her purse down beside her and took a seat myself.

"Are you okay?"

"Yes. Thank you."

"I can leave you out of this from now on. Let you know once I got it all figured out."

"No. I really think I can be of help. You're not as familiar with scriptures as I am."

"Hey, I'll have you know I did go to seminary... for a while at least."

"I didn't know that. Well, all the better, two heads are better than one."

"I think I'm startin' to see a pattern. An' I don't like it one bit."

"I don't understand any of this. The Edwards family goes back to the early days of the church. They're very important members of the congregation, and they've been integral in the expansion of the church."

"How so?"

"They're our largest single benefactor."

"How large?"

"Very large. The Word says 10 percent of your gross income—the tithe—belongs to the Lord," she explained. "The Edwardses donated 25 percent of their *total* income."

"Why did you stress 'total'?"

"Their income is a lot larger than most people realize. You know how busy the shop is, but that's only the tip of the iceberg. They supply the meat to almost all the restaurants in a 50-mile radius. Then there's the investments they've made in the stock market... very lucrative investments."

"I'm on to somethin' here. It's gonna sound crazy, but you'll have to bear with me. In the meantime, I need some bourbon... a bottle of it. Meet me back at my office in half an hour. I need you to bring me them church records and the genealogy charts. I'll explain everythin' then. We need to explore how far this goes."

As Claire walked up the street back to the church, I sat in the car, befuddled. I opened the dash and pulled out the flask I kept there for emergencies... like this one. I'd lived in this town my whole life, and I didn't remember any of these murders. I remembered going to the Edwards butcher shop every week growin' up. When Joseph and his wife took over, Sarah gave me a peppermint stick every week when I picked up my mother's order.

The biggest mystery had my head spinning. I'd been curious about everybody's business since I was young. Been reading the paper since I started school. More important, I'd started workin' as a paperboy when I was eleven. After I finished my deliveries, I'd run through town bellowin' the headline, hopin' to catch a few more sales. I woulda been twelve when Joseph and Sarah were killed. There's no way I would have forgotten a headline like "Azrael's Assassin Strikes Again." It simply wasn't possible. I knocked back the last of the gin in my flask and headed out to get more booze.

I had just sat down at my desk after pickin' up a bottle of Wild Turkey at the liquor store when in walked my brave little church mouse. Even exhausted and shaken, she was still breathtaking. I wanted to wrap my arms around that little darlin' and then...

Gotta get my head on straight. She's nearly young enough to be my daughter. And she paid me to work a case.

Her arms were loaded with leather-bound books, sign-in books, and a volume labeled "Compassionate Truth Temple Genealogy." "I think I have everything you wanted to see." She dropped them on the desk with a resounding thump. "What's first?"

"Let's see if my theory stands up to the first test. We know, from experience, that Olivia is missing from the books. Did you ever check the genealogy for Randall Williams, an' Candace an' Delilah Matthews? While we're at it, what about Nathan? Or Sarah and Joseph?"

She flipped through the book, organized alphabetically, to where the Edwards family should have been, then went on to the Matthews family after that. She looked up at me, fear in her eyes, and then back down at the book, flipping page after page.

"What's wrong?"

"They're gone. All of them!"

"What do you mean by all?"

"Well, almost all of them. Candace isn't missing, but her death date has changed. And the same goes for Sarah and Joseph. They aren't even listed as ever being married. And their entire family... there's no trace of them—all ten children and 22 grandchildren."

"Ten? Sarah and Joseph were busy... getting busy."

I couldn't help but chuckle at my joke. Claire didn't even notice.

"We're encouraged to be fruitful and multiply."

"Apparently. Next question, was Delilah an only child?"

"Yes. Candace became barren after Delilah was born."

"One last question: Did you see that picture in the newspaper of that other victim named Jud Williams?"

"I did. Why?"

"Didn't you notice his striking resemblance to Randall...?"

"Williams! Yes, I did. I think I see where you're going with this."

"This is where you might think me crazy. I think Jud was their father. And I'm no expert, but takin' a wild guess at the ages of our missin' people, it appears to me as if one or both of their parents were murdered *before* any of the children were born. Thereby erasin' them from existence... entirely."

"But how? They *did* exist. You and I remember them. I know my father does too, even if he won't admit it."

"Never said I had it all figured out. Whooo-oooooo-ooo! Cue the sci-fi movie music. That's the part I can't explain."

"But why were they murdered?"

"That's a good question. It seems as if someone is systematically targetin' all the members of the church. But to what end? And who? Got any theories about that?"

"No. This is all too much. Believing in magic is heresy."

"Or madness. Not sure which is better right about now."

Claire slumped in her seat, the events of the day wearing her down. She checked her watch and jumped up, lookin' worried. "I've got to get home. It's after 8. My father is going to want to know where I've been."

"By the way, shouldn't Olivia's parents be back from Maui by now?"

"Yes. Why?" she asked impatiently.

"Humor me. Before you go, can you look up one more thing?"

"Yes. Quickly!"

"When you noticed Olivia missing from the photo, did you ever look for her parents in any of the records or the genealogy?"

"NO! I never thought to look for their names when Olivia disappeared. I was so focused on Liv herself, I didn't think about checking for her parents' names." She quickly riffled through the genealogy book, breakin' into tears when she turned to the previous page and found the death dates for Michael and Patricia Dunphy had changed, just like the others.

"That's what I was afraid of. We need to go back to the stacks tomorrow, and check these dates against what we can see in the papers. I'll call you in the morning sometime to arrange a time to meet."

I gave her my hand to help her as she rose with the stack of books in her arms. She walked out, silent, with the weight of the world on her shoulders.

"Get some rest, sweetheart. I mean Claire."

"I was beginnin' to feel like this case was FUBAR... utterly hopeless. *How do you even begin to work a case when the past is changin'? How do you stop a murderer that was active over 30 years ago?* Maybe I'd had a little too much of that Southern comfort and lost touch with reality. Hopefully all of this would be helped with a good night's sleep. I could return to this nightmare case in the sober light of day.

STEPHEN H. and SHARON MARIE PROVOST

The Detective
Folie à Deux

A good night's sleep? The "sober" light of day? Who was I kidding? The way things had been goin' lately, I wasn't gonna get even twenty winks, let alone forty, without a stiff nightcap or two or three. Hell, I really just wanted to drink myself into oblivion. None of this shit was possible, and part o' me couldn't shake the notion that Claire might be puttin' me on. She sure knew how to distract me with those legs, those curves, and that angel face of hers. There was no arguin' that. And she was the one who'd been feedin' me all the information: the church registry, the member list, the photos. Everything... except for those photos that had changed *after* she gave 'em to me.

Even if I figured out how she'd faked the stuff at the church, it didn't account for that. No one had broken into my place, and they hadn't been touched or disturbed. Was she usin' some sort o' newfangled photo developer that erased parts of a picture after the fact? These mad scientist types were splittin' the atom an' shootin' up satellites. Who's to say they couldn't pull off something this nutso?

And it didn't account for those newspaper pieces, either. She couldn't have got into the morgue and planted them... could she? I rubbed my eyes, reached into the liquor cabinet and pulled out a nearly full bottle o' Smirnoff. Vodka wasn't my usual poison, but it didn't taste like nothin', so you could go on a bender without noticin' so much... except for the burn goin' down, an' I was used to that.

I poured myself a glass of the stuff and downed it, then walked over to the phonograph, droppin' the needle on "Sing, Sing, Sing," by Benny Goodman. Then I poured another glass an' took the bottle with me to the couch, settin' it on the coffee table beside me for easy access before I plopped my ass down on the old blue cushions. The couch had been Granny Bea's before I got it, and I chuckled to think that she'd be havin' a conniption fit if she knew I was drinkin' on it. She'd been all hot to trot about that teetotalin' temperance crap.

By the time I'd downed my fifth glass of vodka, "Sing, Sing, Sing" had been sung, sung, sung for a while, but I was still hearin' ol' Gene Krupa pounding them drums in my head. I closed my eyes and saw Claire leanin' over me, kissin' my forehead and tellin' me not to worry. To relax... right before she started laughing in my face. I opened them up again, but the room was spinnin', and I wasn't feelin' so good. I shut them tight again, and the next time I opened 'em, I felt a cold shiver and saw I was starin' up at...

Ginger.

Ginger was my older sister—twelve years older, to be precise. She'd always been protective, but since mom had passed, Ginger acted like she was tryin' to *be* her. She'd made me give her a key to my flat and told me to call her whenever I needed her. I never called, but that just made her worry more, and she'd started to drop by unannounced every now and then, usually when it wasn't convenient. Like now.

The cold shiver had come from a cold compress Ginger was holdin' on my forehead. The room wasn't spinning anymore when I looked up at her, but the light seemed brighter than normal and was makin' me squint. Gene Krupa was bangin' the bongos again, louder than ever, and my brain felt like it was tryin' to break outta my skull and make a getaway—not that it was doin' me much good when it came to figurin' out Claire's rabbit-hole of a case.

When I opened my eyes again, she was waggin' that bottle of Smirnoff back and forth a few inches above my face. It was empty.

"Looks like you went on quite a bender, brother of mine," she said. She wore this expression of hers that was both angry and satisfied at the same time. Angry at me 'cause I'd been drinkin', and satisfied 'cause it gave her another excuse to feel better'n me.

I forced myself to sit up, and had to hold back a tidal wave wantin' to come up out of my belly.

Ginger rolled her eyes. "Drink this," she said, handin' me a glass of water.

"What happened to the hair of the dog?"

"The dog that's eatin' away that yellow liver of yours? Or the one that's got almost as much hair on his face as you do? When was the last time you shaved?"

"It's just a five o'clock shadow," I muttered.

"More like midnight," she cracked. "You can't keep living like this, Elijah. You've been drinking yourself under the table ever since you left the force. Isn't it time you got over it and owned up to your mistakes?"

That sobered me up then and there, or came close. "I was set up, and you know it," I growled. "Why the hell do you always wanna think the worst o' me?"

"Maybe 'cause you keep proving me right." She threw the empty vodka bottle down into the trash can by the sink for effect. "I don't care what you did or didn't do three years ago, brother. It's in the past and you need to stop moping about it. That early grave's just waiting for you halfway between that vodka bottle and Nick's place. I could just let you walk into it, but I'm responsible for you since Mom died."

There it was again. She always said it like I was a burden. She had some kind of duty to me for Mom's sake, not because she actually cared about me.

I rubbed my head again. "I'll have you know this has nothin' to do with me getting run off the force. It's somethin' else. But don't bother askin', 'cause it ain't your concern. You wouldn't understand none of it anyway."

"You're right, Elijah. And I'm *not* concerned about it. I don't care. But I'm not gonna have you drinking yourself into a coma. You need help, and you shouldn't need me to tell you. But since you seem to, here I am." She went over and opened the liquor cabinet, and started pourin' all my stash down the drain in the kitchen sink.

"Hey!"

"Hey nothing. You'll have to earn some more money if you wanna replace this, and you'll have to be sober to do it. Maybe by the time you've dried out for a while, you won't need this crutch of yours. In the meantime, go find yourself a shrink. You won't talk to me, but maybe you'll talk to some stranger who doesn't give a damn about you," she huffed. "This is one helluva way to treat your sister."

Yeah, I was just a burden. A stain on the prom dress of her perfect life.

She turned on her heel and sauntered out of the room, all holier-than-thou. Almost like she belonged to that church of Claire's. She slammed the door—which set off Gene Krupa drummin' on my skull again—without so much as a goodbye.

But maybe she was right. I sighed, pulled myself to my feet and staggered over to the phone book in the kitchen. Blinking a couple o' times to clear my vision, I flipped through it until I came to the page with the listing for headshrinkers. I let my finger drop onto one of the names. That'll do well enough, I said to myself. But first I had to call Claire, like I promised, and tell her I wasn't gonna be able to meet her. I had to get my head screwed on straight first, and I didn't have any idea how long that was gonna take.

The shrink had a second-story office in the Collier Building, an art deco low-rise in the Gaslamp District. It wasn't much to look at—the office, that is. No reception desk. No secretary. Just one small room with a chair, a sofa, and a side table holding up a small, abstract piece that was a poor excuse for a white elephant. The ears were flat bulges on the sides of its head, and the tusks curved out of a nonexistent mouth, then back into what must've been the trunk; the rest of it was all smooth and featureless. It was a white elephant, all right. This guy had probably gotten it regifted to him at a Christmas party.

The shrink had a desk, which wasn't much more than a table with a couple of drawers. On top were a quill pen, telephone, humidor, and appointment book on top of a desk pad. A couple of folders sat off to one side.

On the wall hung a single painting of daffodils in a field against a pale blue sky. I figured it was supposed to be comforting. It wasn't. At least not to me.

I was having second thoughts about this already, but I'd

come in the door and found the shrink waiting for me. He walked out from behind his desk, and stuck out his hand.

I took it.

No turning back now.

"Do I sit on the seat or the couch, Doc?"

"Whichever you'd like," he said.

I chose the chair and pulled it up to the desk so I was directly across from him. I liked to be on equal footing with whoever I was talkin' to, shrink or no shrink, and I wanted to look him in the eye.

"What brings you here today, Mr. Kirk?" he asked.

"You gotta promise you won't think I'm nuts," I said. "I've heard of that quack and his icepick lobotomies. I don't wanna end up in no straitjacket or locked away in the looney bin."

"I can assure you, Mr. Kirk, that our meetings here are strictly confidential. I only refer my clients for medical procedures or other forms of treatment with their full consent. And to further set your mind at ease, I do not perform, nor do I approve of lobotomies—using an icepick or any other implement."

"How long you been practicin'?" I asked. "I don't see no filing cabinet. You just open the place up?"

"No, I've been in practice for three years now. I take my files home with me to ensure that no one breaks into my office. You can't be too careful when it comes to confidential material, and you'd be surprised how many spouses, family members, or other 'interested parties' would like to get their hands on my clients' records."

I chuckled. "No, I wouldn't. I'm a private dick. I see a lot of the same kinda thing."

"That must be a stressful job," he said, opening the humidor and extending it for me to take a cigar.

"Thanks," I said. "That ain't my vice. I got too many others."

"Very well," he said. "I find that smoking relaxes some of my clients."

"I prefer a shot of whiskey. Across the table from a leggy blonde, if you know what I mean. No offense, Doc."

He laughed. "None taken. But you still haven't answered my question of why you sought out my help—I should tell you that my sessions last an hour and twenty-five minutes. Have you come here to discuss an alcohol problem?"

"Yeah... well... not really. What I mean is, yeah, I can lay the sauce on too heavy. But it's what's causin' me to drink that's really drivin' me nuts." I leaned forward. "A client came to me with this case. I can't go into specifics, but it looks like people been disappearin' without a trace and no one knows what's become of 'em."

"What do you mean?"

"Just that. These people are here one day, then, like that"—I snapped my fingers—"they're gone."

"And this client has hired you to find these missing persons, I assume," he said. "And since I also assume you have yet to find them, you're feeling pressure to solve the case. Am I correct?"

"Not pressure so much as... none of it makes any sense. I'm the only one who seems to know they're missing—me and my client, that is. Everyone else is actin' like nothin' happened. And here's the weird part: One guy who disappeared, he and the missus owned a butcher shop. You musta heard of it, Prime Cuts. But now, all of sudden, it's got new owners who're callin' it Pierce Meats. Redid the whole interior. Shoulda taken 'em a couple of weeks at least, but it happened overnight."

The shrink's brow furrowed.

"I've never heard of Prime Cuts. It's been Pierce Meats as long as I can remember."

I blinked. "So you don't remember Joe and Sarah Edwards ownin' the place?"

"No, but I do remember those names. Let me think... Yes, that's it. Someone named Edwards *did* own the place before the Pierces. I just didn't remember what it was called. I was a kid at the time."

The shrink *did* seem young. From the look of him, I mighta had ten years on him. Prob'ly more.

But he was talkin' again: "And... yes... I've heard the name Joseph Edwards, and Sarah too. But her name was Danvers, not Edwards. One of the most famous cases anyone's ever seen here. Again, it was before my time, but I'm sure you've heard people talking about it. They called it the Butcher Block murders because Joe worked at his father's meat market."

"Yeah," I said, sittin' up straighter. "I went down to the *Trib* an' found a story about it in the archives. "The headline said 'Azrael's Assassin Strikes Again.'"

"Yes, now that you mention it, I remember that too. I don't think they ever caught the guy. But you see? There's proof positive that it happened, and that your memory is playing tricks on you. Now we just have to pinpoint what triggered this delusion of yours and find a way to restore the real memories you've either lost or somehow suppressed."

"What *triggered* it, you say? Listen, Doc, I know how you guys think. My father musta hit me, so I wanted to off him and marry my mom. Do I got that right?"

"We've come a little ways in our field since Freud," he said. "Every individual is different. Some neuroses are triggered in childhood. Others are based on later events, like wartime trauma, or even occurrences in the present day. I know you don't want to talk about your alcohol, but since you brought it up, perhaps it's worth exploring."

I rolled my eyes and glared at him, but it didn't stop him from goin' ahead with it.

"This could be a case of you losing time," he said. "Some people black out and wake up miles away in a totally different place. They have no idea how they got there. Have you ever blacked out after drinking and had that happen?"

"I've *passed* out after drinkin', but my client ain't had a drop of the stuff. She don't drink at all. And it was her that ordered a delivery from the butcher shop when it was Prime Cuts. She called the place when it didn't show up, and the line had gone dead. Operator said there was no such number. So we went over there and saw it for ourselves. The owners said they'd had the place for somethin' like twenty years! And get this: The couple that shoulda been there? The new owners said they'd been murdered even longer ago'n that. I mighta lost a couple of hours to the bottle, but no way in hell did I lose twenty years. That woulda put me back in high school."

The doc started drummin' his fingers on the table, starin' toward me... but more like over my head.

"I admit that seems out of the question." He sighed and looked me in the eyes again. "You referred to your client as 'she,' which must mean she is a woman."

I nodded, kickin' myself for lettin' that slip.

"Tell me, do you find this woman attractive?"

I shrugged. "Yeah, but what's that got to do with it?"

"Have you ever heard of a shared delusion?"

I hadn't, and I told him so. Sounded like a bunch o' quackery to me, but it couldn't be any more bizarre than what I was tellin' him.

"A shared delusion, or a folie à deux, is when two people view some event or situation in the same way, even though their common perspective is entirely false. The details can be very specific, and the delusion can be... disorienting, especially when one or both of the people involved are confronted with the truth. But that doesn't mean they will abandon their delusion. The human mind can be a stubborn thing. Once we adopt a belief, it's very difficult to dislodge it—especially when someone we trust or admire reinforces it.

"This is why, for example, nations support tyrants, even after they've revealed their true nature. It isn't just fear of the tyrant's wrath. It's the fear of being exposed for believing a lie. Rather than changing their viewpoint, they cling even more tenaciously to their false idea that the tyrant has their best interests at heart, even though nothing could be further from the truth. This shared psychosis can become even more deeply ingrained when the tyrant invokes an authority higher than himself, such as patriotic duty or God's will. By equating the will of God to his own, he introduces the threat of damnation for those who dare oppose it."

I put my hands on both sides of my head. I'd heard some of this stuff in seminary, but it was still givin' me a headache the way the doc was sayin' it. Either that, or I wasn't completely done with my hangover yet.

"What does that have to do with my client?" I asked.

"It's the same principle operating on a much more intimate level. You trust your client and want to please her by solving the case for her. From the little you've told me about yourself, this instinct is present for you with any client. It's part of your moral code. Someone pays you, and you deliver."

I nodded.

"But if I'm right, the attraction to your client is amplifying this sense of duty—and making you vulnerable to her psychosis. That's how a shared delusion works. It's not a case of two people looking at a mountain and seeing a skyscraper instead. One of them develops the delusion independently, then passes in on to the second person: someone who is invested in the deluded person's well-being. In cases where two people are close, that investment can include the psychotic person's perspective and, with it, the delusion itself. The more time they spend together, the more the delusion is reinforced, until it becomes more real to them than the truth."

I'd never heard of anything like this, but the way he was sayin' it, it kinda made sense. At least it made more sense than people disappearin' twenty or thirty years ago... but *after* you'd been standing in front of 'em yesterday. If what he said was right, I was flippin' out because I'd been spendin' too much time with Claire. She'd gotten me to believe her crazy ideas because I wanted to—because I was getting' too close. That would mean the photos she'd showed me, the newspaper clippings, even the butcher shop, had been what I'd *wanted* to see, not what was really there. Or else I was too drunk off my ass to think straight. Either explanation made more sense than all the crazy shit Claire had been feeding me... and that'd I'd been lappin' up like a good little puppy.

It wasn't her fault. With everything I'd found out about the Temple, it was no wonder they'd done a number on her. Her father, the Prophet, was doin' to her exactly what the shrink said she was doin' to me. The only difference was he was doin' it on purpose, and she was just passin' it on.

Not everything made sense. Like why Claire's delusion seemed to be at odds with the Prophet's agenda to keep the church's dealings hush-hush. But maybe she'd come up with this bizarre story of hers to justify gettin' out from under his thumb. I was no fuckin' shrink, though, and I was in over my head tryin' to figure *that* part out. All that mattered was I needed a break from Claire to clear my head. To look at all this more objectively. If I was just feedin' her delusion, I wasn't doin' my job. And the job came first.

"Has any of this helped you, Mr. Kirk?" the shrink was sayin'. "Would you like to schedule a follow-up appointment?"

I stood up and extended my hand. "I don't think so. I think I can take it from here, Doc."

"Well, I'm always here if you need to touch base," he said.

"Thanks, Doc Donovan. I'll keep that in mind."

The Assassin
13
Out of Sight, Out of Mind

I walked home, my mind still spinning from my last session of the day. He was new to my practice. I'd fit him in for his first appointment when he called this morning for an emergency session. He claimed to be losing his mind. Sadly, it didn't seem too much of a stretch to worry that it might be true.

This town was full of corruption, from the crooked cops to the multitude of crime families who owned them, to the biggest scammer of all, the Compassionate Truth Temple. The minority in town who didn't fit into one of those categories just kept to themselves, too bullied too many ways to put up a fight.

Mental illness, especially paranoia, anxiety and depression were common; I'd treated many such cases in my office. But shortly after he began his story, I knew this man wasn't crazy. And he wouldn't let this go unless I gave him a push in the direction he was already headed... the way I needed him to go.

I just let him get it off his chest. Asked the right questions. Then I expressed my concerns about a shared delusion with this troublesome church member, and my worries about his declining mental state if he didn't abandon this obsession. I couldn't believe how easy it was to bring him closer to the brink of a breakdown.

When he mentioned the butcher shop changing, I told him I remembered the change in ownership. I even told him how my parents talked about the overwhelming fear in town when those murders were occurring. He believed every word, even though I'd made up all of it on the fly, of course. I didn't even *have* any parents. After an hour and a half, I was confident I'd convinced him to let this go—for the time being at least.

I wished I'd known the identity of that woman at the church. If I had, maybe I could have changed my plans to address this issue sooner. It was odd that she'd left her prayer closet and taken her concern about the disappearances to a private investigator, a former cop at that. The church was usually so secretive—and with good reason. The upshot of all this was, if I'd convinced him to avoid her, she wouldn't dare take this anywhere else. The consequences were too high if she got caught by one of the elders or the Prophet.

As I reached for the doorknob, it was pulled open from the other side by Sally—a very angry-looking Sally. "Finally! You're home."

"It's been a long day. Can we talk about this later? Let's just have dinner and some normal, easy conversation. What do you say?" I walked down the hall and unlocked my office to put away the day's patient files. Sally entered behind me, her face still red with anger.

"What do I say? Why don't we start with this: What's the

big secret in your office that you keep it locked?"

"I've told you before, Sally. My patient files, like these here." I lifted my hand with the stack of charts.

"What's in those locked cabinets?"

I walked over to the cabinets and unlocked them. I lifted the doors and slid them back on the track for each shelf, one by one, showing her row after row of patient charts. "See? All patient records. Nothing sinister. I have a legal and ethical obligation to keep these confidential from *everyone*. I don't understand why you don't trust me. I would never cheat on you. I intend to make you my wife."

"Fine. How about telling me why you're late *again*? You have an office downtown. You have office hours. I've seen them posted on the door. You're supposed to be out of there by 5. So, what's with all the late-night meetings?"

"I can't really talk about this, Sally. Remember doctor-patient confidentiality? I had a late-afternoon emergency appointment with a new client. I couldn't turn him away. OK?"

"And what about all the other nights you've been gone?"

"You do realize I have a really full schedule, don't you? I'm a busy man. You know how screwed up this town is and how many people need help because of it. I try to stick to my office hours, you know, maintain the whole work-life balance, but not everybody is available during normal work hours. I feel a responsibility to help everyone out."

"Why do you have this overblown sense of responsibility? You can't save the world, Brantley. At some point, you have a responsibility to yourself and to me."

"I understand that. I love you more than you know. I'm working to make this world, and especially our little corner of it, a better place for us and for our children... when we have them. I know I haven't given you a lot of details about my childhood, but

I've told you how difficult it was for me."

"*No* details, Brantley. None at all."

"Fine. You're right. None. But I'm not hiding it from you, I swear. I'm just not ready to share it yet. I will tell you everything I experienced... soon. I'm working to make sure no one else experiences what I did."

"So is that your secret project? Your *mission*? The one you can't talk about. The one you said was 'assigned' to you, yet you say there's no one I can speak to about it?"

"Yes." I sighed. I feared I'd already said too much. Sally could be a bit pushy and nosy at times, especially when it came to those she loved. But I loved her dearly. *Who among us is without sin or faults?*

Then it came to me: The answer to all three of my problems lay in one simple solution. The detective *and* the woman from the church would have to back off if I laid low for a while. No more murders. No more disappearances. I'd just stop as quickly as I started. The easiest way for any person to deal with the unexplained, the impossible, was to forget it. The good old "out of sight, out of mind" principle.

And Sally would be pleased if I spent more time with her.

My mission was of great importance to me. I'd been assigned this duty because of my faith and tenacity; I couldn't abandon it, especially so close to completion, but a short break would ensure my success. Sally was a good woman, and she'd been there for me through many hard times. I wouldn't be living up to my oath to be an honorable man if I didn't see to her needs as well.

I had a weeklong psychology conference coming up in ten days, so I'd invite Sally to come with me. It would be her first plane flight, which would be exciting for her. I'd change my reservation to a suite, so she'd have her own room. When I was in the conference sessions, she could hang out in the hotel, go to the spa, maybe do some shopping. Then I'd take her out to dinner each night. Really wine and dine her, like she deserved.

I could set my mission aside for a couple of weeks, maybe a month. I'd keep my schedule light when we returned, so I could plan a big surprise proposal. We'd dated for seven years and talked about getting married frequently. But it was time we made it official. That would keep her busy planning the wedding, and she wouldn't notice my absences as much when I resumed my mission.

Besides, a little extra time to solidify my plans for my final targets would allow me to expedite my mission when the time came. With any luck, I'd complete my preparations before the detective's interest was piqued enough to draw him back in.

And I could make that meddlesome whistleblower at the church disappear... one way or the other.

STEPHEN H. and SHARON MARIE PROVOST

The Detective

The Fix is In

I'd been keepin' my distance from Claire for a few weeks, ever since I talked to the shrink. It was just as well, since nothin' new had happened with her case in that time. No disappearances. No new leads. I was thinkin' more than ever that Doc Donovan had been right. Things had cooled down since I stopped seein' Claire.

Besides, it gave me time to spend on my other cases.

Not that I had any.

But that changed on a Monday morning when this sap walked into my office out of the blue, plunked five C-notes down in front of me, and told me he wanted to procure my services. I say he's a sap because he's dressed way too spiffy for this side of town, in a silk tie and a tailored pinstripe suit. This *might* have meant he was one of the Carboni Boys, 'cause they're always dressed to the nines, even when they're doin' a job. But none of Carboni's goons, or Vinnie Lombardo's, or Pretty Boy Parker's would just throw down five C's without layin' down conditions. They respect me 'cause they think I was a dirty cop, but respect only gets you so far when you're dealin' with the mob.

So, yeah, this guy was a sap. The way he talked just confirmed it. All straight-laced like some accountant or tax man. But as long as he wasn't with Internal Revenue, he was OK by me. He was givin' *me* revenue, after all.

Underneath his natty duds, the fellow was an odd duck. His left eye was perpetually half shut, and he had a large mole on his right cheek.

"What brings you down to the Left-End District?" I asked him. "Take a wrong turn at the country club?"

The guy's mouth twitched a little bit on one side just before he opened it to speak, and his jaw moved back and forth. He was grinding his teeth: He was nervous, and not good at hiding it. "I'm here on behalf of... a certain gentleman who wishes to engage your services," he said, pursing his lips tightly when he'd finished.

Christ, was he one of those fuzzy-headed statue guards on leave from Buckingham Palace? This guy was as stiff as them, but a lot mouthier.

"Now ain't that illuminating," I said, reachin' forward and pullin' the C-notes to me like a card sharp collectin' his winnings. "Who is this mystery man?"

The sap shifted back and forth on the balls of his feet. "He doesn't wish to disclose his identity."

"Well, I ain't workin' for no damned phantom."

Buckingham Palace cleared his throat. "The gentleman is paying you $500."

He had me there.

"Then what's *your* name, wise ass?"

Buckingham Palace pulled out his wallet and laid down another C-note. "The gentleman is now paying you $600."

"Not to ask who the fuck *you* are?"

He nodded once. "That's correct."

I smiled.

"Make it a G, and you got yourself a deal." I figured I'd overplayed my hand, but if Buckingham Palace was as much of a sap as he was givin' off, he wouldn't know a bluff from a hole in the head. Which meant I'd be a sweet G richer.

He pulled out his wallet again and went through it, pulling out four more C's and slapping them down on the desk.

Jack-fucking-pot.

I swept up my winnings and pointed to the chair across the desk from me. "So, whaddya got for me?"

He stayed standing.

"Are you familiar with..." He cleared his throat, and I thought he was gonna dish me somethin' about some bigshot. Maybe a dumbass who got caught with his snake in some floozy's cookie jar. But it wasn't that. "...the Friday night cards at the Palladium?"

I leaned back and laughed out loud. "Ho ho ho, and Jiminy fuckin' Christmas. Who ain't?"

"The boxing matches there are fixed."

"Yeah? Well you coulda fooled me, Buckingham." The sarcasm was almost drippin' off my tongue, but if he noticed, he didn't react.

"Buckingham?" He looked confused.

"Forget it. Listen, Mr. Smart Guy, it's the fights. Palookas take payoffs. Mugs take a dive. It's part of the game. If you're paying me a thousand bucks to tell you that, I almost feel bad takin' your money. Almost." I laughed again and shook my head.

He frowned. "The gentleman I represent lost $20,000 on the main event last week. Bam-Bam Cassini won every round going into the 10th, and then, out of nowhere..."

"Marty Sullivan floors him outta nowhere. I know. I follow the fight game. And yeah, the fix was in. I can tell you that right now. It was clear as the nose on your face. But let me ask you somethin': How'd you know about the scorecards? It wasn't in the papers."

"I..."

I leaned forward. "You went pokin' around, didn't ya? Maybe talked to one of the judges?"

He nodded nervously.

"Well, let me give you some advice. It's won't even cost you another Benjamin. Half the judges at the Palladium are on the take, and you know who's buyin' 'em off? Vinnie Lombardo, that's who. And if Vinnie catches wind of it, he'll have it dealt with. He'll have *you* dealt with. And before his goons are done with you, they'll be usin' brass knuckles on you, pryin' off your fingernails and God knows what else till you tell them who this 'gentleman' of yours is. Then they'll thank you by offing your sorry ass and dumping your body in Briarwood Canyon."

He opened his mouth to say something, but I wasn't finished.

"I'm guessing you went to the bunco squad, and I'm also guessing... no, this ain't a guess... that they didn't do Jack shit about it. You know why? Because half of the boys in blue are on the take just like the boxers, and those who ain't, well, they just look the other way. That's how it works. Get the picture?"

Buckingham nodded slowly.

"So you come to yours truly." I spread my arms wide. "Tell me, just what do you think it is I can do for you?"

Buckingham hesitated. "I was hoping you could tell me who was fixing the fights."

"I just did. And...?"

"We are going to get the gentleman's money back."

"We?" I wanted to laugh. This guy was just too much. But he was startin' to get under my skin. I leaned forward and slammed my hand down on the desk.

Buckingham jumped and took a step back.

"You idiot! Haven't you heard a God damn thing I said? You don't mess with fuckin' Vinnie Lombardo. I don't even mess with Vinnie Lombardo. I got no wish to be fitted for size 11 cement overshoes and dumped in Lake Ossagon. Catch my drift? You wanna go an' 'talk' to Vinnie? Be my guest. It's been nice knowin' ya, dumbass."

He chuffed and did his best to look put out, pulling down on his vest. "Then I suppose we have nothing more to discuss," he said. "I will relay your advice to the gentleman." He turned toward the door.

"You do that," I said to his backside. "An' if he sends you out to talk to Vinnie, he ain't no fuckin' gentleman. Be seein' ya."

Buckingham was done with me, but I wasn't done with him. I figured he'd given me a thousand smackers, so I could afford the luxury of doing my own investigating. Something seemed off about him, beyond him bein' a Class-A boob. I recognized him from somewhere, but I couldn't put my finger on it. Maybe I should be the one talkin' to Vinnie's people. As long as I wasn't snoopin' around *his* business, Vinnie wouldn't give a god damn.

Vinnie actually owned the Palladium, and there was a gym

out back called the Vesuvius where some of the fighters trained. Vinnie ran that too, and was known to frequent the place to check in on them... which really involved makin' sure they did what he expected of 'em when fight time rolled around. Not all the outcomes were "prearranged." That woulda been too obvious. The ones that weren't served as set-ups for bigger paydays—orchestrated by Vinnie through intermediaries.

I went in through the backdoor of the Vesuvius. The "doorman," a 6-foot-6, 300-pound bruiser named Augie DeCarlo, just nodded and let me pass. They knew me here. There weren't nothin' inside I hadn't seen before.

The gym was halfway underground, so I went down five or six steps before I got to a corridor lined with locker rooms on both sides. Once I'd got past these, I walked out into the main gymnasium, a windowless cube lit by maybe a dozen halide bulbs under silver domes. Brick walls on four sides. Racks of old leather gloves for sparring partners who didn't have their own. Posters of big fights: Tony Canzoneri vs. Kid Chocolate, Canzoneri-Berg, Jack Sharkey vs. Primo Carnera, Carnera-Uzcudun, Carnera-Loughran... Lots of Italian pugs, which was only natural in a place run by a guy named Lombardo. None of those fights was at the Palladium, but Vinnie liked to pretend they were.

A pale-skinned, redheaded club fighter named Pepper McGrath was working the small bag. A welterweight who no one ever thought would amount to much. But he won just often enough—sometimes because Vinnie "arranged" it—to stay in the game. Bulldog Harrigan, a heavyweight whose belly was bigger than all the muscles in his body put together, was throwin' haymakers at the heavy bag. He looked like he was punchin' in slow-motion, but that was his regular speed.

As luck would have it, Vinnie was there, leanin' in on the ropes from the apron as a couple of kids I didn't recognize went at it in the ring. He was always bringin' in new blood to get spilled for entertainment and profit. Vinnie's, that is. "Hey, hey! Elijah T. What's the news from the cop shop?" He reached out a big hand, grasped mine and pulled me to him, clappin' me on the back. "Oh, that's right. Silly me," he said pullin' away. "Y'ain't down there no more now, are ya?" He winked at me. He knew full well I'd been off the force for three years.

I shrugged, letting it pass. It was one of his tests; he'd insult you to see if he could get under your skin, and if you came back at him, he'd have Augie show you the door. Roughly. "Same old shit, different day," I told him, shrugging. "How's everything in your world, Vincente?" Everyone called Vinnie 'Vinnie' behind his back, but no one said that to his face without gettin' on his bad side. And you did *not* want to be on his bad side, so in person it was always Vincente. It was Italian for "winning," and—no surprise—he liked that.

"Can't complain," he said. "Although we did have some chump poking his nose around down here the other day."

"What about?"

"Wanted to see the scorecards for Sullivan-Cassini. Freddie Baron, one of the judges, happened to be here. He brushed him off, and Augie escorted him out, but I think he got a peek at the cards. The nerve of the guy. Like it wasn't on the up and up. Nothin' shady goes down at the Palladium."

I played along, even though he knew I was the wiser. It was all part of the game.

"That's the guy I wanted to ask you about."

"Oh, really?" He raised his eyebrows, no longer just feigning interest.

"Yeah. Did you or Freddie happen to catch the guy's name?"

Vinnie laughed. "He was bein' all cagey, tryin' not to give himself away. Just told Freddie some 'gentleman' had sent him...

which, of course, meant I put a shadow on him. Louie Carvallo. Very discrete. Interesting thing is, he went back to a church. Don't ask me what it was called. It wasn't the Holy Mother Church, so I didn't concern myself. Figured if he was from some *Protestant* church, he wouldn't be causin' no trouble. Them's a bunch o' numbskulls, anyway. Don't know their piehole from their shithole. Figured if he came back, I'd deal with him. Just might be stupid enough to do it, too."

"Where was this church?"

"A few miles outta town, on the north side, Louie said. Hey what do you care? What's this about, anyway?"

I wasn't about to tell him the guy had come to me. I was nervous enough about the prospect of Buckingham being dumb enough to try an' get his money back, which could very well lead to him spillin' the beans about me. I couldn't let that happen. I'd have to track this guy down before he made a spectacle of himself—and made Vinnie reconsider his nonchalant reaction.

"It's personal," I said. "I think the guy might be mixed up in some second-rate kidnapping scheme. A client came to me with a missing persons case and thinks there might be some hanky-panky goin' on. It's probably nothin'. Nine times out of ten, it's just a runaway or a gal who finally got sick of gettin' knocked around by some loser. But I know these skirts. They get all wound up at the drop of a hat, then you gotta calm them down an' reassure them. I just gotta follow it up so I can tell her I ain't found nothin'."

Vinnie nodded. "Got it. Then you take their money and maybe 'reassure' them into givin' ya some tail."

I smiled, still playing along, but picturin' Claire's leggy physique in my mind—despite bein' determined not to. "Maybe."

"If ya hear anything that concerns me, do me the courtesy of cluin' me in, will ya?"

"You got it, Vinni—"

It was out of my mouth before I could stop myself.

Vinnie flashed a warning glare at me, then smiled and clapped me on the back. "That's your mulligan, Ellie. No more free passes. Got it?"

"Of course. I apologize."

"Think nothin' of it." He flashed another smile. "Remember, clue me in."

Vinnie had been a big help. The church "a few miles out of town on the north side" could only be the Compassionate Truth Temple. By bein' so secretive about the so-called "gentleman" who was pullin' his strings, Buckingham had raised Vinnie's hackles and supplied me with the answers he didn't wanna give.

Some of them, at least.

If Buckingham was actin' on behalf of someone at the church—which, given the church's preoccupation with secrecy, seemed likely—then it might tie in to somethin' else. Chris had told me it was common knowledge on the force that the church was cookin' its books, and Buckingham had been eager to throw a buncha C-notes at me and not even complain when I took 'em for doin' almost nothing. Then there was that $20,000. Where could that have come from? Was it church money bein' used for gambling? And if so, who had his fingers in the cabbage pie?

I decided to get Chris on the blower to see what he might know, and we met down at Nick's after he got off his shift. I asked the barkeep for a dry martini, and he ordered a Manhattan. Ginger woulda killed me, but as long as I wasn't fallin' down drunk, I figured, what's the harm?

We sat in the back corner where no one could listen in.

"I got a new case," I told Chris.

"Oh?"

"Turns out could be tied into the old case—the disappearances."

"I thought we'd hit a dead end there. I couldn't find anything about those people, and I haven't heard nothing new from you for nearly a month now. It's probably all just a red herring anyway." I wasn't about to tell him Ginger'd found me passed out drunk on my sofa or that I'd seen a shrink who told me the disappearances were all in my head. Or Claire's. So I played along. "What's this new case, and how does it tie in?"

I filled him in about Buckingham, and how he'd come to me about a fight bein' fixed at the Palladium. "Said he was workin' for some other guy he wouldn't name. Mister Mysterious wagered twenty grand on Cassini against Sullivan, which I'm sure you know wasn't such a good idea. Vinnie didn't do a very good job of makin' it look legit, so Buckingham had questions. Anyway, with you bein' from the church and all, I thought maybe you'd have a line on this guy. He came in dressed sharper than Cary Grant, and he had a lazy eye with a big dark mole on his cheek. Ring any bells?"

Chris sat up straighter but looked perplexed. "You say this guy's name is Buckingham?"

"Nah, he wouldn't tell me his name. That's just what I call him for convenience's sake."

Chris nodded knowingly. "Then I know him, all right. That's Roderick Birch. He's one of the elders at the Temple."

"Oh? That must mean he has some pull there."

"Yes and no. The elders are just paper tigers. They act all high an' mighty, but they don't so much as sneeze without askin' permission from the Prophet. Hugh Cassidy. He's the one callin' the shots, and if Birch was actin' on anyone's orders from the church, it woulda been him. It just confirms all the talk about the church playin' fast an' loose with the purse strings—and about Cassidy bein' behind it. Like I said, he's behind everything there, so why wouldn't he be? They even call him the 'for-profit prophet' down at the station." He laughed.

Finally, things had started makin' sense. I wasn't about to tell Chris about the past changin' and all that shit. He wouldn't believe it, and I was tryin' not to think about it myself. I didn't want Chris to drag me back into Claire's delusion—if the shrink was right about that.

I pushed my martini away from me. I'd already finished it, but it was the principle of the thing, right?

Chris frowned. He suddenly looked dead serious. "What if," he said, "Vinnie's boys are behind these disappearances?"

That did it. Claire had convinced *me* people were

disappearin', and I'd convinced Chris. Maybe I'd brought him into her delusion. I didn't know what the fuck to think. But if I had, I needed to play along and work through the what-ifs with him. I figured I owed him that much.

So, Vinnie's boys...

I thought for a moment, but it didn't add up. Vinnie had passed this Birch guy off like he was nothing to worry about, and he didn't give a rat's ass about the Temple. He didn't even know what the damned church was called. Yeah, he might've been playing dumb. But why? He didn't know I was looking into any disappearances, so there was no point in him putting on an act for me. And he was a pretty shitty actor in any case.

"Maybe it's time we look into this down at the station," Chris suggested.

"C'mon, Chris," I said. "If Vinnie is behind this, you know they'll just look the other way." I wasn't liking the sound of this. If people *were* disappearing, I was sure Vinnie was just an incidental player in it all. But I didn't want to let Chris know that. If Vinnie *wasn't* involved, the department would be *more* likely to go nosin' around, not less. And this was *my* case. I was startin' to feel proprietary about it... whether there was anything to it or not. Besides, I had a duty to protect my client, whether she was on the level or batshit crazy. And if Chris found out Claire was the source of the whole thing, he'd track her down and start askin' questions. Then she'd think I'd spilled the beans—even though I hadn't. I couldn't let that happen, for her sake or for mine.

But Chris wasn't gonna let it go that easy. "This thing is startin' to blow up, Elijah. If more people go missing, I won't be able to keep a lid on it. Especially if we start gettin' reports from folks outside the church. They won't be as secretive about everything as the Temple has been, and they'll want answers."

I took a deep breath and raised both hands, palms out. "Hold on. Slow down, Chris. You yourself said we'd hit a dead end. There haven't *been* any new reports of people missing, so maybe whoever was doing this has stopped. Nothing can blow up if nothing new has happened. And even if he starts up again, there's nothing to suggest he'll target anyone outside the church. He sure as hell hasn't so far. Besides, who knows? Maybe the missing folks will turn up."

If anyone did go missing, I wasn't about to tell Chris. He'd been an asset so far, but he was starting to become a liability. Now that I had access to the *Tribune*'s archives and the church's records, I didn't need him.

All those people disappearin' outta photographs and missing records wouldn't matter if I could solve this case by following the money. I already knew it led straight to Hugh Cassidy, who would have to be cash-poor now that the Edwards money was gone—apparently had never existed. I still couldn't wrap my brain around that one. But it wasn't important. People had started disappearing long before the Sullivan-Cassini fiasco and before Vinnie even entered the picture.

Cassidy had been suspected of cooking the books long before that, too. Maybe some of the church members had gotten wise to this. Maybe they'd threatened to expose him. And maybe, just maybe, this was why they were disappearing.

If they were.

I decided to head back to the *Tribune* an' look up the two murders we'd figured out on our own by lookin' at the Edwards article. For some reason, I hadn't thought to look for those stories back then. An oversight. Not like me. Jud Williams was one, and Candace Matthews was the other. Sure enough, both stories were there. The headline for Willams read: "Local Man Found Dead with Eyes Gouged Out," but it didn't say anything about

Azrael's Assassin.

Neither did the one for the Matthews case. It just read, "Killer Feeds Woman to Piranhas at Zoo." Apparently they hadn't started callin' him Azrael's Assassin yet. Not that any of this mattered. It didn't shed any new light on the case, so maybe I'd been too hard on myself for neglectin' to look at 'em. But somethin' *mighta* been there. And if it had been, I'd be kickin' myself about it down the road.

One thing was for sure, I couldn't let somethin' like that happen again.

The Detective

Into the Lion's Den

*I*t was risky as hell, but there weren't no other way. I had to see for myself what was goin' down inside the not-so-hallowed halls of the Compassionate Truth Temple. I'd have to make sure Roderick Birch wouldn't recognize me, and I hadn't been in touch with Claire, but I had to hope that she'd keep her mouth shut if she did. If I did my job right, she wouldn't.

My idea of a disguise was a bit more sophisticated than Claire's wig and bug-eye sunglasses. I'd run into this Hollywood makeup man, Ted Larsen, a while back, when I was still with the department. He ran a diner, too, an' had his daughter workin' there, waitin' tables. She was a looker, like Claire, but even younger, so when I wanted to order a cold one, she had to get her father.

We struck up a conversation and, long story short, he told me if I ever needed help with anything, to get on the blower and he'd see what he could do. I'd sent him a mold of my face, and he'd shipped me back a couple o' fake noses, a bald pullover dome, a cauliflower ear, bushy eyebrows, and two beards an' a moustache that looked natural as hell. Even gave me instructions on how to apply all the pieces. We lost touch, an' I never knew what happened to him after that, but I'd kept all the stuff he'd sent me, and it still fit like a glove.

Now it was about to come in handy.

I chose the neatly cropped beard, not the shaggy one, the Roman nose, an' the bald topper. I wore a hat over the top of it. Not my usual fedora but a pork pie number. I knew I'd be takin' it off inside; I'd just have to be careful the hairless honey Larsen had made for me didn't come off along with it. It felt pretty snug for now.

Other than the hat, I dressed up in my Sunday best: a three-piece suit which I'd kept in the back of my closet for court appearances.

I didn't wanna chance anyone makin' my car, so I took the Red Line out to a stop at the end of the city route, across from the Temple, which was just up the hill.

Out front was a marquee sign, like on a movie theatre, that read "Today's sermon: The Lord Loveth a Cheerful Giver."

I chuckled to myself: *How fuckin' appropriate.*

The Temple itself was one of them old-style churches, built outta big gray blocks, with a square bell tower and a cross stickin' out from the top of it. That was the sanctuary part, but they'd added onto it a low-slung annex off to the right, built in mid-century modern style. Off to the side was the Prophet's house—Claire's house too—but it weren't no simple parsonage. It was a three-story mansion with a fountain out front and topiaries shaped like two lions, a dog, an elephant, and a hare. It was all outta proportion, though: The dog was bigger'n the elephant, an' the hare was the same size as the lion.

I saw Claire come out the front door, so I ducked into a group of parishioners who were milling about in front of the main building. They'd gotten there early and were yammerin' at each other about whatever it is churchy folks yack about. The weekly potluck. Sunday School lessons. Typical shit. Nothin' at all about the missing members, though. They were actin' for all the world like everything was right as rain.

Me bein' new, they picked me out right away. The men started clappin' me on the back an' callin' me "brother," askin' me if it was my first time even though they knew the answer. The women stayed back, their eyes down, pretendin' not to notice me. They all wore dresses that ended at the top o' their bobby socks, with no leg showin' and not a pair of panty hose in sight. I'd thought Claire was a wallflower, but these gals acted like they were permanently stuck to the side of the building, like they were wall*paper*. Two-dimensional. And mute. I wondered if their husbands gave 'em a thrashin' if they stepped outta line, or if the Prophet reserved that privilege for himself.

I nodded, bein' polite and dismissive at the same time, as I stepped through the crowd and up to the church entrance. They were still talkin' behind me... and *about* me, but I didn't care what they were sayin'. I'd never see most of them again—especially if they kept disappearin' the way they had been.

"Well, well, who do we have here?" said a leggy woman standin' at the lectern with a book layin' on top of it.

I looked up to see Claire starin' back at me an' smilin'. Had I been made? I couldn't tell, and I had to force myself to act casual.

"Colin Hayes," I said. "I'm visiting from out of town. Was lookin' for a place to worship, and I found your church in the phone book."

"Welcome to the Compassionate Truth Temple, Colin." Claire didn't miss a beat, which meant she hadn't recognized me. And if she didn't, no one else would. "Can I ask you to sign our attendance sheet, with your phone number, address, and date of birth?"

"Date of birth?"

"So we can send you a birthday card from the congregation," she explained.

I scribbled down my bogus name, alongside a phony phone number—RIchmond 6428—my childhood address in Kankakee, and a birthdate that was a little over five years later than mine. I told myself it weren't vanity, but of course it was. If Claire ever found out it was me, she wouldn't think of me as some late-model Studebaker. I might not be a Mercedes, but hey, a guy can dream.

Claire smiled that angelic smile of hers and handed me a Xeroxed church program that read "It's the Lord's Day at the Compassionate Truth Temple!" Underneath was a rundown of the morning's agenda: an invocation, songs from the hymnal, holy communion, the "Word of the Lord"—which I supposed must be the sermon—tithes and offerings, "the Moving of the Spirit" (whatever that was), prophecies, and a benediction. Below all that was a bunch o' names of people who were to be "kept in prayer." I looked for any of the missing members, but none of them was listed.

Ushers showed us all to our seats: Everyone else's seemed to be assigned or reserved, but bein' a visitor, I got to sit in the second row. Not ideal if I wanted to stay inconspicuous, especially since I was right behind the Prophet's wife and Claire;

Roderick Birch, who was there by himself; and the organist's wife and seven kids. I didn't seem to have any choice in the matter, though. When in Rome...

On the other side of the center aisle, the pews were filled six deep with a bunch of people who all had the same ruddy complexion and strawberry-blond hair. The oldest sat in front, with younger folks behind them and younger ones in the next row back, and so on. They *had* to be related. Inbreeding? No way to tell. But they all sure looked like they came outta the same cookie-cutter.

Everyone was facin' a stage with a fake mini palm tree on either side of a lectern. Behind the podium was a baptismal with glass in the front, so you could see the faithful bein' dunked, and behind that was a giant stained-glass window of Christ holdin' a lamb an' a shepherd's staff. He had a dead look on his face that gave me the creeps, like he was starin' out through them crystal blue eyes at nothin'. Not that Christ really had blue eyes, o' course, but it looked better in the stained glass and to the congregation, which looked a lot like him, except for the beard.

I wondered if I'd made a mistake wearin' the fake beard Ted had given me, since all the men there seemed to be free advertisin' for Burma-Shave. But it was the best part of the disguise, and I couldn't risk anyone recognizin' me. Besides, I didn't give a shit about bein' judged by these Bible-thumpers. I'd be here today an' gone tomorrow, like a thief in the night, so to speak. They'd never even have a chance to tell me what they thought o' me.

Some guy walked in from a side door and sat his ass down behind an organ, then raised his hands an' held them still above the keys for a minute, like he was Liberace or somethin'. I almost expected to see a candelabra up there. When his hands came down, it was like they was lightnin' bolts strikin' out of nowhere, resulting in a single, held note that was a cue for everyone to stand up.

I followed suit, and the organist launched into "How Great Thou Art." The congregation started singin' without even openin' their hymnals. This musta been the way they always kicked things off. I didn't remember all the words, but I knew the chorus, so I chimed in there and just moved my lips to the rest of it, hopin' no one would notice. As the song reached its climax, with the singers slowin' it down for a final "how great thou art," a tall, imposing figure who looked in better shape than he shoulda been at his age stepped out from behind a curtain, his chest puffed out like a big ol' rooster.

This had to be the Prophet. Hugh Cassidy. Claire's pops. I could see why she was afraid of him.

The congregation kept standin' until he got behind the podium an' looked out over all of us, stretchin' out both hands and lowerin' 'em, palms down. "Brothers and sisters in Christ, welcome to the Truth! Please be seated."

There was a shuffling of feet as everyone took their seats. I nearly tripped over the kneeler on the back of the pew in front of me, which'd dropped down while I was standin'.

"Christ is risen!" the Prophet declared.

"He is risen indeed!" the congregation nearly shouted, all together.

The Prophet raised both hands again. "May the Spirit of Christ dwell within you today and for all days to come. Lean not on your own understanding, but the Word of the Lord and his holy prophets. May they guide you in your steps and make straight your paths, that you not stray into the wickedness of temptation and be consumed by his wrath. I am his instrument!"

"We are his instrument!" the congregation replied.

"I am his chosen one, anointed as his shepherd."

"We are his chosen ones, called to be his sheep!"

"This is my home, the one true Temple."

"This is our home, the one true Temple!"

"Amen."

"Amen!"

"Please remain standing and open your hymnal to Page 180. Join me in singing praise to the Lord, who is 'Holy, Holy, Holy'!"

A bunch of hymns and choruses came next, most of which I knew from when I was a kid. Then everyone sat back down, and they passed around some loaves of sourdough bread and a cup of red juice. It weren't real wine, though. These holy rollers were all drier than fuckin' Death Valley in a drought. Then everyone looked up expectant, like a dog waitin' for a treat, as the Prophet opened his mouth to speak.

"...the Lord commands us to set aside his tithe before we pay our obligations to mortal men, that His Name may be glorified first in all things. We teach that this tithe must come from a believer's gross income. You shall not pay your debts, figure your taxes, pay for your food or housing, or even clothe your children until the Lord receives his portion. But fear not. This is an act of true faith, that the Lord may provide and multiply your blessings as a good and faithful servant. Do not withhold for yourself God's glory or his portion, and give not grudgingly or from a spirit of bondage, but with gratitude, for God loveth a cheerful giver. This is the word of the Lord."

The organist played and held a single note for several seconds, then the congregation shouted all together, "Amen!"

"Give freely now, that ye may be blessed in abundance."

The ushers came forward and picked up a pair of golden platters, which they handed across the pews and picked up at the other end. I noticed that everyone who put somethin' in the plate, whether it was greenbacks or a check, kinda did so in a way that everyone else could see what they were givin'. Peer pressure at its best. The guy next to me frowned when I didn't put nothin' in, and it made me feel guilty despite myself. Another reason I didn't hang out in places like this on a reg'lar basis.'

Maybe the most interestin' part of the service came next. The movin' of the spirit started with the Prophet readin' from the book of Acts: "And they were all filled with the Holy Ghost, and began to speak with other tongues, as the Spirit gave them utterance."

Without any more prompting than that, everyone started talkin' gibberish at once. These weren't no actual languages. It all sounded like a bunch o' babies at playtime, mixed up with barking dogs, chatterin' birds, an' screamin' monkeys. I couldn't make heads nor tails of any of it. When all this racket finally died down, the Prophet said some mumbo-jumbo nonsense of his own, then did us all the favor of speakin' again in plain English— with a few bits o' King Jimmy-ese thrown in for kicks an' grins.

"After being appointed by Paul the Apostle, Titus did set in order those things that were wanting, by ordaining elders in every city. By his example have we ordained elders to oversee our Temple. Elder Reynolds, Elder Birch, if you would please come forward and sanctify the Lord's Prophet by the laying on of hands, that his words may be pure and true and righteous, not his words, but the words of the Lord Himself."

I was afraid Birch might be lookin' down at me, but he was too wrapped up in what Cassidy was tellin' him to do. He and the oldest guy from the other side of the aisle got up on the stage and stood beside Cassidy as he knelt down beside the lectern, puttin' their hands on the top of his head an' lookin' up to heaven. "Oh, Lord, hear our prayer. Sanctify this, your servant, to deliver thy words in the spirit of holiness to these, the children of the New Israel, grafted onto the tree of Life by thy grace and mercy. Hallelujah!"

The two men returned to their seats, and the Prophet stepped forward with a look in his eye that seemed a lot like the zombie Christ in stained glass standin' behind him.

"Hear the word of the Lord!" he said. His voice was louder than before, like he was tryin' to make himself sound even more important now than he'd been doin'. Kinda like the phony baloney Wizard of Oz getting' all blustery behind that curtain. "This charge I deliver unto you, as your leader and Holy Prophet. I decree unto you in this holy place that the tithe is to be doubled from this day forward, that the glory of the Lord might be manifest more fully. Hear the word of the Lord!"

"We hear the word of the Lord!" they all shouted back.

"And this covenant I shall make with thee, that the doors to this holy house are to be closed to all men not already among our number. The day has passed when strangers shall receive shelter among us, for the harvest is nigh, and the time has come to separate the wheat from the tares, that the tares may be cast out from among us and burned in the unquenched lake of fire. Hear the word of the Lord!"

"We hear the word of the Lord!"

I tried like hell not to get antsy at this, bein' a visitor and all. I imagined 'em slammin' the doors and boltin' 'em shut, then comin' to grab me and carry me off to be roasted like a pig on a spit.

Fortunately, that didn't happen. Instead, Cassidy fell to his knees and put his forehead down to the ground. After a minute, he lifted his head, speakin' in his normal voice again, announced that the offering plate would be passed around a second time so everyone could make up the difference between their tithe and the one the Prophet had just decreed. I resisted the temptation to roll my eyes, an' I had to go through gettin' the evil eye from the guy next to me a second time.

I was gettin' bored as hell, and a little nervous, so I was glad when Cassidy told the church to rise again so he could give the closing benediction.

"We are the body of Christ, one in purpose and in deed. Go forth now and be in the world, but not of it. The secret things belong unto the Lord our God, but those things that are revealed belong unto us and our children forever, that we may do the words of the law. Reveal not these secrets to the profane and the blasphemer, but guard them in your hearts, where the Lord resides, until he calls us forth into his heavenly kingdom."

"Amen!" said the congregation, and the organist started playin' the recessional, "Washed in the Blood."

Now that was uplifting.

This place was even more nutso than I thought. How could Claire even stand it? Washed in the blood? I felt like I needed a shower after listenin' to all that crap. But there was blood bein' spilled. Maybe by the Prophet's own orders. He had these sheep so completely bamboozled that they'd do anything he said—maybe even kill for him. That was like what the shrink had told me about people bein' caught up in someone else's delusion, but it wasn't Claire's in this case, it was her father's.

The question was how much she was still caught up in *his* delusion. It wasn't a question I could ask her outright. I'd have to figure it out by observation, usin' my trusty private eye.

The Detective
Curveball

T he Cheetahs had just blown another one. They'd been stuck in the cellar all season. They were so bad, more fans showed up from out of town than from just across the tracks.

They'd yell shit like "Cheetahs can't beat us" and "Cheetahs never prosper." The home fans just sat there on their keisters, lettin' the splinters bite into their asses from them old wooden bleachers. All 500 seats, half of 'em empty.

Now, Class-C ball ain't the bigs, but it *is* the goddamn national pastime, an' it's all we got in this two-bit three-horse town. Ya gotta appreciate what ya got, but everyone here's so fuckin' scared of the mob an' the crooked cops an' the Bible nuts, mostly they stay in and mind their business.

They think Vinnie or one of the other "families" are fixin' the games. But they don't get how it works. If the mob was makin' the Cheetahs pull a Black Sox, they wouldn't be losin' all the time. Ain't no profit in that. But when they're paranoid, folks don't think straight. They're suggestable, an' if they trust the wrong person, they'll believe bullshit over their own eyes an' ears.

Hell, maybe *I* shoulda been the shrink. But I was startin' to think I'd been trustin' the wrong person. Was it Claire? The shrink? Chris? *Now who's actin' paranoid?*

Not me. Paranoid schmoes were suckers who swallowed the bait hook, line, and sinker. I rolled it around in my mouth to get a taste for it before spittin' it back out. I just hadn't got to that point yet.

Some folks are just born lackeys. It's like they wanna be lookin' up to someone, anyone, 'cause they're either too damn lazy or too damn pathetic. They think they *deserve* to be the shit under someone else's shoe. An' there's always a someone or someones willin' to oblige.

Take the Cheetahs. They weren't near as bad as all them losses would suggest, but they'd got inside their own heads an' made 'emselves what they thought they were. They didn't need no help from a Vinnie Lombardo; they did it to themselves. Better to fail on your own terms than let somebody beat you, right?

That's what happened here. The one time the Cheetahs actually started actin' like big cats instead o' pussies, they go an' pull a disappearing act in the ninth.

Lefty Hudson, who hadn't thrown a complete game all year, was nursin' a 2-0 lead an' had a no-hitter goin' into the ninth. Got the first batter to whiff on three pitches, but the catcher dropped the ball, then threw three feet over the first sacker's head. Batter legs it out an' makes it all the way to second.

Hudson walks the next guy, then gets tagged on the first pitch for a three-run shot to straightaway center. That was the end of it. The visitors crossed home plate eleven more times, an' the kittycats went meekly into the late afternoon.

Now night was falling. I thought about headin' to Nick's, but I had to dry out... at least long enough to see if that shrink was right about the booze.

The game had been better therapy than Doc Donovan had ever been. This wasn't a case of a shared delusion between me an' Claire. It was bigger than that. It was a mass delusion by sheep who *wanted* to have their own wool pulled over their eyes. Members of the Compassionate Truth Temple... which had less to do with truth than the Sazerac Lyin' Club.

Like the Cheetahs, but worse.

Every clue pointed straight back at the temple. I just had to put 'em all together. I needed to think, but first I needed a good night's sleep.

I had a feeling I wasn't gonna get one. That Packard sittin' outside my place was Ginger's. She'd come back to check on me. It was thoughtful an' all that, but I didn't need the distraction.

I turned the knob and opened the door.

"Hey, sis. Back so soon? I swear I'm good. You didn't need to..."

I stopped in my tracks. Ginger was sittin' there, in a kitchen chair, whimperin' like a baby. It was the only sounds she could make. She was gagged. Arms tied behind her. Legs strapped to the chair with a coupla my ties.

There was a guy standin' beside her. A guy in a mask. A guy with a gun.

His hand was shakin'. This weren't no professional.

"Stay out of it, Mr. Kirk. It's none of your business." He was tryin' to sound all scary. He didn't. Goons from the mob didn't talk like that. Sounded formal, an' his voice was shakin' too.

"Out of what?"

He didn't answer.

"I ain't got time for this shit." I pulled out my own gun an' pointed it at him.

"I *will* shoot her," he said. He was point blank to Ginger, but his hand was shakin' so bad now he might still miss.

"You don't wanna do that, jack. You shoot her, I shoot you. An' if you stand around too long, I'll shoot you first. Then I'll call the cops. You better hope this is your lucky day, pal."

This guy weren't no killer. He wanted me to back off somethin', but he wouldn't say what it was. Not too effective. But I had a pretty good idea. It had to do with the Temple, an' I wasn't about to back off there. 'Specially not now.

Ginger was starin' at me, pleadin' with her eyes. She didn't deserve to get dragged into this mess, and I had every intention of draggin' her out of it.

"I'll give you one chance to do this," I said. "You can walk out that door free an' clear, like nothin' happened, and I won't smear your sorry ass all over this floor. I don't wanna have to clean that shit up."

He was starin' wide-eyed at the gun now, barely noticin' Ginger. She'd managed to get one o' them tiny ankles o' hers free from my necktie. I guess dumbass hadn't counted on silk ties bein' slippery—even if they weren't real silk.

I couldn't tell her not to do what I knew she was thinkin' about without givin' her away. So all I could do was stand there and hope this cheeseball would take me up on my offer before...

Ginger kicked her leg out, and her stiletto heel slammed into the cheeseball's ankle. She always wore those damned high heels 'cause she was all self-conscious about bein' barely 5 feet tall.

The cheeseball's gun went off, but with him bein' off-balance, the shot sailed a coupla feet over Ginger's head an' into the ceiling.

Plaster rained down. Ginger screamed. Dumbass hit the floor an' dropped his gun, which went skitterin' away like a daddy long legs.

I fired but missed too, owin' to the fact that joe palooka was now on the floor and not where he had been.

Ginger kicked her other foot loose an' tried to stand up, but with the chair still tied to her back, she didn't have a prayer in those damned stilettos. She came crashin' to the floor.

This distracted me. I shoulda known better. 'Cause in that moment, dumbass lunges at me, hits me in the shins, an' lays me out on the floor.

Now my piece is the skitterin' spider.

I lunge for it, thinkin' he'll be goin' after his. But he doesn't. Instead I see him jumpin' up and runnin' past me out the door, like one o' them three blind mice tryin' to get away from a carving knife.

I didn't wanna cut off his tail, so I let him go.

I had a feeling he wouldn't be back.

I went over and untied Ginger's arms and ungagged her.

"Who the hell was that, Elijah?"

That was the $64,000 question. Unfortunately, I didn't have an answer.

The Detective

Let's Make a Deal

I tried to ring up Claire, but she wasn't answerin', which left me with a conundrum. I couldn't go to the church, and I damn sure couldn't try her house—which also happened to be the Prophet's house—without givin' myself away.

I wanted to give her the skinny on the attack. If I was right, and the church was behind it, she'd have to be careful.

Where else could she be?

I tried the butcher shop, Nick's, the diner... no luck. Then, as I was passin' the *Trib* building, I saw her car there in the parking lot. I jammed on the brakes an' did a quick turn in before parkin' my heap beside her. She was sittin' in her jalopy. Looked like she was getting' ready to pull out.

"I rolled down my window. Hey, dollface. Long time no..."

She didn't give me no time to answer. Instead, she comes marchin' up to me like she was headin' off to war, and sounds off: "Well look who it is? Isn't it the loser I paid... how much was it?"

I opened my mouth, but couldn't get a word in edgewise or any other wise.

"It doesn't matter. It was a waste of time and money. We're no closer to finding Olivia than we were when we started. You're pathetic, you know that? You're..."

"Whoa! Hold up there, darlin'..."

"It's CLAIRE!"

"Yeah, yeah. Right. But you yellin' at me like this ain't gonna help either one of us get to the bottom of this. It'll just draw attention neither one of us want. Why don't we go somewhere private an' continue this."

She took a deep breath and held it, bitin' her lip and ballin' up her fists. Was smoke gonna start spewing out her nose an' ears? It kinda looked like it. She bent down next to the window and whispered, "We don't have to go anywhere. This is exactly where I want to be. You know what I've been doing while you've been sitting on your rear end with your head in a bottle? I've been doing some investigating of my own. And guess what? I actually found something here in the morgue.

She strolls around to the passenger side of my vehicle, opens the door and plops herself down beside me. "Look at this."

She produced a Xerox of a newspaper clipping dated twenty years ago. The headline was kinda familiar. "Police Stumped as Ruthless Killer Strikes Again."

"Read it," Claire hissed.

"That's what I'm doin', doll."

She made a growling sound under her breath. "Out. Loud. I want the satisfaction of hearing you read it."

"Whatever floats your boat." It'd been filed by a *Tribune* reporter named Milton Crowley, but it had a tagline that read "for the UPI." That meant it had gone national, so it had to have been a big deal.

I started reading.

The latest in a series of grisly murders committed by the killer police have dubbed Azrael's Assassin was discovered Saturday morning in a campground northwest of here. Michael and Patricia Dunphy were found dead beside a picnic table in Longvale Park, a two-foot-long, tent-spike embedded in each of their skulls so deeply that it had gone all the way through and pinned them to the earth.

Park superintendent Damon Lafayette discovered the bodies at daybreak as he was making his rounds. He said the couple had checked in at the entrance gate and paid the overnight fee the previous afternoon, then had pitched their tent beside the picnic table in their campsite. He reported seeing and hearing nothing unusual overnight, but confessed that he does not check on the campsites after 9 p.m. The park is situated in the forest, and shaded by a stand of tall trees. Not being equipped with artificial light, it is dark during the nighttime hours and, being fairly remote, is typically quiet, authorities said.

The campground was nearly empty, and sheriff's deputies questioned the few occupants they contacted on site. One witness said they'd seen man wearing a dark hooded cloak that obscured his face, but the man was only there for a moment and disappeared. The witness, whom authorities have refused to identify, told deputies he thought at the time that he was seeing things and was unable to provide any further description.

Local police, who have dealt with similar cases in the past, were brought in to consult on the case, but have few leads beyond a calling card left at the scene bearing a circular symbol inscribed with Greek lettering on the perimeter and a series of marks inside the circle. Among these are five crosses with arms of equal length, what appears a stylized lowercase H, the numeral 2, and an 8 set on its side.

Greek translators have said the lettering at the top is likely a name, AΖΙΑΕΛ, which they render as Aziael but which others have suggested should be read as Azrael. The lettering at the bottom spells out ΑΔΟΝΑΨ. Translators render this as Adonaps, which is similar to Adonai, the Hebrew word for "lord."

Police are continuing to reach out to the community for any help in solving the case and are now working with the FBI. The Bureau's task force is under the direct supervision of J. Edgar Hoover. Anyone who has any information should contact the FBI or Lt. Raphel LaRue at the downtown police station.

Michael Dunphy leaves behind a brother, Gerald, and two sisters, Carla and Bernadette. He is predeceased by his parents, James and Maeve Dunphy. Patricia Dunphy is survived by her brother, Conrad Borg and her mother, Alice Borg. She is predeceased by her father, Linus Borg, and a sister, Caroline Borg Harper. Services are private. Arrangements are through Walter E. Cummings Funeral Home.

"See?" Claire was givin' me that I-told-you-so look. "Olivia isn't mentioned. If she'd been alive, she would have been listed among the survivors. It's like she never existed. We must be onto something. But it still doesn't make sense because I saw them just before they went to Maui. They should have been back weeks ago, but dead for *twenty years*?"

I leaned back and looked up at the roof of the car. I couldn't be drawn back into all this. What use was there in tryin' to solve a cold case that had stumped everyone right on up to J. Edgar Hoover? If they hadn't caught the What's-His-Face Assassin by now, with all their men and money, I sure as hell wasn't gonna do it. An' with these cases all bein' such a long time ago, the guy was probably dead or livin' in Bolivia.

These church folk had all gone missing in the past coupla months, not twenty or thirty years ago. There had to be some rational explanation for it in the here and now, and we weren't gonna find it by diggin' through old newspaper stacks an' microfilm. If we were ever to get to the bottom of all this, it would be by usin' old-fashioned investigatin' and surveillance. The tried and true stuff. Follow the money trail and see where it leads. And I already knew where it led: right back to the Temple.

I looked sidelong at Claire. "So whaddya suggest we do about it?" I asked. "You think you can solve this case without me, then be my guest, sugar. You won't have to pay me another dime. I only flagged ya down here 'cause I happen to give a shit about you. You need to start lookin' over your shoulder an' grow some eyes in the back o' your head, or what happened to me just might happen to you."

She frowned at me. "*What* happened to you?"

Now it was my turn to look smug. "I got home last night, an' who do I find inside my home, holdin' a gun to my sister's head?"

She gasped.

"That's right, dollface, there was this numbskull in my livin' room who'd tied my sister to a chair and was threatenin' to shoot her if I didn't back off. I managed to extricate myself from said awkward predicament and Ginger got 'im good with a kick to the shins. No one was hurt, but the sonofabitch got away. Never got a good look at him, neither. He was wearin' a cloth mask over his face, and..."

"A cloth mask?! Don't you see? It was in that story you just read, about the man who killed Olivia's parents. He was wearing a hood that hid his face!"

"Christ on a cracker...!"

"Please!"

"All right then, great Caesar's ghost? That better? Girlie, that was decades ago! This was just last night. And the guy wasn't wearin' no cloak. Just a pair of slacks, a collar shirt and an overcoat."

"Which could have been mistaken for a cloak in the dark."

"It ain't uncommon for a criminal to hide his face. It's kinda expected, actually. Listen, I'm tryin' to do you a favor here. Forget about all that, just for a minute. The guy who busted into my place weren't no professional. He was shakin' in his shoes the whole time. That means he wasn't one of Lombardo's goons, or Pretty Boy Parker's, or King Keller's. It also means it couldn't have been the Whatchamacallit Assassin..."

"Azrael's."

"Whatever. It couldn't've been him 'cause that guy knew what he was doin'. If he didn't, he wouldn't've given everyone the slip for thirty or forty years or however long it's been."

"Well, this guy gave you the slip, didn't he?"

"That's beside the point."

"Then what *is* the point, exactly?"

"It's that the guy wanted me to lay off, and what I ain't told you yet was what I've been doin' since last we met."

"Oh?"

"Yeah, this guy shows up in my office outta nowhere and wants me to look into some fishy fights at the Palladium—one in particular. Tells me Bam-Bam Cassini took a fall against this bum named Matty Sullivan in the 10th. I've seen Sullivan in the ring. Couldn't fight his way out of a torn paper bag if someone put razors on his gloves, so the guy was on the level. I told him that's how it works. Fighters in Vinnie's stable throw fights on occasion. They feed bogus info to his bookies, who pass it along to their regulars. Then, once the money's on the table, Vinnie scoops it all up when the fight goes his way."

"What's that you once told me?" Claire said. "Daylight's a-wastin'? What does this have to do with anything?"

"I'm gettin' to that. See, the guy who paid me to look into this wasn't actin' on his own behalf. He was sent there by a mystery man who'd blown twenty large on the fight. Wanted me to help him get it back. I told him not to go messin' with Vinnie's people, 'cause it wouldn't end well. Whether he took my advice or not, I ain't got a clue. Never saw him again after that. But somethin' was naggin' at me, so I decided to go to the horse's mouth and ask Vinnie about it. He'll let me come askin' questions if I make it brief and keep it under my hat. So I'm tellin' you and expectin' you to keep it under yours, got it?"

Claire drew a line with her finger across her closed lips. Maybe she was startin' to cool down a bit.

"Good. Long story short, I find out that the mystery man wantin' his money back is some guy from this church a few miles north of town. Sound familiar?"

If she'd been coolin' down, she heated right back up to a boil. "What are you insinuating? Gambling is a sin."

"Then someone's sinnin' pretty good. I ain't insinuating nothin'. I'm tellin' ya straight. I went down to the station and talked to Chris, and when I described the guy who came to see me, he knew who it was. The name Roderick Birch ring any bells? Snappy dresser with a lazy eye an' a big fat mole on his cheek?"

"You're lying."

I put up my hands. "Hey, the guy never told me his name. I just described him to Chris, the way I did to you just now, and he came up with the name like that."

"Then Chris is lying. He left the Temple. Maybe he is holding something against us. As it is written, the Lord hates the false witness that speaketh lies and the one that soweth discord among the brethren."

I nodded. "Proverbs 6. He also hates a heart that cooks up nasty plans, hands that shed innocent blood, and feet that go runnin' toward evil. I'm paraphrasin'. I do remember some of what they tried to teach me in seminary. Point bein', you might wanna start blamin' Roderick Birch an' the guy who sent him runnin' toward evil Vinnie Lombardo, and whoever's cookin' up the nasty plans in the first place."

"Azrael's Assassin."

I laughed. "You think some guy who went around killin' people a long time back sent your Mr. Birch to go snoopin' around at the Palladium? There just ain't no connection. No motive. No nothing. Yesterday, today, an' forever, it's always gonna be the same."

"Don't mock the Scripture. That's what it says about our Lord and Savior."

"Apologies. But I ain't gonna beat around the bush no more,

doll. Chris told me Roderick Birch wouldn't so much as sneeze without approval from the Prophet, so I'm sorry to break it to ya, but it stands to reason that your father's the mystery man who bet those twenty G's on Bam-Bam, and I'd be willin' to make a bet of my own: that he took money outta the church funds to do it. Probably to pay me too."

Claire just sat there, starin' straight ahead at nothin'. I could tell she was havin' trouble takin' it all in.

I didn't wanna say what came outta my mouth next. I dunno if I said it 'cause I felt sorry for her or out of my own morbid curiosity about this Assassin. If that shrink Donovan was right, I'd be steppin' right back into Claire's delusion again. But Chris wasn't part of that delusion—he hadn't even seen Claire since he left the church, and I hadn't told him enough to convince him of jack shit. Besides, the money angle was somethin' Claire didn't wanna believe, so there was no Duke's Follies, or whatever he'd called it, there. An' if I could get her to start lookin' at things from *my* perspective, that would prove she weren't castin' no spell on me with her feminine wiles or nothin'. I'd put this Donovan to the test and see how good a headshrinker he really was.

"I'll make you a deal," I said. "You help me with investigatin' your father an' the Temple shenanigans, and I'll help you try to figure out this Assassin thing. One way or the other, we'll get to the bottom of what happened to Olivia and the others once and for all. Whaddya say?"

"Who says I *need* your help?"

"And who says I need yours. But didn't you tell me two heads are better'n one?"

She smiled despite herself. "Deal," she said softly.

STEPHEN H. and SHARON MARIE PROVOST

The Detective

Angels We Have Heard On High

O f course, the deal we struck involved divin' head-first back into this Azrael bullshit before we looked into diddly squat about the for-profit prophet and his financial finagling. I fully intended to hold Claire to her part of the bargain, but for now it was good just to be workin' with her again. She had a good head on her shoulders, even if she had filled it with too much biblical bullshit to think straight half the time. But who was I to judge? I'd been headed down that road myself when she was in pigtails and polka dots. I had to admit that her knowledge of the Bible could come in handy, with me bein' a bit rusty, and it was good to have her company again. She was quite the looker, even when she was spittin' bullets—maybe especially then. And when we weren't goin' at it, we worked well together.

I invited her over to my digs, thinkin' it would be more private there, but she said it wasn't proper for a woman to be alone with a man at his place. Or hers, for that matter. Not that it had crossed my mind that anything *improper* might occur... well, actually, it had, but only on a temporary basis. Now that she was callin' it untoward, I had a hard time gettin' it out of my head.

That made things difficult. Findin' some privacy without bein' alone together was a tall order, so we wound up back at the diner again, once again cursed to have Freida as our waitress.

Claire was wearing a blouse with a buncha roses on it and a frilly skirt that went down to her knees. She had another wig this time: a straight brunette number that fell down to her shoulders. And those damned shades that made her stand out rather than blend in when she kept 'em on indoors.

"You wanna talk about those Assassin murders," I said as she sat down across from me. "An' you say you did some more diggin' through the stacks. What did you find out?"

She leaned across the table and kept her voice low. "Well, we know that Azrael's Assassin killed a lot of people associated with the Temple, either them or their parents or both. What I couldn't find was anything that indicated he was involved in any *other* killings. Every murder was linked in some way to our church."

"Okay, so he had something against the Temple. But no one ever made that connection. Not the cops, not the press, no one. Don't you find that strange?"

She shook her head. "Remember, most of these murders took place *before* the missing members were born."

I put both hands behind my head and scowled. "I don't wanna go back down that rabbit hole again just yet. How about if we go over the murders one by one. I've never tracked a serial killer before, but from what I know, most of 'em are smarter than the average bear. They follow a pattern, and they like to leave a signature or calling card. It's like they're daring you to try an' outwit 'em. They think they're smarter than you, so they play with ya like a cat playin' with a ball o' yarn. They wanna make you come unraveled.

"They're a contradiction. They take risks and put themselves out there, but they're also really careful. It's like part of 'em wants to get caught, but part of 'em doesn't."

"That sounds crazy."

"Did ya hear the part where we're talkin' about serial killers?"

Claire giggled under her breath. The church mouse got my morbid sense of humor. Part of her wanted to come off all prim and proper, but part of her wanted to live dangerously. Another contradiction. Imagine that.

"So what's the pattern here?" she asked, but from the glimmer in her eye, I suspected she knew the answer.

I shook my head. "I don't see one. One guy gets his feet burned off, his fiancée gets drowned. One guy gets his eyes plucked out an' replaced with a couple glass balls. A woman gets fed to the fishes..."

"And don't forget Olivia's parents."

"Yeah, they're all completely different. Every one of 'em killed in a different place by different means."

"But they all do have one thing in common."

"Yeah, that calling card. What do you make of that?"

"That newspaper article said some of the letters spell out Azrael and Adonai. The first word means 'God's helper,' and the second refers to God himself. But that doesn't make any sense. God doesn't want us to kill people. It's against his commandments. It's a sin."

I smirked. "Not really. Heck, he told the Jews to kill all sortsa people back in the day. He told one guy to kill everyone, even babies and nursing mothers, all the way down to the animals. Then he went apeshit when the guy didn't kill the king and a few donkeys."

"The Amalekites. That was a war, and it doesn't count as murder if God tells you to do it."

"Exactly! And that's what this guy thought he was doin': carryin' out the will of God with these murders."

"I don't know..."

"That has to be it. He's helpin' God kill people, and he's justifyin' it by sayin' this Azrael character brought him a message from the Almighty tellin' him to do it!"

Claire frowned. "It sounds like the name of an archangel, like Michael and Gabriel. But I've never seen that name in the Bible. I don't recognize it."

"Hmmm." That reference to him maybe bein' an archangel *did* ring a bell from a class on angelology I took in seminary. I just had to open up the ol' memory bank an' try to dig it out. "You're right," I said. "He ain't in the Bible. But I do seem to remember he is some kinda archangel. Just give me a sec..."

I tried visualizing the pages from my textbook, *Angelic Beings, Hierarchies, Principalities, and Powers*. That's how I'd always studied for tests. I didn't have no photographic memory, but I could remember certain things an' link 'em to other things, an' so forth. It was like followin' a trail of breadcrumbs, an' it helped if I had pictures to go by... which in this case, I did. The book had charts an' sketches an' paintings by the masters. One of 'em had stood out to me in particular, because it looked like the grim reaper— with a creepy hood and a big ol' scythe in his hand. Except it *wasn't* the grim reaper. It just looked like him. There'd been a name an' description underneath the picture. All I needed to do was make it come clear to me in my mind's eye. It came into focus gradual-like.

"Azrael!"

Claire had been fixed on my face, waitin' for me to explain myself, so she jumped when I said it. Then she settled down real quick and started scowlin' at me. "Yes, Einstein, that's who we're looking for."

"And I think I just found him—or at least found out who he is. You're right about him bein' an archangel. We were just lookin' for him in the wrong place." I didn't remember everything about that description under the photo, but I remembered enough. "He ain't in the Bible, but he's talked about in a lot of other places. There's four main archangels in the Bible: Michael an' Gabriel, like you said..."

"And Raphael and Uriel."

"Right. Well, the Muslims got four archangels too. They're all the same except one: Uriel. I bet you can't guess who they got instead."

"Azrael?"

"Bingo! And he shows up in other places too. He's in Hebrew books outside the Bible, an' Christian ones too. Don't ask me which ones, but he's there. An' y'know what else? Our friend Azrael wasn't just any angel. He was the angel of fuckin' death!"

Claire winced, but I ignored her. More of it was comin' back to me as I was talkin' and I didn't wanna let her bein' a nice Nelly throw me off my train of thought.

"He looked just like the grim reaper, and his job was to escort people into the afterlife whenever God told him to do it. An' you wanna know the topper? He was in charge of a scroll that lists the names of everyone alive on Planet Earth. He writes 'em down when they're born, an' then when they die, *he erases them.* Sound familiar."

Claire was listenin' so closely she'd almost stopped breathing. In fact, she looked like she was about to hyperventilate. "The names in the attendance records and the registry."

"Yep. He can't seem to make all of 'em disappear, but he is wipin' out all traces of the younger generation."

"But how...?"

"That's what I still don't get. The only thing I can figure is this assassin thinks he's doin' the work of Azrael for him, and he's goin' around erasing every trace of them in the records, just like Azrael himself does when people die. But what doesn't add up is how he has access to the photos an' all the public government records."

The only person I knew with ties to both the official records and the church was Chris. It'd never even occurred to me that he might be a suspect, but Claire *had* called him a Judas, and he clearly had no love for the church either. Could he possibly...?

Freida interrupted us, droppin' by with a basket of cold limp fries. The kind with the ridges on 'em. We hadn't ordered 'em, but she said they were on the house. Probably sent back by someone who didn't want 'em.

Claire was white as a marshmallow an' shakin' like a leaf about ready to fall. I reached across the table and took her hand. "You OK?"

She didn't say nothin', but nodded, so I kept goin'. I wasn't gonna say anything about Chris. She already didn't trust him, and I wasn't about to sell him down the river for a smile on that pretty face of hers. Apart from bein' my friend, he was my only contact down at the station, and I couldn't afford to lose that.

"So, we know who Azrael's supposed to be, an' we know this assassin thinks he's doin' the work of God by offin' people," I said. "But maybe there's more of a pattern than we're seein'. Maybe that calling card of his is just the signature. Maybe the killing itself, the way it's done, is the letter he's writin'."

"To who?"

"To God. To us. I dunno. Maybe we'll figure that out if we figure out the message. It's gotta be somethin' religious. Maybe something from the Bible..."

After lookin' nearly comatose a few seconds earlier, Claire suddenly sprang to life. In fact, she practically jumped right up outta her seat. "Yes!" she shouted, and half the people in the diner turned around and looked at her like she was nutso.

"Keep your shirt on."

She sat down, straightening out her skirt nervously. "Think about it," she said, lowering her voice but talkin' a mile a minute. "Joe and Sarah's murders are straight out of John's Gospel. The disciples had already been baptized, then Jesus washed their feet. Sarah was 'baptized' when the Assassin drowned her, then he 'washed' Joe's feet in a bucket of acid." She shuddered as her mind caught up to what her mouth was sayin'.

This guy thought he was Jesus. He was getting his jollies playin' God.

What Claire was saying made sense.

"And the guy whose eyes got plucked out?" I prodded her.

She shut her eyes tight. I was guessin' she didn't like the mental image. "It could be a couple of things," she said, opening

151

her eyes finally. "I think he's referring to the Gospel of John again. In the ninth chapter, when Jesus was asked why a man had been born blind, he told his disciples that it was so that the works of God might be displayed in him. Then, a few verses later, he says, 'I have come into this world for judgment, that the blind shall see and those who see shall become blind.' Who do you think the Assassin was talking about?"

I shook my head. "It has to be the people at the Temple. They think they can see, so he blinds them to show they do not. Then he forces them to see with new eyes."

"So you're saying that this person has ties to the Temple?"

"You said it yourself: That's what connects all these murders."

"And the man who attacked your sister and warned you to stay away. He's connected in the same way. He has to be the man who's been doing this."

I nodded slowly. I didn't think so, but there wasn't a point in arguin' with her. I'd laid it out for her plain enough before. We'd figure out who that dumbass was sooner or later, but the Assassin weren't no dumbass. He was the opposite. He fit the mold of a serial killer: shrewd, cunning, and two steps ahead of everyone.

"What about the piranhas?" I said. "Ain't no piranhas in the Bible that I remember."

"No, but there are fish. Let me think. The miracle of the fishes and the loaves? No, that doesn't fit."

"Yeah. There were a lot of fish in that one, but the people were eatin' them, not the other way around," I cracked.

She didn't seem to hear me. She was thinkin' again. Then, after a minute or so, her eyes suddenly brightened. "What about the Book of Jonah?"

"That's a whale, not a fish."

"Didn't they teach you anything in that seminary? The Bible never actually *calls* it a whale. People just think it of it like that because whales are the largest creatures in the sea. But what it really says is that God prepared a great *fish* to swallow up Jonah. Piranhas are fish, but whales aren't."

"I know that, sugar." I put a little more oomph on the last word. I didn't appreciate her talkin' down to me like that. I *knew* the difference, an' I knew the verse about it bein' a fish too. The thing was, I'd been hearin' people call it a whale for so long I'd picked up on it without realizin' it. Maybe that's what Doc Donovan had been sayin' about delusions. They sneak up on ya without you even realizin' it. Then, before you know it, you're talkin' like everyone else, even though you oughta know better.

But who was havin' the delusion here? Was it me an' Claire, or was it everybody else? It was like an endless loop of unanswerable questions.

"Argh!" I said, shakin' my head vigorous-like to jar myself loose from the vicious circle.

"Sorry," Claire said, leanin' back again. "People tell me I can be condescending. I guess I should listen to them more. Pride goeth before the fall."

"I call it autumn," I said, tryin' to lighten the mood.

It worked. She laughed and leaned forward again, grabbin' both of my hands on the table. "I really *am* sorry," she said. "This whole thing has made me feel like I'm wound up in a thousand knots. You must think I'm terrible."

I squeezed her hands. "Not at all, Claire."

She smiled at that and leaned forward further, plantin' one on my cheek. I smiled back, tryin' not to let my face show what I was thinkin'. But I must not have done a very good job of it, 'cause she giggled and blushed.

I cleared my throat nervously. "So," I said, "what about

Olivia? I mean, what kinda sicko kills a couple of innocent people by ramming tent spikes through their skulls? He woulda needed a sledgehammer to make that work."

Claire shook her head. "I can't think of anything from the Gospels, and he hasn't used anything from the epistles of Paul."

"Unless you connect the glass eyes to Paul goin' blind on the road to Damascus."

"Showing off, now, are you?"

I shrugged. "I got my pride. In the autumn, the winter, or any other time."

She laughed again. "I don't doubt it."

"But he ain't shy about referrin' to the Old Testament, neither," I said. "Jesus talks about Jonah regardin' the resurrection, but Jonah himself's in the Tanakh, not the New Testament." I was showin' off some more. The Tanakh was what Jews called the Old Testament, bein' that they didn't have a new one. I remembered that from seminary too. The more we were talkin' about this shit, the more it was comin' back to me.

"You're right, but what in the Old Testament...?"

"It was probably a gruesome murder, an' the Assassin had to be makin' a point."

"Like every other time."

"Right."

"Let's see... Jezebel was eaten by dogs..."

"That would be pretty hard to arrange, though I'll admit the piranhas took a bit of doin'. I gotta admire him for that. But he prob'ly chose tent spikes to get in an' out fast. That'd be a lot quicker."

"OK," she said, "Absalom was run through with spears after being hung by his hair from a tree for betraying David."

"No tent spikes there."

"I've got it!" she said. "Sisera!"

Even with the stuff comin' back to me, that didn't ring a bell. "Enlighten me."

"Sisera was the top general in King Jabin's army. He built a fortress and iron chariots, but the Israelites ambushed his army and had them on the run. Sisera tried to get away and took refuge in a tent that belonged to a woman named Jael. Her husband was an ally, so he thought he could trust her. But she gave him some milk to put him to sleep, then used a hammer to drive a tent peg through his skull."

"Just like our assassin did with Olivia's parents."

"Yes," Claire said, her face turnin' sad again.

"My mama used to give me warm milk when I couldn't sleep. Maybe I shouldn'ta let her." I laughed, but my bad joke didn't lift her spirits this time, so I dropped the jokin' an' got serious again.

"I don't remember that story too well," I told her. "What message do you think our assassin was tryin' to send?"

Claire looked up at the ceiling for a moment, thinkin', then back at me again. "There's not a lot about it that I remember. Just that Jabin and Sisera treated the Israelites harshly and oppressed them for twenty years."

"Twenty years. That newspaper clipping was dated twenty years ago... but that can't be important. The killer couldn't've known we'd find it that long after the murders, or even that we'd be lookin' for it, for that matter."

Claire frowned. "Well, maybe the killer was feeling oppressed by the Temple, and he took it out on Olivia's parents..."

"And all the others."

"...because they were members of the church."

"I gotta tell you, if what Chris told me is right about your pops havin' complete control over the elders an' everyone else in the church, I can't blame the guy for feelin' oppressed."

I could see she felt all offended. "I don't feel oppressed."

155

"You *did* say you'd be on your knees beggin' forgiveness if daddy-o heard you say your secretary gig was boring."

"Please don't refer to him like that. He's the Prophet. Or my father. Not 'daddy-o' or 'pops.'"

I sighed and nodded. This wasn't a battle worth fightin'. At least we were workin' together again, an' makin' progress about figurin' out our assassin's M.O. Not that it mattered, since all of it happened so far back, but it showed Claire I could work with her, and that was a good sign. Maybe now she could work with me, too, in dealin' with the problem in the here and now.

The Assassin

Snakes In the Grass

I watched Elizabeth King cross the street, clutching the hand of her daughter Tabitha. The sight of her made my blood boil. While not elders of the church... yet... Elizabeth and her husband, Thomas, had ascended the leadership ranks rapidly. Easy to do when you worship a false god with blind devotion. Whatever words the Prophet let slither from his forked tongue, the Kings believed and followed without question.

I knew all about them. I'd done my homework.

They'd arrived in town, newly married, at only seventeen years old and had joined the church within a week. From the first moment, their lives had been consumed with following the twisted doctrines set forth by the Prophet. From that time forward, the two of them had worked long hours to help fund the church's mission and their own: starting a family. Within a few weeks, they were on their way to being fruitful and multiplying, especially now that their second child was on the way at only twenty-one years of age.

That snake Thomas landed a job with an ad agency in town, and it soon expanded—which meant he was away more often, making pitches to companies across the state. Elizabeth had supplemented their income by working as a waitress at Jill's Diner. This went against the Scripture. A woman's place was in the home, as Paul had written to Titus: Young women were to be sober and love their families as chaste and obedient keepers of the home. But the Temple allowed it because it meant a larger tithe.

I spat in disgust at the thought of it. "No one can serve two masters," the Lord had said. For "where your treasure is, there will your heart be also."

God in judgment had sent an affliction to visit Elizabeth, but the filthy Prophet and his Temple still made her work... for them, of course, and with only a pittance as a salary. When she had health issues carrying her first child, the Prophet hired her to help with administrative duties, acting like he was doing her a favor by sparing her long hours on her feet at the diner.

But she was complicit in their iniquity. She knew firsthand about all the church's underhanded activities, but played an active part in sweeping it all under the rug. Quite simply, they had turned away from the true God in favor of a money-grubbing charlatan.

Part of me hated what I had to do next, at least when it came to the innocent. But innocence only lasts so long. Thomas, away on a business trip, would miss the day's events, but he would meet his end in time.

Elizabeth entered the ice cream shop and sat her daughter down at a small table while she went up to the counter to order. The little girl played with her dolly while she waited, and I took a seat on a planter in the courtyard next door. A few minutes later, they exited and sat on a bench in the bright afternoon sunshine to enjoy their chocolate-dipped cones.

I was close enough to overhear their conversation.

"You've been a very good girl today, Tabitha. That's why I got you ice cream," Elizabeth said, smiling down at her.

"Thank you, Mommy."

"After dinner, Mommy has to go do a little work at the church before bedtime. Will you be a good girl and play with your toys for Mommy while she works?"

"Yes."

"You are my blessed little girl. Now let's go put you down for a nap before dinner."

What perfect timing! The church was just a few miles outside of town, not far from the zoo. I could pick them up without anyone noticing. I wandered around for the next few hours before making my way out of town, hitting the zoo first to prepare for our final stop. Elizabeth would never expect the surprise I had in store for her.

I arrived at the church just as the lights went out inside. A moment later, the last person in the office emerged and locked things up. I couldn't have timed it better.

About thirty minutes later, I heard a car approaching; the engine cut off after a minute, and I peeked through the thicket to see Elizabeth helping Tabitha out of the car. She unlocked the door, turning on the lights in the office and then heading back into the Sunday school area, where she presumably left Tabitha to play. I waited a few minutes for her to get settled before quietly making my way inside. I could hear music from the radio drifting through the quiet halls. I crept past the office, where Elizabeth was engrossed in paperwork, and made my way back to find Tabitha.

As I approached, I heard a steady stream of talking, some of it gibberish, as Tabitha cooed to her dolly. When I entered the room, I saw her drinking a tiny cup of tea at the table. Her little doll face lit up with a wide smile when she saw me. "Who are you?" she asked.

"I'm a friend."

"My name Tab-a-ta." She held up three little fingers before proudly announcing, "I three."

"I'm Azrael's Apostle. Do you know what an apostle is?"

"No."

"Apostles are teachers. They spread the word of God... the true God. Azrael entrusted me with this mission."

"Mmm hmm."

"Do you believe in God, Tabitha?"

"Yeessss! The Pofit says..."

"I don't care what the Prophet says. He is not God. He's an idolator, worshipping a false god. You all are."

Why was I even having this conversation with a little girl? She was too young to understand, but she was already indoctrinated, her innocence compromised.

Her little eyes filled with tears, ready to spill over at any second. I couldn't afford to attract her mother's attention before I was ready. I ruffled the hair on the top of her head and knelt down in front of her. "Can I have some tea with you?"

Tabitha sniffled twice and reached over to pour me a cup.

After I finished my imaginary tea, I set her on my lap and spent the next twenty minutes captivating her with stories from the Bible. When I heard a door close and footsteps approaching, I turned in my little seat and waited for Elizabeth to enter.

Elizabeth gasped when she saw me. "Who are you? How did you get in here?"

"The front door... same as you."

"I asked who you are. What are you doing holding my daughter?"

"He a possil, Mommy."

"What, darling?"

"It doesn't matter who I am. You don't know me. I've been taking excellent care of your sweet, little daughter. Now it's time we get down to business."

"Please put her down, or I'll have to phone the police. If you need some food or help, I'm happy to oblige. Just please don't hurt us."

"I don't need anything from you. Any of you."

"Then why are you here?"

"I'm here to cleanse this place of the abomination you have birthed here. It is just as Daniel foretold: You have polluted your sanctuary and made it desolate. And as our Lord himself has said it: 'My house shall be called a house of prayer, but ye have made it a den of thieves.'"

"I'm familiar with Scripture, sir. You are in the Compassion-ate Truth Temple."

"Truth... this place has nothing to do with the truth. Their wine is the venom of serpents, the deadly poison of cobras. You should know that better than anyone. You help this false Prophet of yours hide all his sins—and yours—in this den of iniquity."

"I really don't know what you are talking about. You

obviously don't know anything about us. All the charitable work we do and witnessing to unbelievers. The Temple is a pillar of this community, but you? You're a predator, a son of the devil himself, prowling around like a roaring lion and seeking someone to devour. Well, sir, you will *not* devour my daughter! In the name of Jesus, I command you to release her. She is an innocent babe. You can't seriously hold her responsible for whatever delusions you have about the church."

"The Lord punishes the children for the sins of the parents who hate him, for those children will carry down the lessons they've learned."

Elizabeth's strong façade began to crumble. She was starting to realize the gravity of the situation... the depth of my resolve. Still, she fought to hide her fear from her impressionable little girl. The tears tracked a slow trail down her face as her voice cracked, "You can do whatever you want with me. Please just let me put her to bed in the back where she'll be safe."

"If you want to keep your daughter safe now, you will do as I ask. Is that clear?"

The last of her façade gave way and crashed down like Humpty Dumpty.

"Yes! Yes, of course. What do you want?"

"Let's go out to your car now. I'll sit in back with little Tabitha. You'll drive us out to the zoo." I turned to Tabitha and asked, "Would you like to go to the zoo, sweetheart?"

"Oh! Can we, Mommy?"

"Sure, baby," Elizabeth said as she held her hand out for her daughter to join her.

I stood up at that moment with Tabitha cradled in my arms. "Nice try. Don't try that again. Are we clear? You're *both* coming with *me*." I bent over to pick up my backpack and slung it over my shoulder.

"Yes. I'm sorry. Just please don't hurt her."

"That's up to you," I retorted as I brushed past her roughly. I held open the church door and waited for her to lead the way to the car. When she unlocked it, I slid into the backseat, Tabitha still clutched in my arms. Elizabeth got in the front seat and stared back at me through the rearview mirror.

"Idle hands are the devil's workshop, Elizabeth. Shall we go?"

"Uhh... yes." She wrung her hands before turning the ignition and backing the car out of its parking space.

"I doubt we'll see anyone at this hour outside the city limits, but don't do anything stupid if we do."

"I won't."

The brief car ride was quiet. It was past Tabitha's bedtime, and she had fallen asleep shortly after the car started moving.

After Elizabeth pulled into the parking lot of the darkened zoo, I climbed out of the car and walked her over to the gift shop entrance. As I switched arms holding Tabitha before opening the door, Elizabeth tried to pull Tabitha from my grasp. I reached into my pocket and pulled out my pocket knife, flicking it open. "I wouldn't do that if I were you."

She backed up, fear in her eyes, and I opened the door, ushering her inside first. I'd left the door unlocked when I was here earlier to facilitate our entry.

We walked through the park and entered the Reptile Rotunda, securing the entrance door behind us.

"Don't move a muscle," I growled.

I walked across to the far exit that led to the Amazon exhibit to check on the setup I had prepared earlier: It was still in place by the closed door. I lay the sleeping Tabitha on the floor a few feet away. She murmured in her sleep and shifted slightly... which drew his attention, just as I had hoped.

When I returned, Elizabeth was standing in the center of the room, looking around nervously. "I don't like snakes. They terrify me. Why are we here?"

"When the Israelites spoke against God, the Lord sent venomous snakes among them; they bit the people, and many died. The people came to Moses and said, 'We sinned when we spoke against the Lord and against you. Pray that the Lord will take the snakes away from us.'"

"Don't quote more Scripture to me. What are you trying to say?" Elizabeth angrily turned to face me directly. "Oh God! What did you do with Tabitha? Where is she?" She ran toward me, trying to dart around to get down the hallway. I caught her and dragged her over to the far wall.

"Quiet down. This will be far easier if you let her sleep."

"What? What will be easier?"

I shook her by the arms. "Stop it. Now!" Her muscles were coiled tight like a spring; she was ready to make a run for it if I released her. I wasn't going to do that. Instead, I turned her around, pulling her arms behind her back, interlocking them in the crook of my elbow. I bent down to my backpack and removed the two lengths of rope I had brought, quickly tying her wrists together and then her ankles, leaving a tiny amount of slack so she could still her shuffle her feet.

As I turned her back around, she lost her composure. "Where is my baby?" she screamed before dissolving in tears. At that moment, Tabitha woke from her nap and released a blood-curdling scream.

"Mommy! Mommy! Moooommmmmy! Help!"

Elizabeth lunged past me but fell in a hopeless heap at my feet with a grunt. "You bastard! What did you do to her? Take me to my baby."

I hauled her to her feet and looped my arm through hers to

help her shuffle down the hall into view of the python exhibit. My eardrums nearly bled at the piercing scream she let out when the full weight of the scene dawned on her.

The fifteen-foot reticulated python was wrapped tightly around Tabitha, squeezing the last bit of breath from her tiny body. Her eyes bulged from her purple face. Its massive jaw was gaping open as it swallowed the small child, her legs already consumed up to the knee, having vanished from sight inside its swollen body.

Elizabeth finally came to her senses and stopped screaming, once again trying to lunge from my grasp. "You've got to save her. There's still time. Let me go!"

"It's too late. She's gone... or soon will be."

Elizabeth's screams and struggles diminished over the next hour as she watched the hungry python devour her toddler. As the snake slithered farther into the corner to rest after its large meal, Elizabeth collapsed onto the floor in the fetal position, her eyes glazed over.

"Are you ready, Elizabeth?"

There was no answer. I snapped my fingers in front of her eyes and saw only the slightest blink in response. I yelled her name again as I slapped her face, once on each cheek. "Wake up! It's your turn."

She slowly lifted her head up and rolled her eyes to look at me. "What else can you do to me? You already took my precious daughter." She looked down at her stomach. "I can't believe I— or my unborn child—will have any better fate."

"Well, I have to give you credit for not holding on to false hope, even if you do worship a false prophet. You are correct. I just have to do one little thing first." I reached into my backpack and pulled out my calling card and a small cross, tucking them into her skirt pocket. I looked down at her once more.

"Just do it. I don't care anymore."

"Oh, you *will* care. I promise you that."

I walked over to one of the reptile exhibits across from where she lay and pulled out a crowbar I had tucked in my backpack. As the prophet Jeremiah foretold, the Lord will send venomous snakes among you, vipers that cannot be charmed, *and they will bite you!"*

With a crash, I sent the crowbar flying through the glass viewing window of the Desert Horned Viper exhibit. The snake inside, disturbed from its slumber and newly imbued with the wrath of God Almighty, slithered out of the window and down onto the floor. Elizabeth began screaming again and flailed about, trying to scramble to her feet. The horned reddish-brown viper slid sideways across the floor in typical sidewinder fashion, the dark blotches down its back undulating with its scaly skin, as it moved inexorably toward the disturbance in its habitat.

Elizabeth kicked out at the snake, trying to keep it away from her.

"I wouldn't do that if I were you," I called out, just before the viper sank his teeth into her calf. Elizabeth cried out in pain. The snake coiled up beside her, its body tense and ready to strike again. As the pain increased, Elizabeth tried to wriggle away from the snake.

It struck again with lightning speed. The venom spread throughout her body, and the bite wounds continued to bleed as her clotting became inhibited. I watched her moan in pain as the headaches and stomach cramps set in. After a while, she began to convulse in seizures—which only angered the viper more: It struck her twice more before she went into shock and her spirit left her body, bound for the fiery depths of hell where it belonged. I had researched venomous vipers in preparation for this target, but it was still a marvel to see their efficiency at killing.

I backed out of the room slowly, so as not to draw its attention, and shut the door behind me. I needed to get home. I still had a lot of planning to do before I went after my remaining targets.

STEPHEN H. and SHARON MARIE PROVOST

.

The Client

20

Father Knows Worst?

I looked at the current member roster as soon as I rose. I had begun keeping it at my bedside to check each morning when I woke.

As I'd been fearing might happen one day, the murders had started again. More than thirty more members had disappeared overnight. The target this time: the King family. Thomas and Elizabeth King had been longtime, faithful members of the church. Sadly, Thomas had gone to the Lord about ten years ago, after having a massive heart attack while traveling for work. But today, Elizabeth, their eight children, and twenty-six grandchildren were all missing.

I ran across the property from my father's house over to my office in the church to check the genealogy. To my surprise, I found that only Elizabeth's date of death had changed. Thomas was still in there, having passed ten years ago, just as I remembered. Even more unsettling: Their eldest child, Tabitha, was listed with the same date of death as her mother. Could this monster really have murdered an innocent child? The weirdest part of all: their deaths had occurred thirty-five years ago... *after* the Jud Williams murder but *before* Candace Williams and the Edwardses were killed. Why hadn't they been listed in that news story we read as previous victims of Azrael's Assassin?

I just wished I had the genealogy information for Alfred Sanderson and Elsa Franklin, the two people who'd disappeared first along with Olivia. They had joined the church very recently, and I'd wanted to give them time to settle in before asking them for detailed personal information. I had their current address, but both of them had moved to the area within the past year, so there was no way to track where they'd come from—and, therefore, no way to know where to look for any newspaper stories that might explain their disappearances. They'd been erased from all public records, so I could only assume that they met the same fate as Olivia.

And the other missing members.

The longer this went on, and the more people went missing, the more I wondered why my father... the Prophet... hadn't said anything about it. It pained me to even consider that he might be

involved in some wrongdoing, but I had to check the church's coffers. Elijah had raised some questions that I hadn't wanted to face. But given the loss of the Edwardses' generous donations... if they'd never lived to own and expand the butcher shop... it stood to reason that the Temple's bank balance must have dropped precipitously.

But if there'd been a recent withdrawal of $20,000 or more on the church's ledger—the amount Elijah had said was wagered on that barbaric fight—then I had to consider the possibility that he was right.

The only way to find out for sure was to look.

I leafed through the pages and found that the church's assets were, in fact, much lower than they had been. My trepidation mounting, I flipped forward to the present and found a withdrawal that I did not remember or authorize as treasurer. Only one other person had the authorization to take money from the account, especially in these amounts: $20,000 about one month ago and then approximately one week later $1,500.

I called Elijah and asked him to meet me down at the *Tribune* in an hour so we could discuss my findings and see what more we might discover. I ran back over to the house to grab the tote bag with my disguise and headed downstairs to the front entryway to grab the car keys. As I passed the sitting room, my father's booming voice stopped me dead in my tracks. "Claire!"

"Yes, Father?"

"If you would please do me the courtesy of coming in here, instead of yelling down the hall."

I hadn't seen him sitting in there when I walked by. I rarely paid attention to the sitting room because I'd never spent much time there growing up. It was mostly used as my father's den, where he relaxed in the evenings or received visitors— parishioners who'd come to call, elders there on church business, or my mother's friends for afternoon tea.

As I turned the corner into the room, I felt the same oppressive weight I'd always felt there. I'd been taught that a person's home was as much a place of worship as the church. But this room took it to the extreme: It felt as if I was entering the hallowed halls where God himself held court. The light that should have been reflected off the cream-colored walls was swallowed up by the heavy ebony furniture upholstered in dark brown leather. Behind his desk, an ebony custom-built bookshelf held his Bible and other religious texts.

The walls were adorned with several fine works of art depicting Jesus, the Last Supper, the Loaves and Fishes, Paul on the Road to Damascus and the Sermon on the Mount. The Ten Commandments hung beside his desk. As I entered the room to walk over to where my father sat, my eyes were drawn to a depiction of an archangel. Were we all being watched and judged by Azrael? Would he bring the wrath of God upon us to pay for our sins?

"How may I serve you, Father?"

"I hope you're not headed out to meet that private detective, Elijah Kirk."

I was taken aback. How could he have known? "I'm not sure what you're talking about."

My father's penetrating stare bored through me to my very soul. His dark brown eyes with the sharp angular eyebrows drew my gaze to his naturally, but it felt overwhelming. If I lost eye contact, he would know I was hiding something, but I couldn't hold back any longer. The tall, imposing man in front of me, his severe face focused solely on mine, had always both intimidated me and inspired obedience. The fact that he was my father, and that my father was also my Prophet made it difficult for me to stray from his strict rules.

"Have you forgotten your Scriptures... all that I taught you? Proverbs 12:22: 'Lying lips are abomination to the Lord: but they that deal truly are his delight.' Psalms 34:13: 'Keep thy tongue from evil, and thy lips from speaking guile.' Have you forgotten the ninth commandment, Claire? Or are you still the trustworthy, faithful daughter I raised?"

"Of course, I am, Father."

"Then's let shed all pretense here. I know you've been meeting with that man. He's been putting his nose into all the church's private business. You know we keep our private matters in the prayer closet, both personal and spiritual. Our Savior warned us in the Gospel of Mark, 'See that no one leads you astray.' That man, the investigator, is trying to do just that. What is he trying to find out? Is he trying to make you believe falsehoods about the holiness of our faith... about me, the Prophet?"

"I'm not letting him lead me astray. It was I who sought him out. I needed his help. No one else was willing to help me."

"No one? Do you call your Prophet 'no one'? I have always helped every believer in my flock, especially my daughter. What is this matter that you needed help with?"

"You already know what I need help with, Father, and you haven't lifted a finger. Nobody in this church, including you, will acknowledge all the missing parishioners. You can't tell me you haven't noticed that we have over seventy-five people missing from our pews? I can show you pictures we've taken of our congregation at picnics and other celebrations where vast swaths of people are clearly missing now. I've tried to talk to you about it, but you act as if I haven't said a word."

My father let out a sigh, which meant to seem sympathetic but sounded more impatient. "I'm very worried about you, Claire. You're letting this man confuse you with his wicked tongue. Do not let the devil tempt you into sin. I did not raise my daughter to be a liar. Proverbs 17:4: 'A wicked doer giveth heed to false lips; and a liar giveth ear to a naughty tongue.'"

"I'm not the only one who has noticed the missing members. Mr. Kirk knew Sarah and Joseph Edwards as well, and their son Nathan, who used to deliver meat to me for the potluck every Sunday. Are you honestly saying you don't remember them?"

My father nodded, as though it was a silly question. "Of course, I knew Joseph Edwards and his fiancée Sarah Danvers. It really was a tragedy what happened to them. But they were chaste, righteous members of the church who were waiting until marriage before sharing themselves with one another. They never had a son named Nathan, because they never were married. Have you told this salacious story to anyone else? Tainted their good name? Exodus 23:1: 'Thou shalt not raise a false report: put not thine hand with the wicked to be an unrighteous witness.'"

"I'm not spreading lies. I'm concerned about the welfare of our precious flock... dwindling more each day. It all started with Olivia."

"And *who* pray tell is Olivia?"

"My best friend! I've known her since childhood. You know this! Stop lying to me."

"What is this man's hold over you? I hope you don't have an unsavory interest in him. Has he defiled your body, which is the temple of the Holy Spirit? Second Corinthians 6:14: 'Be ye not unequally yoked together with unbelievers: for what fellowship hath righteousness with unrighteousness? And what communion hath light with darkness?'"

"How dare you besmirch my name and honor, Father? You know I have taken a vow to remain chaste until marriage, like all young women in the church. You still haven't answered my question. You keep trying to turn this back on me. Have you or have you not noticed our declining membership? That the younger generation seems to have never existed in many of our most prominent families? How long until *I* disappear? Would you even care?"

"I have had quite enough of your insolence," he said, raising his voice. Then he threw yet another scripture at me. "Ephesians 6:1-4: 'Children, obey your parents in the Lord, for this is right. Honour thy father and mother; which is the first commandment with a promise; that it may be well with thee, and thou mayest live long on the earth. And ye fathers, provoke not your children to wrath, but bring them up in the nurture and admonition of the Lord.' And First Corinthians 11:3: 'But I would have you know, that the head of every man is Christ; and the head of the woman is the man; and the head of Christ is God.' You will show me respect. I will not tolerate any more sinning from you today."

"Stop it with all this incessant quoting of Scripture. After all, I am the *daughter* of the Prophet. I can quote Scripture, too, Father. From the Gospel of John: Let he who is without sin cast the first stone."

"And just what is that supposed to mean?"

"Is gambling not a sin, Father?"

"Undoubtedly." My father shifted uncomfortably and turned his face away from me.

I'd never been so bold before, but I had to know. I walked around in front of him, forcing him to look at me. "You taught me well, Father. You should be proud." I hit him rapid-fire. Proverbs 13:11: 'Wealth gotten by vanity shall be diminished: but he that gathereth by labour shall increase.' Matthew 6:24: 'No man can serve two masters: for either he will hate the one, and love the other; or else he will hold to the one, and despise the other. Ye cannot serve God and mammon.' First Timothy 6:9-10: 'But they that will be rich fall into temptation and a snare, and into many foolish and hurtful lusts, which drown men in destruction and perdition. For the love of money is the root of all evil: which while some coveted after, they have erred from the faith, and pierced themselves through with many sorrows.' Are these not scriptures you have quoted before on Sundays?"

"Umm... uhh... yes. What is your point?"

"I know your secret, Father."

"What secret?"

"I know that you have been gambling with the church's money... that you lost $20,000 in a rigged boxing match. I know that you, too, engaged the services of Mr. Kirk via Elder Birch to investigate the possibility of getting back that lost money."

"I did no such thing. I am the Prophet. I would never fraudulently use the church's money to engage in the sinful act of gambling."

"Don't try to deny it, Father. Did you forget that I am the treasurer as well as the secretary? That the only person with access to our ledgers, besides myself, is you, the Prophet. And," I added with a little sarcasm, "apparently Elder Birch. I saw the $20,000 withdrawal a month ago, right at the time of that boxing match. I'm assuming you hired Mr. Kirk because he has a very good reputation for doing his job. It wasn't difficult for him to identify Mr. Birch, who said he was hired by someone whose identity he was not at liberty to disclose. That would be you. It could only be you. Conveniently, there was another withdrawal of over $1,000 at the time of that meeting... enough money to cover Mr. Kirk's fee and any other pertinent expenses. These are not the actions of a righteous man. Matthew 24:11: 'And many false prophets shall rise, and shall deceive many.'"

"That's enough. I will not entertain this topic any longer. First Timothy 2:11-15: 'Let the woman learn in silence with all subjection. But I suffer not a woman to teach, nor to usurp authority over the man, but to be in silence. For Adam was first formed, then Eve. And Adam was not deceived, but the woman being deceived was in the transgression. Notwithstanding she shall be saved in childbearing, if they continue in faith and charity and holiness with sobriety.' I'm not subservient to your judgments and beliefs. I am the Prophet. I follow God's mandates and lead my flock, not you... a woman."

I couldn't hold back. I took a small breath before blurting out, "Lead what flock? If you keep ignoring these disappearances, there won't be anyone left by the end of the month."

"Claire! You must obey me, and stop this insanity now! Do not interrupt me again."

A thousand thoughts were spinning through my mind. I'd never disobeyed him, but now that I had started, it seemed like I couldn't stop. If he wanted to talk about duties, wasn't it his responsibility to set an example? Why hadn't *he* been fruitful as he demanded of the rest of the congregation?

"You talk about a woman's duty, but what about your duty as one of God's disciples? Why am I an only child? Your sermons say we must multiply. Shouldn't the Prophet be held to account for that as much as any of his flock? If not more?"

His face turned cherry red. He looked like he was about to explode.

He lowered his voice and spoke slowly, almost menacingly. "Be careful what you say, Claire."

"I know Mother wanted more children. I remember one time I overheard her crying and talking to Mrs. Reynolds. She was fearful that she was being punished by God for some sin that the two of you had committed. But she said the doctor had told her she was healthy and fertile. So Father, if Mother was fertile, then what, or should I say *who*, is the problem? And what was that sin?"

"Don't you dare!"

"Did you defile Mother before entering into the covenant of marriage?"

"You have gone too far, young lady. I am your father. I am the Prophet. Have you forgotten your place? I refuse to discuss this further with you. So help me, I will..."

His face was nearly purple. He was sputtering and gulping for air. I knew I'd stepped over a line I hadn't wanted to cross.

"I'm sorry, Father. I went too far. I'm just so frustrated and worried about the congregation. I didn't mean to be disobedient and disrespectful."

He inhaled deeply. "I should hope not. Maybe it's time we reconsider your position as secretary. I'm so busy with running the church, seeing to the flock, and shepherding your mother that I don't have the time to guide you properly. I think we need to find you a husband, someone chosen by God to lead you down the path of righteousness. Then you can spend your time rearing children rather than poking your nose where it does not belong. Your job was to balance the books, not make assumptions about how the money *might* have been spent and the morality of it. Your duty to the Prophet and to God is to be a good wife and a loving mother. You're twenty-one years old—you've already wasted too much time that should have been spent raising God's children. Don't let this devil lead you down the wrong path. It's time for you to be the righteous seed of the Prophet."

I couldn't risk losing my position or, more importantly, access to the records. Besides Elijah, no one else was trying to solve this mystery and save these people. I had to beg forgiveness for my sins and at least buy some time.

"Please, Father, don't take my job away from me. It means everything to me to serve the church, the Prophet, and God. I promise I will change my sinful ways. I must attend to some errands for services on Sunday, but then I will come home and fall on my knees to beg for God's mercy."

My father looked skeptical, but he nodded slightly. "I hope you mean this. Time will tell. We'll revisit this topic again... soon. Remember Proverbs 30:17: 'The eye that mocketh at his father, and despiseth to obey his mother, the ravens of the valley shall pick it out, and the young eagles shall eat it.' We've already had a word with Mr. Kirk. He shouldn't be bothering you again."

"Yes, Father."

I turned and walked out to the car, worried that Elijah might've given up waiting for me since I was already fifteen minutes late. I needed to speak to him more than ever. My father had skillfully avoided answering any of my questions, but he'd accidentally given away some important information. Azrael's Assassin may be responsible for the murders—and, therefore, the disappearances—but he certainly wasn't the one who had attacked Elijah and his sister. Now, it seemed my own father had given me a warning as well.

Part of me felt remorseful about my disrespect toward my father, but I also felt a righteous duty to oversee the wellbeing of the congregation. I had not lied to my father. I knew I would be on my knees this afternoon asking God for forgiveness for my sins, but I was sure he would forgive me for speaking the truth and protecting his flock. If God hadn't sent Azrael's Assassin to collect their souls, then someone needed to stop whoever was committing this atrocity.

STEPHEN H. and SHARON MARIE PROVOST

The Detective
The Kings
Are Dead

C laire ran up to me and threw her arms around me, pullin' herself into me. No. it wasn't like *that*. She was sobbin' like there was no tomorrow.

I resisted the urge to kiss her. I was still a gentleman an' all, even if I didn't like it sometimes—this bein' one of those times. She needed comfortin', not canoodlin', so I just held her there for as long as she wanted and didn't resist when I felt her pull back.

"What happened, dollface?" I asked, pushing the hair back from where it was plastered to her face... except it was a wig, so I almost knocked it clean off.

That broke her mood, and she went from cryin' to laughin' out loud. "No wonder you don't have a girlfriend," she chuckled.

"I don't have one 'cause I was waitin' for you." I hoped she could tell I was jokin', even though there was a hint of truth to it. Claire was the kind o' dame guys waited for—guys with taste, anyway. You know the sayin': There's gals you want between the sheets and gals you want walkin' down the aisle. Claire was the second kind... an' I had a sneakin' suspicion she woulda been the first kind, too, if pops had let her. Me, I was kinda screwed both ways. Claire was the kind of dame that really got me goin', but I sure as hell wasn't gonna *marry* no one. No ball an' chain for me, no siree, no matter how pretty the package.

"Father wants me to wait for a man: one he's chosen for me, of course. But I don't need my life laid out in front of me like some red carpet with barbed wire fences on both sides. I'm my own person. Father just hasn't figured out that yet."

"It sounds like you're just figurin' that out yourself. And he doesn't like it."

Claire rolled her eyes. "You've got that right. I'm sorry to come in here and start crying on your shoulder, but he can just be so... awful."

"What happened?"

"I was going out to see you, and he summoned me into his sitting room for a father-daughter talk. I knew from the tone of his voice that he wasn't in a good humor, and that he blamed me for it, but I wasn't ready for what happened next: Elijah, he knows about us."

"Us?"

"I mean he knows I hired you, and he called me a liar when I tried to deny it."

I ground my teeth together. I was feelin' protective of Claire, but the irony of it was, her father was feelin' the same way. He just had a different way of expressing it. "Nothin' wrong with a little white lie for the greater good."

"Yes, there is. Exodus 20:16: 'Thou shalt not bear false

way up to the desk an' were about to ask about headin' back to the morgue when we were interrupted by someone comin' in behind us. I turned around to see a man in a golf shirt and a straw hat, walking a little hunched over an' usin' a cane.

"Oh, hello, Mr. Crowley!" the dame at the counter called past us, a smile lightin' up her face.

The man raised his hand. "I've told you a thousand times, Martha, you've gotta call me Milton."

Milton Crowley. Where had I heard that name?

"What brings you back to us today?" she asked, still smiling. Whoever this guy was, she knew him well an' had what I'd call genuine affection for him.

"Just visiting the old sweatshop," he said. "I heard something about Old Man Brinkley selling it to the Scripps people."

The woman put a finger to her lips. "That's *supposed* to be a secret," she said. "How did you get wind of it?"

"Word gets around." He shrugged. "I used to be the ace reporter here, remember?"

She laughed. "My memory's as good as ever," she said. "And I can see yours is too."

"Sharp as a tack," he said, tappin' his temple.

"Well you couldn't have come at a better time. These good folks here have been by a couple of times, looking through the microfilm and the stacks. They're very interested in the Azrael's Assassin murders, and since you were the lead reporter on all of them..."

"Yessiree, all four cases. The police started calling him Azrael's Assassin after the swim park murders."

"Four?" Claire and I both said it at once.

"I thought there were only three," she added.

Crowley shook his head. "The glass eyeballs, the piranhas, the snakes, and the double-murder out at Waverly Waves."

I was tickin' 'em off on my fingers as he went through 'em.

"Snakes?" I said. "We hadn't heard of that one."

Crowley nodded. "Yep."

Claire looked scared, but I knew what she was gonna say. She didn't want to, but she had to. "That snakes murder. It wouldn't have involved a woman named Elizabeth King, and her young daughter Tabitha?"

Crowley snapped his fingers. "Yes, that's it. I'd forgotten the names. But now that you mention it, that sounds right."

"Can you tell us anything else about the murder—or any of the others?" I asked.

Crowley thought for a minute, then shook his head. "Fraid not," he said. "It was all so long ago now."

I reached forward and shook his hand. "We won't take up any more of your time," I said. "Thank you for your help. We can find it in the stacks, I'm sure."

We headed back to the morgue and found the article we were looking for right away, on Claire's birthday fourteen years before the fact. Just like the genealogy had said.

"Tragedy at Zoo's Snake Enclosure Claims the Lives of Local Woman, 3-Year-Old Daughter."

It was clear right away that it hadn't been no accident. The little girl had been eaten by the reticulated python. Eaten! Then the glass on the Desert Horned Viper exhibit around the corner from it had been smashed in; the woman's body had been found right beside it, along with that familiar calling card. She'd died from multiple snakebites.

"Why do you think he used snakes this time?" Claire asked.

I thought a moment. "The serpent in the Garden of Eden?"

"I'm not sure. The serpent is the devil, but I don't think he's referring to Satan. I think our assassin wants us to see *God's* judgment."

"'The Lord sent fiery serpents among the people, and they bit the people, and much people of Israel died.'"

"Yes! And there's also this: 'For, behold, I will send serpents, cockatrices, among you, which will not be charmed, and they shall bite you, saith the Lord.'"

"What the hell is a cockatrice? Never mind… Whatever it is, seems like he's referrin' to the Old Testament. Maybe we'll find somethin' about a python… I don't remember anything."

"No, but remember the verse where Aaron's rod turns into a serpent, and the heathen magicians tried to copy him?"

"Yeah, and Aaron's serpent swallowed up the others—'cause they were as phony as a two-dollar bill. Sounds like he thinks you an' your church ain't the real McCoy. They act all hoity-toity, but they're too big for their britches and pretendin' to be something they're not."

Claire frowned. I could tell she didn't like the picture I was paintin'.

"That's pretty much what you think too, isn't it, Elijah?"

I didn't want her thinkin' bad about me, but I couldn't soft-pedal it for her. "If I do, at least I don't go killin' people for it."

"I'll give you that," she said.

"The one thing that don't add up about this whole thing is why that old reporter didn't remember any of the details. How could you cover somethin' like that and not have it seared into your brain for the rest of your life?"

"He's old," Claire suggested. "He could be getting senile."

I wasn't buying it, though. The guy mighta been a little stooped over, but he'd said he was sharp as a tack—and he sounded like it. His speech was clear as a bell, and he didn't sound confused or nothin'. He knew what he knew, an' was sure of it. It was what he didn't know that seemed off. "Senile? I ain't convinced of that," I said. "I think there's somethin' more goin' on here, but I'll be damned if I know what it is."

Claire fixed me with that disapprovin' look of hers.

"Darned," I said. "I'll be darned."

"That's better."

The Assassin

Monkey Wrench

My next targets were the Reynolds couple. It had taken some thought, but I'd finally realized how Azrael wished for me to eliminate these sinners. Now I just had to obtain the supplies needed for my holy mission. I drove downtown to visit the hardware and sporting goods store that had opened there last year.

I found the rope and basin I needed with ease in the

hardware section. Then I moved on to sporting goods to procure the most important item. I'd been standing at the glass case, surveying the selection of hunting knives inside, when an employee finally approached me.

"Welcome to Valley Hardware and Sporting Goods," he said. "My name is Josiah. How may I help you, sir?"

I looked up to see a short, blond-haired man sporting a "Compassionate Truth Temple" T-shirt beneath his navy-blue Valley Hardware vest. That's just my luck. Here was another member of the Temple... one I hadn't even known about.

I maintained an even demeanor. "I'm going hunting soon. I need a good knife for filleting meat once I process the carcass out in the field. Can you point me in the right direction?"

"I'd recommend this one here by Browning. Would you like to see it?"

"Yes, that'd be nice."

He handed me the knife, and I looked it over. The blade was razor sharp and would do the work nicely.

"This is perfect. Thank you for your help."

He smiled the kind of phony smile I'd seen all too often at the Temple. "I'll get this boxed up for you," he said. Is there anything else I can assist you with today before we head up to the checkout counter?"

"No, sir. But hey, I have a question for you. I noticed your T-shirt there. Do you attend church at the Temple?"

"Yes, sir. The Prophet speaks the true word of God. He leads his flock through this world of pervasive evil and shepherds us onto the path of righteousness. Do you want to save your soul from the clutches of Satan? You're welcome to join us at services on Sunday."

"I just may do that, Josiah. I've heard good things about the Compassionate Truth Temple. I've met quite a few members around the area. I'm a godly man. I follow the path of righteousness, and I pray to God every morning when I rise and at night before I lie down to sleep. I've just been searching for the right place to worship. Have you been a member for very long?"

"Yes, sir. My whole life in fact."

"Oh, so your family belongs to the Temple as well?"

"Yes, sir."

"Who are they? I might have met them."

"My parents attended faithfully, but the Lord took them into the bosom of Abraham, and another member of the church welcomed me into her home and raised me."

"My sympathies. It is a blessing that the Lord called your parents home to him, but I'm sorry to hear you missed out on the benefit of their guidance. How old were you?"

"I was seven, sir, far too young, but as you rightly said, it was the Lord who called them home. Who am I to question?"

"Indeed. God works in mysterious ways, and his call took precedence over human grief. So who raised you then?"

"My parents were friends with a kind widow, a longtime member of the Temple who lived down the street. She took me in and raised me as her own, since she had never been blessed with offspring. I was very lucky. Phoebe Wallace was a saint, God rest her soul."

"What a blessing! Thank you for your help today. I appreciate your candor. You've inspired me."

"I hope to see you at services on Sunday, sir. Good day," he chirped as he left my purchase with the cashier.

I paid for my items and walked out of the store. This situation was becoming more complicated than I had anticipated.

Azrael had promised that if the parents were dealt with, their sins would not be passed to the next generation. But

Josiah's parents were dead, and here he was still being brainwashed by the filthy Temple. Had Azrael been mistaken? That couldn't be. Something else must have happened. The only question was what, exactly, it was. Azrael wasn't telling me, so I'd have to figure it out on my own. He was testing me.

Azrael had told me I wasn't the first he had chosen to do his bidding. There had been others before me, an unbroken line across the centuries, each of them charged to stay the hand of Satan by destroying the enemies of God. He had arranged for Elijah to prophesy concerning the death of Jezebel, and ordered Jehu to have her thrown out a window and into the mouths of ravenous hounds. He had issued the command to Moses and Joshua that they slaughter all the Canaanites. And the Lord had spoken through him again to Saul concerning the Amalekites.

But Saul had failed in his mission, and had fallen on his own sword. The one who had preceded me had failed as well. He had gone mad and taken up the sword for his own glory, killing without regard to the guilt or innocence of his victims.

These things were anathema to me. I would not fail in my mission. I would stay true to Azrael's commands, regardless of the personal cost. The heretics at the Temple of Compassionate Truth were the Amalekites reborn, the enemies of the one true God. Unlike Saul, I would smite each and every one of them, sparing not a single soul. Once again, I would prove myself worthy.

I would need to delve further into this to solve the mystery of how exactly to accomplish my ultimate goal. But first things first: I had to deal with the Reynoldses.

The Assassin
Unholy Communion

I'd been looking forward to this day for a while. The church leadership was like a hydra: a serpent with many heads. The largest and most fearsome of those belonged to the Prophet himself, Hugh Cassidy, but he could wait... for now. It was high time to start cutting off some of the others, starting with Obadiah and Nadine Reynolds. Being the elder second in line to the Prophet lent him immense power, which he wielded with an iron fist. Nadine was the proper, obedient wife:

an example to all the other women of how to forsake all independence and submit to her husband's every command.

The offering plates that were passed around the congregation each week somehow never stopped in the hands of the two most senior elders, Birch and Reynolds, or the Prophet's family. But they sure seemed to benefit from the money collected—especially Daddy Warbucks in his mansion next to the church. But the benefits were obvious to the Reynolds family too. Somehow, Obadiah was able to support a large family in style on the modest income he earned through their small farm. How many farmers could afford a large two-story ranch house, two family cars, and a truck?

Obadiah had his family locked in a stranglehold of control. Nadine made no decisions concerning their household other than deciding on the night's menu and her God-given maternal duties. The children's punishments—frequently corporal in nature— were all decided on and doled out by Obadiah. (Not that they misbehaved often. They didn't dare.) He put them to work on the farm at an early age... which left Obadiah himself with far too much free time.

He spent it walking around town and "visiting" parishioners; "spying" was really a better description. He kept track of the congregation's comings and goings, and job promotions, noting any outward signs of wealth. Nadine helped in this mission by inviting herself to tea at parishioners' houses so she could report on any new signs of vanity within the household décor. It was all quite ironic given the ostentatious lifestyle demonstrated by the Cassidys, Reynoldses and Elder Birch in his fine tailored suits. If someone displayed any new wealth that wasn't proportionally reflected in their tithe, they received a private "come to Jesus" talk from Elder Reynolds.

As his family grew and multiplied from eleven children to

forty-six grandchildren and then even more great-grandchildren, his control never waned. He was not above insisting on a grandchild being whipped for the most minor infraction. Power had become his addiction... his obsession.

Obadiah still strutted around town like a peacock. Some days you'd think *he* was the Prophet. Nadine, his ever-faithful spy, wasn't above boasting about their blessed life, her cooking, and any other little tidbit that gave her some sense of pride. But, as the Bible said, "Pride goeth before the fall."

And I was just the one to take them down.

The Reynolds farm was quiet in the evening after the work was done, with Nadine and Obadiah turning in early.

When night had fallen, I walked a mile-and-a-half south of town to their spread. I crept into the darkened farmyard and evaded the notice of the two sleeping border collies by the barn. I turned the knob slowly and pushed the door open, hoping to avoid any loud creaks.

As I entered the kitchen, I heard someone coming down the hall. I ducked into the sitting room and hid in the shadows, biding my time as Nadine opened the icebox and pulled out the bottle of milk. When she turned to retrieve a glass from the cabinet, I lunged out of my hiding place, pressing my hand firmly over her mouth. "Don't scream or try to get away," I growled into her ear. She nodded, eyes unblinking and a few tears sliding down her cheek.

I wrapped my arm around her throat, applying pressure until she sagged limp in my arms. Then I guided her unconscious body down to the floor in silence.

I made my way down the hall to the master bedroom, where I found Obadiah snoring. I picked up the heavy metal "praying hands" sculpture off the chest of drawers and hit him on the side of his head, ensuring that he'd stay unconscious. I dragged his body out to the kitchen and placed him in a chair, tying his feet to its legs. With that accomplished, I duct-taped his hands together before tying a rope around his torso and binding him to the chair. I then repeated the process for Nadine.

As I began unloading the items from my backpack onto the table, both of them started to stir.

A moment later, fully awake, Obadiah roared like a lion whose pride had been threatened.

"Who are you to enter my abode without an invitation? It isn't seemly for you to gaze upon my wife in her nightclothes. Don't put your filthy hands upon her again and sully her virtue. Untie me right now before God strikes you dead, sinner."

I spat in his face. "Don't preach to me about virtue," I roared back. "And you, of all people, calling me a sinner? That's laughable. The proverbial pot calling the kettle black. Shall I list your sins? Pride and idolatry! Those come to mind first."

Obadiah's arrogant spirit was undaunted. Even in his vulnerable state, he still acted as though he was the one in control. "Bow down on your knees and beg forgiveness from your Lord. Jesus forgives sinners who confess and atone for their crimes. It's not too late."

I had an answer for that too. "You took the words right out of my mouth. I came here to help you do just that. To show you the error of your ways. You idolater! The time has come for you to quit worshipping the Prophet... worshipping money... worshipping power... worst of all, worshipping yourself, rather than the Father, the Son and the Holy Spirit. I've seen the way you strut around town, sermonizing to others as if you were above reproach, the very image of a God-fearing man. You see your wife in that same false light."

"How dare you pass judgment on me!"

"I was sent to right the wrongs committed by you and your church. You must renounce that deceiver, Hugh Cassidy, and beg for mercy from the one true God. 'Thou shalt not hearken unto the words of that prophet, or that dreamer of dreams: for the Lord your God proveth you, to know whether ye love the Lord your God with all your heart and with all your soul.'"

"Prophet Cassidy speaks for the Lord. What would a heretic know about true spirituality? Elder Birch and I lay hands on him to bless him so that he may receive the message from the Lord our God."

"There's that vanity of yours asserting itself once again. As if you have the power to bless anyone to receive God's message. God alone decides who is deserving. Proverbs 16:5: 'Every one that is proud in heart is an abomination to the Lord: though hand join in hand, he shall not be unpunished.'"

"And just who do you think you are to quote Scripture to me?"

"An angel on high has tasked me with this mission. Proverbs 16:18: 'Pride goeth before destruction, and a haughty spirt before a fall.' I am the creator of that destruction. Each week at your services, you pass around bits of sourdough bread and cups of red juice to represent Jesus' flesh and blood, which he sacrificed for your sins. But you are not worshipping Jesus or the Father. You worship yourself and the Prophet, a literal golden calf, who profits from the poor for himself, not in service of his Lord. First Corinthians 11:27: 'Wherefore whosoever shall eat this bread, and drink this cup of the Lord, unworthily, shall be guilty of the body and blood of the Lord.'"

"You know nothing about that of which you speak. No holy man would hold a man and his wife hostage, threatening their well-being."

"I am Azrael's Apostle. Listen to what I say. You must atone for your sins. You still have time to seek the Lord's forgiveness before it's too late. Acts 2:42: 'And they continued steadfastly in the apostles' doctrine and fellowship, and in breaking of bread, and in prayers.'"

I pulled out a bottle of red wine and some unleavened bread and set them on the table before them. "John 6:53-58: 'Then Jesus said unto them, Verily, verily, I say unto you, Except ye eat the flesh of the Son of man, and drink his blood, ye have no life in you. Whoso eateth my flesh, and drinketh my blood, hath eternal life; and I will raise him up at the last day. For my flesh is meat indeed, and my blood is drink indeed. He that eateth my flesh, and drinketh my blood, dwelleth in me, and I in him. As the living Father hath sent me, and I live by the Father: so he that eateth me, even he shall live by me. This is that bread which came down from heaven: not as your fathers did eat manna, and are dead: he that eateth of this bread shall live for ever.'

"I'm giving you this one chance now to earn your passage into heaven. I will be sending you to meet your Maker. On what terms, do you choose to do so?"

Obadiah's angry eyes looked like they were boring into the table. He wouldn't look up to meet mine. Nadine's nervous gaze flickered from the floor to her husband. I poured some wine into a goblet I had retrieved from their cabinet and cut off two small pieces of bread. I placed a bite of bread into Nadine's mouth and leaned over, putting the goblet to Obadiah's lips. She held the bread in her mouth, scarcely breathing, as she waited for her husband's reaction. Obadiah turned his head to look at me and spat the wine into my eyes. "Sinner! I will not break bread with the devil." Nadine leaned her head forward and let the bread drop into her lap.

I walked over to the sink and grabbed the dish towel to wipe my face and splash some water into my burning eyes. "Very well!

You've made your choice." I reached into my backpack and removed the basin, setting it on the table. Then I pulled out the hunting knife, eliciting a scream of terror from Nadine.

"Wha... what are you going to do with that?" she mewled pitifully.

"The two of you can't move past your haughty spirit. You are trapped in your pride—an abomination to God—and the wages of this sin, for you, is death. If you had worshipped the one true God... truly partaken of the flesh and blood of his Son, you would have been granted eternal life. Instead, you feed your soul with the love of self. Now your sustenance in this life, or at least what life you have left, shall be that which you cherish most."

I placed the basin in Nadine's lap and slid it under her bound hands, up to the elbows. In one swift motion, I unsheathed the knife and slashed her right forearm open from the wrist to just shy of her elbow. Crimson liquid began to pour into the basin. Nadine let out a bloodcurdling scream as the moment of shock passed and the pain set in.

"Unhand her, you monster," Obadiah bellowed. "Nadine, push that off your lap now." He struggled in his bonds, the rope cutting into his tender flesh without loosening. Nadine followed her husband's command and used her knees to upend the basin, spilling the blood across the floor.

I shook my head in disappointment. "I wouldn't have done that if I were you. Now we are just going to have to collect more." I placed the basin back into her lap and secured it to her legs with some duct tape from my bag. Then I sliced her other arm in the same manner. Her lifeblood began to pour from her in earnest— a veritable river of crimson coursing down her ivory skin and splashing into the basin below. It wasn't long before she began to get woozy. "Don't you pass out on me yet. The best part is yet to come."

I walked over to Obadiah and slashed his shirt with my blade to remove it, leaving a shallow cut across his abdomen and up to his neckline. I began to slice through the flesh on the right side of his abdomen to obtain his offering. Obadiah gritted his teeth, trying not to cry out, but as the knife cut deeper, he couldn't hold back.

He let out a long, deep moan of pain. "Almighty God, I call to you! Save me from this demon! We are your faithful servants."

I could see one of his lower ribs peeking through the muscle and sinew before blood welled up, obscuring the view. I placed the newly severed flank steak onto a plate and began to cut it into pieces. The pupils of Nadine's bleary eyes widened as she saw me pick up a bite and move toward her. She shook her head from side to side, and the muscles in her cheeks tightened as she clamped her mouth closed.

I pinched her nose shut tightly and waited until she gasped for air, dropping the large bite of her husband's flesh into her mouth. I wrapped my hand under her jaw and held it closed so she couldn't spit it out. Her face began to turn red as she fought to breathe. Tears poured from her eyes as she whimpered in terror. Finally, I saw her swallow involuntarily and released the pressure from her jaw. She gagged and tried to bring the 'meat' back up.

"I suggest you don't do that, or I will feed you his flesh until you choke."

She sobbed weakly in her chair as her strength began to wane.

"Now for you, Obadiah." I pulled the basin out of Nadine's lap and set it on the table. Pouring the wine out of the goblet onto the floor, I refilled it to the top with Nadine's blood.

"Stay away from me, you devil."

I grabbed his hair and pulled his head back roughly until he was staring at the ceiling. I pried his mouth open and began to pour the thick, red blood down his throat as he coughed and sputtered. When it was gone, I reached over and grabbed the basin. His anger boiled over as he hacked and sprayed the room with a cloud of aerosolized blood droplets.

I yanked his head back again and began to pour the basin of blood into his open maw. The viscous fluid bubbled and flowed down his neck as he choked, struggling to swallow it fast enough. I could hear him gurgling and wheezing as he began to drown in his wife's blood. His body jerked and flailed; he struggled for air, his face turning red. Tears trickled from the corners of his bloodshot eyes, his oxygen-deprived body fighting for its life.

I looked over at Nadine, who had lapsed into unconsciousness. I felt a slow, thready pulse in her neck as the last of her blood slowly oozed from the wounds on her arms. When I turned back to Obadiah, his pupils had become fixed and dilated.

I removed the bindings from their hands and arranged their bodies as if they had just sat down to a meal. I used the last of the blood in the basin to fill a goblet for each of them. I cut another chunk of flesh from Obadiah's flank and placed it on a dinner plate that I set in front of him. Once I had finished the staging for their last supper, I removed the cross and calling card from my pack, placing them both in Obadiah's hand.

It was time to return home and get some rest after a long night completing my holy task. There was much left to be done over the coming days.

STEPHEN H. and SHARON MARIE PROVOST

The Detective

Once a Cop...
Never a Cop?

*I*t was worse this time.

Claire rang me up in a panic. Said it couldn't wait for in-person. She wouldn't normally call on a Sunday, bein' the Lord's Day, an' all. But there she was on the other end of the line, sobbing into the phone so I could barely make out what she was sayin'.

"They're gone. All of them. Gone. I can't..." More crying.

"Who's gone? Where are you? Aren't you supposed to be havin' services?"

"I... I couldn't stay in there. The Reynolds family didn't show up today..."

The Reynolds family. I remembered them from the time I went there. They took up somethin' like seven rows of seats on one side. But she couldn't mean the whole family... could she? "How many people didn't show?"

"I said *all* of them! Aren't you listening? All seventy-five of them. And before you ask, their names are missing from last week's attendance sheet—when I *know* they *were* here because I signed them in myself. With them gone and all the other people who've disappeared, there was hardly anyone there this morning. Father's always so sure of himself, but he ended up shutting down the service after the benediction. Now he *has to* admit people are disappearing, doesn't he?"

I wasn't about to bet on it. I'd dealt with these Bible-thumpin' types enough to know their M.O. They called it faith but they were actually *refusin'* to believe somethin' that was right under their noses. Kinda warped if you ask me, but that's how they operated. Believin' 2+2=5 wasn't so much the problem as believin' it *wasn't* 4. It wasn't faith. It wasn't even doubt. It was outright denial. And they'd stay in denial till the cows came home, were sent to the slaughterhouse and served up on a bun at Mickey D's.

Before I could answer, though, she was talkin' again, which woulda been a blessing if she'd starting yammerin' about anything other than *this* new thing.

"Does the whole congregation have to disappear before you solve this case?" she asked, her tone changin' from sad to bitter. "I paid you to do a job, and I have yet to see any results."

"Hold up, sister," I said. "Yeah, you paid me, but I charge all my clients by the hour. Except for you. I gotta tell ya, if I'd been followin' my normal practice, you'd be on the hook for three or four times what you paid me up front. If it makes ya feel any better, I won't charge you anything from here on out. Hadn't planned on it anyway. But if you wanna do the hourly thing, just say the word, dollface. I was tryin' to be nice an' all, but if you insist on payin' me more, I ain't gonna object."

"Uh... no. That's all right," she stammered.

"We're workin' this case together, anyway," I said. "Kinda like unofficial partners. Which means I don't think it'd be right to charge my normal rate. But it also means if the case ain't solved, that's on you just as much as me. I'll tell ya, though, this ain't like any case I ever seen before."

"Are you saying it can't be solved?"

"No. *Any* case can be solved. You just gotta know what to look for and where to look."

"Or when."

She was right about that. "You talkin' about the newspapers?"

"Yes." She was all cried out now and seemed more focused.

"Then I guess it's off to the *Trib* again. With as much as we been goin' there, we might wanna pitch a tent in their parking lot. Wanna bring along some marshmallows for toastin'? We can build a bonfire an' everything."

"Very funny," she said. "Very funny, Mr. Comedian."

"When ya figure out everything's a joke, bein' a comedian just makes sense."

Checkin' through the stacks, lo and behold, we found another reference to our assassin's handiwork that hadn't been there before. Stranger still, it was there *before* any of the others. All of fifty years ago. "Farmer, wife, slain in brutal murder," the headline read, and it really *was* brutal. This time, the assassin had killed the woman by bleedin' her out, and her mouth had contained traces of partly eaten human flesh. The man had a bite carved out of him and, the article said, had choked to death on red liquid that had been forced down his throat.

His wife's blood.

The killer had arranged the couple like they'd just sat down for a Thanksgiving meal, with more blood poured into a coupla goblets and another hunk o' flesh on the man's dinner plate in front of him.

We didn't have to do a lot of thinkin' to interpret this particular setup. It was the Last Supper, with the body an' blood taken at face value. This guy was a real sicko. Of course, he'd left that same callin' card and cross that he'd planted at every other crime scene. But this bein' the first murder, they weren't callin' him 'Azrael's Assassin' yet.

A thought occurred to me, an' I asked Claire to look up Candace Matthews' and Jud Williams' murders.

"What for?"

"Just a hunch."

She found the clipping and showed it to me. The headline on the Williams story was familiar: "Local Man Found Dead With Eyes Gouged Out."

But the Matthews headline...

"See that?" I said.

Claire shook her head. "What are you talking about?"

"The headline. It's different. I came down here without you a while back and looked it up. But then it said 'Killer Feeds Woman to Piranhas at Zoo.'

"Now it says, 'Azrael's Assassin Strikes Again.' But I remember seeing that before."

"Not on this story though! Remember what Crowley said?

The cops didn't start usin' 'Azrael's Assassin' till *after* the swim park murders. *That's* where you saw the headline. Not on this story.

"Maybe he forgot and actually started using it for Candace."

I shook my head slowly. "I don't think so. And that wouldn't explain how the headline changed from when I looked at it before."

She had to give me that one.

"There's one other thing we can do," I said. "Let's take a look at the story about the swim park murders."

Claire looked through the stacks until she found it, then her face went all pale. "It says, 'Azrael's Assassin Claims Two More Victims in Fifth Murder Case.' The headline had changed. And more than that, it was now sayin' our assassin had struck five times. Not three. Not four. *Five!*

I was noddin' my head, lookin' at her like I was sayin', "Now you're catchin' on."

"It's just like I thought," I told her. "We're discoverin' these cases in a different order than they supposedly happened. Stories from earlier aren't appearin' in the paper until *after* some ones that came later."

"That's impossible."

"But that's what's happenin'."

"Are you sure we didn't just miss them somehow?"

"That's what I was wonderin', and it's why I wanted to check these clippings again. I think I'll ask the front desk to Xerox these for us, so we can refer back to 'em. Who knows? Maybe they'll change before our eyes, like those pictures have been changin'. This new case regardin' the Reynolds, didn't appear in the back issues—all magical like—until after the swim park case, which happened twenty-five years later. And it showed up after the snake murders, even though it happened before them, too. You see what I'm drivin' at now?"

Claire's face brightened. "Yes! Whenever someone vanishes, a story about someone in their family being murdered *appears* in these old papers."

"Not just someone. The family matriarch, sometimes the patriarch, too."

"What does it mean?"

"I have no fuckin' clue."

I decided it was time to bring Chris back into it. I'd tried to keep him at arm's length, 'cause I didn't want the cops gummin' up the works. But I needed an outside perspective, an' I didn't want to go back to that shrink, Donovan. The more I thought about it, the more somethin' seemed kinda off about the guy. I hadn't quite put my finger on it yet, but it had almost been like he'd been tryin' to throw me off track—get me to drop the case by sayin' *I* was the problem.

Yeah, he'd been right about the booze, but I didn't need no shrink to tell me that. All the stuff he'd been spewin' about shared illusions and Duke's Follies, or whatever he'd called it, hadn't helped me one bit. It'd just gotten me to doubt myself, which I was startin' to suspect was his purpose in bringin' it up.

I had a hunch, but it wasn't enough to act on it... yet. Maybe Chris could help me hash it out.

I didn't like the idea of goin' down to the stationhouse. I wasn't exactly welcome there, since they were still sore at me for rattin' out my partner. Cops had long memories when it came to that kinda thing, and once you were on the wrong side of that thin blue line, there weren't no goin' back. But I was losin' patience with this case, and I wanted to get it solved yesterday. So here I was.

"Hi, Janey," I said to the dame mannin' the front desk. Me and her'd been tight when I was on the force. I'd even taken her out a few times. But now she just looked up from her paperwork, saw who I was, an' said, "Oh. It's you. What do *you* want?"

I ignored the cold shoulder and forged ahead. "I'm just lookin' for Chris."

"Chris who?"

"Don't play games with me, Janey, Chris Reynolds." As his last name left my lips, I had a sinking feeling in the pit of my stomach. Reynolds. No, it couldn't be.

"There's no one here by that name, smartass."

I forged ahead, still hopin' I was wrong. "You know. Kinda short. Brown hair startin' to recede. Ambidextrous. Master of bad puns. Manager of the PAL baseball team an' one helluva poker player." It wasn't like you could miss Chris. He was that one guy everybody liked.

"You're losin' it, Kirk," Janey said. "There ain't nobody here like that, and there never has been. Monroe manages the PAL team, and Jackson is the guy who cleans up at cards. You can't miss it. He's always going on about it. What's your game, anyway, *detective?*" She said the last word derisively. The cops didn't like the fact that I'd gone out on my own. They started off callin' me 'Counterfeit Dick,' but then they just shortened it to 'Dildo.' "When a dildo like you comes snooping around, asking bogus questions, that usually means they want information on something else and are trying to weasel it out of us. I ain't falling for that—especially from the likes of you."

I could see she wasn't gonna be any help, and I woulda been more upset at how she was treatin' me considerin' our past. But I had a panicky voice inside me that kept repeatin' the name Reynolds over and over in my head.

"Thanks, Janey," I said. "You're a doll. Or at least you useta be."

I didn't wait to see her reaction. I just turned away an' got the hell outta there. No need to stay any longer than necessary, plus I had somethin' else I had to do.

I didn't even wait to get home. I stopped at the first phone booth I found, tossed in a dime, and dialed Chris' number. But instead of him pickin' up, I got the switchboard dame sayin' that KLondike 9428 was not in service. I slammed the phone down on the receiver, picked it up, and tried again. Same result.

"Fuck!"

I picked it up again and rang Claire's number.

"Hello?"

At least her line was working.

"It's Kirk," I said.

"Oh, hello, Mr. Stapleton. Do you have a delivery for us today?" That was what she said at work so no one would know she was talkin' to me, but she didn't like it. She thought it was a lie, which I had to admit it kinda was. But I'd told her that, if she wanted this case solved, we might have to resort to such "drastic" measures.

She lowered her voice and said in a hurried whisper, "I asked you not to call me here unless it was an emergency."

"It is," I said. "Can you look in your records and see if there's anything about Chris Reynolds in there? It would be a while back."

"Of course there would be. He's part of the Reynolds clan that..." She stopped short. "Oh my God. He hasn't been part of the church for years. If whoever's behind all this has a problem with the church, why would they care about him?"

"I don't know. It doesn't make sense to me either. But everyone else in the Reynolds family is gone, so maybe our mystery man is just bein' thorough. Or maybe it's just automatic-like. Everyone in the Reynolds clan is just gone, whether they're in the church now or not."

I heard the sound of Claire leafing through some papers. I suspected it was the genealogy. "He's not here," she hissed. "He's gone, just like all the other Reynoldses. I don't want to talk anymore from here. Can you meet me at your office?"

"I'm on my way right now."

I'd barely unlocked the door when Claire burst in.

"I don't know what's happening," she said.

"Neither do I. Chris was my only contact down at the stationhouse. With him missing too now, we're on our own. Till now we've been lookin' at who's been disappearin', but maybe we're goin' at it the wrong way. There's more people gone than there are left by this point, so it's time to start lookin' at who's left—not just now, but outta everyone who's ever been to the Temple, even for just a short time. If they targeted Chris, they could be targeting other past members as well. Can you think of anyone offhand who might be in danger?"

Claire thought a minute. "Well, my family's still there, and then there were a couple of people who came and went, but I don't remember their names off the top of my head. There might be others, too, farther back. How far back are you thinking?"

"All the way back to when the church was founded. We're flyin' blind here, so we gotta be as thorough as possible. I wanna go through all the records you have at the church. Can you get them here so I can look at 'em?"

Claire nodded. "I can sneak them out tonight if you can meet me after hours."

"Good."

"What do you think you're looking for?"

"I'm not sure," I told her. "I think I'll know it when I see it."

She frowned at me. I could tell she still didn't trust me a hundred percent, even now, but she had no choice in the matter.

And I had no choice but to tell her what was naggin' at the back of my brain.

I started slowly: "Claire, I hate to say this 'cause I don't want you to give up hope, but...

Tears started formin' in her eyes, and her lower lip began to tremble. As much as I wanted to spare her, I thought it best to tell her now. To prepare her. It was mostly a gut feeling, but my gut was usually spot-on.

"Doll, I gotta give it to you straight. We been lookin' for these missing friends of yours for a long time, and we haven't found a single goddamn lead... Sorry. Either someone's hidin' 'em real good, or..."

She knew what I was getting' at. "Don't say it," she whimpered.

I reached over an' brushed her hair back where it was fallin' down into her eyes, then wiped a tear away with the back of my finger.

"I'm really sorry, sweet cheeks, but we gotta be prepared for the possibility that we might not be able to find them."

Her tears gave way to red-faced rage as she pulled back from me. "You're giving up!" she wailed, pounding both fists into my chest. "You acted like you cared, but you don't give a damn about my friends. Which means you don't give a damn about me!"

"Claire, that ain't true. None of it. I *do* care, and I ain't givin' up. Not by a long shot. If anything, I'm more determined to crack this case than I've ever been. Now that Chris is missing, it's personal to me. This thing is gnawin' at me like a dog with a bone, an' I ain't gonna stop until I put it outta my misery."

Claire dissolved into tears again an' buried her head in my chest, wrappin' her arms around me tight. I was glad to return the favor.

"It's okay, darlin'," I whispered in her ear. "We'll get through this thing together and come out the other side. I promise."

That's what I said to her. But inside, another voice was sayin' somethin' else entirely: *Don't make no promises you ain't sure you can keep.*

STEPHEN H. and SHARON MARIE PROVOST

The Assassin
25
Tongue-Twister

My mission had been so straightforward up until this point. I thought Azrael had provided me with all the tools and information I needed to complete the job. But now someone had thrown a monkey wrench into the works, and it was time to figure out what had happened. My trip to Valley Hardware had ended with the surprise discovery of a member of the Compassionate Truth Temple that I hadn't known about.

How was he still around? Most of the families had been already been dealt with, and I knew he didn't belong with those still remaining. He had been raised by Phoebe Wallace, who was not a relative, after the death of his parents—who had been members of the church. But he never told me who those parents were. If they'd been dealt with, why was he still around? And if they hadn't, what were the circumstances of these two young people's deaths?

The first step: Find out his last name. I called Valley

Hardware and asked for the manager. When he answered the phone, I explained that I'd received excellent service from his employee in the sporting goods department named Josiah. I asked if he could give me his last name so I could address a thank you card to him in care of the store. The manager was all too happy to provide it, but I wasn't ready for the answer I received: King.

King? How could his last name be King? Surely, he couldn't be related to *those* Kings. Those Kings had been taken care of thirty-five years ago. I didn't remember there being a second family named King. I had to sneak into the church and check the records to solve this mystery.

I waited until after midnight to drive over to the Temple, parking about a half-mile away so as not to draw unwanted attention from the "King on the Hill." The church had long since closed for the night, and all was still. No lights were on, and it appeared as if everyone had retired for the night at the Prophet's house as well. I crept through the yard, keeping to the shadows, until I reached the front door of the church. I put on leather gloves to prevent leaving any fingerprints; I knew I would have to take care not to leave evidence behind that would link me to this murder.

It didn't take long to pick the lock.

Once inside, I entered the front office where the church secretary kept all the records. Of course, they were under lock and key as well. The church insisted on absolute secrecy when it came to all personal matters. After some time, I was able to access the file cabinet's contents.

The member roster was useless. It contained contact information and work history, but nothing about family. I pulled out the genealogy book next and found the name King. As I had thought, there was only one family with that last name. During a quick perusal down the page, I didn't see Josiah King listed as one of Elizabeth's and Thomas' children. But just as I was about to give up, I noticed a small addendum at the bottom of the page.

Josiah apparently had been adopted by the Kings at age 4 from a family outside the church. That would have made him 7 at the time of the murders, which meant he must have been at school the day Elizabeth and Tabitha were killed. It was frustrating that Azrael had failed to warn me about the possibility of such complications. Was he testing my resolve to be sure I would succeed where others had failed him? Whatever his reasoning, I had to get it resolved.

I locked the records back up and left the church, locking the door behind me. Since I was already outside of town, I made a stop at Anderson Farm Goods. Along the highway, at the far edge of a large farm, the Andersons ran a small shop that sold fresh produce, home-baked pastries, and pies. They also operated a small petting zoo from the barn out back. I parked my car in the small lot between the store and barn, out of their sight and hidden from anyone who might pass by on the road. I broke into the barn to collect a few items I would need for the next step.

Thankfully, I'd made note of Josiah's address, so I headed over to his house. The records had not indicated that he was married or had any children—with any luck that meant he would be home alone. Josiah lived on a quiet street with just a few homes scattered along it; only one had a porchlight on. I grabbed my pack from the backseat and scaled his fence, proceeding to the back door.

I slipped inside and went down the hall, checking the other rooms along the way, until I found the master bedroom.

I found Josiah snoring in the room, alone. I snuck up beside him and put my hands on his throat, pressing down hard and digging in with my fingers. He thrashed on the bed, gurgling, as he tried to breathe. After a short while, he passed out. I needed him incapacitated for the next step, so I hog-tied him, arching his back and tying his wrists to his ankles. I would have preferred to gag him to keep the noise level down, but it would have gotten in the way of my plans.

I removed the hunting knife from my bag and knelt on the floor beside him. Josiah moaned as he started to regain consciousness. He pulled at the restraints with his arms and legs, trying to stretch out his limbs. His eyelids fluttered open as I straddled him to hold him in place. I brandished the knife at him. "Don't scream, or I will slit your throat right now."

"Please don't hurt me, sir. You can have whatever you need. Just take it and leave."

"I don't want anything you have."

Josiah squinted up at me, recognition dawning on his face.

"Do I know you?"

"No, you don't."

"Wait! I do. You're that guy from the store. I sold you a knife. That one in your hand."

"That has no bearing on this situation."

"Did I do something to offend you? I'm a righteous man. Please let me make amends."

"Of course, you did. You were sold a bill of goods by that church, and you bought it hook, line and sinker."

"I'm afraid I don't know what you're talking about, sir."

"Don't play innocent with me. You don't strike me as an imbecile. You *must* know how corrupt Hugh Cassidy's Church of the Almighty Dollar is—that he only keeps you around for your money. You were spouting their filth to me the other day, extolling the virtues of that church. The Temple must be stopped... all of you."

"We tithe to support our church."

"Like building the Taj Mahal for the Profit?" I gave him a playful slug in the arm as I snickered. "You get it? 'Profit'?"

"No sir, I don't. The Prophet, Mr. Cassidy, is a very honorable man. You must be confusing him with someone else."

Josiah's eyes were pleading with me to believe him. He looked like a sad little puppy whose favorite toy was being taken away from him. He couldn't let go of his misplaced faith.

"I wish I could believe you were just toeing the company line, but it's obvious to me that they've thoroughly brainwashed you. A lifetime in the church, and you believe every word they say... which is why I have to kill you. First Corinthians 13:1: 'Though I speak with the tongues of men and of angels, and have not charity, I am become as sounding brass, or a tinkling cymbal.'"

"The Prophet leads the church in performing many charitable activities... we run a food closet for the poor, we supply milk and produce from our farm to underprivileged children, and so much more. I swear it's not just talk. I help out myself every Sunday after services."

"You poor, confused man. You seem nice enough to me. I'm sorry I have to do this to you, but you really have no idea what you're supporting. Jeremiah 9:3: 'And they bend their tongues like their bow for lies: but they are not valiant for the truth upon the earth; for they proceed from evil to evil, and they know not me, saith the Lord.' You are worshipping a false prophet who parades himself around like a false God. I wish I could lead you to the path of righteousness."

Tears trickled down Josiah's face. He still thought he could convince me of the error in my thinking.

I grabbed his hand and held it as I closed my eyes and prayed to God for his eternal soul. It was too late for him, since I could not convince him to repent for his sins. But I could still feel sorry for him.

"Josiah, to eradicate the church, I have to eliminate all of you. The church is like a grove of quaking aspen. It looks like it's composed of many trees, but in fact, they're all one single organism—and Hugh Cassidy is at the root of it all. I can't stop this evil unless I exterminate each and every one of you."

"I'm begging you to change your mind. I've never hurt anyone."

"That may be true, but the evil that's within you is like a virus. If I don't stamp it out, it will spread, and many people *will* be hurt. So I'm afraid I'm going to have to hurt you instead. And Josiah, this next part *is* going to hurt... a lot. If you want, though, I can make your passing as painless as possible. God will grant you a measure of mercy, but you must ask him."

"That would be like suicide... which is a sin. You're asking me to forsake God."

"I'm asking you to beg for forgiveness from the one true God... to save your soul. John 7:37-39: 'In the last day, that great day of the feast, Jesus stood and cried, saying, 'If any man thirst, let him come unto me, and drink. He that believeth on me, as the Scripture hath said, out of his belly shall flow rivers of living water.' It is your choice."

"I cannot. I will lay down my life for *my* God."

"As you wish."

I reached down and pried open his mouth, pulling out his tongue as far as I could. His eyes widened in fright as he tried to close his mouth when I brought the knife closer.

"You made your choice. Hold still, or I can make this a whole lot worse for you."

I sliced off his tongue with one smooth stroke of the exquisitely sharp blade. A jet of blood squirted onto my face and shirt. Josiah began to choke and cough from all the blood pooling up in his mouth. I opened his jaw as far as I could spread it so I could shove the severed tongue deep into the back of his throat, blocking his airway.

Josiah's face morphed from bright red to purple as he retched and fought to bring up the object in his throat. I leaned all of my body weight on him, holding him down as he slowly suffocated. One last tear streaked down his face as his body became still. His eyes bulged and showed pinpoints of red from the petechial hemorrhaging. He was about to have a mouthful, so I cut the skin at the corners of his mouth back to his ears, widening his smile.

Propping his lifeless shell up against the bed and nightstand, I pulled my backpack over to remove my supplies. The glass jar in the bag contained the severed tongues of barnyard animals at the Anderson farm, one each from a cow, donkey, pig, sheep, and goat. I filled his mouth with the tongues, arranged top to bottom, from smallest to largest. I had to dislocate his jaw to make them fit.

This time, I would not be leaving a cross and my calling card. It was too risky.

Surely, Azrael would be pleased with my progress. I only had two targets left to complete my mission, and one of those was the head of the snake.

STEPHEN H. and SHARON MARIE PROVOST

The Client
26
What's Up, Doc?

I 'd returned home, intent on getting those records together for Elijah to meet him later, but the strain from his cockamamie theory was all just too much. I'd had to turn in early, blaming it on a bit of an autumn cold. Unfortunately, I spent most of the night tossing and turning, unable to fall asleep. The thing that was keeping me awake—his theory made sense.

If the Reynoldses were killed fifty years ago, then that was before their first child was born... no children, then no grandchildren or great-grandchildren... no Reynolds family at all. But exactly how was the family patriarch and matriarch killed in the *past*? We're living in reality, not some *Twilight Zone* episode.

I'd given up on sleep and risen with the sun, intent on getting some church work done before meeting Elijah at 9. When I entered the empty church, the preternatural silence was unnerving, so I turned on the radio for some company. I was unprepared for what I heard next. Instead of the soothing sounds of "The Old Rugged Cross" or some other gospel music, the broadcast was a news flash dedicated to a gruesome murder that had been discovered in the pre-dawn hours.

None of the details were being released yet, but a man had been found murdered in his home. A neighbor had reported hearing terrifying screams, gone over to the house, and come upon the scene of a brutal, ritualistic murder. The police were asking the public to come forward with any information that might be pertinent to the case. Murders didn't happen in our peaceful town. And who had been murdered? I was too scared to contemplate that it might be related to our present predicament. I turned off the radio and tried to work on balancing the ledgers.

The phone rang, dragging me out of the daze in which I sat. It was the police department. I felt a sinking feeling in the pit of my stomach.

"Hi, ma'am. I need to speak to Hugh Cassidy or someone in charge."

"I'm Claire Cassidy, his daughter, and the secretary in charge of all church matters. How may I be of assistance?"

"Ma'am, I'm not sure that you want to be involved in this matter. Maybe I should speak to your father."

"I'm perfectly capable of handling whatever you need. It is my job to complete tasks for the Prophet. He is resting. Please tell me what you need."

"Well, ma'am. I'm not sure if you've heard the news, but there was a murder last night."

"Yes, I did. And how does that concern the Temple?"

"I need someone to do the identification. The deceased has no next of kin, but we know he's been a lifetime member of the Temple."

"I know all of the members. Who's been murdered, may I ask?"

"Josiah King, ma'am."

"Oh my God! When do you need me and where should I go?"

"Come down to the coroner's office behind the police station at 10 a.m. Will that work?"

"Yes, officer. I'll be there."

I couldn't believe it. Josiah King. How had I forgotten about him when Elijah asked me who was still left in the church? It was more important than ever to figure out who was left. I needed to talk to Elijah now... before I made the identification. I dialed his home number; he was no early riser, that's for sure, but there was no answer. I tried calling his office, but no answer there either. I hoped nothing had happened to him. Only one way to know for sure... I had to go looking for him. I packed up all the church records in a large tote bag and ran out the door.

I made it to his office in ten minutes and started banging on the door. He wasn't answering, but his car was out in the lot. I pounded harder, but still nothing. The roller shade on his office door wasn't pulled down all the way. I peeked underneath it and saw him passed out on his desk, a bottle of Jack by his hand. So much for being on the wagon! This was the last thing I needed right now.

I pounded on the door and screamed, "Elijah, dammit! Open the door!"

The door opened slowly. "Relax there, kitten. I'm right here. Better watch that pretty little mouth of yours, church mouse; you've been hangin' around me too much."

I wanted to yell at him, "My name's Claire," but I didn't have the patience to argue with him about that. Instead, I fell into his arms, sobbing. After a moment, I gathered myself together again.

"Have you heard the news? Probably not... you were too busy drowning in the bottom of that bottle over there," I said, venom dripping in my voice.

I collapsed into the chair, sobbing uncontrollably.

"There, there, Claire. I'm sorry. Whatsa matter?"

"Josiah's dead."

"Slow down there. My head ain't on straight yet. Who's Josiah?"

"Josiah King was killed!"

"Did you say King? King as in *the* Kings?"

"Yes."

"How was he related?"

"He was Elizabeth's son."

"How can that be? We didn't see him on the family tree. I thought they were all gone, just like all the other families who lost one or both parents."

"It bothered me all night. I can't explain it. It's impossible. Yet you're right. I don't think they were ever born... the missing people, I mean."

"So... then what's up with this King character then?"

"Neither one of us noticed the little addendum at the bottom of the page. He was adopted. I've been under so much pressure, I'd forgotten about that. I'll never forgive myself. Maybe we could have saved him if it wasn't for my mistake."

"You can't go thinkin' like that. We've been doing everything we can. Runnin' like chickens with our heads cut off. We still have no explanation for how any of this is happenin'. I don't even know if it was possible to stop it. Wait a minute! You asked if I heard the news. Do you mean to say this *just happened*? This ain't some old news story we need to look up in the *Trib*?"

"Exactly. I couldn't sleep, so I went to do some work in my office until it was time to meet you. When I turned on the radio, there was a news story about a murder. The police called a few minutes later. They want me to come down and identify the body."

"Why you?"

"Try to stay on track here, Elijah. Remember, his entire family was obliterated. The church is the closest thing he has to family."

"Oh yeah, yeah. Makes sense. So what's the story? You been down there yet?"

"They didn't tell me anything. They want me to go to the coroner's office at 10. Will you go with me?"

"Of course. Phil, the coroner, is a good friend of mine. Maybe I can get some information outta him."

"Even better. And thank you. To be honest, I'm a little nervous. I've never seen a dead body."

"Don't worry, darlin'. I'll hold your hand and everything."

"You are absolutely incorrigible, Elijah, but thank you for being there. I don't know how I would have gotten through these past few months without you."

"Don't go makin' me blush now, dollface."

"I don't understand what's happening. This must be related, but how? The other murders happened over a thirty-year span of time, with the last one being twenty years ago. Could it really be the same killer?"

"That's some good detective logic there. Simple answer... it beats me. I've never heard of one killer keepin' it goin' for that long. I mean... he'd have to be, what, at least seventy years old now? Seems unlikely. Could there be a copycat? Possible... We must be missing somethin', but what?"

"That's what I was thinking. What's this about a copycat though?"

"Hold your horses. Let's get on down to the coroner, and see what he has to say. We'll discuss the rest later when I've had more time to think. That bag over there contain what I think it does?"

"Yes, I brought all the records. I thought we could pore over them together, in depth."

"You finally trust little old me to look through your private church records."

"Why not? There isn't much left."

I couldn't suppress a sad little laugh at my joke.

I drove us over to the coroner's office. Elijah still wasn't fit to be behind the wheel. When we entered, the secretary at the front desk greeted us.

"Hello. How may I help you?"

"Detective Robins told me to come down here at 10 to meet with Dr. Allen. I'm here to make an identification."

"Oh yes, he's expecting you. One moment, please."

A few moments later, a short, balding man with spectacles entered the room. "Miss Cassidy, I presume?" he asked as he held out his hand to me. He looked over at Elijah and smiled as recognition dawned on him.

"Hey there, Elijah. What are you doing here? You ain't back on the force, are ya?"

"Hi, Phil. I'm helpin' Miss Cassidy with an issue. She asked me to accompany her here. That okay?"

"Absolutely! It's good to see you, even if it is under such horrific circumstances."

Dr. Allen led us back to a private room with a viewing window. On the other side of the glass, a body covered in a sheet lay on a gurney. An attendant was standing nearby, awaiting further instructions.

"Miss Cassidy, I must warn you that what you're about to see will be quite disturbing. Are you ready?"

I latched onto Elijah's hand, squeezing tightly. "Yes, doctor."

Dr. Allen motioned to the attendant, who pulled down the

sheet. I cried out and buried my head in Elijah's shoulder. I couldn't bear to look another second. His mouth had been slashed open, giving him an unnaturally large smile like that Joker character. I'd been nearly as disturbed by the Joker's image in that comic book I'd taken away from one of the kids during Sunday services.

My stomach was roiling; the coffee I'd had on an empty stomach was making it burn. I dove away from Elijah and fell to my knees by the waste can in the corner, retching up bile until my abdominal muscles cramped.

Elijah hurried over and pulled my hair back, tentatively patting my back. "Are you alright, darling?"

"Miss Allen, let me get you some water," the coroner said. "I'll be right back. I shouldn't have shown you that part of the body. Your delicate feminine sensibilities weren't made for such a sight."

"No, please wait, Dr. Allen. I just want to finish this and get out of here."

"Certainly."

"Yes, that is Josiah King. Do you need anything else from me?"

"No, ma'am. Let me just escort you out."

"Just a minute, Phil," Elijah cut in. "I have some questions for you if that's okay?

"Yes. If you'll just wait right here, I'll take Miss Cassidy out and be right back."

Dr. Allen left me sitting in a chair in the lobby with a small paper cone of water. I must have been as pale as I felt because the secretary kept looking over at me. About ten minutes later, Elijah emerged from the back, looking perplexed... and sobered up. He led me out to the car and climbed behind the wheel. I was too weak to argue. I wanted to forget I'd ever started this investigation, but I had to know what had happened.

"So, is it related?"

"I'm not sure. I think so... it must be... but there's some discrepancies."

"Discrepancies?"

"The killer didn't leave behind any callin' card... or cross."

"But would there be if this was done by a copycat?"

"Not necessarily, but possibly. I don't know. This whole case makes no damn sense."

"I'm not sure I want to know, but why was his face cut like that?"

"I don't think you're up to this, dollface."

"Don't you dare leave me out of this now. I can handle it."

"Okay. The killer cut out his tongue and shoved it down his throat."

"My God! But..."

"You didn't let me finish. His mouth was sliced open so the killer could stuff it full of animal tongues. Phil clued me in about it. They'd cleaned it all up by the time we saw it."

"That's barbaric! But why? This case must be connected. Murders don't happen here. Even if they did, what are the chances a church member would happen to be the victim of some other killer? And the brutality of this crime is off the chart."

"Any thoughts about what the message might be?"

"On this one, I'm stumped."

"I know you guys do that whole 'filled with the spirit' junk where you start speakin' in tongues. I think the killer believes you're saying all the right words but not to the right God."

Just when I started to think Elijah could act like a grown man, he had to prove me wrong.

"And just what is that supposed to mean? And don't think I don't know you were at my church that one Sunday back when you ditched me!"

"You *did* recognize me! Why didn't you ever say anything?"

"At the time, I couldn't risk anybody realizing who you were. Since then, it just didn't seem to matter. I figured out that you were just trying to get some more information. Now, Mr. Kirk, I asked you a question."

"You must have noticed how your father spent so much of the church's tithes and offerings on that large, beautiful home of yours, furnishin' it with only the best décor. Your lawn is perfectly cut. Then there are those topiaries and flower gardens. You've already told me you buy the best, but most expensive, meat in town. He rules that church, his flock, and you with an iron fist. A fistful of dollars, that is."

My anger was boiling over. I would've gotten out and stomped away, but we were in my car.

"That's not fair."

"I live out here in the real world. I see how people fight to keep their heads above water. What ain't fair is how your parishioners struggle to meet their own families' needs after they give away so much of their *gross* income to the church. You've never had to support yourself. You don't know what it's like. I'm not blamin' ya. I just want you to understand. And then there's the way your father and all the men in your church treat women. It's abominable."

"And you're just the pillar of virtue, right? Calling me 'dollface' and 'darling' but rarely my God-given name."

"I don't mean anythin' by that, *Claire*. But I know you're smart as hell and got the right to make your own decisions. I'd never tell you who you can or can't see. I'd never insult your intelligence by actin' like you're crazy or lyin' to ya."

Just when I wanted to hate Elijah most, he had a good point. He'd always been honest with me... to a fault even.

"Let's just drop this conversation for now. We've got more important matters to consider, right?"

"Yes. Let's get back to my office and go over those records. Whatever's happenin' seems to be speedin' up. I don't think we have much time left. And I don't want nothin' happening to you." He looked away when he said that last part.

We stopped off at the diner and picked up two cheeseburgers and fries to go. It looked like we had a long day of research ahead of us.

We started with the roster of current church members. I opened the book and read off the names as Elijah took notes on his legal pad.

"There's my father, mother, and me of course. Orion and Mary Bauer. Frank and Edna Pierce. Wait a minute... Pierce? Who are they? Why does that sound so familiar?" My brow furrowed as I dug through my memory bank. I've known almost all the church members since I was a child."

"How am I supposed to know? You're the secretary. Now that you mention it though, it does seem familiar. Wait... isn't that the people who bought the butcher shop from the Edwards family?"

"You're right. But they weren't members before. Or were they? I feel so confused. It says they've been members for nineteen years. How can that be? I don't remember them being there at services... ever... not even this past week. Like I told you, father ended after the benediction because the church was nearly empty. But on the other hand, it feels like I *did* know they were members. *Were* they there? I feel like I'm remembering two opposite things at once. Am I making any sense at all?"

"Strangely enough, you *are* makin' sense. Do you remember what I was sayin' before about that reporter's memory gaps down at the paper? He remembered those killings but was all fuzzy-headed about the details. Details he had no business forgettin'. But he wasn't senile, and you sure as hell ain't either. Now don't you go locking me up in no looney bin after I say this, but it looks like the present has changed, just like the past has with all these murders."

"But..." I had opened my mouth to ask the next logical question, but he cut me off.

"Don't you go askin' me how. I ain't no Einstein or Heisenberg. Is that all the members left?"

"Yes."

"What about the organist and his family? I remember them bein' there when I visited."

"Gone."

"Whaddya mean, 'gone'?"

"I forgot to tell you the other day: That's one of the reasons Father ended services early. An empty house was awkward enough, but with no organist to accompany us, there was just no point."

"What happened to him, though? He and his family were sitting in the front. They musta been some kinda big shots, right?"

"Yes," I said. "They *were*. They were part of the Reynolds family. So *poof!* Gone like the rest."

"Okay. At least I got this straight. As to the rest of it... we'll come back to these double memories and fluctuatin' timelines later... after I ponder it more. Let's move on to anybody who visited the church but didn't stay."

"I keep track of anybody new who signs into the church attendance register each week, so I can follow up with them and answer any questions they may have. It's a short list because we rarely have newbies."

"Will you have contact information for them?"

"Usually, but not always. Let's see... there's Adeline Foster, Robert Castor, Lucas Fisher and Brantley... hmm... I can't quite make out the last name. Adeline was a traveling nurse who was only in town for a few weeks, so we can eliminate her. Robert and Lucas each came only once over ten years ago. I think they're unlikely to be a threat or in danger. Now Brantley attended a few times over a couple of months just about a year ago."

"Now I'm the one experiencing déjà vu. The name Brantley seems so familiar. Any chance you can find a picture of him or his last name somewhere else?"

"Well, here's all the pictures taken over the last year. You look through those while I dig through the weekly attendance records."

Elijah started with the oldest pictures first while I flipped back through the log. He held up a picture to show me.

"There's the Pierces, right here in this picture. Everything *has* changed."

He was right. They *were* there.

I turned my attention back to the attendance log.

"Here it is..."

I jumped when Elijah slammed his fist on the table. "Well, I'll be goddamned! Fucking Donovan, right?"

His reaction startled me. I wasn't used to angry outbursts like that. My father could grind you into dust on the heel of his boot, but it was all about his tone of voice and wording, rather than being loud or hitting objects.

"I'm sorry about that. Takin' his name in vain and shit. Remember when I didn't contact you for a few weeks...?"

"Do you really want to remind me of that right now?"

"I know, I know. I apologize again. I went to see a psychologist because it felt like I was losin' it. None of that shit that was happenin' made sense. If only I could go back to those good ol' days because it has gotten a hell lot more complicated. Anyhow... wanna make any guesses as to who that psychologist was?"

"I don't know."

Elijah raised his eyebrows at me.

"Oh no. You don't mean Brantley Donovan?"

"Good ol' Doc Donovan. That bastard, pardon my French... that bastard made me think I was losin' it. And you too! In fact, he blamed my problems on you sharin' your craziness with me. Called it some bullshit like Duke's Follies. I don't know. It don't matter. He claimed that he remembered the change in ownership at the butcher shop years ago. Even said he remembered hearin' about them murders of Edwards and his fiancée. I knew I didn't like that guy. He just gave me that hinky feeling."

"He never told us he was a doctor. That's so strange. He seemed like such a nice man."

"Classic wolf in sheep's clothing. I don't know who murdered people in the past, thereby changing our present in more ways than one. I dunno how those murders in the past occurred. But there's certainly someone murderin' now. Maybe Doc Donovan is a copycat pickin' up where that other one left off. That's what I meant when I talked about it earlier. Josiah may only be the tip of the iceberg. The question is: what's his beef with the Temple?"

"I'll trust you. You're the expert. Whatever it takes to make all this stop before..."

"Before you go poof into thin air or meet some grisly end? Damn right!"

I stood up and gave him a quick hug. "Thank you, Elijah."

"I'm goin' to do some diggin'... see what I can find out. I need you to take care of yourself. Stay in the company of other people.

Lock the doors whenever you're alone. No goin' out at night by yourself. Watch that cute little ass of yours."

I opened my mouth to object at that last comment, but it was useless. There was no changing him. Besides, he was already on his way out the door. As he trotted down the hall, he called out, "Can you lock the door behind you on your way out, Claire? Hurry home, Red Riding Hood. The wolf is out, an' he might be comin' after you."

The Assassin

Dog Day

I was looking through the refrigerator for something to eat
when Sally arrived. I'd had the door open for a couple of
minutes already, having become distracted from whatever
I was looking for by more thoughts about my mission. I
didn't even notice when Sally came in. She finally caught my
attention the third time she said my name—very loudly—as she
dropped her keys on the kitchen counter in dramatic fashion.

"There you are," she said, a snide tone in her voice. "For a
minute there, I thought you were going to get swallowed up by
Miss Frigidaire there. Enjoy the peep show? I guess you're not

imagining what's behind *my* door anymore. Not that you've shown any interest lately. I guess you prefer your ladies... *frigid*."

"Sorry," I said, nearly bumping my head on the top of the fridge as I extricated myself. I whirled around and put my hands on Sally's hips, but she resisted my attempts to draw her to me.

"Oh, no you don't, mister. I've had enough of your games. You haven't even called me in three days. I don't need to chase a man, Brantley. You probably don't even notice the guys staring at me. If you did, you probably wouldn't care. You're always too stuck inside your head." She reached up with her index finger and tapped my forehead. "Hello. Anybody in there?"

"Look, Sally, I really am sorry. I've just been so caught up in my assignment..."

She wouldn't let me finish. "There you go with that assignment of yours again, Mr. Self-Employed Psychoanalyst. Maybe you should analyze yourself for a change. What would you say you are? A narcissist?"

"No."

"Then what?"

"From your point of view, it would probably seem I'm a schizoid: absorbed in my own thoughts, distant, slow to connect with others."

"Then, since you love the Bible so much, maybe you should follow its advice: Physician, heal thyself."

"I said I probably *seem* like a schizoid from *your* point of view. That doesn't make it true. It wasn't true for Jesus, either. He said it to make a point: No prophet is accepted in his own country."

Sally put her hands on her hips and just stared at me. "So you're a prophet now, are you? Like that crazy preacher at the Compassionate Truth Temple—that place you hate? Doesn't he call himself a prophet too?"

I could feel my fists balling up involuntarily and the blood rushing to my face. My heart was beating faster. She didn't want to go there. "I am *nothing* like that charlatan!" I shouted. "He is a *false* prophet. A wolf in sheep's clothing."

Some of the anger melted out of Sally's face; she looked genuinely concerned. "Who's to say he wouldn't think the same thing about you?" she said. "I'm not saying you're wrong, but you've been wrapped up more and more in religion lately. You weren't like this when we were in school together, or even a year ago. You didn't want to even talk about religion. I'm worried about you, babe. I…"

She paused and turned toward the backyard.

"Brantley, did I just hear a dog bark out there?"

I nodded slowly. I hadn't told her, but Azrael—the dog my foster parents had left me to care for—had returned. I hadn't seen him for fifteen years, and I thought he'd found a new home or been taken to the pound. But he'd shown up on my doorstep out of nowhere just two days ago, wagging his tail and staring up at me. He was still wearing the same tag on his collar, the one with the sigil that identified him belonging to his namesake.

I knew immediately it was a sign. I hadn't left Azrael's calling card at my last assignment because I'd been afraid of drawing attention to myself. Of getting caught.

Fear.

"The fear of man bringeth a snare: but whoso putteth his trust in the Lord shall be safe."

I couldn't allow myself to get caught before my mission was complete, but I had to give the glory to God. "For God hath not given us the spirit of fear; but of power, and of love, and of a sound mind," Paul had written to Timothy. "Be not thou therefore ashamed of the testimony of our Lord."

I took a deep breath and tried to reel my anger back in. I wanted to tell Sally that everything had changed when I received my mission, but every time I mentioned it, it just set her off. She didn't understand, but I sensed she wanted to. I had to honor that, yet I knew I couldn't tell her everything. She would never accept it, and it would put the mission in peril. I had to limit myself to things she could accept and approach the subject in a way she could understand—even if doing so might be painful... might bring up things I had tried hard to bury.

She had mentioned the dog, so I decided to start there.

"That's my old dog," I said.

"Your *old* dog? You never told me you had a dog."

"I never told you anything about that part of my life, Sal, because it's all just too painful. But if I want you to trust me, I'm going to have to be honest about it."

"About what? I don't understand. You told me you were in an orphanage... a group home. I know how difficult that must have been." She reached out and took my hand.

"It's not that, Sally. It's from before that. I was placed in a foster home with a couple from the Temple. It was the worst experience of my life." I could feel something pounding inside my head. *This* was why I never wanted to talk about this. I couldn't talk about it without reliving it, so I suppressed everything about it—forced it down deep inside myself and buried it there, so I wouldn't have to think about it. I felt waves of nausea roiling my stomach. I had to hold it together, but Sally could see I had bent forward slightly, trying to control it.

"Brantley, are you OK?" She squeezed my hand. "I'm here."

I nodded several times quickly and forced myself to stand up straight again.

"I'm sorry, honey. You don't have to talk about it if..."

I waved her off. I'd already brought it to the surface, and it would take great effort to push it back down again. That could wait until after we'd talked. With any luck, she would see how hard it was to discuss my time with my foster parents and wouldn't press to hear anything more. I could make it through if I could get my head to stop pounding. I couldn't afford to black out again, the way I had the first time. It had been worth it—God works all things together for good—but I couldn't let it happen again now. Sally would think there was something wrong with me, and the last thing I needed was more scrutiny from her. Or anyone.

That first time... the man had come downstairs and beaten me with a switch. I don't remember for what, but I remembered what he did like it was yesterday. He'd pulled down my pants with such force he'd ripped them and knocked me off my feet so I fell forward, hitting my head on the wall. I was barely conscious, but I felt him beating me... beating me so hard it left welts on my buttocks and the back of my legs. At some point, I blacked out, and when I came to, I wasn't afraid anymore. When I read about Paul being blinded on the road to Damascus, I knew that's what had happened to me. God had struck me blind so that I might see with new eyes, to his eternal glory.

It was later that day that the man had given me Azrael. He seemed to have been treated poorly himself, his fur matted and one eye always half-closed. He came up to me with his head cocked, one ear up and the other down, then started to wag his tail. It was like he was delivering me a message. And I saw that message on his collar tag: his name and the heavenly sigil of Azrael.

It had been a sign. Just as it had been a sign when he returned to me two days ago.

"The man—my so-called 'foster father'—gave him to me when I was staying there. He told me to take care of him, but if you want to know the truth of it, the dog took care of me. And now he's come back to me after all these years."

Sally looked confused. "How could he have found you after all those years?" she asked. "Are you sure it's the same dog?"

"Completely. He looks exactly the same as the day I last saw him."

She had this weird look on her face, but she didn't say anything. I didn't want to give her any more time to process it, so I forged ahead, beating the nausea back. "My foster parents weren't parents to me at all. They just wanted the money they got from the government for looking after me. I went there at the start of the summer, right after school let out, and they locked me in their basement right away. They never let me out." I paused, gulping at the feel of bile rising toward my throat. "The man beat me for no reason. With a switch. With his belt. With a flyswatter. With his bare hand... and the woman didn't do anything to stop him. She was always spouting Bible verses to justify cowering before him like some sniveling sycophant. 'Wives, submit yourselves unto your own husbands, as unto the Lord,' she said. 'Children, obey your parents in all things: for this is well pleasing unto the Lord.'

"But they didn't know a damn thing about what the Lord finds pleasing. For him, it was just an excuse to take out his frustrations on a helpless child; for her, it was just a reason to placate him. She tried to make me feel better by saying he treated her the same way, but the woman was just a coward. I swore I'd never be like her: weak and groveling. It made me sick. Still does."

Sally pursed her lips and furrowed her brow. "Maybe he *did* mistreat her, the same way he mistreated you. Maybe he was abused as a child."

She was trying to be empathetic toward them, but I needed her to be empathetic toward *me*. She didn't even know these people. Why did they matter more to her than I did? She was supposed to be *my* girlfriend! She was supposed to support *me*.

"Don't give me that crap!" I nearly shouted it, and she took a step backward. I lowered my voice; she did not have ears to hear, for the Lord had not yet opened her eyes. He would... I had faith that he would, but until then, I needed to be patient. "I'm sorry." I reached out and took her hand, and she relaxed a little. "This is just hard for me. I've heard so many people—even my own colleagues—try to excuse bad behavior by blaming it on a difficult childhood. That's far too simplistic. Any *good* therapist will tell you that each case is different. Most of us experience trauma as children in one form or another, but not all of us project our anger and frustration onto innocent people. Most of us don't. I don't blame other people for the abuse I experienced; I hold the abusers themselves responsible."

Sally nodded slowly. I could tell she was weighing whether to say something or not. She was scared of me... but not too scared: Ultimately, she decided to ask. "What about the Temple? You seem to be angry at them, too."

I forced myself to speak calmly. "They were hardly innocent. They were complicit. Enablers. The teachings of the Temple freed them from any guilt they might have felt if they had acted on their own. Maybe they wouldn't have acted at all if the Temple and its false prophet hadn't given them permission."

"So, did they drag you to the Temple every week?"

"No, they never took me there. They didn't want anyone to even know about me. They wanted to be the ones to 'discipline' me the way they saw fit. The Temple's teachings were just an excuse."

Sally looked puzzled. "I don't understand. If they were concerned about your salvation..."

"They weren't. That's what I'm trying to tell you. They were only concerned with having a reason to abuse me."

"But if you never went to the Temple, how do you know its

teachings played a role?"

"They told me," I said. I was trying not to lose patience. I knew I had to let Sally in on some things; I owed that to her. But once I started opening up—about anything—she always latched on like a prosecutor, asking question after question. It felt like she was trying to poke holes in my story. "Besides, I attended the Temple myself for a short time as an adult."

"Since we've been together? You never told me about that. I thought we weren't supposed to have secrets."

I tried to avoid smirking. If she only knew. "I didn't want to expose you to that shit. It's toxic."

She stood up straighter. "I'm a big girl, Brantley. I can take care of myself. And if it's that bad, why would you expose *yourself* to it?"

"I needed to see for myself. To be sure. And I wanted to look at their genealogy records."

"They let you do that? Isn't it private?"

"They give you access if you belong to the church. That's why I became a member: I wanted to see if the church was hiding anything." I didn't tell her I'd broken into the church more recently to see whether the records had been updated. "I just went there a few times over a couple of months. That was enough, believe me."

Sally's eyes narrowed. "It's like you have this secret life I don't know anything about."

"*Had*. I *had* things that I've kept private. Not just from you, but from everyone. As I said, they're simply too painful."

Her expression softened. "I understand, babe." She leaned into me, and I wrapped my arms around her. It felt good. Maybe, just maybe, I'd been able to put her mind at ease.

"Oh, hey," she said suddenly, pulling back. "I went over to Pierce Meats yesterday. They're expanding from being just a butcher shop, so now they have a limited menu if you want to eat there. They've taken the displays off some of their tables and put them up on new shelves lining the walls, and they've made those tables for seating. I ordered one of their meat pies. They're really good. I hope you don't mind me going there."

"Why would I mind?"

"Well, you know the Pierces are members of the Temple, right?"

I didn't. "No," I said slowly. "That's news to me."

"They even have a new sign up, with a plaster cow on top of it, painted gold."

I tried hard not to let my anger show. A golden calf. The nerve of those people. It wasn't enough that they worshipped the god of mammon. They had to go flaunting it like Aaron and the Israelites with their false idols. If they were members of the church, that made it all the worse. But they hadn't been members before. The Edwardses had been, but not the Pierces. They hadn't even lived in town until...

I hadn't accounted for this. Had Azrael made a mistake?

No, he was just testing me. Again.

I was so wrapped up in my thoughts that I hadn't noticed it, but Sally had gone to the back door and opened it. In came Azrael, wagging his tail.

"Hi, boy!" Sally said, bending down on her haunches and rubbing his ears as he licked her face. At least he liked her. That was a good sign.

"Hey, babe," she said, standing up and looking at me. "What's that weird tag on his collar? I've never seen a symbol like that before."

"It's just a rabies tag. The vet is using some weird kind of code. I don't understand it, either." I laughed.

She looked slightly offended. "Why didn't you take him to

my vet's office? They'd even give you a discount. And they don't use weird symbols like that."

I didn't tell her I'd been trying to keep her at arm's length from everything involving Azrael... the angel *or* the dog.

She shrugged. "Well, he's a nice dog," she said. "Maybe we can take him out for a ride sometime."

I sighed inwardly. *That was a close one.*

The Assassin 28
Butchered

Now I understood why Azrael had come back to me. He'd lost faith in my ability to complete my mission. I'd let fear rule my actions and withheld the glory that belonged to God when I expelled Josiah King. I'd already screwed up by missing him in the first place. I couldn't blame Azrael for sending his dog to watch over me... to help me. I needed to get my act together and stop making mistakes. Now I had to prove myself by resolving this new difficulty he'd brought to test me... the introduction of new members, the Pierces, to replace the Edwardses.

After Sally's big revelation of the golden calf on display at the butcher shop, she'd wanted to go bowling after dinner. I was anxious to get back home and take care of this issue post haste, but I couldn't put her off again. Still, Azrael and God were counting on me. I feigned a headache after three games so we could end the night early. We parted in the driveway, with a promise to meet for dinner the next night at Luigi's Italian Eatery. I made a quick stop in the house to gather the supplies I needed and to check on Azrael.

I would have to be even more careful on tonight's mission. The butcher shop was at the edge of downtown. Weeknights were typically quiet after 8; at least I had that in my favor. I parked in the lot at the town square, only a block from the butcher, and a short walk from my office should I need an alibi. I had dressed in dark clothes and kept to the shadows as I headed over.

The Pierces lived above their butcher shop in a small apartment. It was nearly 10 by the time I arrived, and all the lights were off—both in the shop and in the windows above. I planned to use the back stairs to access the apartment through their private entrance. However, I was surprised to find a large wheelchair ramp with multiple turns and landing platforms leading up to the door. When and why had this been installed?

I picked the lock and entered the Pierces' living room. The fancy furniture and décor inside didn't match the simplicity of the exterior. No wonder they had put a golden calf on display to boast of their wealth.

I made my way through the apartment until I found their bedroom in the back corner. When I entered, I saw a wheelchair sitting next to Frank's side of the bed. This was an unexpected but pleasant turn of events; it would make my job much easier. I quietly wheeled the chair out of the room and walked over to

Edna.

I placed my hand over her mouth, waking her with a start. She tried to scream, but I pressed harder and covered her nose.

"I'll let you breathe if you quit struggling. Got it?"

She nodded her head and looked over at her sleeping husband. "Try anything, and I will kill him." She nodded once more. "I'm going to remove my hand. No screaming." I uncovered her mouth as tears slid down her face.

"Please don't hurt Frank. He's been through so much. His life is hard enough as it is."

"What's wrong with him?"

"He had a stroke last year. He can't speak, see, or walk. He's like a small child. He poses no threat to you. He couldn't identify you even if he understood what's happening."

I hadn't expected this turn of events. Frank Pierce had sinned, forsaking the Almighty and turning to the false god sold by the Prophet, but it seemed he was already paying for that. He certainly wasn't responsible for this latest sin: the addition of the golden calf to their store. In his condition, there was no way he could perpetuate the evil being spread by the Compassionate Truth Temple.

I wrapped my hand around Edna's wrist, digging my fingers in, and led her out of the room. She seemed relieved when we left her husband behind. I took her into the small living room and told her to sit on the couch.

"What do you want, sir? I'll do anything. I never saw you. I won't even call the police. Just please don't hurt my husband... or me."

"God has instructed me to grant your husband clemency. He's already living out the wages of his sins. You though... that's a different story. You were people of faith when you moved here. You believed in the one true God. Why, then, did you let that devil lead you astray? That false prophet! Matthew 7:15: 'Beware of false prophets, which come to you in sheep's clothing, but inwardly they are ravening wolves.' You've committed an act of apostasy."

"How dare you question our faith! The Edwards family belonged to the Temple. When we bought the shop, they spoke so glowingly of it. As soon as we visited, we knew we had found our new home."

"How much of your hard-earned money do you tithe to that cash whore? He sells his soul *and yours* to the devil to line his pockets with filthy mammon."

"You are mistaken. The Prophet is a good and righteous man. The Temple does so many good works in the community."

"He has brainwashed you. It seems like you have come to covet money, following his example. That's quite a fancy ramp out there."

"That ramp is for Frank! He needs it to get inside!"

"What he *needs* is to atone for his sin, not to pay for something so elaborate, which he could have built at half the cost."

"But you don't even know how much it cost."

"Silence!" I waved my hand around the room, pointing out the ostentatious display of wealth. "Forget about the ramp. What about all of this? Not that anyone can see it from the outside. But that golden calf... that false God... shows everyone what you truly hold dear. Have you not read the 32nd chapter of Exodus, wherein the Israelites told Aaron to make a god for them out of gold? He melted down their golden earrings and created a golden calf... just like yours. Moses returned unto the Lord and pleaded that he forgive them, and if not that the Lord might blot his name out of the book that he had written in their stead. But the Lord's hand was not stayed, for he said unto Moses,

'Whosoever hath sinned against me, him will I blot out of my book.' That is why I am here: to be the hand of God against the sin of this false Temple. I have been tasked with removing all the tainted worshippers."

"And what do you mean by that?"

"I shall blot you from his book."

Tears slid down Edna's face. I heard her grinding her teeth from across the room. The lines in her face deepened as she became angry.

"Are you that foul murderer? It's all around town. Everyone knows that some beast killed one of our flock, dear Josiah King. God will strike you down! You will burn in the everlasting fires of hell."

"Not I. I am doing God's good work. There's nothing more to discuss."

It was time to tell the rest of town... the whole world... about the evil being executed by the Prophet and the Compassionate Truth Temple. What better way to rally the faithful and eradicate it permanently than to show them the consequences of disobedience? As the Book of Judges said, "And when he was come into his house, he took a knife, and laid hold on his concubine, and divided her, together with her bones, into twelve pieces, and sent her into all the coasts of Israel."

I wrapped my hands around Edna's throat and squeezed. She clawed at my hands, drawing blood, trying to pull them away as she kicked me. But I had the strength of Azrael behind me. I didn't even feel her blows raining upon my body. When at last her heart stopped beating, I laid her body out in the center of the living room floor.

I drew the hatchet out of my pack and hacked at her body, chopping her into twelve pieces—her torso, head, arms, hands, thighs, lower legs, and feet. Blood pooled on the floor and was cast about the room as I thrust my sharp blade downward, piercing her flesh.

Once this was done, I used a quilt laid out across the couch to gather all the body parts together.

It was after midnight by the time I finished. I walked back to my car and found the downtown area dark and deserted. I drove back over to the shop and parked in the darkened back corner of the lot before ascending the ramp again and using the wheelchair to transport the bundle down to my car. Then I drove out of town to the Compassionate Truth Temple.

When I arrived, I broke into the church once more, carrying the package inside with me. I sat her head in the front pew facing the pulpit, where I placed one of her hands holding the calling card and a cross on the lectern. I wanted to make sure that my message was clear. I felt confident that Azrael—and God—would be pleased with my work. The rest of the body parts I spread throughout the pews, in the front office, in the Sunday school classroom, then I left the other hand lying on the sign-in logbook near the door.

I saved the torso for last: I placed it in the Prophet's office, propped up in his chair. Everyone in town, especially the church members, had been ignoring the disappearances. They couldn't brush the murder of that hardware store employee under the rug, but the press had reported on it as if it were an everyday crime. That had been my mistake, and I wouldn't make it twice. They wouldn't be able to ignore me, Azrael's Apostle, anymore. It was time that they faced the truth... retribution was coming for them... all of them. The wrath of Almighty God was upon them.

The Detective
Azrael's Apostle

I t was time to pay my old friend Doc Donovan another visit. I'd had a gut feeling about the guy that was only gettin' stronger, and now that we knew he had a connection to the Temple as well...

If he really had been tryin' to throw me off the scent, this gave him a motive for doin' so. Maybe he had some beef with the church or the Prophet, so he'd decided to pick up where our assassin left off twenty years ago. If he knew about those old cases, maybe he'd found common cause with our assassin and set himself up to continue his mission.

A classic copycat killer.

The Tongue-Twister Murder, as the police were callin' it, was sure as hell sick enough to fit the old pattern. But one thing didn't add up: The murderer hadn't left the calling card and cross that had been the hallmarks of the assassin's killings. If he wanted to follow in the original assassin's footsteps, that would be the one thing he'd be sure to include. Wouldn't it?

It was always possible that the Tongue-Twister case was just an isolated murder. But there were even bigger problems with that theory. Nothing had been taken, so it wasn't a case of a robbery gone wrong. And besides, what kind of thief sets the kind of grisly tableau the Twister had left behind? It had obviously been premeditated. But that still left me without a motive. No one, as far as I could tell, had anything against the victim. Everyone loved him. He was just a nice, polite guy who was always helpful and never bothered anyone. When I went to Valley Hardware to ask his boss, he told me the guy was his best worker. He'd even been employee of the month three times in a row.

He didn't have any debts or ties to the mob. He didn't have a girlfriend, so the jealous lover angle was out. The only ties he *did* have, other than his work, were to the Compassionate Truth Temple.

Which brought me full circle, back to the shrink.

I'd spilled way too much to Donovan in our first session, so he had to know I'd been sniffin' around. But I hadn't said nothin' about Claire, and he probably figured he'd thrown me off the scent with all his talk about shared illusions or whatever the hell he'd called them. In hindsight, I could tell he was tryin' to make me feel like I was nutso—not that I needed much help at that point. But my head was screwed on straighter now, and I'd learned enough to turn the tables on him. If I was careful.

I'd been ice fishin' a few times during the winter, so I knew how to bait a hook. What I needed to do now was apply the same principle to Doc Donovan. I just didn't know if he was the kind of fish to go for minnows or worms. If he was the kind of psycho I thought he was, he probably had a taste for maggots.

I just needed to try fishin' from a different hole.

I hadn't been a threat to Donovan before. I'd been the one

spillin' my guts, which meant he could act all superior and tell me what was wrong with me. He could steer me in whatever direction he wanted me to go. This time needed to be different. I had to put him on the defensive, and in doin' so lay the groundwork for makin' him blow his cool. What better way to do so than to ditch the PI persona and replace it with somethin' that hit close to home?

I'd spent some time stakin' out the Temple, takin' notes on how the people there acted an' the kind of duds they wore. Plus I'd been pickin' up on the way Claire spoke, which would also come in handy. I ditched the trench coat an' fedora in favor of the same three-piece suit I'd worn to the Temple—similar to the one Roderick Birch had worn. Birch himself had recently come to a nasty end, getting' smeared all over the railroad tracks less than a football field away from my office window. No Azrael note on this guy. They'd called it suicide. But I suspected Vinnie'd gotten spooked by his pokin' around and had dealt with him accordingly. No big loss. The guy was a confirmed bachelor with no family to miss him. I knew I didn't.

My outfit was almost complete. Just needed a few accessories to make it right: I went to McGillicuddy Menswear an' picked up a tie tack that was shaped like a cross and matching cufflinks, completin' my makeover with a copy of King Jimmy's Good Book under my arm.

I'd boned up on it, so I'd be ready for him this time. I'd broken out my old seminary textbooks, too, and I hadn't had a drop to drink. I was gonna have to be sharper than a tack to hold my own with the good doctor.

I didn't say it was no emergency, but Doc Donovan set me up for an appointment the same afternoon. Either he was worried or curious or wantin' to reinforce the B.S. he'd been feedin' me at our first meeting.

"Mr. Kirk. Good to see you," he said, striding across the room and grabbin' my hand. "Have a seat. You look quite... different than you did at our first meeting."

"I'm a changed man, Doc," I said, puffin' out my chest and smilin'. "What you said before got me thinkin', and as I was doin' so, I happened to see the Good Book sittin' right there on the bookshelf. I opened it, and I turned right to the page that says, 'Thou shalt not follow a crowd to do evil.' I thought about what you'd said, talkin' about shared illusions..."

"Delusions."

"...and I figured it was a sign. I got on my knees then and there, and I turned my life over to the Lord Jesus Christ, praise his name."

A hint of a frown crossed Donovan's face before he managed to smooth it over. I'd gotten to him, if only for a moment. Time to press the attack. "As it is written, 'Evil men and seducers shall wax worse and worse, deceiving and being deceived.' So we gotta hold on to the church, the body of Christ."

Donovan's frown returned, and this time, it stayed. "This is quite a... transformation."

"Just call me Paul on the road to Damascus. 'He hath delivered us from the domain of darkness and transferred us to the kingdom of his beloved Son.'"

Donovan banished the frown again and just sat there, still as a statue. "What do you think?" he said finally, his face smooth as glass. "Is the church always a refuge, or can it not itself be a source of delusion? Remember our discussion about tyrants equating their own will to the will of God. You mentioned the Apostle Paul. But did not Paul himself also write that there would be false apostles and deceitful workers masquerading as followers of Christ?"

I opened my eyes wide. "I did not know you were a believer, Doc."

"You seem surprised. Most people in this great country of ours are Christians. It would be more extraordinary if I were not. But we are not here to talk about me..."

"But doc," I interrupted. "If you're a brother in Christ, ain't it right that we fellowship together? I trust you all the more to help me out, now that I know that we're on the same page—of the Good Book." I chuckled.

He stiffened. "I prefer to keep my personal and professional lives separate."

I smiled. "But has the Lord not said that what he whispers in our ear, we should shout it from the rooftops?"

"We are not on a roof."

He was tryin' not to let on that I was gettin' to him, and he was doin' a pretty good job of it. Almost perfect, but not quite. I decided to dial it back a notch. I needed him to *think* he was still in control, so I could make sure I had him hooked before reelin' him in. I remembered how confused I'd been during our first meeting, and I put that look back on my face. "Are you sayin' the church is a bunch of false apostles, Doc? If I can't trust the church, then who can I trust? You?"

"Of course you can trust me."

"Then tell me, Doc, what would you do in my position? If you think the church is a scam, who do *you* turn to?"

"I never said it was a scam. I..."

"C'mon, Doc. Level with me. You said I could trust you, so don't hold nothin' back. Give it to me straight."

"Have you thought about finding a mentor to help you navigate this new journey of faith?"

"How about you, Doc?"

"Well... I'm not sure..."

"OK. You musta had a mentor yourself when you were first getting' started. How did you choose him, an' how did it go for you?"

Donovan leaned forward. "He chose me."

I nearly had him hooked. "Oh, really? Why?"

"Because he found me a worthy laborer."

I leaned forward myself, my face just inches from his, an' looked him square in the eye. "How did you prove yourself worthy?"

He lowered his voice like he didn't want no one to hear some kinda secret he was about to tell me. There weren't no one there, but if this guy was as looney tunes as I thought he was, he might be thinkin' Azrael or some ghost-toastie was listenin' in. "He showed me the verse in Genesis, in which God commanded Abraham to make a burnt offering of his son on Mount Moriah..."

Christ on a cracker! Had this guy killed his own kid? I was ready to reel him in, but who knew what kind of monster I'd find on my hook.

"I had no son, so he asked that I prepare myself to sacrifice something else that was precious to me. When I had decided on what it would be, I went on a camping trip and pitched my tent at Longvale Park. There are some large firepits there; they were suitable for my purpose. I was about to light the flame underneath it when, just as it did to Abraham, a large ram appeared. A blue ram. It was trapped in a dense thicket of underbrush off to the side of the campsite, so I freed it and made it my sacrifice instead."

I'd been tryin' to play him, but he'd turned the tables back on me, stayin' fully composed throughout his story. He musta known I was on to him an' made it up just to mess with my head. And he'd done a bang-up job of it: His face was entirely serious, and he never blinked while tellin' it. But I knew it was a buncha bullshit: There weren't no rams in this neck o' the woods, and there weren't no *blue* rams anywhere except in L.A.—they wore pads and helmets an' had names like Van Brocklin and Crazylegs Hirsch. I knew he couldn't've been sacrificin' *those* blue rams.

I wanted to ask him what his original sacrifice had been, but I didn't wanna be too obvious and a big part o' me didn't wanna know anyway.

Instead, I asked, "Do you think this mentor of yours would be willin' to take on another disciple?"

Donovan leaned back again, cool as a cucumber, and said, "No." Emphatically.

I played dumb. "But how do you know if you don't ask him— or tell me where to find him an' I can ask him myself?"

His voice was still even but betrayed the smallest hint of impatience. "I already told you: You don't choose him. Azrael chooses you." He shut his mouth quickly. He knew he'd slipped up royal an' was tryin' to stay calm. I wasn't gonna give him the chance. I'd snatched him off the hook, an' now it was time to gut him an' lay him out on my own personal firepit. "Azrael," I said. "I've heard that name before. Wasn't there a serial killer awhile back called Azrael's Assassin?"

He stood up in front of me, an' I thought we was gonna go at it then an' there.

"APOSTLE!" he shouted. "Azrael's APOSTLE, you fool!"

Now there was a new bit of information I hadn't heard. Seemed like the press had tagged this killer with a name that was different than the one he liked. This nutso shrink was takin' after him an' takin' offense at the same thing. Most copycats I'd heard of just thought they were carryin' on the mission of the original killer. This nutjob seemed to think he *was* the original.

I'd served Fish Donovan up on my plate, but I decided it was time to play with my food a little bit. I could tell he wasn't armed, unless he had a switchblade on him—which meant I had the advantage, seein' as I had a Baby Browning tucked away in my coat pocket. He was standin' there, towerin' over me, looking like he was about to breathe fire like the red dragon in that Blake paintin'. But I just sat there, crossin' my legs and lookin' up at him.

"You call me a fool, doctor, yet 'anger resteth in the bosom of fools' and 'a wrathful man stirreth up strife.' "

I thought he was about ready to lose it on me, an' my hand crept slowly up inside my jacket, toward my pocket pistol. He closed his eyes, took a deep breath, an' raised his hand to his neck. "I will kill you!" he shouted. "He has ordained it!" And with that, he leapt straight at me. The dumbass must not've seen me goin' for my gun, an' I wasn't complainin'. I'd had enough of this shit.

I pulled my pistol and fired at him point-blank...

...into thin air.

The bullet slammed into the window an' shattered it, disappearin' without spillin' a single drop o' blood.

The last thing I heard was the sound of a maniac's laughter, driftin' away as soon as it'd begun.

The Assassin
Soulmate Sacrifice

That filthy animal! How dare he question my faith and the righteousness of my mission. To imply that I was a wrathful fool? What hypocrisy! "Vengeance is mine," saith the Lord. I was the tool the Lord had chosen to wield in exacting his revenge. Kirk thought he could stop me, but he was wrong. Azrael was standing behind me, guiding me.

I thought I had angered Azrael—made him lose faith in me—so that he'd tested me to measure my resolve. I saw now that those unexpected trials had come, not from him, but from Satan. I'd underestimated the strength of Lucifer... his hold over man. Evil was pervasive in this town, running rampant, threatening to overthrow God. I would not let Satan win. Only I could stamp out the heretics and spread God's message of love to save the others' eternal souls.

Mr. Kirk had misjudged how serious I was. When I told him that story about God's test to see what I would sacrifice, I didn't say what my intended sacrifice had been. If only he had known, he would've been more careful about angering me. I had taken Sally out to the park with me. She was sleeping in the tent next to that firepit. I had poured a trail of lighter fluid from the edge of the firepit up to the tent. I'd been seconds from dropping that match when the blue ram appeared.

Sally was my soulmate... the Eve to my Adam. Nothing was more important to me than her... except for God. I would have given anything to prove my honor to God. I may have lost her now anyhow. Only time would tell. One thing was sure: I hadn't been spending enough time with her lately. She believed in God, but I didn't know if she would be able to accept what I had done for him. I was prepared to be a martyr for the cause.

I hadn't intended to let that pathetic detective see my gift from Azrael, but I couldn't let him stop me.

Azrael had gifted me with an amulet that enabled me to travel through time—just like the one the dog wore on his collar. I kept it hidden in my pocket, where I could grab it at a moment's notice, fastened securely on a chain attached to the fabric. But Azrael had told me he wanted me to wear it openly now, so everyone might know the purpose of my mission. When they saw its power, he told me, they would repent of their sins and return to the one true God.

Of course, this made everything more dangerous for me, but had Jesus hidden his light under a bushel? No! He had declared God's truth boldly for all to see, even to the point of upending the moneychangers' tables at the temple. Those charlatans would sell people doves to use as sacrifices, extorting money from the faithful. But what had Jesus done? He had made himself the ultimate sacrifice, and had replaced the doves that were slaughtered with the dove of eternal life that had descended upon him: the Holy Ghost.

Now, despite my unworthiness, Azrael had cast *me* in the

role of messiah, charging me to overturn the Prophet's filthy moneychangers in this new Temple.

Compassion? Truth?

Neither was present within its unclean walls, built with money stolen from men who were told they needed to sacrifice. To sacrifice! Yet Jesus had already paid the ultimate price, made the ultimate sacrifice, with his blood at Calvary. The temple moneychangers had sold false salvation in the form of doves; the masters of this new temple had made the same false promise. They demanded tithes, as though the old covenant was still in effect, because it suited them. Because it made them wealthy. Yet because they rejected the new covenant of Christ's blood, I would write *another* new covenant for them—their testament in blood. Their riches would profit them not in the day of wrath. Only righteousness might have delivered them from death.

But it was too late for that now. For the old things had passed away. Behold! All things are become new!

If I needed to die for the cause of Christ, then so be it. I would fulfill Azrael's mission. He had gifted me with his own sigil as my means to accomplish his mission, and I owed him a debt—one I would not shrink from repaying.

If that accursed detective thought he could get in my way, he had another thing coming. He thought he was clever. But he knew not the mind of God, whose ways surpassed mortal comprehension, just as the heavens were higher than the earth.

Azrael had recognized my humility, and as a reward had let me know the mind of God.

No sauced up, washed-up amateur sleuth was going to stop me.

I didn't know how he'd figured out I was involved. I wasn't sure he understood the full implications of what he had just seen, but I didn't think that would last for long. Being an ex-cop, I didn't know if he would drop the dime on me and involve the police. But given his tumultuous history, I didn't think that was likely. I was so near the end of my mission. I couldn't fail now.

I had to accelerate my timeline. I couldn't go home again, and I couldn't come back to the office. Tonight would be the night. That pair of abusive heretics would be going down. This one was very personal, but I couldn't let my feelings of rage cloud my judgment. I had to be clearheaded for this portion of my mission.

Once those worthless heathens were out of the way I, would have to find someplace to hide out for a couple of days. Then it would be time to cut off the head of the snake. I had to lay low, let the heat die down, so that I could succeed where others had failed. Azrael was counting on me.

I had one final task to complete after I wiped the Compassionate Truth Temple from the annals of time. It would be of great personal pleasure to exterminate that impostor... that Pharisee... that detective masquerading as a Christian. He was probably using that façade to woo that client of his. And if he was still working the case, that meant the only person who could have hired him must be the fair Claire, daughter of the Prophet of Lies. Mr. Kirk was no more religious than I was a circus clown. He was going to see who had the last laugh.

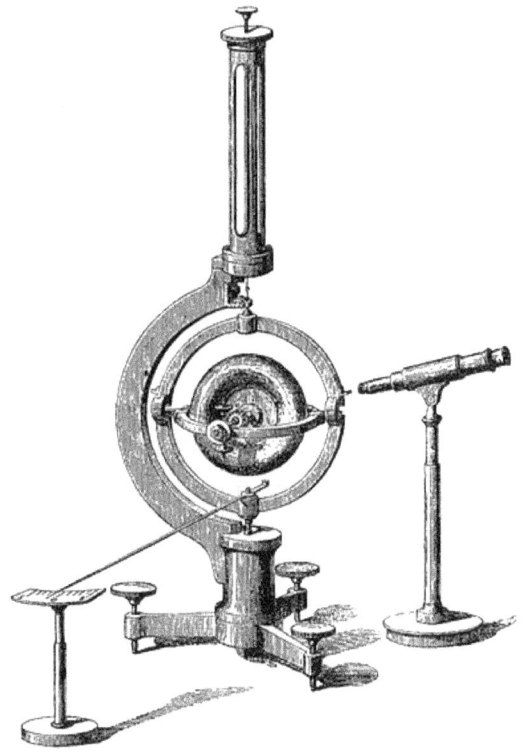

The Detective

It's About Time

I n the end, Brantley Donovan's house wasn't hard to find. I didn't want to tail him myself; a guy this smart would be lookin' over his shoulder, so I went back down to the *Trib* an' strode up to the front desk. I was in luck. The lady there wasn't the same one who'd been workin' the day I came in with Claire, so she didn't know me from Adam... or Donovan, which I was countin' on.

I was also countin' on her not knowin' what Donovan looked

265

like.

I rang the bell 'cause she was turned away from me, eating a tuna fish on rye durin' her lunch break. "Excuse me."

"I'll be right with you," she said, wolfin' down the last of her sandwich and scootin' her chair over to the counter. "Now, how may I help you?"

"I'm Brantley Donovan, ma'am," I said, puttin' on my most disarming smile. "I haven't gotten my paper the last few days, and I was wonderin'..."

"Oh dear," she said, reachin' up to adjust the hairpin on the back of her head. "Which dates are you looking for? I can ring circulation and have them bring you up some replacement copies."

I waved a hand in front of my face. "That won't be necessary. I was actually worried about my paperboy. He's always been so punctual-like, and I wanted to check in to be sure he's OK. I forget his name."

"Here, let me look... You're at 3928 Briarton Road... No, I show that Samuel's been on his route every day this week." She huffed. "We get this all the time. Someone next door picks up a customer's paper or one of the neighborhood kids throws it in the bushes. I'll have his route supervisor speak to Samuel and let him know what happened. If he is missing the porch, we might need to let him go."

"No, no. Please. Don't do that." This was better than I'd hoped. I thought I was gonna have to track the kid down and slip him a coupla bucks to give me the address. But this dame had served it up on a silver platter. "Samuel's never missed the porch since the day he started. I'm sure it's some kids playin' a prank, like you said. I'm just glad to know he's OK."

The dame nodded and smiled. "That's very kind of you. Just let me know if you have any further problems, and we'll look into it. Are you sure I can't have one of the boys in the mailroom bring you the copies you missed? My ledger shows you've always been on time with your payments, so we're more than happy to make things right."

"That's fine," I said. "Just don't get Samuel in any trouble over this. I already picked 'em up at the Bill Daly's newsstand, an' I don't need yesterday's news. No offense, ma'am." She didn't know that I'd already been down here lookin' for news a whole lotta yesterdays back—news I still swore hadn't existed till it turned up on their microfilm. "Have a good day."

The way Donovan had disappeared on me—literally—it seemed likely he'd gone to ground. It was just as well, since that would give me an opportunity to do some up-close an' personal investigatin'. When I drove by his place, sure enough, there weren't no car in the driveway. I had to be careful in broad daylight, that some nosy neighbor didn't see me snoopin' around, though, so I pretended to go up an' knock on the front door, blocking the knob with my body while I used a feeler to pick the lock. Then I turned the handle slowly and pushed the door back away from me to make it seem like someone was openin' it from inside. I nodded like I was greetin' the phantom Donovan an' stepped inside through the half-open door, closin' it again from the backside so I was out of view.

I wasn't sure what I expected to find at Donovan's place. It was a typical single-story tract house on a narrow lot, so it was deeper than it was wide. The front room was on the small side, with a brown carpet, fireplace, an' a 14-inch RCA tube with rabbit ears sittin' on a stand across from a lovey-dovey-seat. That meant he was used to entertaining. My guess was he had a squeeze—prob'ly not a wife: I hadn't seen no ring on his finger or picture on his desk at either of our sessions. Maybe more'n one.

He brought her, or them, over for smoochin'... an' maybe somethin' more. A look down the hall in the bedroom confirmed the somethin' more: Ol' ladykiller Donovan had a queen-size bed, all turned down an' ready to go.

That told me a little bit about him, but there wasn't much so far that tipped me off to anything. Coat rack in the front room. Coffee pot on the kitchen stove. The other thing I did notice was a print of that famous Scream painting over the hearth. Was that some psychology thing, or was that what Donovan himself felt like doin'—screamin' at the world or someone in particular? Maybe he just liked that impressionist shit... or was it expressionist? But if so, it was still pretty damn weird. Me, I was partial to landscapes an' paintings of topless dames.

But hey, whatever floats your boat.

There was just one room left to explore, and that's where I hit the jackpot. It was his office, and it was locked up tight. Well, not so tight when ya got a feeler and a feel for pickin' locks, which I did. A few seconds and, presto, I was in.

The room was dark, with wood paneling on the walls an' a brown leather chair behind the desk. First thing I noticed were the horns of a buck stickin' out of the wall behind his desk. Maybe ol' Brantley was a hunter, only now he was huntin' humans. He had a picture on his desk, which wasn't of a dame, like I expected, but a dog. It was no huntin' dog, either: not a spaniel or retriever. Just some mangy mutt that looked like a mix of shepherd and border collie.

There was a filing cabinet—dark wood like the paneling— sittin' off to one side in a corner. That would be my first stop. It was locked, too, but it was even easier to jimmy open than the two door locks I'd picked. Inside, I saw folders marked with the names of all his patients. I didn't recognize none of 'em except one: mine. I pulled the folder out and started flippin' through it, expectin' to see somethin' about my "condition." What I found was partly that, but mostly a whole lot different.

> *September 25:* "*Patient is a private detective who exhibits signs of paranoia and delusion, which is convenient considering my mission. He seems ignorant of that mission, which indicates he sought my services not to investigate me, but for legitimate reasons. This is also quite convenient. He himself seems convinced that he has been experiencing some sort of hallucination, so it was a simple matter to nudge him further in that direction. Should the patient seek further care, it is advisable to discover the identity of the woman who engaged his services. Discovering this, while not strictly necessary, will facilitate the completion of my mission in short order.*"

So he'd been feedin' me a line o' bull all along. *Figures.* There was another entry after this one.

> *October 9:* "*Patient has not returned for a follow-up session. This can mean one of two things: Either he was satisfied with the answers I gave him, or he has grown suspicious of me. The former seems to me more likely. His personality is not one to seek help in the first place, so it is probable that he accepted my little nudge and considers himself 'cured' now that I have taken a break from my mission. This would be exactly as I hoped. I can see no reason for him to have*

269

grown suspicious of my motives, as no rational person would connect any of those murders with someone like myself, who hadn't even been born when they occurred. From this, I conclude that I will be free to resume my mission shortly and, ultimately, complete it, without any interference from this oblivious so-called 'investigator.'"

He hadn't made an entry followin' my second visit, which he wouldn't have since he'd disappeared into thin air right in front o' me. I still hadn't puzzled that one out yet, but if he could do *that* he was one helluva... something. Illusionist? Manipulator? Hypnotist? I still didn't know what the fuck he was. But I did know that anyone who could pull that off was dangerous as hell. What else he might be capable of was beyond me. I tried not to let myself think he wasn't just a copycat; that somehow he'd been able to mastermind murders thirty or more years ago. Maybe he was a lot older than he looked.

And maybe, since he hadn't bothered to make an entry about my second visit, he was gone for good. But somehow, I didn't think so.

I pulled out my Kodak Brownie and snapped a few photos of my files. If I mailed 'em to the cops, it would put 'em onto the guy. An' they wouldn't do shit about it anyway. But I could always send 'em to the psychiatric board. I didn't know if they followed the same rules of evidence as the boys in blue did, but even if they did, they'd still start keepin' an eye on him. Fruit of the poisonous tree be damned. You could always eat it, plant the seeds, and watch 'em grow without anyone bein' the wiser where you got 'em. If nothin' else, I could get the guy's license pulled. But that was just insurance. I had bigger fish to fry, and I figured I could find the skillet and a nice big-mouth bass around this office of his

if I looked hard enough.

My eyes drifted back to the desk, next to the dog picture. I picked up right away on a few items: a book, a rolodex, and a small notebook.

The book was flipped over so the spine was bent backward, holdin' his place for him, so I decided to start there.

The cover read: *The Eternal Gyroscope: Matters of Time and Space*. Whatever the hell that meant. It was by someone named Dr. Julia Parmenter, which didn't mean shit to me either. I shook my head and turned it over to the pages he'd been readin'.

It said a whole lotta weird stuff about time bein' like a ball of yarn with a buncha different strands wrapped around each other. What a mess. Sounded like somethin' by that Isaac Asimov guy, who wrote a bunch of books about robots and outer space and galactic empires. It was just as far-out as any of that, but this Parmenter dame was dead serious about the subject.

I read a bit of it.

"The more closely entwined two strands are, the more often they will come into contact, connecting past, present, and future. This is, I believe, why close friends can pick up right where they left off, even though they haven't seen each other in years. It is why some musical groups achieve the kind of chemistry that changes the soundtrack to our lives. It is why some business partnerships work so well. It is why some couples stay together, almost effortlessly, while others go through divorce. And it is why many of these same couples feel they've known each other far longer than the calendar says they have.

"What, therefore, are the ramifications of all this?

"In theory, it should be possible to 'leap' from one strand to another at the contact points I mentioned. This is, in fact, something I believe occurs without us even realizing it, because we are on the gyroscope rather than viewing it from the outside, as observers. It is happening to us, so we do not even realize what is occurring. But if we could somehow become aware of this process, and learn to participate in it consciously, the implications would be profound.

"We could, in theory at least, avoid marrying the wrong person, making bad business deals, signing bad peace treaties—any human contact that didn't align with how the strands of time and space naturally connect. We would not eliminate all mistakes (how else could we learn?), but we would eliminate many of the needless errors that lead to so much senseless tragedy."

I chuckled to myself. This dame sure had a rosy fuckin' picture of the universe. She seemed to think the people on these strands of hers would use the power to leap through time an' make the world a better place. She might know about physics or whatever the hell was behind this theory of hers, but she didn't know a thing about human nature.

Power corrupts.

I'd read about this in seminary, in a class called Spirituality and Morality. The point was that faith was fine... until it wasn't.

Believin' ain't enough. It makes a difference *what* you believe and *why* you believe it. Do you believe in somethin' for moral reasons or selfish ones? Or just because the church says so. And if a church says it, that doesn't make it moral. Hell, the Pharisees *were* the church before Jesus came along, and these holier-than-thou bastards wanted him crucified.

That sure as hell wasn't moral. But was it moral to burn so-called witches?

Of course not. But the church said so. In fact, the guy who talked about power corruptin' was talking about the Spanish Inquisition when he said it. A bunch of Catholics who rounded up so-called heretics and tortured 'em, killed 'em, or threw 'em in prison to rot. That guy who said power corrupts... I forget his name, but I remember his words 'cause they rang truer than a dinner bell on Thanksgiving. Havin' power didn't make a thing moral. It was the other way around. According to this guy, extreme power made people *immoral.* It just meant some clown at the top of the food chain could do whatever he wanted, even if it meant steppin' on the people underneath him. Sometimes especially then.

That's how the mob worked, and it was how the Temple worked too.

Donovan had marked another page with a folded newspaper clipping, so I turned a few pages and started reading there:

"The strands on the ball of yarn represent not only individuals but states of existence. Parallel universes, if you will. In theory, I should be able to leap from one strand to a nearby strand—a universe very nearly the same as the point of origin, but with a few minor differences. Similarly, I should be able to retrace my steps on

the current strand, using my memory as a roadmap, and jump from an earlier time to the corresponding time on a strand in close proximity to my own. With enough information about the past, I might even be able to leap from the beginning of my strand to another and trace IT back further into a time before I was born.

"As of this writing, such scenarios remain hypothetical. What remains to be discovered is the means to accomplish it. Some additional factor must be necessary to facilitate these leaps. One possibility lies in extremely close relationships, such as identical twins or soulmates. The connection between the two strands of their lives could act as a catalyst for making a leap in time. The other possibility is an external force, such as a talisman of time, that is imbued with the power to stimulate a jump. Such an amulet might be tied to a deity or supernatural being, such as Chronos from Greek mythology or the Norns in Norse folklore, who have influence over time.

"I realize that this quest has taken me outside the realm traditionally occupied by science and onto a more metaphysical path. But the less we know about something, the better advised we would be to explore those horizons, and I intend to continue to do so."

Out of curiosity, I unfolded the newspaper clipping. It was a story dated a few years after the book's publication about none

other than the author herself. It seemed she'd gone on a vacation to Yellowstone but had never arrived there. Her car was discovered on the edge of an isolated area that was givin' off bizarre energy readings, but there was no sign of her. The last thing she'd written was a letter to her sister sayin' she'd gone off lookin' for a place where she suspected she might be able to test her theories. From the look of it, she'd vanished without a trace.

I shook my head. Was *this* why Donovan had been tryin' to throw me off the scent? Because of some cockamamie theory about travelin' through time like old H.G. Wells, but without an actual time machine?

I picked up the diary, hopin' to find somethin' more concrete there.

The first page started with one big punch to the gut. I'd heard of serial killers leavin' a manifesto, but I'd never read nothin' like this.

"This is my design," he'd written: "to purify the earth of the Temple's charlatans by making it as though they had never been born. By the time I have accomplished my mission, they won't have been. I plan to fulfill my holy charge, in the service of Azrael, by using his amulet to transport myself back in time and destroy their forebears. I will, in the manner of Christ, drive out all the sheep from this 'Temple' and overturn the tables of the money changers before they even have a chance to establish them. In this manner, I will destroy this church of Satan and its 'Prophet' masquerading as an angel of light. 'Vengeance is mine, saith the Lord,' and he has given me, his good and faithful servant, a share in it."

Was it possible I was reading the words of Azrael's Assassin, the man who had never been caught? Or was Brantley Donovan the one suffering from a delusion? Did he *think* he was Azrael's Assassin and, if so, had got it in his head to become a copycat killer? I checked through the rolodex to see if it held any clues, and I stumbled upon a name I thought might hold the key to this whole puzzle: Sally Bennett. It looked like any of the other cards except for one thing: It had a heart drawn beside it.

This had to be Brantley's squeeze, the gal he'd been lockin' lips with on that lovey-dovey-seat of his and maybe even doin' the nasty with in the queen-size bed. She was close with him, so I'd be takin' a chance by talkin' to her. But if it could help me put the rest of the pieces together, it just might be worth the risk.

The Detective
32
Caught Red-Handed

I heard a noise and spun around. Turned out I wouldn't need to go lookin' for Sally Bennett at all: She'd come to me.

"Who are you, and what are you doing here?" she demanded. She was holdin' an ashtray in her hand, which I assumed she meant to use as a weapon against me. Havin' a gun, I wasn't too concerned. Not that I wanted to shoot her. I was hopin' she might provide some of the answers I was after—and maybe I'd get a chance to clue her in on a few things too.

"Listen, sister, I got no beef with you. I'm just here to..."

"To what? Steal from Brantley?"

"There's nothin' here I wanna have. Just doin' a little window shopping, so to speak."

Sally looked past me, taking in the room like she hadn't spent much time there.

"Don't tell me you never been in here before," I said.

She shook her head. "Brantley keeps it locked. He's never let me in here alone. I've just seen it from the doorway. It's his place; I don't live here. He tells me it's his work business, but I have to admit I've been really curious."

"So have I. That's why I'm here."

"But you're not supposed to be, "Sally said. "I'll call the police." Her voice was quavering, and she was shaking that ashtray in her hand, trying—without much success—to look menacing. She was a small gal, maybe 5-foot-2, and no more than a hundred pounds. She had straight brown hair that went down past her shoulders and a plain-Jane face without any makeup. She wasn't the kind of dame who was lookin' to attract attention.

"I used to be a cop myself," I said. "Now I'm a private dick. I been hired to work a missing persons case, except now a whole lot of people have gone missing, and more might go missing unless I find a way to stop whoever's behind it. There's even been a murder now."

"All the more reason to call the police."

"Sister, half the force is on the take. They think the mob is behind this, in which case they ain't about to do shit—pardon my French—because they're paid to look the other way." That part wasn't exactly a lie. It was what you might call an educated guess. Large-scale crimes in town could usually be traced to Vinnie's goons, the Carbonis or some other "family," so the cops tended to leave those things alone. I'd been worried about Chris pushin' for an investigation, but with him no longer on the force, there was no incentive for that crooked crowd to go pokin' around.

Unless there was a public outcry... which wouldn't be forthcoming as long as the church, or what was left of it, kept tryin' to keep everything hush-hush.

Sally still wasn't convinced, though.

"If you think the mob is behind this, how would Brantley be involved?"

I smiled. "I didn't say that's what *I* thought. I said that's what *the cops* think. That's why I left the force"—okay, this part was a lie, but it *was* what I was thinkin' at the time—"so I didn't have to go pussyfooting around in situations like this." And now, time for another lie. "I don't think Brantley's involved the way you're thinkin', but how long has it been since you've seen him?"

"Yesterday. We had dinner here and went bowling at Riverside Lanes."

That was weird. I'd never thought of Mr. Psychotherapist as a bowler, but pretty much everyone was into the sport these days, so who was I to judge? Learn something new every day.

"Okay. See, everyone who's gone missing so far has some sort of tie to that church outside of town, the Compassionate Truth Temple. I know Brantley went there himself for a while, so I was worried he might be in danger. I came over here to warn him, and when he didn't answer the door, I let myself in. I'm just tryin' to look out for his welfare."

"Brantley hates that place. With a passion. He wants nothing to do with it."

I knew that myself from my most recent visit with him, but I wasn't gonna tell *her* that.

"I didn't know that," I said. "I was just followin' up on a lead an' wanted to make sure he was okay."

"I see." Sally's voice was hesitant, but she'd put that ashtray down by her side. I could tell I was finally gettin' through. "Why did you break into his office, though?"

"Just lookin' for evidence. If he was abducted here, I thought whoever'd done it mighta left some clues behind."

"And I assume you have a PI license."

I pulled mine out and showed it to her, along with my driver's license so she could see it wasn't counterfeit.

Sally took a deep breath. "Fine," she said. "You can look on two conditions: you put everything back the way you found it... and you let me look around with you."

She really *was* curious.

"That's copacetic with me, sister. An' you can even keep that ashtray handy, in case I get outta hand. The thing is, though, I've already seen most of what I came here to see before you got here. I didn't find no evidence he'd been abducted, but I did find some pretty weird shit in here, and it ain't just about his work."

She gave me a suspicious look.

"Then what...? Please don't tell me you found a little black book. He and I aren't married, but we *are* exclusive."

"No," I chuckled. "Nothing like that. The only thing I did find in that regard was *your* name in his rolodex with a heart drawn next to it."

That made her smile.

"What I did find was a whole lotta stuff about time travel."

Her eyes got wider, all of a sudden like.

"Does that ring a bell in your belfry?"

"Well... he did talk about it a couple of times. He asked me once if I thought it was actually possible, then he asked me where I'd like to go if it was. I told him I'd probably go to Stonehenge, to find out—don't laugh—whether aliens had something to do with building it."

I shrugged. "That's no weirder than time travel."

"Yeah, and that's the thing. At first, I thought it was just talking hypothetically, like 'Where would you like to go on vacation if you could go anywhere in the world?' I could say Bora Bora or Timbuktu, knowing good and well I'd never get there. But he actually seemed serious about it, as if he planned to take me to Stonehenge someday, back when it was being built. I passed it off at the time; he was usually serious and stuck in his own head anyway, so I didn't think about it again."

"What about the other time you talked about it?"

"He said he thought time didn't run one direction in a straight line, it was more three-dimensional, like... I forget what he called it."

"A gyroscope? A ball of yarn?"

"Yes! He mentioned both those things, but he dropped the subject when I told him it didn't make sense to me."

"Look over here," I said, and took her over to Brantley's desk, where the time travel book was still sittin' open. "I think he got those ideas in here. At first I thought, the way you did, that it was just a science fiction sorta thing. But now I'm thinkin' there might be somethin' more to it. Maybe he really does think he can travel through time, and he's usin' this as a blueprint to get wherever the hell he's goin'."

"But that's impossible."

"Is it? Most people would laugh at the idea of aliens buildin' Stonehenge. But who knows? When you eliminate everything else, whatever's left—however absurd—has gotta be the truth."

"Sherlock Holmes."

I winked at her. "I learn from the best."

What I didn't tell her is that I'd all but convinced myself that Brantley *was*, in fact, traveling through time. It might seem impossible, but it was the only explanation I could come up with for why so many people had gone missing without a trace. Why those pictures kept changin', and the church records too. Why Azrael's Assassin suddenly appeared in newspapers where he hadn't been before, and why those cases had never been solved. Then there was the fact that so many people who'd been killed were at the head of families that had been goin' to the church for generations.

I knew that somehow the past was changin', but I had no idea how in the blue blazes it could be.

Now I knew.

By travelin' back in time and killin' all the church pioneers an' longtime members before they had any children, Doc Donovan could make sure those children would never be born. He could eradicate the church by pullin' it up from the roots.

He wasn't a copycat killer at all. He'd been killing *everyone* all along—even the ones that'd died before he was born.

But I wasn't finished questionin' Sally just yet.

"Have you ever heard your squeeze mention the name Azrael?"

She laughed. It wasn't the response I'd been expectin'. "As a matter of fact, that's his dog's name."

"His dog?"

"Yeah, he's kind of a mutt, but he looks a little like a border collie."

I nodded, impressed. "You know your dogs."

"I work at a vet's office, and I've picked up on a lot of things. The boss even said I should go to veterinary school, but I don't have the money for that and all the vets are men anyway."

"I'd say you could go to the police academy, but I wouldn't be doin' you any favors. If you don't know the right people, it don't matter how well you pick up on things. And I wouldn't wanna see you jaded like me." The small talk wasn't gettin' me any new info, but I'd learned to use it on people so they let their guard down. Miss Bennett seemed to be more relaxed now, so I figured it was workin'.

"About that dog... Is there anything else unusual about him?"

"Well, Brantley says he had the dog a long time ago, when he was living in a foster home. It ran away, but then it showed up again out of nowhere yesterday. Azrael seems like a nice dog. It's at least fifteen years old, but his teeth are perfect. There's no tartar on them at all. It doesn't make sense."

It didn't... unless the dog had been time traveling too.

"Anything else you noticed?"

"There is one thing: Azrael doesn't have a dog license, but he does have some weird tag on his collar. It's a circle with some foreign-looking writing around the edges and some crosses and squiggles inside."

"Have you ever heard of Azrael's Assassin?"

She shook her head.

"He was a serial killer in town who struck several times over a period of three decades, killin' people who were members of the Compassionate Truth Temple. Or people whose kids became members."

I reached into my pocket, where I still had the Xeroxes of those stories I'd made at the *Tribune*. I pulled out my copy of the story about the Dunphys and showed her the description of the Azrael sigil.

Her face blanched whiter than rice at a weddin'.

"That's the same symbol. Here, I can show you."

She led me to the back door and opened it, callin' for Azrael, but the dog wasn't there. He musta been hidin' somewhere, or maybe he'd run off again, or... It didn't matter. I believed her when she said it was the same symbol.

"You lied to me," she said suddenly. "You said you didn't think Brantley was mixed up in this, but you do, don't you?"

In this case, the only remedy for one lie was to tell another, despite how Mom had lectured me about tangled webs. "No. I didn't say that. I don't have enough evidence yet to know who's behind it. All I can tell you for sure now is that your boyfriend ain't been abducted, and there's no evidence linking him to anything." *Except that time travel book, those magical pictures, the church records, the Azrael sigil...* I couldn't rule out her reachin' the same conclusion I had. In fact, if she was as sharp about piecin' clues together as she was about the veterinary business, she probably would.

Which meant she'd probably tell Doc Donovan about it.

Which meant we were runnin' out of time. It wasn't lost on me that Claire could be the next one to disappear, so I'd have to work fast. I'd have to contact her and fill her in first thing the next morning.

Little did I know that our assassin would strike again in the meantime.

The Assassin

Home Is Where the Hurt Is

A t times, it had been difficult to complete certain steps in my mission because some of the targets assigned to me had been good people who only became corrupted later in life. It was not my place to question Azrael about who should be punished. However, God forgive me, I was feeling some personal satisfaction as I prepared to exterminate my next targets, the Bauers.

A lot of satisfaction, if I were honest.

Only one person was more deserving of God's wrath than these two, and he was next on my list.

Orion and Mary Bauer lived in a small ramshackle house on the edge of town. The old subdivision had mostly been abandoned as people moved on to newer homes with more amenities close by. In the fifteen years since I'd lived there, it had deteriorated so badly that a stiff breeze might have blown it down. It hadn't always been that way though. Once, Mary had come down to the storm cellar with a photo album and a flashlight. She must have been lonely because Orion was passed out drunk... as usual.

As she began to talk, I realized she was trying to make excuses for her husband's bad behavior. She'd shown me pictures of the house just after they'd built it. It'd been a cute little two-bedroom bungalow house with flower beds in the front. But then the Depression had hit; work had become scarce, and times were hard. On top of it all, the Bauers had been unable to conceive. They had attended church faithfully every week and continued to tithe, even when they didn't have enough to eat. Still, they believed in the Prophet and the Compassionate Truth Temple. It was God's love they had come to doubt.

Little by little, Orion had sunk into his own depression, and with that depression had come alcohol... lots of alcohol. Eventually, the tide had turned, and the economy improved. But Orion didn't. He blamed God for their misfortune rather than his own sloth. He'd forgotten that God helps those that help themselves, and that He doesn't tolerate a drunkard or a glutton. As it is written in the Book of Job, "He hath swallowed down riches, and he shall vomit them up again: God shall cast them out of his belly."

Orion had never quite finished the storm cellar. He never got the drywall put up; last I knew, it was lying in the corner moldering. He had poured cement across most of the floor, but the large nook under the stairs was still only a dirt patch. Moisture had seeped in through the cracks in the foundation; that, paired with the water damage from a broken pipe one winter, led to thick patches of black mold that grew across the ceiling.

Being a storm cellar, it had no windows, and Orion had only

installed a single bulb that hung down from a fraying wire in the center of the room. It was amazing that the place hadn't burned down long ago. The room was dank, dark and foreboding. That made it the perfect location for the Bauers' final resting place.

I'd used my amulet to go back home at a time before the heat was on to get a few items I needed. I was camping out in the dense forest a few miles from town. I'd been staking out the Bauers' house for the past couple of hours, waiting for my opportunity. If they'd stuck to their usual routines, Mary would be leaving soon to do the shopping after stopping off at the Temple to pray. It would probably be a short trip, though, with the Temple shut down. Orion was probably half a dozen drinks into his bottle of Jack and well on his way to passing out.

I saw Mary leave, and the house seemed quiet. As I walked through the yard, I picked up a thin branch that had broken off the weeping willow tree. I snuck up to the back door and tried the handle.

It was unlocked.

Before entering, I peeped through the window and saw Orion asleep in his Barcalounger in front of the television. I opened the door, watching to see if he stirred. He was out for the count.

I slipped past him and headed down the cellar stairs. It was just the way I remembered it, if not worse. I found the shovel in the back corner; it didn't look as if it had been touched in years. He'd taken it out when I was living there, so I wouldn't "get loose," but he probably took it back down, intending to finish the cellar. He never did. But I knew how to use a shovel, even if he didn't. I started digging a large hole in that dirt patch under the stairs. I was about halfway through when I heard Mary return. I'd left the door open at the top of the stairs so I could hear.

Just as I had hoped, the open door also drew her down to the cellar to see *why* it was open. I hid in the back corner behind where he'd propped up my old mattress. She walked into the center of the room, looking around. When her attention was focused on the hole, I leapt out of the shadows and cupped one hand over her mouth and wrapped the other around her neck. "Welcome home, you whore of Babylon," I growled in her ear. I slammed her head off the underside of the stairs, knocking her out.

I threw the mattress on the floor and laid her down, all trussed up with the rope from my pack. I'd gagged her with an old dirty rag I found lying in the corner. No reason she should have something clean when I'd always been left to sleep on a mildewed mattress. Once she was immobilized, I returned to digging.

It wasn't long before the hole was ready.

Now I just needed the guest of honor.

Before heading upstairs, I threw a rope over an exposed beam in the ceiling. I would need it for later. I could hear Orion still snoring away in the living room. As I approached, I saw how much he had changed. Even though he was an older man, he'd always seemed so intimidating to me. His thick, muscular arms had wasted away. His cheekbones jutted out, and his eyes appeared sunken in his yellowed, emaciated face. The once-powerful, overbearing man now looked small and weak.

I undid my belt and removed it, folding it in half, with the metal buckle hanging loose. I raised my arm high above my head and brought it down hard across his chest. "Wake up, spawn of Satan!" I screamed as he startled awake with a groan. "I'm here to pass God's judgment upon you for your sins. You shall receive thirty-nine lashes with this belt for your sloth and gluttony."

"Who are you? Get away from me!" he roared back.

"1... 2... 3... 4..." The leather belt rained down upon his body, leaving large red welts. "5..." The buckle landed on the thin skin of his arm, ripping open the flesh.

"Help! Mary, there's a madman in the house!"

"No use calling her. She's otherwise engaged at the moment. 6... 7... 8..."

More blood oozed from other gashes in the skin. He struggled to get up from his reclining position, but he was too drunk to coordinate his movements. Blow after blow struck his body, with devastating results. Tears ran down his face, mixing with the crimson flow from the cut above his eyebrow.

"Mary! Mary, are you okay?" he cried out.

"I told you she's busy. She's unable to answer you. Just as she never answered my call for help. Proverbs 21:13: 'Whoso stoppeth his ears at the cry of the poor, he also shall cry himself, but shall not be heard.' 20... 21... 22..."

"Didn't answer you? Who are you?"

"I am Azrael's Apostle!"

"What in God's name is that supposed to mean?"

"Ah ah ah... don't take the Lord's name in vain. I have been sent here by Azrael on a mission from God to eradicate the idolators and sinners from the Compassionate Truth Temple."

"Please stop! I beg of you. I'm sorry for whatever I may have done to offend you."

"Offend me? You've done far more than that. You abused me... neglected me... starved me... all for your profit. First Timothy 5:8: 'But if any provide not for his own, and specially for those of his own house, he hath denied the faith, and is worse than an infidel.' You're a monster. Not only did you torment an innocent child. Me! Your sins of sloth, gluttony, and worshipping that false god, the Prophet, speak for themselves. And let's not forget your covetousness, bending low in supplication to the god of mammon. First Timothy 6:10: 'For the love of money is the root of all evil: which while some coveted after, they have erred from the faith, and pierced themselves through with many sorrows.'"

"Are you that little bastard we fostered for a while?"

"Not so little anymore, am I? And I'd watch what you call me. 33... 34... 35..."

"You were more trouble than you were worth... literally. They didn't pay us shit for you, and we had to clothe you, feed you, and put a roof over your head."

"You can't be serious!" Those last four blows came down upon him with renewed vigor and strength. "36... 37... 38... 39!" That last one tore a three-inch gash down the withered skin of his thigh. I yanked him up out of the chair by his upper arm. "Let's go see Mary."

I could call them by their names now... now that I was the one in control.

Orion stumbled and nearly fell several times as I dragged him through the room and down the stairs. Mary whimpered and screamed through the gag when she saw him. I grabbed my rope and tied his hands together, and then his feet as well. I used the rope I'd hung over the beam to suspend him in a standing position in the center of the cellar.

"Well, Mary, it's time I let you in on the party. Do you recognize me?" I asked as I walked over and pulled the rag out of her mouth. She lifted her tear-stained face and searched mine, but I could see no sign of recognition. She shook her head no. "No surprise. Neither did your wonderful husband over here. Why would you? You two only saw dollar signs when you looked at me. You saw me as trash, like gum on the bottom of your shoe."

I looked up as I heard him coming down the stairs, the telltale click-click of his nails on the wood. I knew he'd come. I'd even left the back door open in anticipation of his arrival. "Oh yes, the last member of the party is here! It's old home week for you two. Ring any bells now, Mary?"

Her wide eyes told me everything. "Azrael? How can you still be alive?" she whispered.

"Ding ding ding! We have a winner... well maybe. It won't bode well for you if you can't remember my name as well."

Fear was coming off of her in waves. "Umm... uhh... you're that boy... my uhh son. My boy! They took you away from me." She forced herself to smile. I could hear the desperation in her voice, hoping she could fool me. But I knew. She was a liar.

Azrael came and stood by my side, surveying the scene. I reached down to pet him.

"And my name?" I asked.

She started to speak and stopped. She just stared at me; it was obvious she didn't know what to do next.

"Brantley! My name is Brantley! You were no mother. You didn't protect me. You didn't provide me with real food *or* love." I pointed over at Orion hanging limply from the rope. Too drunk and weak to support his own weight. "You didn't protect me from *him*... all those beatings with the belt and the switch... the flyswatter... or his own two hands. You put Azrael down here with me, but you gave him no food or water. I had to care for him with the small amount of stale bread or rotten bananas you gave me. That is no diet fit for a dog, yet alone a growing boy. Let's not even discuss my living conditions down here in this sunny lap of luxury. I can see you are as disgusted to be on that bed as I once was."

Mary cried harder as she leaned forward toward me, but they were the crocodile tears of a sinner only concerned about her own welfare.

"My only friend besides Azrael was God. You left me with that tattered old Bible as my only recreation. The two of you were always spouting Bible verses at me. All that spare the rod, spoil the child bullshit. But that is about discipline for disobedient children, and I only ever did as you asked. You tried to use the Bible as a weapon... as an excuse for your bad behavior. God had come to me through Azrael so you didn't destroy my love for him. Now he's sent me here for retribution. Matthew 18:6: 'But whoso shall offend one of these little ones which believe in me, it were better for him that a millstone were hanged about his neck, and that he were drowned in the depth of the sea.'"

Mary tried to back into the corner, as if that would shield her from what was to come. I turned back to Orion, who had regained his footing... at least for a moment. "So Orion, what have you to say in your defense? I think we left off with you saying how you had to provide for me."

Orion couldn't meet my eyes. He must have known where I was going.

"Clothed me with the dirty, holey clothes you'd worn as a child forty years ago. Fed me with the dry crusty ends of bread and spoiled fruit you'd gotten from the food closet at the Temple. And the accommodations," I waved my hand around the musty, dim room. "Now *those* were stellar. Not the small bedroom next to yours but this shithole where not even rats deign to enter. My only saving grace: an angel didn't fear to tread."

"I'm sorry. We needed the money. It wasn't my fault. God abandoned us in our time of need. He didn't provide for us when I lost my job... when everyone did."

"James 4:3: 'Ye ask, and receive not, because ye ask amiss, that ye may consume it upon your lusts.'"

"What is that supposed to mean?"

"God doesn't test you beyond your strength. And even though there may be temptation, he will give you an escape so that you may bear it. It's a test of faith, and you failed. Times changed and the situation in the world improved, but you had gotten lost in your shiftless and greedy ways. Proverbs 23:21: 'For the drunkard and the glutton shall come to poverty: and drowsiness shall clothe a man with rags.'"

Orion gritted his teeth in anger and spat at my feet.

"I see you feel no remorse, as I expected. It's time for another thirty-nine lashes with one of those switches you so loved, as punishment for what you did to one of God's innocent children and another of God's creatures." I pointed to Azrael and gave him another pat on the head.

Orion tried to kick out at Azrael, but the dog ducked away from his feet, baring his teeth as he settled again. I picked up the weeping willow branch and whipped Orion thirty-nine times, until the blood ran down his back in rivulets from the open wounds on his skin. His back was a crosshatch of torn skin, swollen and oozing blood. I bound his feet together with rope and undid his binding from the ceiling.

He was too weak to stand or walk, even with assistance. I grabbed his wrists by the rope binding them together and dragged him over to the hole, pushing him into it. He landed with a grunt as the air was knocked out of him. I walked over to the corner where Mary was trying to hide and pulled her out.

"Please don't do this to me. I'm so sorry. I know I'm a sinner. Let me beg God for his forgiveness. I'll do whatever you ask of me."

"It's too late for that. Although you can try asking God for his forgiveness when you're in there," I said as I dropped her into the hole next to Orion. "Hopefully it won't fall on deaf ears as my pleas did with you."

"It is now time for me to carry out God's punishment for defying his will. Numbers 16:33: 'They, and all that appertained to them, went down alive into the pit, and the earth closed upon them: and they perished from among the congregation.'"

I ran upstairs to collect Orion's liquor bottles and pipe tobacco and Mary's cigarettes and gossip rags. I returned to find the two of them struggling to inch their way up and out of the hole, but to no avail. It was too deep. I threw the magazines on top of Mary, sprinkled the tobacco and cigarettes across them, and then poured the alcohol into the pit.

I snickered as I began to scoop the dirt back into place, shovelful by shovelful. "Pray, Mary, pray." Twenty minutes later, I was patting the last of the dirt firmly into place. I pulled out the cross and stuck it into the center of the grave and set the calling card up against it.

I despised this house, but it seemed like a good place to hole up for the night. Even if someone showed up, I'd be able to pop out in the blink of an eye, thanks to Azrael. I turned to head up the stairs to see if there was anything to eat in the fridge. "Come on, boy, " I called out to Azrael, patting my hip as I climbed.

As I waited for the oven to heat for my TV dinner, I wrote a quick note to the *Tribune* letting them know where Azrael's Apostle's next victim could be found. It was time they learned how to address me correctly. I put it out in the mail and sat down to make one more phone call. I didn't know if she would even answer or be willing to speak with me.

The Client

Memories Are Made of This

All of a sudden, it had become more difficult to stay in contact with Elijah. Father was starting to lose it. The church he had spent so many years building was crashing to the ground all around him, so he was trying to hold on to what little he had left. That meant Mom and me.

Mother was at her wits' end. Between Father's ill humor and

her own crisis of faith, she had become increasingly withdrawn. She had always waited on Father hand and foot because that's what she thought the Bible dictated... and because she really did love him. As time went on, he'd come to take that for granted, and she'd become accustomed to his cold, distant demeanor. That had begun after Mother passed her childbearing years, making it certain they would never have a son. He blamed her for that, and because he did, she blamed herself.

That's the way he'd been toward her—and me—most of my life.

But ever since the Reynolds family had vanished, his moods had become darker. It didn't help that the church's other senior elder, Roderick Birch, had been killed on the tracks in what police had ruled a suicide.

Then Mrs. Pierce had been found—in pieces—spread throughout the sanctuary. The church was still locked up as an active crime scene, but it was supposed to be released later this morning. I'd never seen Father look so pale as he did when he came running back up to the house to phone the police. I didn't even know Father *could* still run. I found that I missed doing my work down at the office; I missed my freedom even more. Father had forbidden me from leaving the house. But it was nearly impossible to convince myself to enter the church knowing what had been found there anyhow.

Father felt more alone now than he ever had before, and he took his mounting misfortunes out on us. He would berate Mother for not ironing every single wrinkle out of his 'Sunday shirt,' of misplacing a sock, or serving him the same dinners he'd always loved.

He had done so just this evening.

"How long did you let this cool?" he demanded. "It tastes like something you dredged up from out of the sewer! As the Lord has proclaimed, 'I know thy works, that thou art neither cold nor hot... so then because thou art lukewarm, and neither cold nor hot, I will spue thee out of my mouth!'"

He spat a mouthful of omelet out onto his plate, but he wasn't just talking about Mother's food, he was talking about *her*.

She ran crying to her room, where she had been sleeping separately from Father since she had gone through the change.

I started to run after her.

"Stop!" Father commanded.

I froze, as if I were in a game of Musical Chairs, but I didn't have anyplace to sit. I felt exposed. Naked.

"If you go after her, Daughter, you will have no portion with me."

I looked at his plate of spewed-up omelet, and had the thought that I didn't *want* any of his portion. The absurdity of it distracted me from my growing anxiety, if only for a moment, and I wanted to laugh but dared not do so.

"Solomon says that 'evil pursueth sinners.' Are you evil that you would pursue after your mother, a sinner? Will you do evil unto me?"

"No, Father."

"Then show yourself worthy and take our soiled vestments and make them clean again."

Soiled vestments. The angrier he got, the more he started speaking in what I called 'Biblese.' Whether it came from the Bible or not, everything started sounding like it had been King Jamesified. I don't know whether it was conscious or not, but I'm sure he thought it made him sound more authoritative. To me, he just sounded more ridiculous—and desperate.

"Yes, Father."

I retrieved Father's overflowing laundry basket and took it to the mud room. He insisted that his clothes be washed separately from ours, so as not to be "defiled" by "unclean women." He feared any drop of menstrual blood that shared the spin cycle with his "holy adornments" might contaminate them, even though he knew Mother's monthly cycle had long been a thing of the past. Knew it too well. He called her "barren" to her face.

I began unloading the laundry into the washer, then pressed the button and reached for the box of Rinso. I was about to pour the powder detergent into the machine when I realized there wasn't any water running into it. I pressed the button again, but nothing happened. Then I remembered: Mother had told Father last week that the washer was broken. Obviously, he hadn't gotten around to having a repairman come out. That's why his basket had been so full. It was unlike Father to let something like this go so long before having it fixed. He was a stickler for running "a tight ship," as he called it, even though our house was nowhere near the ocean.

I dreaded having to tell Father I couldn't fulfill the task he had assigned me. I knew it wasn't my fault—if anything, it was his for failing to ring up the repairman—but he was a master at deflecting blame. I would get called out on the carpet for some transgression he'd concocted to explain why it was my fault.

"Father," I called out. "The washer still doesn't work."

"Do not yell in my house!" he shouted, missing the irony of doing so himself. "Come and speak plainly to my face, child."

I put the clothes back in the basket and went out and stood before him, feeling like a soldier in bootcamp who was about to be told I needed to scrub the floor with a toothbrush. "The washing machine isn't working," I repeated.

"You don't think I know that?" he said. "I need you to take the laundry to the Washeteria." That was what they called the laundromat in town.

"I'm sorry, Father. I should have reminded you to have the repairman out."

"Repairman!" he screamed, raising his hands and waving them wildly in the air. "We can't afford a fucking repairman!" It was the first time I'd ever heard him curse. "Or don't you realize that my job as minister pays for everything around here? When the offering plate is empty, we don't have the money to fix any stinking old washer!"

I took a step backward.

That must have meant we didn't have any savings. But how was that possible? I knew Father had set aside money in his savings account for emergencies and to pay for future purchases. I didn't dare ask him what had happened to it, but there was part of me that felt vindicated: I would *never* have let that happen, which meant I was more competent than he was to serve as church treasurer.

"Get those clothes washed!" he demanded, so angry now that he had abandoned his King Jamesified language. "See to it!"

He shot up from his chair and went stomping out of the room.

I was relieved to see him go... and more than relieved, I saw an opportunity. I called Elijah right away and asked him to meet me at the Washeteria in fifteen minutes. We had a lot of catching up to do.

When Elijah arrived, he seemed a little confused.

"Why the coin-op, toots?"

Toots? That was a new one. He seemed to have an unending repertoire of demeaning names for women. I ignored it. I didn't have the time or the energy to fight him. Father knew exactly how long the wash and drying cycles took, so I couldn't afford to return late—not with him watching me so closely.

"I'm afraid my father is..." I wanted to say "losing his mind," but I settled for "not in the best of moods."

"Oh?"

"Yes. He's been watching me like a hawk. His financial problems are even worse than I thought. That's why I'm here. He couldn't even afford to hire a repairman to fix our washer."

I nodded. "I was afraid of that. He ain't got no stream of revenue comin' in now that the church has dwindled down to nothin', so he's losin' his marbles."

"It's still my father we're talking about."

"Apologies."

"On top of that, Father is paranoid about me leaving the house—he won't even let me go down to my office in the church once they release the scene. To be honest, my skin crawls just thinking about..."

"Wait a minute, cutie pie! Release the scene? What are ya talkin' about?"

"Have you been so busy with your investigation of Dr. Donovan that you didn't hear?"

Elijah looked at me expectantly. "Yes?"

"I don't how else to say this other than Mrs. Pierce was butchered and her body parts were left throughout the church. In the pews, on the pulpit, the table in the front entryway, and her torso in Father's office. It was absolutely horrifying what was done to her. Father couldn't even speak of it. I only know what happened because I overheard the uniformed officers discussing it out in front of the house."

"I'm so sorry, Claire. I didn't know. I've been so busy... Never mind, no excuses. I'm so happy that you're okay."

"And guess what?"

"I can't fathom what you're gonna say next."

"This time the calling card and cross were left again."

We had to speak louder than normal to hear each other over the whirring and thumping of the machines, and people were staring. They must have overheard us. "Maybe we should step outside."

Elijah shrugged. "It's a bit chilly out there, but sure."

"If I have to deal with my father, you can deal with a little cold weather," I told him, half-playfully and half-annoyed.

"I'll take the weather," he said, and followed me out.

The streetlamp shone down on us, forming a circle around us on the sidewalk, so we ducked off into the shadow of the building. I didn't want any friends of my father to see me talking to Elijah... not that there were many left.

"I'm glad you got in touch with me, toots... er... Claire. I got some pretty... interestin' news of my own: I think I got this whole thing figured out."

My ears perked up, but I could tell by the look on his face, even in the shadows, that the news wasn't going to be good.

"I paid a visit to Brantley Donovan's house and showed myself inside."

"You broke in?"

"Nothin's broken. I picked the lock. But listen, there's some shit in there you wouldn't believe. It seems like our friend the good doctor has been... now hold on to your hat, sister... traveling through time."

I put my hand over my mouth to stifle a laugh. Had he been boozing again? "Be serious," I said. "We don't have much time."

"I *am* serious. Dead serious."

He told me about a time-travel book he'd found on Donovan's desk, his notes, and about his encounter with the girlfriend, Sally Bennett.

"One of the things that book said was that someone might be able to hop around in time usin' some kind of... what did they call it...? A talisman of time. An amulet linked to some deity or supernatural bein'."

I couldn't help but shake my head. "Do you know how ridiculous that sounds?"

He grinned. "Ain't you never heard of that verse, 'With men this is impossible, but with God, all things are possible'?"

"Elijah, you *do* realize you're talking about faith."

"I'm talkin' about findin' the best explanation there is for all the shit that's been goin' down, an' this is it, dollface. There is no copycat killer, like I thought. It's all the same guy. Donovan. He's found a way to go back in time and kill off your church friends by uprootin' their entire family tree. Kill the mother, and the kids never get born. It has to be possible because it's the only way any of this makes sense. As the good book says, a day is like a thousand years to the Almighty, an' a thousand years is like a day."

"Look at *you* quoting the Scripture to *me!*" I said. "But, Elijah that's not just a leap of faith, it's a quantum leap. Besides, do you realize what you're suggesting? You're saying this animal... this monster... has been killing people by jumping around through time because God is letting him, even *making* him, do it?"

"Well, that's what *he* thinks. That explains that Azrael sigil he leaves. He believes the archangel of death has appointed him to this mission. That don't make it so. But ain't it also true that faith can move mountains? Maybe he's got so much faith that it don't matter *what* he has faith in. He was probably talkin' about delusions because he's livin' in one himself. And he believes it so strongly that he's made it come to pass."

"That's ridiculous."

"Any more ridiculous than some Jewish rabbi turnin' water into wine or walkin' across the top of a lake?"

"But that's God!"

He sighed. "We can go 'round and 'round on this till we're both blue in the face, and we won't get nowhere with it. The point is, it's happenin'. Knowing the mechanics of it won't do us any good. But maybe, if we can get our hands on that talisman of his, we can stop him from doin' any more damage. And there's one more thing about this that I think I might be startin' to understand. I dunno how, or even if it will help us, but it's got to do with our memories. That reporter, he remembered all those old murders, but not the details—even though it's the kind thing you shouldn't never forget."

I nodded.

"And you said you remembered the Pierces being members of the church, but you couldn't recall the specifics of them ever attending?"

"Yes, that was... weird."

"And you *do* remember the way the butcher shop looked when the Edwardses owned it, even though, since Donovan killed them... in the past... none of those things ever existed during your lifetime."

I hadn't thought about that, but I did. I remembered the décor had been different. So had the cuts they offered. I could even remember going into the store and ordering rack of lamb or a ribeye steak and paying for it. I remembered how much it had cost, but the price was higher after the Pierces took over.

I nodded again.

"I can't exactly put my finger on it, but I think you're havin' ghost memories. You don't forget how things always were, *for you*, because that's all stored up here..." He tapped his forehead. "...in the old belfry. Things mighta changed on the outside, but that don't erase the way they exist in your memory. It operates independent like. You don't know how many times I seen some goon testify in court about somethin' he *knows* he saw, even though the evidence says otherwise. It ain't that he's lyin'. It's just the way he remembers it... an' he remembers it wrong."

"Okayyyyyy."

"Bear with me, sugar. So here's the thing: When someone tells him it weren't really the way he thinks it was, the guy will start changin' his own memories so they fit with this new reality. Retroactive-like. You don't really remember the Pierces ownin' that butcher shop or coming to services, but you *think* you should, so you convince yourself you knew about it all along so you don't have to deal with feelin' stupid. But of course you never knew any of the details, 'cause they never existed for you. Make sense?"

"And the reporter, Mr. Crowley?"

"Probably the same thing. He probably looked back in the archives, just like we did, saw his byline on them stories, and figured, 'Hey, I musta been there.' But he can't recall it from actually bein' there, 'cause he wasn't."

I put my hand up to my face and rubbed my eyes. "You're saying that our memories don't match reality..."

"Just some of the time, but never exactly."

"Then how can we ever be sure that what we remember is true?"

"We can't. We just work it out the best we can. But some of us have better memories than others. That book in Donovan's office talked about usin' memories as a roadmap to hop through time. Maybe he's got such a good memory he figured out how to do it. Maybe it ain't the talisman at all, but that thing just helped him have enough confidence in himself to try it out."

"We're back to faith again," I said.

"That's what I was tryin' to say. Maybe it don't matter what you have faith in; if you have enough of it, you can make shit happen—even the kinda shit most people would say is impossible."

I couldn't go that far. Having faith in God was still better than having faith in the devil. But I didn't have any other explanation, so I just nodded slightly.

"Now," he said—the man was on a roll—"if all this is true, but if you ain't got no roadmap, you can't go nowhere."

"I suppose not."

"Therefore..."

I raised my eyebrows and stared at him. "So you're saying if we find this guy, and find a way to wipe his memories, we can keep him from jumping through time. Even if we just make him doubt himself, that could be enough."

It would probably be easier just to get hold of that amulet, but I didn't say so. That sounded dangerous to me. Everything was starting to sound that way now, and *my* confidence was being shaken as a result. *C'mon, Claire*, I told myself, *you've dealt with challenges all your life. Father's anger. Mother's depression. Olivia's disappearance—and now the knowledge that I'll probably never see her again. She's still there in my memories, but maybe that's the only place she's ever existed. Does that make her an imaginary friend?* My head was spinning.

Then, out of the corner of my eye, I saw a movement in the shadows off to our left.

I pulled Elijah close to me and whispered in his ear. "I think someone's been watching us." I tilted my head slightly. "There, in the bushes next to the building."

He turned his head slowly, careful not to alert our spy that we knew he was there.

Elijah's eyes widened as he looked me straight in the eye.

"Run to your car," he hissed, his breath hot in my ear. "Don't look behind you, an' step on the gas once you get there. This guy's gonna come after you, but I'll hold him off. Understand? Now run. Do it now!"

I ran, breathless from fear, toward the car.

I heard footsteps behind me, then the sound of a scuffle. Elijah was shouting; so was the other man, but I couldn't make out what they were saying. I heard the heavy thud of a body slamming into the ground, but I didn't know who it was. Elijah had told me not to look back, and I didn't. My hand was shaking as I put the key in the lock, got it to turn, then opened the door and jumped inside.

Key in ignition.

Foot to the accelerator.

My tires squealed, and I was off.

It was only then that I dared take a fleeting glance at where Elijah was.

Had been.

He was gone, and so was the attacker.

I realized halfway home that I'd left Father's laundry back at the Washeteria, but at this point, I didn't care. For the first time in my life, I was less scared of him than I was of something else.

Of whoever or whatever had just attacked us.

The Assassin

The Wrath of Sally

I was about to hang up the phone as it rang for the fifth time; she either wasn't home or didn't want to talk to me. Then I heard a faint click as someone picked up.

"Sally?"

Silence.

"Sally sweetheart? It's me."

I heard a couple of sniffles.

"Baby, please talk to me."

"What do you want?"

"I want you... always... and forever."

"You really expect me to believe that? I haven't seen or heard from you in days. You disappeared without a trace. You don't just vanish on your fiancée without warning, not if you want to keep her. But really, what did I expect from you? You've been ducking out of this relationship going God knows where and doing God knows what for months. Why should now be any different?"

"I know. I'm sorry. I've told you I have an important mission."

"That you never explained... no matter how many times I asked."

"It's complicated."

"Murder usually is!"

"Murder! What are you talking about?" My fingers were gripping the table so hard they began to cramp. I fought to control my breathing so she wouldn't hear my anxiety.

"I came by your house the day after we went bowling. I was going to surprise you when you came home from work before we went out to Luigi's. You weren't there, but someone else was."

"Who? Who was at my house?"

"*In* your house."

"What?"

"You heard me. A private detective was in your office looking around. He found some interesting material on your desk."

"Sally..."

"Don't even try to make excuses. He asked me about time travel. I remember you talking to me about that a couple of times, but I thought it was just that: talk. Then he told me about this serial killer named Azrael's Assassin..."

"Azrael's Apostle!" She was starting to make me angry. I hadn't meant to yell at her.

"My God, you did do it! Didn't you?"

"Don't take the Lord's name in vain, Sally. You know I don't like that."

"What are you going to do—kill me? Is that what's important right now? That I took the Lord's name in vain., not that you are a serial killer! Are you out of your mind?"

"I..." Sally cut me off again before I could answer her.

"I looked around your office more after he left. I found that diary of yours that you always keep so secret. Now I know why. It's a literal confession of your crimes. Nobody would believe it because they think time travel is impossible. I did too, but not anymore. That's one of the things I loved most about you: your tenacity. Nothing's impossible to you. I don't know how... I don't even want to know, but you figured out how to travel through time and kill those church members."

"But Sally..."

"No, I'm the one talking right now. You're listening. I questioned my own sanity at first, like, 'How can you believe this, Sally?' But your own words convinced me. You talked about 'making it as though they had never been born' and 'overturning the tables of the money changers before they establish them.' The detective showed me the articles about the Azrael murders. I went and did more research myself. I knew, or at least knew of, most of those people who were murdered, but most of them were murdered before I was even born. How is that possible? Unless... unless you went back in time to kill them."

"It had to be done."

"You murdered a child, Brantley! In front of her mother! You let a snake eat her alive. You're a monster!"

"I didn't want to do that, but I couldn't let anyone survive to keep the church alive. That girl might not have been a sinner yet, but she was going to be. Another idolator who followed the will of men without questioning, all the while adoring the worst sinner of all, the Prophet."

"What about Jud Williams? He wasn't a member of the Compassionate Truth Temple or any other church. You poked his eyes out."

"No, he wasn't, but his son was going to be a member. Besides, like you said, he didn't believe in God. I gave him new eyes so that he could see the glory of God."

"You're sick and insane. That's not some holy mission. That's just plain murder!"

"I'm sorry you don't understand. I was assigned this mission by…"

"Azrael? A fucking dog?"

My frustration was mounting. She wasn't listening to my side or even trying to understand. It wasn't okay for her to mock Azrael—the dog or the angel.

"No! The dog was just sent to me by Azrael, one of God's angels. He was a sign. He was meant to help me get through the hard times and find my purpose."

"I've never heard of this Azrael."

"So, you claim to know everything about God now?"

"No. Do you?"

"No, I would never say that. I'm a vessel for God's wisdom. But I don't need to know it all; all I need to do is follow His will."

"You're delusional."

"So now you're a psychologist too?"

"No. I know crazy when I see crazy—or hear it."

"You're wrong."

"I heard about two murders in town the past few days. Josiah from the hardware store and Mrs. Pierce. We just talked about them a couple of days ago—the last night I saw you, in fact—the night that they were murdered. So you killed her too?"

"Yes, she was a member as well. I must pull these weeds up by the roots. Leave no traces behind. They all have to be exterminated."

"Like cockroaches? Is that what you think of them?"

"They're worse."

"Good God, Brantley, just how *far* does all of this have to go?"

"What do you mean?"

"How long until you kill that detective?"

"He will be last. I have no choice. He is a heretic, an apostate. And he knows too much. I must remove all witnesses so that life can go on as it should."

"So when do you kill me then?"

It felt like my heart stopped. I couldn't catch my breath. How could she believe that of me?

"Sally, I would never." I tried to repress the thought that I had nearly killed her before, made her a sacrifice to God.

"I'm a witness," she shouted into the phone. "You're asking me to believe that God put you on this 'holy' mission. Even if I *could* believe that, I would never worship a God who could do that. Isn't God supposed to love all his children?"

"Sally, you just need some time. I know you'll come around. You're a good Christian woman. God brought you to me. I'd never hurt you. You must know that, right?"

"I don't know what I believe anymore. I don't think I can trust myself. I thought you were an honorable man, not some sick bastard who kills children and feeds a pregnant woman to piranhas. I'm done with this conversation."

"Are you going to call the police?"

"Of course that's all you're worried about. No, I'm not. They'd just think I was crazy. I'd never be able to convince them of the truth. It's over, Brantley. Don't call me again. Stay away from me!"

Sally slammed the phone down in my ear. I just stared at the handset, my ears ringing with the incessant buzz of a disconnected call. I didn't move until the annoying rapid off-the-hook beep started. I got up and hit the wall repeatedly with the phone before dropping it back on the hook.

That fucking detective had gone too far. It was bad enough when he got in the way. Now he'd destroyed my relationship with Sally. I was going to enjoy inflicting pain on him—a lot of pain—before I ripped him apart, limb from limb.

I had one more call to make before I went to see that viper.

But I'd make that one at my next stop. This was going to be a glorious day. The angels on high were singing of God's glory in anticipation of his triumph over evil.

The Detective 36

Buried and the Mob

When I walked up to the Vesuvius gym, the muscle put himself between me an' the door.

I made sure he saw my gun—and the guy whose head was next to the barrel. "I think Vinnie'll wanna see me," I said.

The muscle scowled at me, but he wasn't about to try

anything.

"Is he here?"

"Who?" They didn't call 'em muscle for their brains.

"Vinnie, dumbass."

The muscle grunted, which I took to be a yes, and waved me on through.

I walked past him, lookin' over my shoulder to make sure he didn't jump me.

My hostage was the guy who tried to ambush me outside the Washeteria. He was big—a lot bigger than me—but he was young an' stupid. Once he thought he'd got the drop on me, he relaxed just enough for me to break free of his grip and slam the back of my hand into his nose. I broke it... which was unfortunate in case Vinnie decided to play hardball. But I still had the gun, an' it was pointed at this guy's head.

It had shocked him when I hit him, which gave me enough time to bust outta his grasp completely, turn on him an' deliver my patented "doughboy" punch to the gut. When he doubled over, I jerked my knee upward an' connected with his chin. *Crack!* That'd laid him out on his backside, out colder than a corpse— but, fortunately, still breathing. I needed him alive to get to Vinnie... and just as important, to make sure Vinnie didn't put his goons on my tail till the end of my days, which in that case woulda been sooner rather than later.

Loyalty runs one way in the mob. Except when it comes to blood. Then even the boss looks out for his own. Vinnie's own blood ran through Zito Lombardo's veins, which meant he'd fuck me up good if I let anything happen to him. Even the broken nose mighta been too much, but I had to take my chances. If I'd just left him on the street, he woulda run back to Daddy-o an' snitched on me, which woulda been curtains then an' there. This way, I could say I was just defendin' myself but I was also lookin' out for his welfare by deliverin' him back to Vinnie in person.

It was chancy, but there weren't no other option at this point.

When I walked into the gym, Vinnie looked more like a ragin' bull than Jake LaMotta ever was.

"What the fuck did you do to my kid?" he demanded, as three big goons surrounded me.

"Temper, temper." I pressed the gun hard against Zito's temple, makin' him grunt. "Why the hell did you send your son to do your dirty work?"

"To prove himself, that's why!" Vinnie shouted, then dialed it back a notch. "Which he didn't, I see. I wanted to give him an easy mark, but looks like he couldn't even handle the likes o' you. Pretty goddamn pathetic, ain't that right, kid?"

Zito grunted again.

"What did you say?" he bellowed.

"Yes, sir," Zito managed, though it came out slurred.

It was Vinnie who grunted this time, sounding more disgusted than anything else. Then he looked at me. He still looked all bent outta shape, but was directin' his wrath more toward Zito than at me. He smiled that threatenin' smile of his and told me, "We're good, Goombah. Drop the gun an' hand him over. Then we're all copacetic. Capeesh?"

I nodded and laid my gun down on the floor, shovin' Zito over toward Vinnie. Callin' me Goombah was his way of lettin' me know we were kosher. It was kinda like his guarantee word, and he always honored it. Plus, I'd become keenly aware that two of his goons were pointin' Remingtons in my direction, nullifyin' my threat to Zito. If I shot him, I'd lose my leverage *and* they'd gun me down where I stood.

Vinnie nodded to the goons, and they lowered their

weapons. He hugged Zito, then slapped him hard across the side of his face, whisperin' in his ear... but loud enough so everyone could hear: "Don't you *ever* fuckin' embarrass me like that again. Got it?"

"Yes, sir."

"Kids!" Vinnie said, shakin' his head.

"Now," he added, turnin' to me, "we got business. Get outta here, you bums." That was directed at the goons.

Vinnie sat down on the ring apron and patted it for me to join him.

"What's with the muscle, Vincente?" I asked. "I thought we had an understanding?"

"We did," he said, fixin' me with a stare. "But you been pokin' your nose around in things that ain't your business, an' it's costin' me. I can't have shit costin' me, Ellie boy." I hated when he called me that, but I wasn't in a place to object. He patted me on the cheek. "The muscle can be useful. Got your attention, didn't it? And it lets ya know there's somethin' at stake, Goombah."

I nodded. "But whaddya mean about me costin' you?"

"You gone too far with that whole church thing. Ya gotta lay off it, got me?"

I was confused. "I thought that Prophet had paid you your twenty big ones."

Vinnie laughed. "Oh, he did. He did. It ain't about that. He was into me for a whole lot more'n that, though. An' he took it on credit, meanin' he had to repay it—plus my standard fee of twenty percent a week, of course." He put an arm around my shoulder. "Now, listen, Goombah, he ain't paid that back, an' with people disappearin' from that church left and right, I can't take a chance on him welchin'. Get my drift?"

"Yeah, but it ain't like you never had someone try to skip out on you before. They always pay—one way or the other."

"But the one way's a lot better for my books than the other," he said. "An' these churchy folks, they always pay up. It's like they think they'll be disappointin' God or somethin' if they don't. Gotta respect 'em that way. They got a code of honor, which I can appreciate—'specially since it means I'm gonna get paid. But here's the thing, my friend." He squeezed my shoulder hard. "They can't pay up if they're dead, right?"

He had that right.

"If I deprive 'em of a pinky or slash a tendon, ain't no skin off my nose. Can be persuasive, like I said earlier. But I already lost a mark from that church before now—a lucrative one, too—and I ain't about to lose another."

"Lost a mark? Who...?"

"Them Pierces. I had 'em signed up for protection on the standard take of ten percent..."

"The same amount they pay to the church."

"Right. Which was another problem. The church had ta squeeze their marks for twenty percent instead of ten to keep up with the Prophet's debts when everyone started disappearin'. That put the squeeze on the Pierces, who felt obliged to pay the church before they paid me. That was bad enough. But when they disappeared too, it put a real crimp in my operations."

I had to admit, that made sense. Vinnie was nothing if he weren't cash savvy. "But what does that have to do with me? I ain't killin' anyone. I'm tryin' to make these people *stop* disappearin'."

Vinnie squeezed my shoulder again. "No offense, but you ain't been doin' so hot in that department. And if whoever's disappearin' them knows you're onto them, that just makes him more careful, which makes things harder for me."

"Shit."

"Now you're gettin' the picture. All I'm askin' is that you lay off for a little while so I can collect what this Prophet o' theirs owes me. Then you can go back to bein' the same old pain in the ass you've always been—as long as you ain't a pain in *my* ass. I been in touch with the boys down at the station, an' told them to be on the lookout for this fuckin' fly in my ointment. They'll send me word, an' I'll take care of the rest. You can do the same. But just look, don't touch. This fucker's mine. Capeesh?"

I capeeshed all right, but I wasn't about to let this alone. Claire's life might be dependin' on it. But I gave Vinnie the thumbs up to keep him off my back.

"Good boy," he said, like I was his dog or somethin'. "Keep in touch."

"I'll do that," I told him.

I was just glad to get out of there with both my pinkies intact.

I tried to contact Claire, but I couldn't get ahold of her—which started me feelin' skittish. No one answered the phone at her house, and when I drove by, the car was in the driveway, but everything seemed quiet. All except that damned terrier of theirs, which was barkin' away in the back yard without anyone tellin' it to shut the hell up.

Yeah, this was definitely a cause for concern. If Vinnie had put Zito on to me, he'd probably sent someone else to find Claire. Someone with more experience.

I was scared shitless for her, but I couldn't go lookin' all over creation for her and risk missing a call. So I decided the best thing to do was go back to my office and wait for her to ring me up. I sat there, drummin' my fingers an' starin' at the phone for a couple of hours before it finally rang. When it did, I grabbed for the handset and knocked it off the receiver by bein' too hasty. I picked it up, expectin' to hear Claire's voice, but it was someone else instead. Someone I had definitely *not* been expectin'.

"Hello, Mr. Kirk."

I froze in my seat. I knew that voice.

He didn't need to announce who he was, but he did anyway.

"This is *Doctor* Brantley Donovan. Are you sitting down? I hope you are, because I have some news for you. News I believe you will be interested in."

I felt a stabbin' pain in my chest. Was he about to tell me Claire was dead?

"I have dispatched two more members of that lying Temple of Satan, just as Azrael has instructed me. You can find them at 623 Bamboo Lane, down on the southside. Do you know how to find it?"

I said nothing.

"Answer me, you fucking sinner!"

I didn't. I wasn't gonna give him the satisfaction of thinkin' he could order me around. Instead, I just left the handset lyin' there on my desk and headed out, lockin' up the office. Time was of the essence, and I wasn't gonna waste it askin' that scum if he'd killed Claire. I could find out for myself when I got there. But I was a little relieved at the address he'd given me. It was in a rundown neighborhood on the edge of town, the Lafayette Tract. So he hadn't driven my doll to some warehouse somewhere an' offed her there, and she definitely didn't live in the Lafayette Tract.

My doll. She weren't my doll, but she might as well have been for the way I felt all protective over her.

I hopped into my jalopy and put the pedal to the floor.

When I got there, the place was crawlin' with cops. Either Donovan had tipped them off or Vinnie had heard about it an' told 'em. He'd said he wanted our town's finest to keep an eye out for developments, an' he could be counted on to do just that.

Sergeant Conroy saw me comin' and came up to intercept me. "Move along, Kirk," he said. "Can't have your filthy ass contaminatin' our crime scene."

I tried to push past him, but he blocked me again. "I said *move along*."

"No dice, Dexter." He hated bein' called by his first name, which was actually short for Poindexter... and he liked that even less. "Who's in there, an' how bad is it?"

"I ain't at liberty to divulge..."

"And I ain't got time for your procedural bullshit. Just tell me, is Claire Cassidy in there?"

He musta heard my tone changin' to one of real concern, 'cause he let down his guard. For a moment, he was the same ol' Dexter who useta join me for a bottle o' Stroh's and a game of 8 ball at Paddy's Palace. "No one by that name in there, Elijah. But the bodies were fresh, so we were able to make a tentative ID. They was buried under the cellar, and the killer did us the courtesy of pointin' us right to 'em. Left a note right on the doorstep. It's almost like he wants us to catch him. He'd better fuckin' pray we get to him first, 'cause Vinnie's boys won't waste no time just lockin' him up. They'll be sizin' him up for cement shoes right away if they get their hands on him."

"A lot of blood?"

Dexter shook his head. "Not much. Ain't no official cause of death, but I can tell you they were buried alive."

"They?"

"Older couple. Can't tell you their names, but you can look up the deed to the house, and I'd say the owners fit their description pretty good."

"Find anything else?"

"Oh, yeah. Just a calling card and a small cross."

I didn't have to ask him what was on the card. I already knew. Azrael's Assassin was getting bolder, which probably meant he was gettin' ready for his coop de grass. He'd been leadin' up to it all this time, an' there was only one family left. He'd saved the best for last: The Prophet an' his family. Claire was safe for the time bein', but she wouldn't be for long. Or at least, I *hoped* she was safe. I *had* to find her.

Problem was, she was nowhere to be found.

STEPHEN H. and SHARON MARIE PROVOST

The Assassin

The Head
of the Snake

inally! The day I'd been waiting for all this time was here. Hugh Cassidy had to be last, so I could maximize his suffering and stress. He had to watch his flock dwindle to nothing... which meant his true gods, money and his pride as "The Prophet," had disappeared as well. I'd take care of Claire and the wife he had forsaken afterward. They didn't matter to him, and, as women, they held no real power in the church anyhow.

Under the cover of darkness, I'd broken into the high school gym last night to access the track supplies, and obtained one item there that was crucial for my mission. Afterward, I walked over to the railyard, which was surrounded by a chain-link fence covered in razor wire. I'd brought wire cutters from my toolbox, which I'd retrieved from my home to cut out a piece. That gave me access to the yard. It only took me a few minutes to collect the items I needed there.

Late this morning, I'd called that asshole private detective, leading him away from my intended destination. I wouldn't have a lot of time to dispatch the Prophet, but I didn't need a lot of time—just a lot of pain. When I arrived at the church, it looked dark inside except for a light in the back corner where the Prophet's office was located. I tried the front door and found it unlocked. Even now, that cocky sinner thought God would protect him—even though he had abandoned his teachings.

Wrong, heathen!

I didn't feel any need to hide my presence. It wasn't like the old man could get away from me. I closed the door and walked down the hall, my steps echoing through the silent building. The police had cleared out the evidence of my previous crime, removing all traces from the scene. It was spic and span, but I was about to dirty it up again.

"Claire? I thought I told you to stay home. Do you disobey me in all matters now, Daughter?"

But Claire wasn't here. It was only me, and I wasn't going to give myself away just yet. Let the old heretic worry... he should. That feeble excuse for a prophet *should* be scared—when I was the one wielding the sword of retribution. This was his last day on Earth, and he certainly wouldn't be passing through those Pearly Gates.

"Child, answer me now!"

"Claire isn't here."

"Hello? Who is that? The Temple is closed."

"A place of worship is always open to God's faithful."

Hugh Cassidy strode around the corner, annoyed and ready to escort an intruder out, but I wasn't leaving.

"Like I was saying... Wait. Do I know you?"

"Yes, you *should* recognize someone sent by one of God's avenging angels."

"What? What are you talking about? Didn't you come to services earlier this year?"

"I'm impressed you remember me. I would have thought you only cared about those who brought you money—the more the better."

"I make it a point of remembering all my flock."

I laughed heartily. "Must be pretty easy now that there's no one left."

"That's it! You really must leave. I don't find that matter funny."

"I do. It took a lot of work. Once I finish with you and your family, I will have fulfilled my mission from God."

"Excuse me? I haven't lost my entire congregation. There are still a few left. And you won't be going anywhere near my family!"

"Don't you listen to the radio or watch television?"

"No. Most of the filth they put on there is the work of the devil. As for the radio, I only listen to gospel music and God's word. What's your point?"

"The past few days I've systematically wiped out the last members still in existence... Josiah King, the Pierces and yesterday, the Bauers."

"You can't be serious!"

"I'm dead serious."

"I'm calling the police. Get out of here now before they come and arrest you."

"I think you'll find them busy. They're at the Bauers' home

extracting their bodies from the bowels of the earth."

"My God! You *are* serious!"

"Serious as a heart attack. By the way, you shouldn't be taking the Lord's name in vain. You're in enough trouble already. But at least you're finally starting to get it. Your days on this earth are over. The day of judgment has come for you, and I can tell you God hasn't found you worthy to enter heaven."

Cassidy turned to run into his office. I arrived at the door just as he was starting to shut it. I slammed into it at full speed, bouncing the door off his forehead and knocking him out.

Well, that was easy. I grabbed his arm and dragged him down the hall and into the sanctuary. His head bounced off the pulpit as I pulled him up onto it and laid him down behind the lectern. I removed my backpack and set it down, pulling out the rope I needed.

I tied it around his chest and under his arms; then I threw the remaining coil of rope over a beam in the cathedral ceiling. I began to heave him upward until he was right in front of the large wooden cross that hung on the wall, pressed almost right up against it. I tied the loose end of the rope to one of the heavy pews in front. He moaned as he came around.

"What are you doing?"

"You'll see soon enough."

"Why did you kill my congregation? Why did you do this to me?"

"I wouldn't have expected anything less from you. It's all about you. That is precisely the problem. You don't worship God and his son Jesus. You worship yourself. Everything you do is in furtherance of feeding your ego—by making your flock adore *you*. You are proud in heart, which is an abomination to the Lord, and this will not go unpunished. Second Peter 2:1: 'But there were false prophets also among the people, even as there shall be false teachers among you, who privily shall bring in damnable heresies, even denying the Lord that bought them, and bring upon themselves swift destruction.' *I'm* the means of your destruction."

"Sinner, you know not of which you speak. Who are you to question my faith and my teachings?"

"As it said in chapter eleven of Second Corinthians, false apostles shall meet their end according to their works. Your works are evil and self-serving. You shall spend eternity with Satan. In Ephesians, it says no unclean man, or covetous man—no idolater—shall have any place in the kingdom of Christ and of God."

"My lot was set in heaven before you were even born, young man. Your soul shall burn in the eternal fires of damnation for your atrocities. For murdering my followers."

"Your followers or God's followers? You tell those followers lies in the name of God. You claim you're giving them prophesies from the very mouth of God. But yours are *false* prophesies to benefit you and line your pockets. Jeremiah 14:14: 'Then the Lord said unto me, The prophets prophesy lies in my name: I sent them not, neither have I commanded them, neither spake unto them: they prophesy unto you a false vision and divination, and a thing of nought, and the deceit of their heart.'"

"You can't know my private conferences with God. A sinner such as you would never be privy to such communication."

"You require your parishioners to give an enormous percentage of their income as a tithe. Recently, you decreed that God had told them to double it. Proverbs 22:16: 'He that oppresseth the poor to increase his riches, and he that giveth to the rich, shall surely come to want.' Azrael has told me God's true will. He does not wish for his hard-working followers to suffer for the benefit of a money-grubbing Prophet of Lies. That is why you must be stopped. Deuteronomy 18:20-22: 'But the prophet, which shall presume to speak a word in my name, which I have not commanded him to speak, or that shall speak in the name of other gods, even that prophet shall die.'"

"My parishioners' tithes are not given for my benefit. We do many good works to benefit the community."

"How does that mansion on the hill benefit anyone but you? Your luxurious furniture and fine décor don't feed the poor. They feed your rotten, corrupted soul. You ask your followers for money because you covet it. No amount of money will ever be enough for you. You eat the finest meat in town. The only time many of your parishioners ever get to partake of such luxury is at the potluck after each service. You've ensured that they can't afford it themselves."

"How do you know what my home looks like?"

"Because I've been there. I'll be returning there shortly. I don't have any more time to waste. The best part is yet to come, but I need to grab some things first. I'll be right back."

"You come back here this instant and let me down!"

I ignored him and walked down the hall to the utility room. I'd helped out at the church once after services, so I knew just where to find the ladder. I grabbed it and stopped in the lobby to pick up the item I'd set down there upon my arrival. We had walked right by it earlier, but the Prophet hadn't noticed it.

"What is that?" I could hear the fear in his voice.

"A ladder, silly. Don't tell me senility has slipped up on you already"

"No, sinner. In your other hand."

"That's a very special item for later. I wouldn't want to ruin the surprise."

I set up the ladder next to where he was hanging. I grabbed the three railroad spikes out of my bag and tucked them in one pocket, slipping the three-pound sledgehammer into my belt. I climbed the ladder and pushed him up against the wall, with his arm outstretched. I grabbed the first spike and pounded it through his hand, affixing it to the wall.

The Prophet roared in pain.

"God Almighty, please save me from this devil!" he wailed.

"Your prayers are falling on deaf ears. God sent me here to do this to you."

Blood seeped from his hand and dripped on the floor below. As he struggled to pull his hand free, the crimson trickle began to flow freely.

I climbed down and moved the ladder over to impale his other hand. I saw his jaw muscles tense as he fought to control his outbursts. "Nothing to say this time, Prophet?"

"I shall not feed your sadistic desire to hear me scream."

"Oh, you will!"

I climbed down from the ladder and removed his shoes. I placed his feet pointing downward, one atop the other, with the sole of the bottom foot plastered to the wall. I used the third spike to complete his crucifixion. As the spike protruded from the bottom of his top foot and started to pierce the other, he let out a long, low moan.

"Lord, have mercy on me."

"Told ya. I knew you'd have something to say. But wait, there's more."

I walked back over to the backpack and removed the length of razor wire I had cut the other night. I placed the ladder in front of him and climbed up again. I coiled the razor wire tight against his head. Then I twisted it until it was in just the right position. Blood poured from the deep wounds I'd inflicted in his forehead and scalp. He blinked repeatedly as it ran into his eyes. It looked as if he was crying tears of blood. The flesh on his temple puckered open, exposing his skull.

"Mark 8:36: 'For what shall it profit a man, if he shall gain the whole world, and lose his own soul?' I hope it was worth it, Reverend Profit From the Fruits of *Others'* Labors."

"I regret nothing. You are not in judgment of me."

"No, *Azrael* is."

At that moment, the dog entered the sanctuary and stood by my side. He nuzzled my leg. I had made his master proud. Now I just needed to finish Cassidy off.

"I wish you alone could have died for your sins as well as those of your parishioners, but we couldn't risk someone else taking up your mantle. You brought to bear the horrific, painful deaths of your flock. For that, you shall burn in hell. Matthew 19:23-24: 'Then said Jesus unto his disciples, Verily I say unto you, That a rich man shall hardly enter into the kingdom of heaven. And again I say unto you, It is easier for a camel to go through the eye of a needle, than for a rich man to enter into the kingdom of God.'"

With my final word, I picked up the javelin I had taken from the high school and plunged it into his side with deadly accuracy. Cassidy let out an ear-piercing scream. I'd studied human anatomy in college, achieving a perfect grade—as I had in all my classes. The tip of the javelin skewered his liver and then passed all the way through him, embedding itself in the wall.

As he struggled to free himself, he tore the wound in his side open. Blood began to pour from his body, splashing onto the tile below. Within a few seconds, his body sagged limply from the spikes.

I felt relieved that the asp had been decapitated. One more step, and I would be free to seek out Sally. I didn't know if she could ever forgive me, but I had to try convincing her. I walked out of the Temple, leaving the doors open. Azrael walked beside me as I climbed the hill to the Cassidy Mansion.

The Assassin
Ring of Fire

I'd already been by the Prophet's house to grab Claire and her mother, and I'd moved them to a secret location. That damn dog of theirs had started barking when I got there and never did shut up. I'd worried it might incite the Prophet's wrath and bring him up from the church to check it out. But I should have known better; he didn't give a shit about anyone but himself. Now I had to make that dog quiet down before it attracted any outside attention.

I left Azrael on the porch and entered the house again to find that cursed animal cowering under the end table by the couch.

I walked into the kitchen and found where they kept the dog food. I poured him a large bowl and brought it out to the living room.

He dove in greedily and even wagged his tail as I approached.

That would keep him busy for a while.

I left the house and closed the door behind me, heading over to the church recreation room at the back of the annex. I'd left Claire and her mother tied up, sitting in chairs I had placed in the bottom of the empty pool. The pool had been drained a month and a half ago for maintenance. However, the project had been put on hold as the congregation—and, therefore, the money—dwindled.

It'd been easier to subdue Claire and her mother than I'd expected. The Prophet had abandoned his wife and stopped caring about her needs long ago. She'd been of no use to him when she failed to produce an abundance of children... although it had been whispered around town for years that the issue was more his than hers.

His temper would have only become more foul and his attitude toward her more dismissive over the past few months as things got worse for the church. By the time I got to her, the last flicker of life and joy in her had blown out, especially after a lifetime of passivity. She'd offered no resistance.

Claire had been a little more... boisterous. But even she responded to the pocket pistol I brandished. I'd found the gun in my foster parents' closet when I had stayed there after killing them. I didn't even know how to turn off the safety—if there even was one—but the very sight of it had intimidated Claire. I had grabbed her by the elbow and marched her down to the rec room, her mother following us listlessly like a cowering dog. I had the chairs and rope already set up in the pool, so it'd been quick work to restrain them.

As I returned to the rec room with Azrael at my heel, I could hear Claire faintly calling for help. I opened the door and walked inside, slamming it behind me.

"Help! Please help us! Father, please come help us."

"Help! Help! Dear God, help me!" I whined mockingly back at her as I looked over the edge at Claire's tear-stained face. My laugh sounded a little unhinged, even to me. "God won't be answering your cries today—or ever. You've forsaken the one true God in favor of that false apostle you call the Prophet. Matthew 24:24: 'For there shall arise false Christs, and false prophets, and shall shew great signs and wonders; insomuch that, if it were possible, they shall deceive the very elect.' I must eradicate this scourge, the entirety of the Compassionate Truth Temple, from the Earth, as God has commanded me."

"You're insane!" Claire screamed at me. "God would never tell you to murder an entire congregation... an innocent child... two pregnant women... all the others. It's an abomination. *You're* an abomination!"

I softened my tone, if only for a moment. "I can tell you have what it takes in your heart to be a good Christian woman. But you let yourself be brainwashed by that heathen, the Prophet. That's why I can't show you mercy. It's not safe to leave any of you around to restart this Temple of Filth. Revelation 20:15: 'And whosoever was not found written in the book of life was cast into the lake of fire.'"

"Stop talking about the Prophet that way! Where is my father? What have you done to him?"

I cackled wildly as I pictured him crucified to the wall of his Temple of Iniquity. "Oh, he's hanging around down at the church."

"What?"

"He learned what it felt like when Jesus died for all of our sins. He paid for all of his sins—and the congregation's as well."

"Nooooo! Father was not perfect, but he didn't deserve that."

"See... that's the problem. It's not *your* place to judge what he deserved. That is God's job, and I'm his instrument. Your father deserved everything he got. Revelation 20:10: 'And the devil that deceived them was cast into the lake of fire and brimstone, where the beast and the false prophet are, and shall be tormented day and night for ever and ever.' You'll be joining him there soon."

"Please let us go."

"I'm afraid that's impossible."

Claire waved toward her mother. "Then at least let *her* go. Look at her. You can see she's no threat. She's a shell of the woman she used to be. I won't fight you."

"For growing up under your father's controlling thumb and misogynistic ways, you seem to have forgotten your place. None of this is *your* choice. I have the upper hand—*I'm* the one in control."

I walked to the corner of the room, where I had stored the two large gasoline cans that morning. I poured a ring of accelerant all the way around the pool. Claire flinched as she heard it splashing onto the tile; some of the gasoline dribbling over the edge and down into the basin. I then poured a trail of gas leading to the stage at the back of the rec room that was used for Sunday school recitals. I shook gasoline up onto the curtains that hung from the ceiling, then continued pouring gasoline about halfway down each side of the gym.

I only left one exit clear, out through the front door. I wanted to watch their mounting terror as the flames grew higher and the roof started to cave in on them. I returned to the edge of the pool. Claire's pleading eyes stared straight into my soul.

"Please don't do this. I can see you're a righteous man. We can work this out. It doesn't have to end this way. You're a good man, Brantley."

"Nice try, Claire. It's not going to work. You can't get into my head. I'm the psychologist here. Then again, I'm sure you already know that from that friend you *had*, Mr. Kirk."

"Had? What do you mean had? You didn't hurt Elijah, did you? Please no!"

"Elijah? That's awful familiar for a chaste reverend's daughter. Or are you not as pure as you should be? Do we need to add 'Whore of Babylon' to your list of sins?"

Her eyes flashed at me in anger. There was that spark of defiance I'd seen earlier. She had a fiery spirit, that girl.

"Don't you dare question my honor! He's the only friend I've had during this horrific experience... the one that *you've* put me through. You've erased the existence of Olivia, my best friend for life. He stepped in and helped me when no one else would."

"Helped or provided the service you paid him for? Let's get real, Claire!"

"He has more honor in his pinky finger than you have in your whole body. The pittance I paid him originally didn't even cover his first week of work. He's stuck by me for months as we tried to figure out what was happening. So help me, if you've hurt him, I will..."

"You'll what? You can't even save yourself or your mother at this point. False bravado isn't becoming, Claire. I'm done with this little game of cat and mouse. It's time to finish this. Azrael has waited long enough. *God* has waited long enough."

I stepped back from the edge and pulled a match out of the

box. Just before I struck it, I said, "Second Thessalonians 1:8-9: 'In flaming fire taking vengeance on them that know not God, and that obey not the gospel of our Lord Jesus Christ: Who shall be punished with everlasting destruction from the presence of the Lord, and from the glory of his power.' Goodbye, Claire!"

I tossed the lit match down. Flames shot three feet into the air and raced around the edge of the pool. The gasoline that had poured down into the pool caught fire and licked at the women's legs. Before long, the fire began to follow the trail of gas leading to the stage in back. Within seconds of its arrival, the curtains caught fire, and the fire raced up them, A couple of minutes later, waves of flame were rolling across the ceiling. I heard Claire screaming for help, as if there was someone coming to her rescue.

As I climbed up into the lifeguard chair for a bird's-eye view of their last moments, I heard the front door slam off the wall.

"Claire! Dollface, are you in here?"

Claire was screaming, but it was unintelligible over the sound of the roaring flames.

I turned to him and started to laugh. "You're too late. You hear that, Mr. Kirk? That's the sound of her dying."

Azrael dashed out of the rec room as Mr. Kirk launched himself at me. "You talk about retribution, Donovan. You ain't seen nothin' yet. I'm gonna tear you limb from limb."

The Detective

39

Up In Smoke

Moments earlier…

My search for Claire had brought me here. Not to her, but to this grisly sight in front of me. Everything I'd read about before—even the Tongue-Twister Murder, even the little girl bein' swallowed by that python—weren't nothin' compared to what was starin' down at me from behind the pulpit.

Hugh Cassidy just hung there, limp, blood makin' a trail down from each of his hands, and crusted on his forehead, below a crown of razor wire. His mouth hung open in a silent scream. His feet were nailed together against the wall. An' what was that? A javelin buried in his side and pinnin' him to the golden cross that hung behind him.

"Jesus Christ!" I whispered.

It weren't Jesus. But the message was clear enough. This was straight outta Mark's Gospel: "And some began to spit on him, and to cover his face, and to buffet him, and to say unto him, 'Prophesy!'"

Jesus had been crucified as a false prophet, a false messiah. Our assassin was sayin' the same thing about Cassidy. Jesus had been the Christ, but Cassidy was the Antichrist—at least to Donovan's mind. He had to reflect everything Jesus had been in reverse. Here I was, starin' into some dark mirror universe, created not by God but by Donovan's twisted imagination.

And Cassidy was starin' back at me with them vacant eyes, lookin' empty an' pathetic, a shadow of his own deluded 'glory.'

Those vacant eyes held me for a second, hypnotizin' me till I shook my head to jar myself loose. I didn't have time to waste. To even think. If he'd done this to Cassidy, what would he do to Claire... what might he have done already?

Fuck.

Fuck!

FUCK!

I whirled around and headed back out the front door. I ran down the steps, nearly fallin' over my own feet as I tried to take 'em two at a time. That worked better goin' up.

I looked up at the mansion. That stupid dog wasn't barkin' no more. Wait. Why had it been barkin' before? Had Donovan been there? Had he left her there... dead?

Fuck and double-fuck.

I sprinted across the parking lot, found the door locked and kicked it in.

"Claire!" I shouted. "You in here?"

I ran from one room to the next, callin' her name and gettin' no answer. But she wasn't here. The only thing I found was an envelope labeled "Azrael's Manifesto." I jammed it in my pocket and ran outta the place even faster'n I'd run in. If Claire wasn't here, he'd taken her somewhere else. But where? My eyes darted left an' right while I tried to think.

Think.

Think!

THINK!

Best to start lookin' at the closest place. I ran into the church annex, pausin' to open each door as quietly as possible in case Donovan might be in there. But he wasn't. Not in the office. Not in the kitchen. Not in the Sunday School room. There was only one place left: the rec room at the back of the church. I remembered scopin' it out when I'd been here before. It was a big, bloated place with a curved roof like a permanent Quonset hut. There was a locker room, a stage for Sunday School plays, storage closets, and a big ol' pool in the middle.

I saw smoke curlin' up from the space under the door.

He hadn't...

As I ran to the room, I heard the sound of voices inside. Donovan's voice... Claire's voice! She was still alive.

The door handle was hot, so I just lowered my shoulder an' slammed my way through.

"Claire! Dollface are you in here?"

Donovan was sittin' up in a lifeguard chair, grinnin' like the cat that swallowed the canary.

"Ah, so kind of you to join us," he said. "But you're too late. You hear that, Mr. Kirk, that's the sound of her dying. Of your dollface going up in flames." He cackled madly, like the Wicked Witch of the West or somethin', and I could tell I'd need to be a real wizard to get Claire outta this one.

For a second, I hoped he'd stay up there. Smoke rises, an' I could already hear him coughin'. But I didn't have no time for nature to take its course. I launched myself at the chair an' sent him tumblin' like dice at the craps table.

That gave me the time I needed.

I ran to the wall an' grabbed the fire extinguisher and yanked the handle at the pull station next to it. An alarm started blarin', but there weren't no sprinkler system in the damn place. The Prophet musta been too big a cheapskate to put one in. Prob'ly sold the congregation on it by sayin', 'You gotta trust in the Lord' or some other BS. Like what he told 'em about goin' to the hospital. The Prophet said you had to pray 'for a fortnight' before resortin' to actual medicine, Claire had told me. How many people didn't last that long before keelin' over and kickin' the bucket? I didn't even wanna guess.

I slid down on my keister into the dry pool at one o' the places he hadn't poured gasoline, rippin' off the rear of my pants in the process.

Claire was screamin', but her mother was just sittin' there like she wasn't feelin' nothin'. I pointed the fire extinguisher at Claire and let the foam fly, puttin' out the flames in short order. Then I did the same for her mom. I untied them both, and Claire jumped into my arms, an' I heard Donovan cussin' up a storm above us. Somethin' about needing more gasoline and there not bein' any.

I sprayed the extinguisher out in front of us, clearin' a path to the steps, but Donovan was waitin' for us there at the top. He'd recovered from his fall and had grabbed a baseball bat from the equipment room, but the smoke was gettin' thicker and he was coughin' up a storm.

He took a swing at my head, but I dove at his ankles to knock him down.

Then he just... wasn't there.

I scrambled up the stairs, with Claire pullin' her mom along behind me, but then he popped up again beside me and slammed a fist into the side of my face. I reeled backward, crashin' into

Claire and sending both her and her mother sprawling. Somehow I managed to avoid fallin' on my ass, but the fire had spread across the ceiling, and a burning beam came crashing between Claire and the door.

I was running out of time. I could try an' help Claire get out, but Donovan could just pop out on me... and back in again to stop us. Or I could go after him, but the fire might spread in the meantime, and we'd all be trapped. It was a no-win situation; I had to guess, and there was no way of knowin' which option was better.

I turned to face Donovan in a fightin' stance.

He grabbed that amulet of his, poppin' out and back in again right in front of me. "I can keep doing this all day, Kirk," he taunted.

"Doing what?" I was playin' dumb, but I had somethin' in mind.

"You *know*, you bastard! Sally told me she caught you going through my papers."

I laughed, then coughed a little myself. "That bullshit? Are you kiddin' me? Don't tell me you actually *believe* you been travelin' through time."

He looked confused for a second, then smiled and nodded. "Believe it? Of course, I believe it! I've done it." He started comin' forward, and I could see he was wearin' somethin' around his neck. It was that goddamn talisman, like the one on his calling card. "All I need is this," he said, holdin' it out to me, "and I can go anywhere I want. Poof!" He laughed maniacally, but I just laughed right back at him.

"And you wanted to lecture *me* about self-delusion!" I roared. "You're livin' in fantasy land, pal. It's all in your head. I can take you out anytime I want to." I reached inside my coat and grabbed my pistol.

He froze.

"You believe in the angel of death and H.G. Wells. I believe in *this*. Wanna see who's right?"

He hesitated a moment, then grabbed the amulet.

But nothin' happened.

He grabbed it again, an' clutched it hard against his chest, shakin' it he was squeezin' so hard.

Again, nothing.

I'd planted that seed of doubt in his mind, broken through that wall of faith he'd built up around himself. And without that faith, he couldn't leap.

It was my turn to taunt the bastard. "What are ya scared of, Mr. Therapist? O ye of little faith!" I threw my head back and laughed. "This little ol' gun?"

His eyes widened.

I wasn't a cop no more, and I knew how to make somethin' look like self-defense. Mercy? That was for them godly types. I wasn't about to let this bastard get away. Not if I could help it.

The smoke was gettin' thicker, and I couldn't see Claire no more.

I could barely see Donovan.

"You wretched sinner!" he shouted in a voice that was half defiant and half desperate—so desperate I thought he might shit his pants. "You'll pay for this," he shrieked. "Azrael shall have his vengeance."

I pulled the trigger and a shot rang out.

Then everything was quiet like a morgue.

I got down on my hands and knees, wheezin' and chokin' as I crawled toward Donovan... or where he *had* been.

But he wasn't there no more.

He musta blinked out after all, I concluded. Just like I always thought: Faith was just another word for desperation.

I wandered around in the smoke, but there weren't no sight of Donovan.

Claire, either.

The whole church was on the verge of goin' up in flames, but that fallen beam had burned itself out, leavin' me a path to the door. I staggered toward it and pushed my way through, then made my way outside. I'd get a few breaths of fresh air, then go back in. I wouldn't leave Claire there to die. I *couldn't.*

Just then, though, that mutt of Donovan's appeared outta nowhere and ran up to me, whinin' and jumpin' on me like he wanted attention.

"OK, boy," I said. "Sorry, but I don't have time to pet ya right now."

The dog didn't get down, but started lickin' my face, and in such close proximity I noticed somethin': He was wearin' that same Azrael symbol on a tag around his neck. The one I'd seen on Donovan. It was almost like he was *trying* to make me notice it.

I reached out and unclipped it from his collar, slippin' it into my pocket, and he started barkin' as if he was givin' his approval.

I didn't have time to think about it.

Where was Claire?

I whirled around at the sound of a familiar voice.

"Looking for someone?"

Claire was standin' there beside her mother, her arms all wrapped around her. The woman had a vacant look in her eyes, not too diff'rent from the look old Hugh Cassidy's eyes had as he hung there on the cross.

"Thank God!" I said.

"You've finally figured that out," Claire said, tryin' to joke so she could keep puttin' on a brave face. But it didn't work. She dissolved into wave after wave of uncontrollable sobbing.

I put my arm around her, hearin' sirens in the distance. The fire department was respondin' to the alarm. Engine No. 1 pulled up, an' its crew started rushin' around, connectin' a hose up to the hydrant outside the church. It was too late to save the annex and the rec room, but it looked like they might be able to salvage the sanctuary.

I helped Claire and her mom up to the house, and I sat 'em down on the porch swing, pullin' up a chair across from them.

"I thought I'd lost you," I said, starin' into her eyes.

Claire just sat there for a minute, then a slow, sad smile crept across her lips.

"I'm pretty good at taking care of myself," she said between sniffles. "I don't usually need a man to come to the rescue."

I smiled back at her, chuckling. She had that one right.

"Still, I'm glad you showed up when you did, Elijah." She reached out and put her hand on mine. "I thank God for that."

The Detective
Epilogue

*C*laire had called me, all excited. It was good to hear that kind of life in her voice again. She'd been pretty shook up by her father's death an' all, but she was soundin' like herself again now for the first time since Azrael's Assassin had disappeared.

I loved the irony of it. Donovan had vanished just like he'd made his victims vanish. But it left me with a nagging feelin' in the pit of my stomach: Where had he gone? Would he be back? It'd been three months since he'd disappeared, and we hadn't heard nothin' from him during that time. Not a peep. But that didn't mean he wasn't bidin' his time somewhere—or some*when*—just waitin' for us to let down our guard so he could pop back up again.

I had no way of knowin' where he was right now, and that gave me the heebie-jeebies. He'd threatened to come back an' make me pay for gummin' up the works in his plan with one last monkey wrench. If I ever wanted to breathe easy again, I'd have to find a way to track him down eventually, but now was not the time. And it sure as hell weren't the time to go sharin' my concerns with Claire.

When I drove up to the church, I was shocked by how different it looked. Claire had hired painters to slather on a new coat of white paint, and she'd taken down the sign in front. That cross was still sittin' up there on the roof, but other than that an' the shape of the old building, there was nothin' to say it was a church anymore. A big new sign was sittin' there on the front of it, announcin' it was the Compassionate Community Center.

She'd kept the "compassionate" part of it, but had dropped the "truth" and "temple."

Her house next door looked different too. It wasn't her house anymore: She'd converted it into a shelter for widows an' orphans. Said she got the idea from Donovan's former squeeze, Sally, who'd told her about how the old Lost Hills Orphanage group home had helped him when he was a kid. That place had closed down a few years earlier, so Claire had decided the town needed a new one. Square Pegs Home she called it.

"So many people feel like square pegs trying to fit in the round hole of this sinful world," she'd told me. "No one feels more like that than widows and orphans. So why not make a place they feel belongs to them? A haven. A sanctuary."

Yeah, she was still talkin' all that religious-speak, but she was usin' it for good instead of tryin' to rip people off and control them."

"Elijah!" she shouted, runnin' out of the old church building to greet me. "I'm so glad you could come." She opened her arms for a hug, then kept 'em open, showin' off all the changes she'd made. "What do you think?"

"I think it's aces," I said. "Lemons into lemonade, if you're askin' me."

She beamed at me, partin' her lips in that bright smile of hers that I swore could set the world on fire if she weren't careful. Then her face turned all serious, and she looked at me like she had somethin' important to say. "Father was wrong," she told me. "He let the enemy come in and pervert his good intentions, twisting them so he could justify giving in to his temptations."

The "enemy" was the devil. I still had to do some translatin' upstairs: They hadn't used that kinda evangelical lingo in seminary.

She told me to follow her into the old sanctuary, and I saw the changes she'd made weren't just on the outside. She'd hung a curtain across the raised platform where the pulpit used to be and turned it into a stage, replacin' the one that had burned down with the rec room. She'd even ripped out the baptismal in back to make more room for set pieces. It was a real bona-fide theater. Some of the pews were still there—at least the front few rows of them, but the back rows had been pulled out and the floor smoothed over for half-court basketball. Foldin' chairs stacked in the corner could be pulled out onto the floor if a big crowd showed up for one of the theater events. That was her way of improvisin' now that the rec room was gone. I had to hand it to her, she was one helluva go-getter. And she knew how to inspire folks, too, the way her father did... but better. She wasn't inspirin' them to empty their pockets, but fill their hearts.

I smiled at the thought of that. It was a weird twist of fate, but she'd actually reached the same conclusion Donovan had—'cept without all that bloodshed. He'd been so hell bent on killin' her and her mother, but neither one of 'em woulda been a threat to his mission. He'd made it clear what that mission had been in that letter of his I'd found in the mansion when I went up there.

I hadn't told Claire about it till now, 'cause I didn't know if she could handle it. But I figured she was ready, and now was as good a time as any to show her.

"What's this?" she asked, as I handed her the paper.

"Just read it. I found it the day of the fire. It's Donovan's manifesto."

She took it and unfolded it.

I write this to the minions of the lord of this Earth, those who have drunk from the waters of wormwood. For ye have tasted the fruit of mercy, and have spat it from your mouth; ye have seen the signs and wonders wrought by His holy hand, yet have ye shunned them. For the Lord hath not given you a heart to perceive, nor eyes to see, nor ears to hear. He hath hardened you as he hardened Pharaoh, that ye might witness the glory of his wrath and suffer the plagues that ye have brought upon yourselves.

Ye hath worshipped the god of mammon and the lord of your own temptation.

And now, behold, God hath sent the rider whose name is Azrael, astride the pale horse of death, to sore afflict thee: the one who kills by sword and with hunger and by the beasts of the earth. He hath swallowed thee up into the belly of the snake. He hath caused you to hunger for the word of God, yet made thee to accept the bitter cup of wormwood in its stead. And he hath brought thee to me, who wieldeth his mighty sword, that ye might taste the fire of his blade, ye apostates and ye heathens.

Think not that I have done this of my own will. For I have acted on the command of Azrael, as ordained by the word of Almighty God. Would that there had been another way. But this is God's will. Ours is not to reason why; ours is but to do and die. My work here is finished; my glorious task complete. This is my legacy. My testament in blood.

—Azrael's Apostle

We sat down in the front row facin' the stage, where her parents an' the elders used to sit. It was kinda surreal rememberin' that and seein' how different it was now.

"What kind of shows you plan on puttin' on?" I asked her.

"Community theater. Musicals like *Singin' in the Rain* or *State Fair*, and Bible re-enactments for Easter and Christmas, and Sunday School."

"You're still having Sunday School here?"

"Yes. It was one of the things Father got right. I made friends there..." Her lip started quivering and I could tell she was fightin' back tears.

"Olivia," I said, puttin' my arm around her shoulder.

She nodded and tucked her head against my chest for a moment.

"I named it for her: the Olivia Dunphy Memorial Sunday School." She smiled again, a melancholy but satisfied smile.

"Who's the teacher?" I asked.

"You're looking at her."

Somehow, I wasn't surprised.

"You know what I can't figure out," I said, "is how you can still have faith after everything you been through. I ain't been through near as much, an' it was enough to turn me off religion."

That twinkle in her eye told me she had somethin' to say on the matter.

"Okay," I said. "Spit it out."

"I just can't believe that, after everything *you've* been through, you still *don't* have faith. You've seen someone travel through time, and you still don't believe in anything that doesn't fit into you're preconceived notions about the universe."

"Ain't that how your people look at the Bible? That's one big, fat book full of preconceived notions right there."

"I'm not just talking about the Bible. I'm talking about anything you can't figure out for yourself. You won't accept it till you understand it. Just look around you: 'All things work together for good to them that love God,'" she said. "Romans 8:28. Our assassin's not the only one who can quote Scripture."

I laughed. "I think I've had my fill o' the Bible for a bit."

But I couldn't deny what she was sayin' with the evidence right in front o' me. As I looked around, I saw everything she was accomplishin', and as capable as she was, she couldn't've done it without... God's blessing, dumb luck, or whatever you wanted to call it. Between her father's life insurance, which had paid out a pretty penny, and the fire insurance on the rec room, she'd had enough dough to rebuild the old church as somethin' new and a whole lot better. Her mom had kept her own room at the old mansion—Square Pegs was a place for widows, after all. There wasn't much left of the poor ol' gal now: She lived mostly inside her head. But at least she was smilin' out from the inside, and she seemed a whole lot happier bein' Annette again, instead of just a handmaid livin' in old Hugh Cassidy's shadow.

Claire told me she wouldn't respond when she called her 'Mother,' but she brightened on up whenever she called her 'Annette.'

"Seriously, though," Claire was saying, "how can you not have faith in *something*?"

I thought about it for a moment. "I suppose I have faith in myself," I said finally. "I did finally crack this case, y'know... well, we cracked it together. I'm a regular Sherlock Holmes, ain't I, Watson?" I winked at her and tapped myself on the chest. "Everything I need is right in here."

"In your heart?"

"Yes, ma'am. That's what I'm sayin'."

"Ma'am is it now? Well that's a whole lot better than toots or dollface. Maybe you *can* teach an old dog new tricks after all."

I made myself look all offended, even though I was just playin' with her. "I ain't *that* old."

"Of course not," she chuckled. "And that heart of yours won't ever get old, because you might *think* you're having faith in yourself, but you're *really* having faith in God. 'Know ye not that ye are the temple of God, and that the Spirit of God dwelleth in you?' Father thought this place was the temple, but it never was. He forgot that God made the whole world, and no temple built by man could ever contain him."

"I bet that's in the Bible too," I said sarcastic-like.

"Acts 17:24."

I shook my head, smilin'. "I shouldn't have asked."

As I walked away, I stopped and turned back around. "Oh yeah, Claire, I may be a poor substitute for Olivia, but you got a friend in me."

The Assassin

It'd been three months since I'd traveled back here to escape the clutches of that meddling private detective. I could only assume that he'd managed to save that harlot and her mother. I'd gone here to hide out and right the wrong I'd committed on my mission. It could and should have been so simple to complete it. If only I'd been thinking right in the first place, I could have ended it all in one fell swoop.

But I'd let my own selfish needs get in the away. I'd been afraid that changing the past in just one step might have kept me from meeting my soulmate, Sally. I'd wanted so badly to see the Prophet suffer through the anguish of watching everything he'd built come crumbling down, piece by piece. And worst of all, I'd reveled in the idea of watching some of the others suffer. Like my foster parents. I condemned them to endure the same kind of pain they'd put me through, languishing in fear and isolation.

Now I'd failed, just as all the others had before me. And it seemed as if my Sally was lost to me forever. I was stranded in a time long before either of us had been born. I'd tried to get back, before she hated me, so I could have a clean slate, but it hadn't worked. I'd clutched the amulet to my heart and thought about the destination in time and place a hundred times. At least. But nothing had happened. I couldn't understand why.

I'd thought about all the possibilities. What if the amulet had been damaged during the scuffle with Kirk? I didn't know the first thing about repairing a magical amulet given to me by an archangel. Being magical, could it even be fixed—like the crystal on my wristwatch? I'd prayed in my heart and out loud, begging Azrael to answer me. Surely, I thought, he could help me get back home. Yet my calls had gone answered.

But why?

That was territory where my heart feared to tread.

Had I angered Azrael by failing him? Had he lost all faith in me?

Was he punishing me for my selfishness? Had I crossed the line by trying to use the amulet for my own purposes before righting my wrong?

Most worrisome of all, I couldn't even believe I'd given words to this thought.

It was something that damn "private heretic" had said.

Coupled with something that Sally said during that last fight over the phone.

Did Azrael even exist? Had he ever given me a magical amulet to travel through time and space? Or had I done it all through the power of my own mind... my tenacity as Sally had put it? What if I'd needed this ability to accomplish my task, to eradicate the Compassionate Truth Temple, and it had existed because I wanted it to? Now that I was all but done, and with the knowledge of my failure in the last step, had I lost my motivation and the faith I needed to travel through time?

How did an accomplished psychologist, such as myself, start to question his own sanity? Mr. Kirk... that's how. How I hated that man! He had to die in the worst way possible. But that would have to wait.

First, I had to rectify my misstep. That's why I'd traveled back forty-eight years... a few years before that fraudulent Prophet had founded his Temple of Lies. Before he'd even met and married that woman whose spirit he had broken. My mission had been to stop that false apostle and his followers. There'd been no need for the collateral damage that had occurred. No one else had needed to suffer and die for their sins—not if the Prophet had never bewitched them in the first place.

I wouldn't have to suffer the way I had at the hands of my heartless foster parents. It might mean I'd never meet Sally, but that was a chance I had to take. It also meant that I might not have had the same opportunity to become a psychologist. But that didn't matter. My love and faith in God were far more important. Reviving Azrael's faith in me was paramount.

It was time to search out where Cassidy held those tent revivals.

About the Authors

Sharon Marie Provost specializes in horror, thrillers, and speculative fiction. Beginning her career in late 2023, she has published a novella, two short story collections, and two collaborative collections of short stories with her husband. Her first novel, *Dark Arts: Love Me Tinder*, was published in 2024. It has received acclaim for its detailed and chilling story of a serial killer who turns his victims into works of art. Sharon is the chief operating officer of Dragon Crown Books. She has lived in Carson City since 1987.

Stephen H. Provost is a former reporter and columnist with more than 30 years of experience at daily newspapers. Over the past 11 years, he has written more than 50 books. In addition to six novels and three novellas, he has produced an extensive collection of nonfiction works on topics ranging from

Nevada's pioneer days to the history of retail in the United States. He has written more than 20 books on U.S. history in the 20th century focusing on highways, towns, and culture. Stephen is the founder and publisher of Dragon Crown Books. He lives in Carson City.

Books by
Sharon Marie Provost

Dark Arts
Shadow's Gate
Shades of Love Vol. 2
The Last Train to Clarksville
All Hallows' Nightmare's Eve (with Stephen H. Provost)
Christmas Nightmare's Eve (with Stephen H. Provost)
The ACES Anthology (contributor)

Books by
Stephen H. Provost

Fiction

   Meteor Ridge
   Crimson Scourge
   The Memortality Saga
      Memortality
      Paralucidity
   Academy of the Lost Labyrinth
      The Talismans of Time
      Pathfinder of Destiny

The Only Dragon
Identity Break
Nightmare's Eve
Christmas Nightmare's Eve
     (with Sharon Marie Provost)
All Hallows' Nightmare's Eve
     (with Sharon Marie Provost)
Shades of Love, Vol. 1
Need
Death's Doorstep
Feathercap

Nonfiction

Mark Twain's Nevada
The Comstock Chronicles
Virginia City Then & Now
The Legend of Molly Bolin
California's Historic Highways series
     Highway 99
     Highway 101
America's Historic Highways series
     America's First Highways
     Yesterday's Highways
     Highways of the South
Highways of the West series
     America's Loneliest Road
     Victory Road
     The Lincoln Highway in California
       (with Gary Kinst)
     Sierra Highway

STEPHEN H. and SHARON MARIE PROVOST

Bonanza Highway
Roadside Illustrated series
    Happy Motoring!
    Signpost Up Ahead: The East
    Signpost Up Ahead: The West
Fresno Growing Up, 2024
A Whole Different League
The Great American Shopping Experience
Martinsville Memories
The Century Cities series
    Cambria Century, Carson City Century
    Charleston Century, Danville Century
    Fresno Century, Goldfield Century
    Greensboro Century, Huntington Century
    Roanoke Century, San Luis Obispo Century
50 Undefeated
Please Stop Saying That!
The Phoenix Chronicles
    The Osiris Testament
    The Way of the Phoenix
    The Gospel of the Phoenix
The Phoenix Principle
    Forged in Ancient Fires
    Messiah in the Making

Praise for Other Works

"The writing was superb, the attention to detail shows she knows what she's doing when it comes to police procedure, and the kill scenes are very detailed and disturbing... For fans of serial killer stories with plenty of graphic imagery. Highly recommended."
— Justin Boote, author of *Soul Searchers*,
on Dark Arts by Sharon Marie Provost

"One of the best books I have EVER read! Messed-up, cringy, tense, sickening, thrilling, exciting, disturbing and complete!"
— Kim Sloan, author of the *Billy Bob Adventures* series,
on Dark Arts by Sharon Marie Provost

"Haunting and beautiful. This book is so good! All the stars!!!"
— Angel Van Atta, author of *In the Tall Trees*,
on Dark Arts by Sharon Marie Provost

"I read this book in one sitting, something I rarely do. The story is fast paced and crisply written, the description of the crimes, though tough to read, are expertly and vividly written. There are plenty of believable twists and turns. The ending is fabulous."
— Catherine Riddick, former *Fresno Bee* assistant managing editor,
on Dark Arts by Sharon Marie Provost

"Heartwarming, heart-wrenching. The romance broke my heart and then mended it."
— Carol Purroy, author of *Tiara*, on
The Last Train to Clarksville by Sharon Marie Provost

STEPHEN H. and SHARON MARIE PROVOST

"I loved the story and the twist at the end. It's my kind of book! I had no idea and I love to be tricked and intrigued by an ending! Highly recommend it if you are a fan of everlasting love!"

— Sue C. Dugan, author of *A Slow Climb Up the Mountain*, on **The Last Train to Clarksville by Sharon Marie Provost**

"The complex idea of mixing morality and mortality is a fresh twist on the human condition. ... **Memortality** is one of those books that will incite more questions than it answers. And for fandom, that's a good thing."

— Ricky L. Brown, Amazing Stories

"Punchy and fast paced, **Memortality** reads like a graphic novel. ... (Provost's) style makes the trippy landscapes and mind-bending plot points more believable and adds a thrilling edge to this vivid crossover fantasy."

— Foreword Reviews

"The genres in this volume span horror, fantasy, and science-fiction, and each is handled deftly. ... **Nightmare's Eve** should be on your reading list. The stories are at the intersection of nightmare and lucid dreaming, up ahead a signpost ... next stop, your reading pile. Keep the nightlight on."

— R.B. Payne, Cemetery Dance

"Provost sticks mostly to the classics: vampires, ghosts, aliens, and even dragons. But trekking familiar terrain allows the author to subvert readers' expectations. ... Provost's poetry skillfully displays the same somber themes as the stories. ... Worthy tales that prove external forces are no more terrifying than what's inside people's heads."

— Kirkus Reviews on **Nightmare's Eve by Stephen H. Provost**

"The story feels so close, so intimate, we as readers experience the emotions, the events, and the conflicts, in what feels like real time. Gut-wrenchingly so."

— Stephen Mark Rainey, author of *Blue Devil Island*, on **Death's Doorstep by Stephen H. Provost**

"**Memortality** by Stephen Provost is a highly original, thrilling novel unlike anything else out there."

— David McAfee, bestselling author of *33 A.D., 61 A.D.,* and *79 A.D.*